MAC DU ROSE

The Hana Du Rose Mysteries –
Generation Z

K T BOWES

Acknowledgment

This novel has risen from the ashes of 2022.
So much has happened.
But amid all the crazy, I stopped for long enough to watch
my eldest daughter walk across a stage and graduate with her
hard-won doctorate. Covid had delayed this special moment for
more than two years, but the wait also blessed us.
Because third from the end, having also waited patiently, her
father stepped onto the stage in his gown to complete his late
foray into academia and claim his prize.
And our doctor rose from her earned seat on the stage, a single
standing figure before of a crowd of thousands. And the big
screen reflected her pride and her smile.
And she acknowledged him.
And I will never forget it.
This novel is for them.
Dr R & Mr A.

1

Assist

He sat on the low wall bordering the soccer turf and focused on the game. Grunted complaints rose as the players contested for the black and white ball which rolled ahead of them like a prisoner evading capture by an army of sweaty soldiers. The girls resembled bees around a honey pot as they surged in a knot of chaos behind the spherical object of their desire.

A shrill whistle sounded close enough to make him jump, and he rose from his perch with significant difficulty. A haze of sweat and floral spray deodorant surrounded him as the girls arrived for their team briefing. They reached for the rack containing their plastic drink bottles before settling to listen. The occasional slurp of mineral fortified water cut across the steady voice of the sports teacher.

"What do you think, Mac?" She directed her first question to him.

McGillivray Du Rose considered his words before releasing them into the atmosphere, aware of their significance. "We're not playing as a team," he stated, his voice gruff against the female whispers from the back of the group. He tried to pronounce the sentence without the inflection caused by a childhood of deafness. "For one touch football to work in this league, we need to know all the information before we send the ball. Who are we sending it to? Are they ready?" He frowned and shook his head, bothered by the chafing of the uncomfortable sling across the back of his neck. "We can't just hoof it into orbit and expect someone to collect it." He moved his gaze around the group, waiting until he got eye contact with each of the fifteen girls gathered in an arc. "We'll work on it during training over the next few weeks. We'll be ready." He forced his lips to curve into a smile and the girls relaxed. His chest hurt when he released his held breath, wondering how he'd gotten into this. He hated the jerkiness of his speech and the way everyone stared at him. His differences filled him with mortification which emerged as a pink flush on his freckled cheeks and neck.

Oblivious, the girls readied themselves for leaving. Optimism filled the group as they bent to gather bags and belongings in lieu of the inevitable bell, signifying the end of lunchtime.

The teacher clapped her slender hands, the faint pink nails glistening in the sunshine. "Hurry to the changing rooms and I'll follow behind you." She dropped the key into the palm of a nearby blonde girl and glanced at her watch. "You have ten minutes if you don't dawdle."

"Yes, Miss Andrews," the girl replied. But she didn't move, standing on one leg and chewing her lower lip. "Miss," she began, her gaze darting to Mac and then back to the teacher. "Did you see Mr Simms about the thing?"

The teacher paused. She seemed to formulate the reply in her mind before releasing it. "Yes," she said. "Hurry to class now. Nine minutes and counting."

The girls ambled in the direction of the school building, the key holder bringing up the rear at a jog. The teacher sighed and watched their slow progress. "Rockets on the pitch and snails off it." She turned to him and smiled. "I hope their aim will improve once the goalposts go up. We can always hope. Thanks for agreeing to coach them. We'd appreciate your input, especially after your success with the First Eleven boys last year."

Mac's mind presented an image of the goal mouth into which he'd placed the ball in the final winning kick. The other team lodged a protest about faulty posts and divots on the high school's inferior pitch. But the Football Association governing schools didn't uphold the complaint. Mac's team kept the cup which would spend a year growing grey and tarnished in the trophy cabinet in the reception area.

The teacher ran the back of her hand over her damp forehead and sighed. "I'll speak to the other coach about taking our spare forward. I hate to do it to her, but she's not at the same level. Nice kid, but she can't place the ball. We already make too many errors near the penalty box as it is. Some of these Year 10 girls have potential and natural talent. Unfortunately, she doesn't. She must have fluked her performance during the muster." Miss Andrews rolled her eyes. "I hate this job sometimes. Breaker of dreams and hearts." Eager to distract herself, she reached out to touch the cast encasing his left wrist, her touch gentle. "Speaking of broken dreams, you'll miss the start of the boys' season."

Mac nodded. "Yep." Not a fan of wasting words, he didn't qualify her observation. He'd hated the limelight of goal scoring. The adoration of his team members caused him massive discomfort.

"How did you do it?" She cocked her head and her blonde curls tumbled sideways to cover her right shoulder.

Something shifted in Mac's stomach and sent a spark of excitement along his spinal cord. He stared at her, his green irises glittering in the sun's glare. A million thoughts spun through his mind, but he held onto the sentence which landed uppermost on his tongue. Unable to tell her she was beautiful, he swallowed the sentiment with an awkward gulp and concentrated instead on the black cast funnelling heat to his painful bones. "Fell off a horse," he said, lifting his lips in a rueful smile. His nose wrinkled and irritation bloomed as a pink haze across his cheeks. "Shouldn't have happened." He exhaled and flexed his right hand to lift the hem of his grey shirt. He used it to mop his brow before realising he'd just given the sports teacher an eyeful of his impressive abdominal muscles. Flustered, he dropped the hem and dipped his head to use the top of his sleeve instead.

She nodded, and her lips flattened into a wistful line. "You have a horse?" She exhaled and lifted her hand to shield her eyes from the glare. "I miss riding. Should have kept it up, but there isn't much opportunity in Auckland City. Or energy after spending all day here."

The bell rang, and she hissed in irritation. Mac hefted his rucksack onto his right arm one-handed and turned to walk with her across the field. Squeaks of alarm sounded through the open windows of the girls' changing rooms. The teacher crossed her arms over her chest and smiled up at him. "What do you want to do when you've escaped school?"

"Farm." The one-word answer hadn't changed since the first time he'd uttered it at the age of four. He'd been deaf since birth. Cochlear implants gave him access to a world containing sound, but the farm offered him peace. He'd delighted his mother by repeating the word after years of silence. No one realised it was the essence of it which gave him joy and not the formation of the letters on his lips and tongue. He shared his deafness with his paternal great-grandfather, Jacob. Too many similarities existed for him to dismiss their mutual love of his father's mountain and their inclination to hide in its safe folds forever. Pity his mother couldn't tolerate Jacob D'Arcy's name.

"Right." A familiar response from Miss Andrews. His life goals both frustrated and infuriated his teachers. They wanted him to study further, and accrue an unmanageable debt for courses which held no interest to him. His exceptional grades dictated a future which included a university postgraduate degree and a soulless career in the public eye somewhere. He'd had the same tutor teacher for the last six years, and the mantra hadn't changed.

"What do you like about farming?" A breeze lifted Miss Andrews' blonde curls and tossed them around her face. She turned her head into the wind and used both hands to get her hair back under control.

Mac faltered. No one had asked him that question. He sifted through the possible replies before landing on the truth. "I love everything. It's peaceful, unhurried. I can be myself."

Girls emerged from the changing rooms at a run. With wet hair and bag straps trailing, they fled across the courtyard toward the main building. One girl dropped her towel, and another picked it up and flung it towards her. She caught it in one hand and its fringe licked the concrete paving slabs as she continued her journey.

"Bye Miss Andrews!" The last girl banged the door behind her and dropped the key into the teacher's palm. "See you tomorrow after school." She fluttered her eyelashes in Mac's direction, her effort wasted. "Bye Mac." Her sing-song chorus invited his attention and adoration glowed from her face.

"See ya," he replied, but only because it seemed polite.

2

CLEAT

Mac struggled through his maths class. The pain in his wrist ramped up to a nine despite the painkillers he'd smuggled into school in his rucksack. Squashed between the graffitied wall and his sweating neighbour created a claustrophobic tick in his chest. The heat didn't lend itself to concentration and his mind drifted back to Miss Andrews and her glittering blue irises.

"Hey, Du Rose!" His neighbour nudged him, catching the cast in his carelessness. He'd refused to take the space next to the wall and Mac lacked the energy to fight with him. He hissed in a heady mixture of anger and agony. "Sorry." The raven-haired teenager dipped sideways, his scent loaded from a garlic sated lunch. Mac held his breath and glared at him without replying. Oblivious, the boy continued his quest. "What's the answer to number eight?" His hand snaked across the desk, dirty nails and nicotine-stained fingers snatching at Mac's worksheet and turning it to face him. The boy recoiled. "How did you get that?"

"No talking!" Grant Simms rose from his desk, fat rolls piling over the belt which fought to prop up his trousers against the landslide of flesh. He dipped his head and peered over his wire-rimmed spectacles at the boys. Everyone in front of Mac spun around to face him. He willed away the promised red flush already heading from his chest to his throat. His mother said he'd grow out of it. One day it just wouldn't happen and he'd forget the beetroot cheeks which accentuated his vibrant auburn hair and embarrassed him. But not today. The heat, the pain, the scrutiny and the scent of garlic conspired against him.

The teen next to him who'd caused the ruckus leaned back in his chair and jabbed his dirty finger at Mac. "He's gone all red," he chortled. Heads bobbed as a titter flew around the room. Simms glared at the speaker.

"Shut up, Masters!" he snarled. "Detention after school for you." His lips flattened as he spoke, ejecting spit amid the words. Mac studied the angry glaze over the man's eyes.

"Aw! Sir!" The boy half rose in his seat and it skittered backwards to hit the desk behind him.

Grant Simms removed his spectacles. "And tomorrow. Want to make it the next day, too?"

Masters sat down with force, missing the chair and landing on the floor between the desks. Dust rose around him in a haze. Mac turned back to his worksheet and ignored the murmured chuntering which he imagined emanating from between the boy's lips. When Masters reached for Mac's sheet again, he snatched it away at the expense of the bottom left corner.

"Why?" Masters hissed. Indignation shone from his glittering brown irises.

Mac leaned towards him, noticing the way Masters gulped and his expression faltered. He used his right hand to retrieve the ripped corner of his sheet and snatched it from the desk. Without speaking, he used the remaining minutes of the lesson to tape the corner back into place. Masters didn't interact with him again. Whatever latent violence he'd seen in Mac's eyes wasn't worth the risk of copying his test. Mac finished the last question, adding the written longhand after he'd already worked it out in his head. He turned his page over so Masters couldn't copy and sat in silence.

His mind wandered to his family home in the mountains and the hospital drama of the previous weekend. The ridiculous, freak accident which caused his broken wrist shouldn't have happened. Something had distracted him and he missed the horse's cue. She'd warned him of the impending buck by bunching her power into her back legs and he'd altered his weight too late to save himself. His father blamed the stranger who'd arrived unannounced. Mac hadn't worn his implants, and the mare demanded all his attention. It meant he missed the end of the altercation as he hit the ground.

Mac blew out a breath and sensed his desk companion turn towards him. Movement in front of him suggested the bell had just rung.

Mac slipped on his blazer and patted the speech processor units in his top pocket. He tugged them free and fitted them back over his ears. Masters' eyes widened as he realised Mac had heard none of his whispered protests. The words *test conditions* scrawled on the whiteboard had prompted Mac to invoke his own silence after Simms finished giving instructions. He hadn't wanted to sit next to the bullish boy, but Simms had decreed the seating arrangements.

Masters mouthed something unrepeatable, but this time Mac heard it as well as reading his lips. He pushed his pen into his rucksack and rose, staring down at the other boy with an impassive expression. "Weirdo," Masters muttered. "You speak like a moron, you deaf idiot."

"Pardon?" Mac ground his teeth together until his jaw jutted through his cheek. His wrist smarted as his knuckles clenched into a fist. He abhorred violence. But maybe just this once would soothe the foreboding in his heart. His analytical mind ran the probability of repercussions and called it as a foregone conclusion. Mac relaxed his fingers. The data was never wrong. He focussed on a massive white-head in the centre of Masters' speckled forehead. It somehow diminished the sense of urgency and threat.

"Test papers on my desk before you leave. Dan Masters stay behind." Simms lifted his voice to carry across the chaos of thirty boys exiting the classroom.

"You think you're something special," Masters hissed. He remained seated, his pen hovering over the empty answer box for question number ten. His eyes flashed with threat as he glared up at Mac. "The disabled Du Rose. Everyone just pities you."

Phoenix would have cried from her tender spirit, as would his mother.

Wiri would have punched him.

Edin would have buried Masters' battered body, and so would Logan.

But Mac laughed. It burst from him as though Masters had told a joke. He noticed the fear reaction in the other boy's eyes and forced his muscles to relax. His lunch box dug into his ribs through the rucksack fabric, and he released a sigh. "For me to react to anything you have to say," he whispered, his tone confidential, "I'd need to care. And I don't."

Mac used his thighs to push past him, shoving the chair with enough force to make Masters lurch forward in his seat. He hoisted his rucksack higher, but it still clipped the boy's head as he passed. But he'd lied. Because he did care.

Simms accepted the test paper Mac laid on his desk, snatching it up to speed-read the neatly scribed answers. A nod of satisfaction punctuated their interaction as Mac left the classroom. He heard the teacher yell out behind him, "Pen down, Mr Masters! Try doing your homework occasionally. I'm sure it would help!"

Mac stepped through the throng in the corridor. Every muscle and tendon seemed to protest as he followed a crowd of younger boys towards the exit. A slender reed of a child, he'd grown into a powerhouse of an adolescent. The Du Rose genetics had kicked in late, chasing away any hint of sickliness. But they hadn't dulled his auburn hair or brushed away the freckles from his high cheekbones. He was Hana's son, too.

"Hey! Du Rose!" The shout issued from behind him. The surrounding crowd turned to face the sound. He swivelled on the soles of his shoes and suppressed the ready groan rising in his throat.

"Sir?"

The barrel-chested male stamped towards him as though the grid locked corridor couldn't impede his progress. Teenage bodies bowed left and right on either side of him as he cut through the mass. The sports teacher's eyes blazed with venom and fury, and he raised a pudgy finger and jabbed it at Mac before reaching him. "You can't coach girls!" he snarled. "What are you playing at?"

Mac stood his ground, his muscles locked and rigid. He'd expected the onslaught, but fooled himself into believing he had more time. The flush threatened to spill through his nerve endings and turn his face into pulsing flesh. He willed it not to. Just this once. Heat prickled at the underside of his jaw and he battled to keep his nerve.

Arthur Darian fixed his hands over his hips and glared at Mac, tilting his flaccid chin to peer into his eyes. He blinked as though in surprise that the summer had given his star soccer player a height edge he hadn't anticipated. "Why are you coaching girls?" He spat the gender word with a grating wisp of disgust.

"I'm injured." Mac raised the cast and Darian's eyes flared wider. He took a step closer and his stubbled chin grazed Mac's chest. Sweat beaded his lined forehead. It took every ounce of self-control to stop Mac backing out of range.

"When?" Hysteria laced Darian's tone. "Why did no one tell me?"

Mac stared at the middle-aged acne dotting the man's forehead and pictured driving his fist through the flat bone. He'd imagined the scene many times, but unleashing the action would herald far too many awful consequences. Today, anyway. He'd bide his time until his last day of school and let the man have it right in the face. It would mean breaking his personal code but what the hell.

Mac exuded calm, though irritation and fear swirled in his stomach. He'd loved playing soccer his entire school career until Darian strode onto the pitch at the start of the summer season. The enjoyment ended there for Mac. Darian's slippery nature and unreasonable tempers decimated the team within weeks. Despite having won the national winter league, they'd noped out to lesser skilled schools beneath the sunshine. Many of the regulars were reconsidering their options.

Darian jabbed his finger into Mac's chest. Hard. "You're the team captain. Rally the guys."

Mac cleared his throat. "I'm injured." He raised the cast again, tempted to bring it down hard on the man's smug nose. A gargantuan act of restraint stopped him, but he sensed his resolve weakening.

"So!" Darian dropped his hand and stepped close enough to bump Mac with his chest. "You'll miss the friendly games, that's all. Muster your best men. I don't want the crappy ones from the summer league. They lost us the cup. You can break the news to them." His level gaze ended at Mac's chin and he sighed. "Stop coaching the girls. They'll get nowhere, so you're wasting your time." His irises flickered with a dangerous glow. It back-lit the muddy brown with a yellow tinge. He ran a fat tongue across his lower lip. "I'll tell Andrews for you. I'll break it to her in bed later."

Bile rose into Mac's throat at the thought of such an interaction. He prevented his mind from straying in the direction the lecherous man had intended. Miss Andrews regarded Darian with the same level of disgust as the rest of her colleagues. Management had squashed rumours of his inappropriate interactions with younger female students the previous year, hence his appearance in the senior boys' soccer league. But there was something disquieting about the man, and Mac sensed a lack of preference in his barely disguised depravity. Neither gender was safe.

Mac took a step back, turning his feet and sending his body after them. He didn't grace the teacher with a reply, battling to swallow the knotty ball which had blocked the back of his throat. A timer ticked in his mind on a gentle loop. It warned of the impending snap of his patience with school and everyone in it.

"Don't forget!" Darian called after him.

Mac's lips twitched, the only sign of his hidden distress. The broken wrist had halted his farm work, and the clown behind him had robbed him of his other passion. He couldn't play soccer, but he would have trained with the team to maintain his fitness. Darian's presence on the side lines and in the changing room nixed that. He refused to undress in front of him.

He dragged his phone from his blazer pocket and sent a quick one-handed text. His rucksack threatened to plummet from his shoulder as he typed with his thumb.

'Ignore what you hear. I haven't quit.'

He didn't wait for a reply, sliding his phone into place and drifting along with the surging bodies towards the exit.

The sunlight blinded him as he descended the steps onto the street. A knot of girls from the soccer team waved to him and he nodded in acknowledgement. They turned in towards each other like a folding blanket to gossip and giggle. "He said hi to me," one squealed.

"No, he didn't," another chimed. "He just nodded."

Mac sensed them hush as footsteps slapped the ground behind him. The girls turned away as one, more united in their movement than they'd been on the pitch.

"Wait for me!" his cousin protested. She arrived behind him in a cloud of frizzing black curls and effervescent energy. Her light touch to his right elbow caused him to slow. "I see your crowd of admirers is gathered again," she hissed. She shot a glare of disdain in their direction. Mac didn't respond, not wanting to fuel Edin's unpredictable fire. He paused to locate their bus, his height giving him an advantage.

"It's over there," he stated, turning his feet toward the single decker headed for the township nestled in the foothills of the mountain range. Edin trotted behind him, her sandals striking the pavement. Teenagers milled around them, some walking home and others seeking one of the gathered buses.

Only one seat remained and Mac insisted Edin take it. He placed his heavy bag on the metal floor and clasped a nearby rail in his right hand, bracing himself as the bus moved away from the curb. He allowed himself to think about the stranger who'd unsettled his father so much the previous weekend. Dressed more for a shopping spree than a farm visit, she'd waved her arms in anger, following Logan as he traversed the round pen. Mac remembered the high heeled red shoes and her fluttering hem. Just a second of distraction proved enough for him to miss the mare's energy change and hit the floor. When he threw up in the dust, he knew he'd broken his wrist.

"Have you got loads of homework tonight?" Edin tipped her face to observe him, a gentleness in her grey eyes which she reserved only for Mac.

He nodded in reply. "I'll get it done," he murmured, more for his own benefit than hers. His greatest task for that long summer evening was to retake his destiny. He needed to get back on the horse.

3

Crossbar

"This needs to stop!" Mac held his breath after delivering the whispered salvo. The tightness in his shoulders bunched his tee shirt beneath his armpits. Sweat slid in a line along his spine, creating an uncomfortable tickle.

Edin froze in his bedroom doorway. Mac regretted the hurt which flickered across her expression as a down-turning of her pretty lips. Then it was gone, swiped away in a millisecond and replaced with a hard sneer. She lowered her head to stare at him from beneath her brows. "What?" Her tone held a characteristic bite, delivered often to others but never before to him. Her gaze strayed to the open buttons of his shirt and the defined pectoral muscles nestled beneath it. Grey irises morphed from the appearance of a stormy sky to the hue of hard slate.

Mac swallowed and lifted his good hand to settle the speech processor back in place after pulling his shirt over his head. His hand shook. Two long strides would carry him across the room. He wondered what one kiss would unleash. Something delicious and explosive. Something destructive. But his father wouldn't tolerate it, Mac told himself. Logan had smashed the blueprint after Phoenix allied with Wiri. Kane's son was bad enough as a partner for his precious daughter, but Caroline's spawn had gained entry to his sacred temple by default. Hana invited her into their home, not Logan. Despite the fizzing attraction which blossomed with puberty, they both knew it couldn't happen. Never. Mac yanked his shirt over the defined muscles of his stomach. "I just got a text from a girl on the soccer team. You know what you did."

Edin's lips pulled into a flat line and danger flashed in her eyes. Not quite an admission of guilt, but enough to make Mac shake his head. Frustration budded in his chest and he swiped his wrist across his face before remembering the cast. The fibreglass dragged across his nose and sent a bloom of pain into his brain. It clouded his vision and his judgement. He'd trained himself to deal with Edin kindly, always putting her needs and wishes first. But her behaviour had crossed a sacred line, causing him conflict and superheating his guts until desire threatened to break free and burn them all. He trod the unfamiliar territory of anger.

"You threatened her!" he hissed. "Told her to stay away from me. How do you expect her to do that when I'm the bloody coach?" He rarely swore. He never raised his voice. But as the words spun into the air, a growing rage accompanied it.

Edin ground her teeth in her jaw and shifted her weight into one leg. A coquettish stance aimed at diffusing his ire. But this was new even to her. She licked her lips and considered her reply with a devious precision. "That's not exactly what I said." She shot a glance towards the kitchen door. Plates clattered as Hana unloaded the dishwasher alone. The scent of meat and potatoes still filled the air from their dinner. Irritation bubbled into Mac's throat and escaped through his lips.

"Why do you never do your chores?" he demanded. His voice rose, and she took a step backwards, confusion causing a shadow across her attractive Du Rose features. Mac jabbed his finger towards the sound of Hana's gentle humming. "Help Ma for once!" He whirled away from her, and his staccato steps carried him along the hallway and into the garage.

His father's voice drifted from the space he'd just left. "Edin, why are you hanging around here?" Logan appeared like a spectre of doom. "Aren't you on dishwasher duty this week?"

Mac leaned against the wall and stared at the white ceiling above him. The blank surface helped to purge his mind of the furious and confusing thoughts rampaging through it. He jumped as Logan stepped into the garage. "Ready?" he asked, a smile lifting the corners of his lips.

"Yeah." Mac added a nod to the response and tugged his boots from the shelf. Dust floated to the floor with abandon, and he sighed.

"What's up?" Logan reached above him for his worn cowboy boots and set them on the mat in front of him. He pushed his feet into them without bending down, but his fingers caressed the shelf where Phoenix's boots sat dusty and unused. "Need help?" He jerked his head towards the boots in Mac's hand. "No shame in needing help with the laces when you have a broken wrist." He cocked his head. "You sure you wanna do this? We can leave it a couple of days."

Mac shook his head. He bent to sit his boots in front of him. His feet folded inside without issue, but the cast impeded him fastening his laces. The bow hung lopsidedly on one and dragged like a washing line on the other. Logan made no comment, grabbing his truck keys and using the side door to exit the house. Mac watched as he waved through the kitchen window to Hana and blew her a kiss. A flare of jealousy rippled through his body, snaking up his spine like a fog of pure envy. He craved a love like theirs, but Edin's territorial behaviour made it impossible for him to even contemplate reaching out to a girl. Now she'd started attacking the younger girls' football team.

Logan didn't speak on the way down the mountain. Mac loved his father's disinclination to make noise for the sake of it.

He wasn't afraid of silence like so many others in Mac's circle. Silence had been his constant companion during the early years before the implant. Sign language and lip reading had satisfied him. The world hadn't cluttered his head like it did since the surgery. He could hold his nose, purse his lips, or shut his eyes if he disliked what he smelled, tasted or saw. Shoving his hands in his pockets negated his touch sense. But the sound took over whether he liked it or not. It sometimes seemed like pushing a moving steamroller back with his hands.

Mac sighed and removed the processors from behind his ears. They jostled in his palm, a blessing and a curse. He held them up so Logan could see he'd removed them. His father gave a nod and a smile to signify he understood. Mac sat them in the cup holder with care and the world felt better. He allowed a smile to curve his lips upwards enough to demonstrate his pleasure at the regaining of control over his world.

Logan waited for a campervan to amble past the end of the driveway before making the sharp right turn onto the lane leading to the hotel. His nose wrinkled, but he didn't need to explain his irritation to Mac. Prominent signposts in the township showed the much easier route to the camp ground, yet once a day one still made the treacherous journey through the hairpin bends and ended up at the hotel entrance.

Logan swung his truck into the empty parking space.

4

FREE KICK

Mac lowered his chin and forced calm energy through his muscles. He closed his eyes for a moment to complete the sense of wholeness which enveloped him. His lips moved as he repeated the familiar mantra without sound. "This is where I want to be. I'm doing what I love."

The mare permitted his approach, tossing her mane and peering at him through first one eye, and then the other. Someone, perhaps Toby, had moved the electric tape and given her access to more of the springy grass in the paddock. Her grey coat shone with the lux of vitality, her range of feed choices expanded with the hay stalks clinging to the hairy underside of her muzzle.

"Work time." Mac spoke the words, his lips moving but his brain recording no sound. The flick of her ears back and forth was the only sign he'd said them out loud. She allowed him to hook the rope's clasp onto her head collar, standing while he checked the underside of her bare hooves for stones and mud. He dragged a pick from his back pocket and tapped her rear offside leg, pausing while she bent it at the hock and fetlock. With a snuff of frustration at his useless left arm, Mac shifted his hips and balanced the heavy hoof over his right knee. With difficulty, he ran the pick alongside her tender frog and dislodged a nugget of grit. The mare sighed and set her foot on the ground. The rope dangled from beneath her chin, the excess coiled like a snake in the grass. Mac left it there as he ran his right hand over her smooth body, checking for cuts, lumps, or ticks.

Her tail swished, and she turned her head to observe his progress. Mac patted her neck as he walked around the front of her powerful body, mindful of her ability to rebel faster than he could anticipate. A steady ache in his wrist prevented him from dodging her shaking head or the spin which would put him level with her threatening rear hooves. "Sassy." He mouthed her name in the same moment it came to him. The word embodied her effervescent spirit, and he smiled. "I'll call you Sassy."

The mare stretched out her neck and inspected his cast. He resisted the desperate urge to pull it out of harm's way. She sniffed the chemical mix of fibreglass and fabric, licking her lips and tasting his scent within it. Satisfied, she lowered her heavy lids and her head drooped.

Mac bent to retrieve the coil of rope from the ground and kept it loose, setting off towards the gate at a steady pace. He smirked to himself as it bumped his hip and the horse mirrored his movements and followed.

Logan loaded his shovel into a wheelbarrow filled with dung. He nodded to Mac and swept it through the open gate of the round pen. Sassy lowered her chin and peered through the tops of her eyes, telling Mac that Rawhiti still hadn't fixed the squeaky front wheel. She didn't remove her gaze from Logan's retreating back until they reached the gate and stepped into the work space.

***

"You made significant progress." Logan sipped from a drink bottle and wiped his mouth on his sleeve.

Mac shrugged, unconvinced by his father's praise. He lifted his right hand and fingered the processor nestled above his ear. His arm jerked as he stopped himself from wrenching it free.

Logan turned in the driver's seat and frowned at his son. Water droplets flecked the black stubble shrouding his chin. "Are they bothering you? We can make an appointment with the audiometrist at the hospital if you want?"

"No." Mac's head jerked from side to side in an awkward movement. He shrugged and stared through the dusty windscreen at the hotel. Hay dotted his clothing, enveloping him in a comforting haze of dried grass and earthiness. "I don't think I made any progress. I wanted to pick up where we left off before I fell." He shaped the sentence to encompass blame for his own actions, not wanting to discuss the shouty visitor who unnerved Sassy with her dangerous energy.

"You wanted to ride the mare." Logan cleared his throat and leaned his head against the rest. His dark fringe obscured his left eye. "It's not always possible to overwrite the past, Mac. We learn to accept the setbacks, get off our asses and start again. I think you did great." He jerked his head at the cast resting against Mac's left thigh. "For a man working with one arm, you impressed me. You groomed her, tacked her, and lunged her. It's enough for a first time back after an injury." His nose wrinkled, and he glanced at the knotty knuckles curved around the water bottle. "I should know." He flicked his head and his fringe released his eyelashes from their embrace. His gentle smile covered his son in warmth. "Maturity is learning when to accept a genuine compliment, kid. I don't give them out like candy." His left index finger shot out to depress the ignition button, and the diesel engine roared to life.

"Thanks," Mac conceded. The cacophony of birds settling down for the night filled his head with squawking. They reminded him to seize the moment. Many of them wouldn't survive the winter, but they didn't care, arguing over perches in the leafy branches and unaware of their fate. He wrestled his seat belt into place and chewed the inside of his cheek. "I'm calling her Sassy," he said, the name sweet on his tongue.

"Good choice." Logan beamed as he reversed from the parking space.

Another campervan lumbered the wrong way around the turning circle in front of the hotel entrance. The chassis rocked as the driver clipped the jutting rock at the bottom of the steps. Logan cursed under his breath and gritted his teeth. "Some people just can't read the signs," he growled.

Mac turned to watch the passenger tumble from the high vehicle. Grey faced and pressing her palms against the paintwork, she looked like someone who hadn't enjoyed the hazardous lane which wound from the main road to the hotel. Her body language oozed misery, and he empathised with her defeated stance. It would worsen once the receptionist pointed out they'd taken the wrong turn five kilometres earlier and needn't have put themselves through the ordeal. Logan spun away from the unfolding drama. They'd have to drive back the way they came before darkness descended around the mountain.

"Wait!" Mac dipped forward in his seat and unfastened his belt. "I'd like to visit with Poppa Alfie."

Logan blinked and his lips parted. "Now? But it's getting dark." Lifting his right hand, he scrubbed at tired eyes, making the inference that he wanted to go home and relax.

"It's fine. I'll find my own way back later." Mac opened the door and slipped from the seat before Logan could object. "See ya soon."

He sensed his father's angst as he slammed the door and strode across the car park without glancing back. But then the diesel engine cut through the night as Logan relented. The passenger from the campervan gave Mac a tired smile as the driver slugged his way up the front steps. Desperate to avoid becoming entangled in giving them bad news and then complicated directions, he overtook the man and jogged through the reception area at a steady clip. The private spiral staircase vibrated beneath his feet as he sped upstairs to the third floor.

Mac likened the plight of the campervan occupants to his error with Edin. He'd missed those signs too and must embark on a similar journey back to where he started. He contemplated the likelihood of their relationship surviving and sadness bowed his strong shoulders.

If he was fortunate, she might just let him live.

5

FOOTBALL

Mac knocked on the door to his Poppa's apartment. He waited a moment before turning the handle and peeking into the long space which occupied a quarter of the hotel's footprint. Vaulted beams soared to his left, taking the roof line to meet with the floor-length windows. He stepped around the door and closed it behind him. It took a second to kick off his dusty boots.

"Poppa?" The comfy furniture absorbed his gentle call. "Nonie? Are you here?"

They'd left the door unlocked at the bottom of the steep staircase. He couldn't remember the last time he'd found it barred to him. His poppa rarely left the apartment. He disliked the stair lift Logan had paid for and used its insulting presence as an excuse for not venturing beyond his eerie.

Nonie Leslie appeared around the partition, which separated the bedroom from the lounge. She jerked in surprise at the sight of Mac standing on the tousled doormat in his socks. "Hey moko." Her face split in a wide grin. "I didn't hear youse there, boy." Younger than his poppa, she'd lost none of her bounce to the years. She approached him with her arms wide, enfolding him into a familiar bear hug devoid of any agenda other than love. He wrapped his arms around her and held on, prolonging the moment more than usual. She smelled of washing powder and summer heat, and he rested his chin on the top of her fluffy head. When he released her, she looked up at him and narrowed her eyes. "Have you got your things in, or do you need me to wave my hands?"

Mac laughed. "I'm wearing my processors." He tilted his head for her to see the connection. It magnetised to the receiver fixed to the bone beneath his scalp. "I wore them, especially for you."

"Good." She smiled and moved towards the sink. "I'm no good at that hand waving thing, anyway."

Hand waving.

Her description of sign language.

Fluent in Māori and less so in English, she claimed a third language stretched her old brain too far. So, she waggled her fingers and Mac lip read. At least she turned to face him as she spoke. "You had your kai? Want some dinner?"

"No thanks, Nonie." He moved off the doormat but didn't venture far. "I wondered if Poppa would let me take him to the hotel bar for a coffee."

Leslie snorted. "Good luck with that. He won't walk past that stair lift Logan installed." She cocked her head to one side. "We could blindfold him and give him a shove, maybe."

Mac grimaced. He knew she didn't mean it, but propriety meant they shouldn't joke about such things. "I'll ask him."

Leslie rewarded him with a slow nod. She didn't request an invitation, perhaps understanding Mac wanted to speak to Alfred alone. She studied his blank expression with a little too much perception. He sensed his ears warming with the irritating blush and cleared his throat. "He in the bedroom?"

"Ae, reading the newspaper. Tell him if he gets print on the bedspread he'll go down that stair lift faster than he imagined. And he won't be coming back up on it."

"Yes, ma'am." Mac used his good hand to give a mock salute and strode across the kitchen and lounge until he arrived at the partition. He knocked on the plasterboard wall. "Knock knock, Poppa. You decent?"

"Define decent," Alfie cackled. "I'm wearing pants. What more do you want?"

Mac groaned and slid around the blunted end of the wall. Alfie lay on the bed with a newspaper spread out across his thighs. His arthritic fingers clutched a biro, and he scratched at the crossword on the back page. Mac couldn't see the pants, just a bare torso, spindly calves and mismatched socks poking from beneath the page. He glanced back at Leslie and saw her hands rising and falling as she dealt with the contents of the sink. Edging closer to the bed, he lowered his voice. "Poppa, can I take you for coffee in the hotel bar?"

"Eh?" Alfie stared up at him, the gaze from his rheumy eyes obscured by the bushy grey brows he wouldn't let Leslie trim. "Why?"

Mac swallowed and stepped towards the bed. "I need help, Poppa. Advice."

Alfie's head jerked back on his stalk neck. "I'm eighty-nine moko. Don't gots no advice suitable for a mokopuna." He tilted his head back and gazed at the vaulted ceiling. "That's not true. Just don't do it. Best advice I can offer."

Mac exhaled and his chest seemed to cave. "Okay." He turned away from the bed and met Leslie on the threshold of the room.

"Miserable old bugger!" she grumbled. She glared at the old man reclined on the bed and shook her head. Her fingers clasped Mac's wrist. "I need to nip to the kaumātua's whare in the township. Can you stay with him just for a while?"

"I don't need minding! I'm not a pepi!"

"Then stop acting like one!" Leslie sent Mac a gratified nod before barrelling towards the apartment door and her ready escape.

Alfie set his pen in the newspaper's fold and sighed. "She was waiting for an excuse to leave me. Now she has one. She took her knitting, did you see? It's her bitch and stitch night, but she said she'd stay here with me." He observed Mac for a moment before asking, "Why do you need advice from an abandoned, broken-down old man like me? Logan's your best bet for stuff like that."

Mac shook his head. "I can't speak to him about this, Poppa."

"You in trouble? You got raruraru?"

"Yes." Mac swallowed. He cleared the blockage in his throat and the words sounded scratchy. "Raruraru. Big trouble, sir." He glanced up at the overhead beams and sensed his hope draining through his socks. His father knew most of what occurred in the apartment, and his children always joked that the renovation included listening devices. He couldn't imagine Logan pouring over recordings of Alfie winding up Leslie and her berating him. But it wasn't worth the risk.

Alfred's shoulders slumped, and he pursed his lips. His closed eyelids prevented Mac from reading his thoughts. He patted the paper covering his thighs. "Well, I lied. I'm not wearing pants." He jerked his head towards the lounge. "Go next door. Give me ten minutes and I'll come with you. Anywhere you want to go."

6

GOALIE

"This didn't happen." Alfred Du Rose wagged his finger at Mac as they settled onto stools in the bar. He tilted his ever-present cowboy hat back on his head. Once a dark tan, it had faded to the hue of dust. "Grass me up and I'll not leave you my favourite hat in my will." He tapped the warped brim with his crabbed fingers. Mac nodded, understanding he meant to keep secret the ride down in the stair lift, which he'd actually enjoyed.

The bartender refused to serve Mac. "You're underage."

"But we only want coffee." Mac eyed the man with a frown. He dipped his chin and channelled his father's authority, noticing the way the man flinched.

The conference centre manager stepped up behind him and touched him on the shoulder. Mac jerked away before recognising the man. "Everything okay, Mr Du Rose?" Blue irises sparkled from beneath heavy lids. He'd run the hotel for almost a decade after the hasty exit of his predecessor. Leasing the listed building had proved a tentative experiment for his father, but it relieved him of the day to day running of a venture he'd never enjoyed.

Mac shrugged. "I just want to buy my poppa a coffee," he said, turning his attention to the manager. "I'm not breaking any licensing laws, Mr Carlisle."

The manager glanced back at Alfie perched on his stool. The old man played a game with a coaster, but his arthritic fingers refused the call to action. It plunged to the carpeted floor, and he glared at it from his high seat. Reggie Carlisle gave a definitive nod and leaned across the bar. "Two coffees, on the house," he said, his tone light.

Mac shook his head and drew the cash from his back pocket. He set it on the bar and walked back to Alfie, retrieving the coaster on the way.

"What's all that about?" Alfie demanded in a loud whisper. Spittle shot through the gaps from missing teeth and landed on the table.

"Nothing." Mac offered him a disarming smile. "Pa said don't take favours from this crowd."

"Ae. Too right." Alfie nodded in satisfaction. "He learned that from me."

Mac exhaled a sigh. Alfred Du Rose had ruined a decent business in his time and it earned him a seat at the bankruptcy court. Logan had rescued the hotel and surrounding land with money earned during his time in London. The old man had accepted more favours than Mac could list. He smirked to himself at the illusion of greatness which time and distance fostered.

The coffees arrived, and the bartender conveyed his discomfort with rapid blinking as he set them on the table. "Sorry about that," he said to Mac under his breath.

Mac shook his head and paused long enough to force eye contact. "No worries," he told him. And he meant it.

Alfie snorted as the man hurried back to the bar. "You do that thing," he cackled.

"What thing?" Mac lifted his hand and fiddled with the processor behind his ear. He tugged at an auburn curl and patted it over the device.

"What your papa does." Alfie forced a gnarled finger through the mug handle. The distended knuckles meant only one finger fitted. He wrinkled his nose and removed it, cupping the mug between both hands instead. "Accidental intimidation. Only, in his case, it's not so accidental."

Mac frowned and blinked at the same time. "No." He rejected the notion offhand. "I don't think that's true."

Alfie shrugged and growled low in his throat. He dipped his head to sip his coffee before asking, "Now, what's this hui about then?"

Mac exhaled and considered his next sentence. The moment's delay caused Alfie to stare at him from beneath his hairy brows. Mac blew out a ragged breath. "It's about Edin," he whispered. "She's become a problem, and I don't know what to do about it." The revelation caused his voice to croak, an irritating track mark of adolescence. It masked his underlying discomfort at speaking about their relationship as something from which he'd divorced himself. He recognised in himself a disturbing trait, pushing Edin outside his circle when things got too difficult.

Alfred nodded, understanding softening his grey irises. "Ah," he replied. His sigh caused bubbles of frothed milk to wobble on his lower lip. "And you don't want to stir up trouble with your parents by telling them about her antics?"

"Yes, sir." Relief sent a shiver through Mac's body and he slopped coffee over the side of the mug as he lifted it. "Ma and Pa don't treat her any different to me and Phoe." Confession produced a catharsis and an uncharacteristic verbal diarrhoea beset his tongue. "I don't want you to think they're at the root of this. If anything, Ma tries too hard to love Edin. She gets very little in return." His brow knitted into a series of lines. "But we hear things."

Alfie nodded. "Those stock men are a bunch of old women," he growled. "They gossip like a bloody knitting circle."

Mac widened his eyes to emerald orbs. "Added to the fact she used to visit her mother in prison once a month."

Alfie recoiled. "Don't get me started on her," he growled. "She's a poisonous wahine. Your mother is the one reason Edin didn't turn out the same."

Mac cleared his throat and shifted on his stool. "That's the problem," he whispered. He dipped his body to prevent his deep voice carrying across the bar to eager ears. "I think she has."

Alfie winced. The tendons on either side of his neck tightened to produce a grizzled effect. With each iteration of Mac's tale, they seemed to constrict more until the old man resembled a tortoise reaching from its shell. He raised his hand to signal he'd had enough, his head shaking as though at the end of a fishing line. "So, every time you get close to a girl, she threatens her?" He coughed over the last word without covering his mouth.

Mac nodded. His shoulders drooped with the monstrosity of the problem. "I got a text after school from the captain of the soccer team I'm coaching." His cast bumped against the table top. "She said Edin cornered three of them in the toilets after lunch. She punched one of them in the stomach. Told them to stay away from me or else." He pursed his lips and fought the tears rising into his throat. His emerald irises glittered with teenage emotion. "I don't know what to do." He lifted his cast. "I can't play, so I offered to coach. Now, she's stopping me from even doing that."

Alfie sighed. "Have you spoken to her about how you see her? Does she know you don't feel the same?"

Mac squeezed his eyes closed. His lashes met like the death grip of a Venus fly trap as he fought to contain the unwanted emotion. "Yes." It hadn't gone well, but then perhaps she knew he'd lied to her. He had felt the same once, until the impossibility of it crowded out all trace of love and left emptiness in its foamy wake. She'd slapped his cheek and left a welt of red beneath his eye. Then continued as though it hadn't happened. The coffee mug shook in his right hand. "What should I do?"

Alfie leaned back on his stool and his answer caused Mac to baulk in surprise. "You're speaking to the wrong man," he replied. "You should kōrero with your father."

"No, no, no." Mac shook his head. He bowed close enough over the table to bump it with his chest. "I can't talk to him about this. Not now." His mind produced images of the angry woman at the round pen. Her jagged mouth had carried the words, 'You can't do this to me,' as far as his lip reading could comprehend. His father had remained silent in the emergency room. His step had lost a little of its spring ever since. Mac rested his forehead on the table. His cast leaned against his left thigh, pain prickling along the edges of the broken bones. "I need to talk to you about it," he groaned. "Just you, Poppa." He lifted his head, his vision blurred by misery.

Alfie conceded with a nod. "Fine," he agreed, "but my story is more like Edin's than yours. I adored Logan's mother, but she never loved me." He flapped his crabbed hand. "Oh, she tried harder than most. I knew my brother fathered Logan, but we all pretended it wasn't true." His eyes sparkled with tears. "I see Miriam sometimes." He lowered his voice and his chin touched the rim of his mug. "I watch her walking along the path towards the bush. She used that track to get to Reuben's house. Do you believe in ghosts, Macky? Because I see her with my own eyes."

Mac swallowed. The question stymied him. He'd attended church and listened to countless sermons. The correct answer was no, but Alfie seemed so convinced. He realised after a pause that his poppa didn't need a response, anyway.

Alfie exhaled. He dragged his mug closer and lifted it again to his lips. "So, I'm Edin, see? I'm the one my woman didn't love." He waggled his brows. "Your pa is you. Caroline wouldn't let him go. She still hasn't. That's why you need his advice."

Mac resumed his determined head shake. "No," he replied. "You're wrong. Nonie adores you, but you don't feel the same. You've chosen to let her take care of you the way she does. Should I just give up like that and accept Edin, even though I feel no love for her?" *No love.* He swallowed the knot in his throat.

The mug clattered to the table and tipped sideways. Mac's cast banged the table as he attempted to lift his hand and met the hard underside of the wood. The bartender appeared at his shoulder with a cloth. "All good," he soothed. He snatched up the mug and used the cloth to soak up the spill. "I'll fetch you another." He'd gone before Mac could refuse.

Alfie sat on his stool like a statue. He resembled one of the gnomes his wife loved so much. She'd scattered them across her roof garden like comical soldiers. Logan detested them, pursing his lips into a line of disgust with each new gaudy addition. Alfie's jaw worked, but no sound emerged. Mac realised too late that he'd accidentally held a mirror up to the old man's marriage and then smashed it to pieces.

"Sorry, Poppa," he breathed. He turned his body to observe the empty bar before jerking his head towards the exit. "Let's go. I'll help you upstairs."

Alfie remained stationary. Agony flared in his stone-coloured irises as his gaze rested on Mac. "I'm a dick!" he shouted, his voice too loud for the environment. "I'm a right dick!"

HEADER

They drank their second mug of coffee and made it to the apartment before Leslie arrived home. Mac helped her to heave a heavy bag of wool up the stairs and ran down to her car to retrieve another.

"Thanks, boy," she said with a sigh. "Marlie bequeathed me her stash of wool to knit baby clothes. Sandy asked me to leave the rest for her when I pop off."

Mac slammed a portcullis over her musings. He didn't want to venture into a thought-world where his grandparents didn't feature. As he set the last bag on the kitchen table, he heard Alfie's voice and turned. The elderly couple stood near the window Alfie spoke about, the ceiling to floor length one in the gable end from where he watched his wife walk up the mountain to her lover. Alfie wrapped his arms around his ageing wife and rested his chin on her shoulder. Mac didn't hear his whispered words, but he read his lips. "I'll be a better husband," he whispered. "I'll use the tūru on the stairs and we'll go places again."

Mac left without speaking. His boots clattered against the wooden stairs as though filled with concrete. His wrist ached, and he remembered an English assignment he still needed to finish.

The balmy air of late summer shrouded him on the front steps of the hotel. He shielded his eyes with his right hand and contemplated his long walk up the mountain.

"Hey, Macky, how's it going?" A gruff voice behind him made him jump, and he whipped around to find Toby emerging from the hotel's front doors. He carried a screwdriver in his right hand. "Door in the mudroom was sticking. Dave's on leave, so I've fixed it." He grinned, proud of his achievement. Mac nodded and smiled. "How's the arm?" Toby jerked his head towards the cast and Mac winced.

"Sore. The doctor said it needs to stay in a cast for six weeks."

Toby flattened his lips. "A bad break then. Do you need surgery?"

"Maybe." Mac stared at the black fibreglass and wished he'd gone for a light reflective colour instead of one which hid the dirt. He sighed. He wished he'd done many things differently.

"You rode the mare again yet?" Toby bounced the handle of his screwdriver against his thigh. He cocked his head and waited for Mac's answer.

"I tried. Tonight." Mac stared at Toby and a light went off in his brain. He licked his lips and considered spreading his problem a little wider than in his immediate family. Everyone knew Toby loved Hana. She'd shown no interest, and so a tentative truce existed between Logan and his farm manager. One wrong move and Toby would disappear into a dark hole in the ground. Yet, still he stayed.

Desperation made Mac clumsy with his words and he burbled them without enough thought. "What should you do if someone loves you more than you love them?"

Toby recoiled. In that moment, Mac realised that again, he'd asked the wrong person for advice. The screwdriver clattered against the gravel and Toby bought himself time by bending to retrieve it. When he rose, a mask of control covered the emotion simmering beneath. His jaw showed through his cheek as he ground his jaw. "Be kind," he said, his voice husky. He jerked his head towards the mountain. "You need a ride home?"

Mac needed a ride home very much. But he couldn't accept one from Toby. Not now.

Dusk arrived fast, a trait of the New Zealand sky. One minute the sun shone on the mountain and then winked out as though someone flicked a switch. The tides behaved the same way, rushing in without warning and stranding tourists in a heartbeat. Mac used the little-known track through the bush. He realised, as he followed the old fence line between Reuben's property and Logan's, that he unwittingly retraced Miriam's footsteps. He paused to stare down at the maze created on the site of Reuben's burned house and wished he could find the right people to ask his questions.

It took him an hour to walk home and darkness lay over the mountain like a tablecloth. He used the data on his phone to dictate his English assignment into a Google Doc and his mood improved.

Hana helped him to wrap the plastic sleeve over his cast before he took a shower. Horse hair and dust washed from his skin and floated into the drain. He let the spray pound his neck and shoulders before the timer sounded from its place next to the sink. The summer drought dictated a three-minute shower, and he obeyed the rule. No one wanted to experience the hell of being unable to flush the toilet when the tanks ran dry. Not after last time, when Leslie had managed to block all three of them following an accidental binge on flax tea.

Mac dried himself and wrapped a towel around his waist. Already tired of performing even the smallest tasks one handed, he groaned as the knot refused to hold. He unlocked the bathroom door and clung to the edges of the towel as he padded along the hallway.

Edin stood in the doorway of his bedroom, her left shoulder resting against the frame. Her grey eyes glittered with an unfathomable danger and he paused in front of her. Tension locked his chest muscles, and he flinched against the water dripping from his curls and speckling the heavy tiles beneath his feet. Edin watched, her red lips curving in a calculating smile. "Your phone rang," she said, her mouth forming the words with added emphasis so he could read her lips. She lifted the device in her right hand and Mac tensed. His keen eyes saw the missed call icon before it darkened to the swirling sand of the lockscreen. Edin didn't know the code. She'd cornered him instead, her soul screaming for answers through the portals of her black pupils.

Her gaze swept over his muscular chest and his death grip on the towel around his waist. With his cast encased in the plastic wrapper, he couldn't take the phone from her and she saw his dilemma. And grinned. "Who's M?"

"Just leave it on the bed," he said. The drips increased around him and the tiles darkened in patches. Edin held the phone by its topmost corner with two fingers and stared at it. Mac sensed the underlying threat. She'd drop it and claim it was an accident. He held his breath, not wanting her to follow through with it. His teeth set up a regular grinding, which created a vibrational beat in his brain. He'd worked all summer to earn enough to buy the indestructible model, but didn't want her to test the advertising claims.

Shock proof.

Water proof.

Edin proof.

A light touch to his shoulder made him jerk sideways, and he clattered his cast against the other side of the door. Hana frowned at him. Her gaze slid to Edin and back again and her hands lifted to sign to him. "What's going on?"

Mac turned to face Edin. Sweat formed a line along his spine despite the coolness of the shower just minutes earlier. "Leave it on the bed," he commanded. She blinked, and he realised he'd sounded harsher than he intended. His words returned to him as a vibration.

Edin glanced at Hana before laying the phone on the tallboy nearest the door. Mac saw Hana's shoulders stiffen in his peripheral vision at the exaggerated care of the act. He didn't hear Edin's reply, but she moved aside so he could enter his room. He sank onto the double bed and faced the door.

Hana stood for a moment. She watched Edin move out of sight. Then she faced her son and tapped her left wrist. He lifted his arm, and she stepped into his bedroom, her fingers already reaching for the sleeve. She extracted his cast with care and held the damp plastic by one corner. "I'll dry this for tomorrow," she mouthed, and he nodded. With one hand, she improvised the sign language for, "Is everything okay?"

Mac nodded and offered her a reassuring smile. If she saw the lie behind his eyes, she said nothing. Her eyebrows twitched, a nothing kind of movement which was there and then gone. A flicker of suspicion. He couldn't ask her his burning questions, either. She adored his father, but equally. They were an unbreakable alliance and always would be.

He hoped.

Again, the memory of the stranger with the accusing eyes rose unbidden. He sighed. All points led back to Logan, yet his father represented the one person he couldn't bother with his questions right then. So he smiled at his mother and hoped she believed him.

Mac donned pyjama bottoms. He hung the damp towel over the handle of his wardrobe to dry, not wanting to encounter Edin again on another trip to the heated rail in the bathroom. He opened his laptop and logged in, resorting to technology to stem his anxiety. The Google Doc he'd dictated needed a little tweaking, but he submitted it on the school's server before the deadline.

Remembering the missed call, he retrieved his phone from the tallboy and unlocked it. Phoenix had cracked his code with disgusting ease a few years earlier, and he'd become much smarter about protecting his privacy. He used a complicated mixture of symbols and numbers before adding a retina scan. The screen flared to life, revealing a call from M. Edin could still have answered it using the power button, but hadn't realised.

Mac ran his left wrist across his forehead before groaning in pain. He wondered how long it would take him to learn not to do that. "Pavlov's Dog," he murmured under his breath. The empty room absorbed the words, but Mac couldn't tell if he'd even pronounced it right. The silence in his head soothed his nerves as he opened the text which had remained behind the lockscreen and out of Edin's view. Unable to speak to him, M had typed a message.

'Thanks so much for your help last week. I feel safer now. Himself is saying you quit coaching but I'm glad you didn't. See you tomorrow. M.'

The realisation hit him like a fall onto concrete. She'd trusted him the previous week. Trusted him not to tell anyone and to help her with the very private matter. Mac clicked the fingers of his right hand in a pattern of agitation.

She could tell him what to do.

Because she'd been there.

8

KICKOFF

Logan drove the teenagers to the bus stop in the township. Edin sat in the back seat with buds jammed in her ears. She spent the journey texting her friends. Mac licked his lips before turning in his seat and observing his father. He formulated the sentence before he released it. "Papa? Who was the woman in the high heels? She distracted me and I fell off Sassy."

Logan ran a hand over his mouth, but kept his gaze on the road. His tongue poked the left corner of his lip and the warning vein pulsed beneath his jawline. "No one important." He sighed and his even tone negated the question. Mac's speech processor delivered the words to his brain, but they didn't match his father's body language. The tension in his shoulders and the stiffness of his neck betrayed the lie.

Mac pressed himself against the seat and focused on the view through the side window. Logan hated liars, and it turned his reply into something else. Either the woman was unimportant and her arm-waving rant irrelevant. Or his father had broken his own rules and covered up something damaging to the family. Mac swallowed and sensed his heart rate tick up a notch. "Does

Ma know?" He dipped forward in his seat to observe Logan's expression.

His father pushed out his lower lip and shook his head. "There's nothing to know yet," he replied. Again, that same even tone aimed to dispel Mac's fears. But his body language stiffened and his biceps bulged through the sleeves of his shirt.

Mac exhaled. Logan had created a cul-de-sac and ended the conversation. Hana didn't know about the woman's visit, but Logan intimated he'd tell her. Just not yet. A veiled warning thrummed behind the sentence, promising consequences if Mac got to her first. It wounded his tender spirit. He pressed his spine against his seat and gritted his jaw. "I have soccer coaching after school," he said, his tone surly. "I'll catch the five o'clock bus back to town."

Edin blanked him at the bus stop. She settled onto the bench, still absorbed in her phone, and ignored Mac. When a car drew up alongside and a group of girls waved from the rear windows, she rose and slotted into a space in the back seat. Mac shook his head and moved towards the vehicle. "You need to wait with me," he said, his speech frustratingly slow and slurred. A hitch in the processors' relay to his brain meant he missed her reply. Her lips turned up on one side and the driver spoke to him through her lowered window.

"I've got my full licence," the girl called. "We'll be fine." She depressed the gas pedal and flung the girls back against their seats. Squeals of glee followed the car along the road. Mac performed a mental head count and realised the car was overloaded. There weren't enough seat belts for each girl. He sank onto the bench and put his head in his hands. His rejection of Edin had sent her back into old habits. Hana deserved better than the constant calls from the principal's office.

Mac sighed and peered at his shoes. Dust had replaced the shine and turned the black to grey. "Taking the shine off," he murmured to himself, turning the familiar expression over in his mind. That's what he'd done to Edin. And he still had no answers to tell him how to handle it better.

As other students appeared around him, Mac cheered at the thought of Miss Andrews. He'd get to spend lunchtime and after school with her. Taller and more senior than anyone else at the bus stop, Mac took precedence in choosing a seat. He stepped up to the driver and presented his card, nodding to the man in acknowledgement before sitting in the seat next to the door. The boy who usually sat there glared at him before walking along the bus to slump elsewhere. Mac had always wanted to sit in the single seat at the front. Edin's constant presence had dictated a double bench near the back. Until now.

As the bus pulled away from the curb, Mac stretched out his legs and savoured his independence. Despite Edin's silent protest, something had snapped deep within their relationship. He'd cosseted and sheltered and mitigated for her for as long as he remembered, not noticing as her influence closed in to hinder and repress him. Everything felt different. Freer and less heavy.

He rested his cast on his left thigh and studied the driver's movements as he indicated, changed gear, and steered the single decker bus onto the motorway. Mac's rucksack nestled between his feet. He loved the wide view of the traffic through the massive windscreen and looked forward to having his cast removed and resuming his driving lessons. The motion of the driver's hands on the wheel and his feet on the pedals gave Mac vicarious satisfaction. He arrived at school happier than he'd felt for a long time.

Edin's friends covered their mouths and giggled as he strode past them. He wondered if she'd told them about his rejection of her, or spun the story to make them think she'd done the severing. He surreptitiously cast his eye over their number, but didn't see Edin. They loitered in their usual place near the steps up to the main building. Mac took the stairs two at a time, his rucksack bouncing on his shoulder.

He placed his bag in his locker in the Year 13 common room, clicking the padlock closed. Then he used the back stairs to access the rear courtyard and wove his way through the myriad static classrooms angled towards the sports field. A game of rugby induced raised voices as the First Fifteen practised before the start of the season. Mac waved and a few of the boys acknowledged him with shouted replies, which made him smile.

"Did you do it?" Arthur Darian swung into place alongside him as he reached the deserted touch line. Mac's right hand ached to disconnect his processors, but he resisted.

"No. Homework." He kept his reply brief and increased his pace, forcing Darian into a lazy jog.

"End of today. I want a list of prospective candidates for a muster. No shit ones, remember? We're already late to the party." He raised a dirty blond eyebrow spattered with curling grey tendrils. It didn't match the bleached yellow of his straw-like hair. He stopped in a cloud of dust, his chest heaving with the effort of maintaining Mac's gruelling pace.

"Hey Mac." Within seconds, a girl joined him on his march towards the equipment shed. It negated the need for him to respond to Darian's demands. Petite and slender, she ran to match his stride. A purple carrot protruded from her fingers and her jaws worked against her cheek. "Want a carrot?" she asked him.

"No, thanks." He smoothed away the lines which littered his forehead at her odd request.

She shrugged. "Keira gets them from her poppa. He's got a place where he grows stuff. We're getting healthy for the season." Her pink lips smacked with a sound like a rabbit eating.

Mac smiled to acknowledge her commitment to the game. He wondered if he should broach the issue of Edin's threat, or pretend it didn't happen. The girl decided for herself, launching into a recap of an English premier league game she'd watched the previous night. She finished the carrot and brushed her hands against her skirt. "You know some of those moves, don't you?" Her dark eyelashes fluttered as she glanced up at him, mismatched against her blonde pigtails. "Are you going to show us?"

"Yeah." Mac nodded and allowed his lips to curve upward at the corners. "We can do that."

The girl gnawed on the inside of her cheek and frowned. Her ponytail swung from side to side as she trotted beside him. A wave of grief doused him in an icy ache. He missed Phoenix and her unruly curls. She was enjoying her first semester of university, sharing a flat with Wiremu and a group of other students. He ached for them both while acknowledging that neither of them could answer his question. They'd loved each other forever. They wouldn't know what to tell him. "What will happen when you go back to your team?"

Mac searched his memory for the girl's name as he considered his reply. Melissa. Maddie. Something beginning with M. He decided not to risk it and didn't add her name to his answer. "I'll still coach." He lifted his cast and inspected it. "It's a bad break, apparently. I'm seeing an orthopaedic surgeon in two weeks and he'll X-ray it again. I might need surgery."

The girl's lips formed a pout of sympathy, but her body language didn't convey dismay. Another girl joined them as the equipment shed appeared after their next turn.

"Hey Mac." The other girl acknowledged him with a wave of a pale skinned hand.

"Hi," he replied.

"Are you meeting with Miss Andrews too?" She dipped forward to see around the girl next to him. "She's finding us some goalkeeping gloves." Her slender fingers tapped the buttons of her school blouse. "Me and Layla are taking turns in goal."

Layla.

Not Melissa or Maddie or any name beginning with M.

"Me and Sammy are best friends." Layla shot Sammy a sideways glance and reached for her sleeve. She slipped her hand through the crook of her elbow and they both giggled in unison.

Mac nodded and wondered if his friend would return to school soon. Deacon's father had joined the population at Waitakere Prison after defrauding his employer of over a hundred thousand dollars. Deacon's last text explained he didn't yet feel ready to return to public scrutiny. He hadn't said that exactly. Mac read between the lines of lame excuses and emailed the homework to his private Gmail address.

"Do you have a meeting with her?" Sammy repeated her question.

Mac blew out a breath and considered his reply with care. His father advocated sticking to the truth and, despite recent evidence to the contrary, Mac respected his advice. "Not a meeting," he said, tugging his shirt collar away from his throat. "I have a question for her. The rugby team stole all the cones from the equipment shed last season. I'll need some for agility training with you guys."

"Oh." Their lips pursed like identical twins. He'd told the truth but merged his answer with another issue. It seemed to work as they tripped along next to him, blazers flapping in the breeze.

The equipment shed's door stood open, wagging like a tail in the wind. A vacant space to the right of its cavernous interior housed a ridge of cobwebs and dead leaves which had sneaked beneath the door during autumn. Rust shavings dotted the debris like cake icing where the goalposts had waited out the spring, summer and autumn in silence. Mac halted and shielded his eyes from the sun. Posts rose from the goal line of the nearest pitch, fixed into place like a skeleton awaiting the shroud of its net. Each of the four soccer pitches sported one at either end. Mac spun on his heel and afforded himself a silent grin. For once, the rugby pitches waited, their touchlines empty of their majestic cross bars. The rugby boys would hate their demotion to second place.

A single cone prevented the door from slamming closed and trapping someone inside with the critters which lurked there. The darkness and the promise of a million spider webs deterred the girls from entering first. Mac stepped over the threshold.

Dust and plastic, overcooked food and sweat rose around his head in an unpleasant haze. Another scent joined them, a familiar, warning odour like burning tyres mixed with the tang leftover from a soldering iron. He peered through the gloom, identifying crates of balls sorted into codes and every manner of bat, stick and racquet dangling from pegs around the corrugated walls. "Miss Andrews?" he called, his voice resonating in his head. Reaching to the left of the door, he located the light switch and flicked it into position. Light should have bloomed from an overhead bulb, but it didn't.

Bodies pressed behind him and an elbow brushed his right hip. "Miss Andrews?" Layla sidestepped him, emboldened by the presence of a male unafraid of White Tail spiders. Her left arm trailed behind her as Sammy clutched her hand. "Are you here? Do we have cones? Mac wants to teach us something." She stepped in front of him and he felt the jolt which went through her body. Her left foot landed hard on his instep and she clattered him as she turned. Sammy's arm became twisted and she let out a cry of pain. Layla's limbs spasmed like a shaking rag doll and her mouth opened wide in a scream. Light from outside highlighted her white teeth encased in metal braces with inset fake gems. It seemed her screams brought dust cascading from the ceiling, but it was the impact of Sammy's body hitting the door frame which rocked the flimsy building.

Mac's arms swept up to catch her as she forced herself against him for a second time. He remained rock steady, his head still reverberating from the high-pitched scream relayed to his brain by the processors. He couldn't think straight, so he held her until she ceased her frantic thrashing. His arms enfolded her and sobs rocked her torso. She slid lower, and he struggled to keep her upright.

Confusion shrouded the teenagers as Mac carried Layla into the fresh air. Sammy's eyes had widened to white orbs in her pale face, her pupils pinpricks against the sunshine. "What's wrong with her?" she whispered, standing back to watch Mac dangling her like a doll. "Did something happen to her legs?"

"I don't know." He dipped his torso and spun on his heel. No safe place presented itself for him to lay her safely down. "Get help," he grunted. Relief sent warmth to his legs as Sammy tugged a phone from her blazer pocket.

"Ambulance or front office?" she demanded, her fingers coasting across the screen.

Mac stared down at Layla's closed eyelids and her gaping mouth. He replied, "Both. Ambulance first and then the school office. So they know it's not a hoax."

Layla's shoulders tugged on the break between his radius and ulna. The excruciating pain occupied his mind, and he ceased looking for somewhere to put her. Sweat beaded on his forehead and his stomach roiled as the fragile healing separated. He lifted his left knee to take her weight and prayed for rescue.

When he swore, Sammy glanced up from her phone. "Oh no!" she breathed. "It's hurting your arm. He caught a flash of a photograph on her screen as she lowered it, and cursed her need to record a disaster before summoning help. He saw himself depicted as a hero with the teenager cradled in his arms. In the space of ten seconds, Sammy had added a sword and a shield to the image.

"Did you call the emergency number?" He spoke through gritted teeth. Laying the girl on the dusty ground lost its appeal. It involved energy already consumed by the agony of his bones grinding against one another. Extracting his arm from beneath her would ensure he needed surgery as he tugged the bones apart further. He berated himself in his own head for not taking care of himself before reacting. It was his father's first rule of bushman craft.

Sammy's voice rose as she gave her details to the operator. "Not me!" she said for the second time. "My friend collapsed. We're at school." Patience and a cool head enabled the operator to extract the salient details of where, when and who before she despatched the paramedics.

"Find something," Mac gasped. "Drag out the vaulting horse or a table. If I don't lay her down now, I'll drop her." His body dipped and his legs sagged. He lost the ability to bend his knees with any degree of control. He imagined adding a head and crush injuries to the girl's woes as they both hit the hard ground.

Sammy stared at her screen. The operator had told her to stay on the line and it caused her conflict. She tucked the phone into her top pocket and added a look of apology which the operator didn't see. "I'm putting you on speaker." She stabbed an index finger at the icon. "I think she saw a spider," she said, giving a visible shudder. She moved towards the flapping door of the equipment shed with obvious reluctance. "Layla hates spiders."

Mac swore again, and Sammy steeled herself before stepping into the shed. Her scream defined the term 'blood-curdling' and his wrist gave way. Leyla's weight separated the bones once and for all, and Mac pitched face first into the dirt.

9

LINESMAN

He rolled at the last second, and Layla tumbled to the floor like a bundle of laundry. Mac groaned and wrapped the fingers of his right hand around the cast. It took him a good thirty seconds to get his heaving breaths under control.

With no help in sight, he shuffled towards the doorway on his knees, still clutching his wrist. He used the door frame to brace himself and slid his spine upwards. Splinters snatched at the fabric of his blazer. He spared a fleeting second of advanced sympathy for Hana as she tried to remove the dust from his trousers and mend his jacket.

Once upright, he lurched into the dark bowels of the shed, not sure if he had enough strength to rescue another teenager. Silence shrouded him and he found Sammy by walking into the back of her. She released a grunt of discomfort.

"What are you doing?" he demanded. The grinding of his bones sent his voice to a higher pitch. She remained silent, standing like a statue next to a crate of cricket balls. The dim light cast all but the top few into inky shadow. The glint of glass and metal caught his attention. Reaching down with his right hand, he found a mobile phone balanced across the corner of the crate. He shoved it into his blazer pocket, freeing up his fingers to seize the back of Sammy's collar. "We need to get back to Layla. My wrist gave way, and I dropped her."

Sirens cut through the stillness as a wail of alarm, rising and falling as the ambulance responded to a dubious distress call from a local high school.

"Do you think she's dead?" Sammy's whisper contained a sob. She lifted her right hand and pointed into the darkness.

"Who?" Mac blew out a breath laced with a groan. "No. I managed to roll to one side, so I didn't squash her. But I've screwed my wrist real bad." He clutched his forearm across his chest and rested his thumb against his shoulder, trying to lessen the pounding of the blood through his fingers. "It hurts," he admitted.

As his eyes adjusted to the darkness beyond the arc of light in the doorway, he noticed a shape in front of Sammy. Trainers, legs and a waist, before the void consumed the torso and head. "What's that?" he whispered. His movement jostled Sammy and seemed to wake her from her stupor. She turned on the spot and lifted her slender face to him. Scattered light danced over her high cheekbones and the tears glistening on her cheeks.

"It's Miss Andrews." Her voice rose by degrees with each uttered word. "I tripped over her foot and she's not moving. Is it my fault? Do you think I killed her?"

A hiccup inserted itself into the sentence and she pressed her face against Mac's chest. Her forehead caught his wrist in its downward pitch and he used a vile swearword banned in their home long ago. A favourite of the stockmen, he fancied it turned the stifled air in the shed a hazy blue.

Then he caught the faint scent of meat in his nostrils. Pork. Roasted on the bone. A metallic, electrical burning. Weird. Realisation dawned as he lifted his right arm and slipped it around Sammy's shoulders. It made no sense in his addled mind that someone would cook a body. He locked his elbow to support his poor wrist and edged Sammy from the equipment shed. She stood mute in the doorway where he left her as he dipped his torso and vomited from a mixture of pain and shock.

10

MATCH

The paramedics arrived, followed by a patrol car. Students gathered at the corner between the changing rooms and the equipment shed, drawn to the promise of drama. Phone screens reflected the morning's rising sun as they filmed, texted, and provided a steady stream of commentary.

Layla woke and sobbed against the shoulder of a female paramedic. As the least mobile of the three, she demanded the most attention. "The spider stung me," she wailed, making little sense.

Sammy stood next to Mac and watched the activity, a blank expression cast into shadow by her limp fringe. "Told ya," she said. Mac slumped on the dusty earth, his legs out straight before him and his throbbing arm resting across his thigh.

A police officer disgorged himself from his patrol car, pausing to check his pockets and lock up his vehicle. He surveyed the scene before ambling across to Mac. "Someone reported an injury." His tone held the bare minimum of interest. With his shirt overhanging his trousers and rolls of pink flesh creeping upwards to touch his chin, Mac figured the controller hadn't taken the call seriously.

"Oh." Sammy tugged her phone from her top pocket. She lifted the device to her ear. "I left it on speaker. The lady must have heard us find Miss Andrews dead on the floor." Jabbing her finger at the screen, she killed the call.

The officer blinked. Sweat already beaded his forehead and spread a darkening stain beneath his armpits. "Wait, there's a body?" He took a step backwards as though desperate to escape.

"Yes." Sammy pointed to the equipment shed. The door clanged against the road cone, the key still protruding from the lock. "Miss Andrews is in there. She's lying next to the cricket balls." She swallowed and looked down at Mac. "My friend screamed and collapsed. Mac ran in after her and carried her outside to safety." Her lips parted and her irises sparkled with the glint of adoration. "He's a hero. I went in to see what happened and Mac came back in for me. Mac's our soccer coach. He's amazing." Her eyelashes fluttered and Mac's shoulders slumped. The police officer continued backing away as though he felt they might be contaminated. He still hadn't pulled out a notebook or asked any pertinent questions. Mac knew his brother would have already closed the scene and moved the students.

The male paramedic walked towards them, dust rising from beneath his shoes. "Do either of you need help?" he asked.

Sammy pointed at Mac. "He broke his wrist again," she stated. The lure of social media distracted her, and she peered at her phone screen as it pinged. Her lips parted in a smile. "My photo just went viral."

The paramedic knelt on the ground next to Mac and pulled open his bag. "Tell me about this," he said, pointing to the cast.

Mac sighed. "I broke it on Saturday. The doctor warned me to take care or I'll need surgery." He stared across at Layla as she blew her nose into a tissue. "I carried her out and felt something twang around the break. Now I can't feel my fingers."

The paramedic nodded. "What's inside there?"

Mac lowered his voice, and the man leaned closer. "Our sports teacher. I think she's dead." He closed his eyes at the memory of the pork scent and his stomach gave a threatening lurch. Grief washed in like a violent tide, bringing with it a jumble of confused thoughts. He longed to rip the processors from his head and plunge himself into a safe silence where he could think.

The paramedic whirled on his toes and peered at the police officer. "Does he know?"

"Yeah." Mac sighed and watched the officer waving his arms at the gathering crowd. His radio crackled, and he dipped his head to speak into it. "But his crime scene is already a mess." He ran his right hand across his top lip, transferring dust from the ground to his face. "Can you take this off, please?" He shifted his cast across his thigh and groaned. "My arm is swelling inside it."

"Sorry mate." The paramedic rose and nodded to his colleague. "That's a hospital job. We'll take you and the other young lady to Auckland City. It's nearer than Waikato Hospital." He blew out a ragged breath, which matched the trepidation of his pursed lips. "Let me just check the lady in the shed."

He walked towards the open doorway and stuck his head into the darkness. The police officer handed responsibility for crowd control to three male teachers who arrived to check out reports of an unusual gathering. "Wait! Wait!" he shouted to the paramedic.

"I need to make sure," the man replied. He frowned at the sight of phone screens lifted in unison to capture his grand entrance. The crowd of students held their collective breath.

"I'll come with you." The officer puffed towards him, dust rising into a choking haze around him. The paramedic coughed and waved his hand in front of his face. Mac wondered how many footprints they'd buried beneath the storm at the officer's feet. He winced, knowing his own prints and DNA covered every centimetre from his sitting position to the body. Again, he thought of his brother and considered calling him. He lifted the fingers of his right hand and touched his top pocket.

Would Bodie come for him?

His fingers dropped to cradle his left arm. The fact he needed to ask himself the question at all fed doubt into his mind. Sammy continued capitalising on her momentary fame, smiling to herself and tapping away on her phone. "Look." She squatted down and spun the screen to face him. Mac dipped his head to negate the glare of the sun. The image of him as a rescuer stared back at him, the ridiculous sword and shield jarring with the formality of his school uniform. The strain showed on his face, his teeth gritted in pain as he supported Layla's limp body with his broken wrist.

"Nice," he commented, for lack of anything suitable.

"No. Look." Sammy pointed to the bottom of the screen. "It's gone viral on Instagram. Over a million people have already liked it. Look at all the hearts."

Mac groaned. "Why did you do that? The police will be really mad at you. It's a crime scene."

Sammy shrugged. "Do you want to see the TikTok version?"

"You filmed?" Mac rubbed his eyes. "Please tell me you didn't film Miss Andrews laying on the floor?"

Sammy licked her lips. "I did. But I'm not sure about posting that one. The light wasn't great."

"Give me your phone." Mac's voice held authority, and he held out his hand.

"What will you do with it?" A twitch began at the corner of Sammy's left eye and she flattened her lips into a line. "I'm trending. That's never happened to me before. I'm an influencer. I influence things."

Mac waggled his fingers. "Then let's use the footage to influence finding out how Miss Andrews died." The words clattered in his brain. A surge of emotion rose and he tamped it down again. He wanted to cry and rail but couldn't. Perhaps he'd never be allowed to show the real extent of his grief.

Sammy smiled. "Okay. But I'm coming with you to the hospital. And you'll need to let me interview you for my Vlog."

Mac ground his teeth and his fingers stiffened. "Phone," he growled, hearing his father's impatience resonating through his tone.

Sammy laid it in his palm with great reverence. He jammed it into the right-hand pocket of his blazer. It continued to dance and vibrate as the post received more hits and interest worldwide.

The men emerged from the equipment shed. They didn't speak to each other, but the medic appeared sad and the police officer looked ill. He pressed a finger over his earpiece and spoke into his radio. "I need an electrician here fast," he demanded.

Sammy watched them with abject interest until she patted Mac's right shoulder. He looked up at her, seeing the sunshine creating a halo around her head. It threw her face into shadow. She paused a moment before asking, "Will you be my boyfriend?"

11

Midfield

Grant Simms snored in the visitor's chair in Mac's cubicle. Emergency room staff milled around beyond the curtain. A healthy dose of morphine dulled the throbbing in Mac's wrist, but also blurred his vision. He lay in the hospital bed with his head tilted back at an awkward angle, lacking the energy to move.

Sammy leaned over and hissed in his ear, causing him to jerk and release a moan of pain. He'd disconnected the speech processors and lost track of them, but her breath and a haze of fine spit landed on his cheek. He turned to face her as she repeated her question. "When can I have my phone back?"

Using his right hand, he patted his chest, seeking the copious blazer pockets containing his phone, processors, and Sammy's phone. A memory resurfaced of another device pushed into a pocket with haste. His eyes widened when his fingers contacted the flimsy fabric of a hospital gown. A nurse helped him out of his school shirt and trousers, allowing him to keep his boxer shorts and socks. He forced his brain to remember where she'd stowed his clothing and looked around the narrow space. "I don't have it," he said.

Sammy jerked backwards, and he figured he'd pitched his whisper more towards the shouty end of the spectrum. Her eyes bugged wide, and she spread her palms in question.

"It's here somewhere." The words vibrated in his jaw and he hoped he'd managed to achieve a normal voice. "Don't worry."

The curtain swished aside in his peripheral vision and his brother's face peered through the gap. He counted his blessings that Bodie wore street clothes and not the full rig of a police officer's uniform. His keen-eyed gaze absorbed the scene of an indignant girl, sleeping teacher and injured brother. The serious expression morphed into one of concern.

Mac jabbed his right hand towards his ear and shook his head, telling Bodie he couldn't hear. His brother switched to a rudimentary form of sign language, which passed as communication. 'What happened?' he demanded with his hands.

Sammy's gaze intensified, and Mac froze. Her scrutiny caused a flicker of embarrassment to pink his ears. Heat began its uncomfortable crawl up his neck and into his cheeks. Bodie read the distress in his eyes and lifted his index finger. He whirled on the spot and disappeared back through the curtain to ask questions of someone else.

Sammy's lips moved, but Mac stopped bothering to decipher her quick, mumbled speech. He closed his eyes and lay his head against the pillow.

Miss Andrews was dead.

And she'd smelled like roast pork.

Despite the limited visibility, he'd recognised her trainers from numerous interactions. A hearing impediment increased his other senses tenfold, and he identified the metallic tang of blood and the awful burned flesh. The switch hadn't activated the bulb which served the cluttered space with its dull yellow glow when he pressed it. He wrinkled his nose at the thought of his fingerprints being lifted by a forensics technician.

Sadness locked up his lungs and caused him to take shallow breaths. His hopes for the future slid away from his grasping fingers like leaves sucked down a waterfall.

Marie Andrews.

Marie.

The contact in his phone listed as M.

He'd intended to finish school at the end of the year and then ask her on a date. The age gap didn't concern him. Four years seemed like nothing. The only obstacle between them was the student teacher relationship. She'd said that when he kissed her, her lips quivering beneath his for long enough to convey something he hadn't understood. She loved her job. It couldn't happen again.

He'd agreed. He'd realised perhaps some part of her recognised the action as him fleeing from the inevitable. From Edin. Though he denied his increasing attraction to his cousin, it hung between them like an electrical aura. He'd allowed thoughts of Marie Andrews to fill his head and heart, forcing out the other pangs and holding them on the periphery.

Only the previous day, he'd learned Marie liked horse riding. Hugging the snippet of information to himself, it added another facet of her character, which meshed with his.

His heart lurched with an unnamed wave of emotion. He'd liked her more than he could explain. Despite the inappropriateness of their growing friendship, or perhaps because of it, she'd approached him for help. Him. A Year 13 boy with a disability. Not just for coaching assistance with the soccer team, but for the other thing, too. The thing he'd promised not to disclose.

Mac gnawed on his lower lip and pondered where that left him in terms of the police investigation. He glanced at Sammy and found her staring at him. Her lips continued moving, and he sensed himself swept up on a conveyor-belt of trouble. She'd seen Bodie signing but hadn't comprehended the full extent of his deafness. With the clunky processors absent from behind his ears, he guessed he looked just like any other teenager in her circle.

Except for his auburn curls, highlighted white in places by the harsh sunshine.

And the hard muscles earned by heavy farm work.

He needed his mother. Hana Du Rose's gentle heart and steady hand could sift through the tangled wool and turn it back into something understandable. She'd defend him against Sammy's unwanted attention and decipher the unintelligible sentences of the surgeon who'd pushed his swollen wrist into a splint and shaken his head. She'd also understand his feelings for Marie. He hoped.

Bodie reappeared, a woman on his heels. With windswept hair and frown lines, she swept Sammy into her arms and bore her away without protest. Bodie winked at him and waggled his black brows in an expression of amusement. He faked a tripping action over Grant Simms' outstretched foot and the teacher woke with a start. It played before Mac's gaze like a mime, comic and without sound. Simms staggered to his feet before pausing to hoist his trousers almost to his armpits. He murmured something Mac didn't catch before tangling with the garish curtain surrounding the cubicle.

Having chased away Mac's motley visitors, Bodie closed the curtain and crossed the short distance to the bed. He didn't bother with the single plastic chair, but eased his right buttock onto the mattress and faced Mac with a quizzical expression. "What happened?" he demanded, mouthing the words for Mac to interpret.

"Mama?" The plea caused a wave of shame to blossom in his chest. It reminded him of his frailty as a not-yet-man in a noisy, confusing world. With his arm strapped into the unforgiving splint, signing complicated replies seemed more impossible than daunting. He needed both hands. Mac jabbed his index finger towards his right ear. "Lost them," he said out loud.

Bodie rose and walked to the other side of the cubicle. He rummaged in a tall cupboard and withdrew a transparent bag, which he set on the end of the bed. He dug through its contents and the tension lessened at the back of Mac's neck as he spotted his shoes, trousers and the dark blue fabric of his blazer. Bodie glanced up at him. "Give me a clue?" he mouthed.

Mac pointed to the blazer as Bodie's brown fingers coasted over the collar. He nodded with as much enthusiasm as he could muster when Bodie tugged it from the bag. But his brother's brow knitted as he searched the garment and pulled out three mobile phones before tugging the processors from the inside pocket. The resulting glare of suspicion told Mac he'd groaned out loud.

It took just a few seconds for Mac to attach the hearing devices. But much longer for him to prepare his speech. Bodie watched him, his eyes narrowed and his hands on his hips as though ready to pounce and snap a cuff around his good wrist.

Sound flooded Mac's head as he activated the processors and he paused for a second to let his brain adjust.

His lips parted, but no words emerged. He still didn't know what to say.

12

OFFSIDE

"So, one phone belongs to that girl?" Bodie took shorthand notes in a pocketbook he'd extracted from his jacket.

Mac nodded. "Yes. She took a photo of me when I carried Layla from the shed. And a video. She posted it online, but I stopped her streaming the one of Miss Andrews." He choked, her name sticking in his throat. Sadness gurgled from the well of emotion threatening to burst free like volcanic steam and decimate him. Bodie winced, mistaking the grief for shock.

"Sorry, mate." His tone held a soothing quality. "Tell me about the other two."

Mac paused. Conflict dimmed his vision. He'd promised he wouldn't tell. The app he installed on her phone would create a wrong impression. Sourced from the dark web, it painted a different picture to the truth. He needed time to think, unable to bear the thought of sullying her character before her body had chilled.

Had it chilled?

His chest hitched and panic zapped through his nerve endings. "What if she wasn't dead?" The processors picked up part of the hissed sentence but not all of it, turning it into something disjointed and robotic. Mac shifted on the bed, swinging his legs over one side. The wrong side. The action tugged his wrist and robbed him of breath as pain flared from the break.

"Stay there." Bodie shifted the pen into the fingers containing the notebook, using his other hand to press Mac against the pillows.

"I feel sick." Mac lifted his right hand to cover his mouth. "I didn't check." His throat constricted, trapping his words in the back of his mouth. "What if I could have given her CPR? I didn't even try."

"Hey, hey," Bodie soothed. "You did just fine. You got the girls out of there and stopped the silly one posting any more compromising videos." He squeezed Mac's shoulder. "Mum's on her way. She's twenty minutes from the hospital. Logan picked her up on route, so they'll arrive before you go into surgery."

"Surgery." Mac exhaled and glared at the splint. "I didn't hear what he said. Hoped I'd got away with it." He groaned and tilted his chin towards the ceiling. "Layla weighs nothing. This is crazy!"

"Just unlucky." Bodie stepped back and clattered with a blood pressure machine. It only delayed the inevitable. "So, who owns the other phones?"

"Me." The lie burned his tongue. A wave of nausea rose into his chest.

"An iPhone and an Android?" Bodie narrowed his dark eyes and turned his head sideways. "That's unusual."

Mac kept his gaze focussed on the slit in the curtains, willing his mother to burst through and rescue him. The lies tumbled free, bitter and damning. If he did this, he couldn't turn back without incriminating himself. "The Android is new. It's supposed to be almost indestructible. But I still have data left on the other one."

"Okay." Bodie didn't sound convinced but he stared at the distinctive chip in the top left corner of the iPhone's screen. He relaxed enough to sit on the end of the bed, bending his right knee and leaning forward over his thigh. "Right. From the beginning again." His fathomless pupils held warning in their depths. "As soon as you're out of surgery, the local detectives will expect to speak to you." His brown lips flattened into thin, parallel lines. "You should get your story straight."

Hana arrived with her red curls and her worried energy. Logan followed her like a thundercloud, parting the sea of porter, nurses, two student doctors, an orthopaedic surgeon and a lone anaesthetist.

Mac lay beneath the stark white sheets, a strange nakedness pervading his senses. The nurse had parted him from his speech processors and his boxer shorts. He'd given up the first without fuss, but not the underwear. His shorts were clean that morning and bore no geographic relation to his wrist. But the argument without his processors proved impossible. A surgical mask hid her lips and she couldn't sign. Mac relinquished his undies with extremely bad grace.

His mother's scent washed over him. Jasmine and midnight orchid. She sat on the bed next to his uninjured wrist, her back to the nurse. "I'm here now," she stated, signing the sentence with practised ease. "Everything is okay." The nurse appeared to her left, trying to force a trolley through the narrow gap between Hana's knees and the curtain. Mac tensed as he spotted Sammy sitting beyond his cubicle. His mother's eyebrows rose. Her lips flattened into a feigned smile. She turned, but Mac saw his father's body language stiffen. He spoke to the nurse, and she nodded before squeezing back through the gap.

Hana reached out and clasped the fist curled on top of the crisp sheet. Her thumb stroked the jagged knuckles and Mac relaxed by degrees. "Girl," he said, knowing by his mother's reaction he'd pitched the volume wrong again. The splint gripped his left hand in a vice, removing his ability to sign and, therefore, his voice.

He was a tiny boy again, locked into a silent world.

A television viewer watching a catastrophe with the sound turned down and the remote control lost.

Tears pricked behind his lids and he gritted his teeth. He'd never understood why the appearance of his mother induced such weakness. It seemed as if the walls he'd built to protect himself contained a hidden gate just for her. She accessed his innermost fears as if by right.

The mattress shifted as Hana swung around to face her husband. He tugged something from his back pocket and Mac dipped his head, curiosity demanding he see the thing Logan handed to his wife.

Hana smiled as she set the notepad and pen on his thigh. Mac heaved out a breath. She understood. He couldn't explain out loud. Sammy's proximity made it too hazardous. He gripped the pen and, in his scrawled hand, wrote out his concerns as a list. Hana supported the pad against his leg as he crossed out one word and selected an alternative. When he set the pen down again, exhaustion nipped at the frayed edges of his nerves.

Hana nodded with understanding. She'd watched him write, deciphering his familiar hand even though it was upside down. Ripping off the top sheet, she passed it behind her to his father. Logan skimmed the list and gave a definitive nod. He folded the page and pushed it into his jeans. Snatching the curtain back, he surveyed the busy emergency department. A nurse stopped and frowned as Logan spoke to him. His head bobbed as he replied.

Logan turned to face Mac and snapped the curtain closed. "The girl went home with her mother," he signed.

Mac exhaled and his shoulders slouched against the pillows as relief took hold of him. It didn't last long as Logan continued. "She's got it bad for you, boy." His eyebrows waggled with mischief, which Mac wasn't in the mood to enjoy. But she'd gone home. "Why do you have her phone?" Logan continued. He jerked his head towards the pad and pen and Mac turned his face away from having to write a lengthy communication.

"Bodie," he replied, attempting a whisper, but not sure whether he achieved it.

The nurse returned with the anaesthetist. Hana rose and leaned across Mac to place a gentle kiss on his forehead. She translated the information about the surgery for him, her hands moving at lightning speed. Gratitude flooded his chest, causing the dreaded tears to threaten to fall. Logan stood at the back of the crowd, arms folded and the fluttering curtain brushing the sleeve of his shirt. He winked at Mac, sending sympathy across the bowed heads of the medics and his mother.

The porter returned to push Mac's bed to the theatre, and the anaesthetist left to take up his post. The nurse raised the rails on either side of the mattress, and Hana wedged herself between the visitor's chair and the curtain. When the bed began moving, she slipped alongside and took Mac's hand in hers. Her green eyes lit with a dangerous fire, inviting anyone to challenge her.

Logan pushed the curtain aside to reveal bustling activity. He raised his hand to the porter in a stop sign before leaning across and pressing his lips to Mac's temple. "Kia kaha," he signed. "Be strong."

Wiremu had found their Uncle Mark waiting to operate on him when he arrived for surgery to a gunshot wound a few years earlier. Nothing so wonderful happened for Mac. But kind strangers put him to sleep, inserted metal rods into his arm, and dealt with the unfortunate surprise of a partially severed tendon.

13

PENALTY

Mac woke to find an unfamiliar face leaning over him. Her lips moved, but tiredness claimed him before his brain could decipher her words. He vomited twice before the porter returned to push his bed to a ward deep in the bowels of the hospital. And once more on the way there.

Faces appeared and disappeared as though on a carousel. Mouths moved and tongues rose and fell, always ending in the speaker's confusion. Mac kept his eyes closed, no longer wanting to witness their concern. He'd planned to have his whakapapa depicted across his right shoulder just after his eighteenth birthday. Logan said he'd pay for the first of his son's genealogical tattoos. But as he lay in the bed being poked and prodded by medics who assumed he was stupid, he decided he'd get 'Proudly deaf' written across his forehead instead.

Was he proud, though?

Another question he couldn't answer.

With the pain in his left arm reduced to a dull roar by the drip, sending morphine into his veins, Mac had time to think. His mind returned to the equipment shed and their discovery of Marie's body. An involuntary sob shook his chest, alarming the nurse fiddling with a blood pressure monitor next to him. She patted his arm and looked towards the curtain.

Hana stepped between the gap in the fabric, the overhead lighting picking out the blonde and grey highlights in her auburn hair. She moved her hands at speed as soon as she reached him. Within seconds, Mac understood the operation went well. The surgeon had pinned his wrist, and he could leave the next morning. The adrenaline stopped pumping around his body and the heightened fear subsided.

Hana's chin lifted as she spoke to the nurse, and the transparent bag appeared at the end of his bed. She dug inside and produced his speech processors. Mac tensed as she attached the left one, waiting for the familiar cacophony to assault his senses. She placed the right one into his open palm. He fixed it into place one handed, grateful to his mother for respecting his autonomy and not fussing. Grogginess from the anaesthetic dulled the squealing of a trolley's sticking wheel against the tiles as its passing caused the curtains to flutter.

"Papa is parking the truck." Hana leaned her elbows on the bed next to him, casting her eye over the new cast and splint. "White," she mused. "That's asking for trouble."

Mac exhaled in a sigh. "Is Bo still around?" He dipped his head to whisper to her, urgency in his tone. "I should speak to him."

Hana frowned and sat back in the plastic chair. "He's holding off two detectives who are desperate to take your statement as soon as you're able." She glanced at the nurse and then back at him. "I'm so sorry about your teacher, Macky. I know you really liked her."

Mac clamped his teeth together. He covered his mouth with his right hand, alarmed at the scratchiness of bristles edging through his skin. His mother didn't know how much he'd liked Marie Andrews. He imagined confessing to her about their illegal kiss in the same sports shed where he'd found her body.

His Adam's apple bounced as he swallowed the sentence, aware of how it implicated him in her death. He'd kissed her. And her phone nestled in the folds of his blazer, less than a metre out of his reach.

The nurse injected painkillers into the cannula on the back of his right hand before leaving. She paused a moment with her fingers touching the curtain and her feet turned towards Hana with seeming reluctance. "We didn't know he was deaf," she murmured, her voice a whisper. "Sorry."

Hana's cheeks flushed an angry pink, and Mac imagined her anguish. She'd spent her life defending and mitigating for his disability. "It says so on his admission form," she managed, speaking through gritted teeth. Tears of rage turned her irises to sparkling emerald gems. Mac sensed her gearing up to say more, but wished she wouldn't. She glanced at him and he offered a slow shake of his head, begging her not to launch into a volley of accusations on his behalf.

His mother pressed her lips together and distracted herself by collecting her long curls into a bunch and forcing a tie from her wrist to contain their tumbled mass. Mac waited while she fixed it to her satisfaction and tossed her head twice to ensure the ponytail didn't slap her in the face. "Sorry," she said, once they were alone. "It gets me every time."

"I know." Mac issued his first genuine smile since he stepped onto the bus that morning. He exhaled. "I woke up and didn't recognise anyone. They were talking to me and at me and I couldn't think straight." He shrugged, and the movement sent an electric jolt through his elbow and along the damaged ulna to its metallic junction with his radius bone. "Ouch!" he breathed. "Why didn't I just tell them I couldn't hear?"

"Not your responsibility," Hana growled. "I told the porter, anaesthetist and the theatre nurse. The surgeon already knew. Pity they didn't see fit to pass on the information."

Mac stared at the cast. His fingers protruded from its end, separated from his thumb by a deviation. His nails required trimming and dirt ridged their white edges. He tutted. "I wanted to wash my hand first. I spent half an hour sitting on the dusty ground waiting for the police and paramedics."

"They took half an hour to come?" Hana frowned and cocked her head. "That's a long time."

Mac cast his mind back to Sammy's antics and winced. "Yeah, well, they weren't given great directions in the first instance. Someone showed too much interest in filming everything and loading the footage onto social media."

"Really?" Hana dug in her handbag for her phone. "Can I see?"

Mac directed her to a Google search, figuring she probably didn't have half the apps available to Sammy. Hana gasped as it instantly pulled up an image of Mac carrying Layla from the shed. "Oh," she breathed. "Apparently, the footage is trending. Everywhere." Her eyes widened. "No wonder Bodie's walking around beneath a thundercloud. Silly girl." Her fingers scrolled across the screen. "Samantha Boyne aged fourteen. Oh, and the usual selfie taken in the bathroom mirror." She groaned. "She looks very young. Is she on the soccer team?"

Mac nodded. "She was. I'm not sure there is a team now. Miss Andrews coached and managed it. I can't do that on my own." He jerked his chin towards his injured wrist. "I thought I could get my cast off in three weeks, pass my restricted and drive to games in one of the old vehicles from the farm." He heaved out a ragged breath. "That plan turned to custard around ten past eight this morning."

"Sorry, babe." Hana patted his thigh through the sheets. "You can still coach. I'll drive you to games."

"Thanks, Mum." He sighed. "I can't think about it at the moment." He prevented his mind from wandering back to the sight of Marie lying so still on the filthy floor. It took more effort than he possessed. He'd just replayed Layla's scream in his mind when the curtain swished aside and his brother pressed his face through the gap.

"Hey Mac," he said. He spoke out loud as well as using his hands and Mac pointed his right hand towards his ear.

"I can hear you," he said, his tone dull.

"Okay." Bodie stepped through the gap and Mac blinked as two more people followed him into the tiny cubicle. Hana's fingers clamped harder over her son's thigh.

"Detective Sergeant Elliot," Bodie said, indicating the male with an outstretched arm. A woman separated herself from the men and edged nearer to Hana. "And Detective Constable Williams." Bodie dropped his hand and his fingers bumped against his thigh. He sighed and the expression he turned on Mac held the down-turned lips of a silent apology.

14

PENALTY KICK

Mac grew bored with answering questions long before the detectives tired of asking them. The nurse interrupted twice to administer painkillers and take his blood pressure. Each time, she shot a glare of rebuke at the officers.

Hana remained silent, but the steady pressure of her palm against Mac's thigh grounded him through the sheet. She occupied the only visitor's chair. A breeze rippled through the cubicle from an open window, causing the surrounding curtain to flutter. Relief formed a lump in Mac's chest at the sight of his father standing just beyond the fabric, listening to the conversation. His muscles bulged through his shirt with his arms folded across his chest. Bodie stood next to him. His eyes narrowed as he strained to listen to the commentary from beyond the curtain.

Mac's vision blurred as the detective sergeant started again from the beginning. "So, you arranged to meet Miss Andrews at the equipment shed?"

"No!" Mac groaned. "No one arranged to meet her. We practice at lunchtimes and after school. The rugby boys took all the cones, and I needed them for an agility exercise." His right hand thudded against the mattress in frustration. "Layla and Sammy just tagged along. There was no meeting."

"Okay." Elliot's pen scratched against his notepad.

Williams cocked her head. For a tiny woman, her voice held a formidable booming quality. "The girls have both said they arranged to meet Miss Andrews at the shed." She pushed her lower lip upward to cover the top one, causing her face to resemble that of a mullet. "Yet, you say no one had a meeting with her."

Mac pressed his head against the pillows and closed his eyes. The thread of a memory drifted back to him and he frowned. "Goalkeeping gloves," he murmured. He lifted his lids and found Hana's intense stare on his face.

"It's okay," she mouthed.

Mac shook his head. "Goalkeeping gloves. The girls had some or Miss Andrews had some. I can't remember which. Layla needed them, anyway." He exhaled and rubbed his eyes with the fingers of his right hand. "I didn't arrange to meet her." His voice caught in his throat. "I shouldn't have been there."

"That's enough." The curtain whipped aside and Logan intervened. Taller than both detectives by a head and shoulders, he peered down at them as though they were inconvenient bugs on the windscreen of his life. "My son just came out of surgery. This can wait until later."

Mac noticed the grimace Elliot sent to Bodie and his raised eyebrow in response. His brother wouldn't take on Logan. Experience told him he couldn't win. Logan's bulk and presence occupied the tiny space, sucking out all the oxygen and leaving the detectives no option but to obey. Williams smiled at Mac as her colleague tussled with the curtain, but the expression didn't reach her brown eyes. "We'll be in touch," she said, almost as a threat. "We'll require a formal, signed statement."

Mac nodded, realising he'd agree to anything if they'd just leave him to recover. The constrictions of the cubicle made him want to scream. The additional bodies crammed into it hadn't helped. His chest rose and fell as though his lungs struggled to get enough oxygen.

Hana patted his leg. "Would you like the curtains opened?" she asked, her tone bright.

His lips parted, and he nodded with gratitude at her understanding. "Please," he said, his tongue slurring the word.

Logan swished back the curtains, yanking them as far as the wall on either side of him. Fresh air flooded into his lungs from the open windows at the end of the room. Beds lined the walls on either side of the ward, patients facing each other as though queuing in a doctor's waiting room. An elderly man opposite lay with his plastered leg raised towards the ceiling as though Mac had caught him half way through a high jump. The other six beds remained empty.

"They'll come back," Bodie said, foreboding in his tone. He blinked at the glare Logan bestowed upon him.

"Then I'll send them away again," he declared, lifting his chiselled chin in defiance. "What's with grilling my son like that? A better use of time might be searching the crime scene."

"Yeah." Bodie pursed his lips. "If it was the crime scene," he murmured.

"What?" Mac used his right hand to push himself straighter in the bed. "What do you mean?"

Bodie waggled his eyebrows. "Her phone is missing. Colleagues say she always kept it on her. The school runs a lockdown system for threats and that's how the staff receive the emergency texts. Someone hit her over the head with a blunt instrument, which is also missing. It's possible she died elsewhere and the killer dumped her body there, thinking they could start a fire. They rigged the wiring in the shed to burn the evidence. One of the girls walked into the live end of the wire and got a residual electric shock."

Mac's lips parted in surprise. "That's why Layla collapsed? But I would have felt the current as I caught her, wouldn't I?"

Bodie shrugged. "She has a burn to the sole of her left foot. Perhaps she earthed it before you touched her. It's just pure luck the whole shed didn't burn to the ground."

"That's not right." Mac shook his head. Dismay sent his pulse rate higher and the machine next to him gave a forlorn beep. The presence of Marie's phone left in the shed indicated a sloppy killer, not someone capable of planning a body disposal to that degree. But the words stuck in his throat. The phone in his blazer pocket called the lie, but he couldn't share it. His cheeks flared pink with the effort of spinning the untruths he'd already told. He couldn't see a way out of his predicament. The machine beeped at his shoulder again, and Hana rose to inspect the numbers flashing red on the digital display.

"Let's not talk about it now," she advised, her tone containing a warning.

The nurse reappeared, making a beeline for the monitor. Her brow furrowed as she lifted the blood pressure cuff and fitted it over Mac's right biceps. "Visiting time finished a while ago," she said, her tone speculative.

Hana tilted her wrist to check her phone and gasped. "Gracious! It's late. We should let you get some sleep." She rose and leaned across Mac to kiss his forehead. He ached to hold her tight and beg her to stay. Fear loomed over him with its tainted fingers, condemning his feelings for Marie and casting him into a pit of despair. Hana blinked as she studied him, her perception eerie. "Would you like me to stay?" she whispered. "I can nap in the chair."

Mac opened his mouth to speak, but the nurse forestalled any rebellious notions. "Parents can only stay on the paediatric ward. It's not permitted here."

Hana licked her lips and Mac sensed her formulating arguments. He shook his head to release her. "I'm okay," he said, though his halting speech indicated the opposite. "What should I do with my processors? Do you think I should keep them on in case someone wants to speak to me?"

Hana glanced up at the nurse, her emerald irises hard and unyielding. "Do you have a staff member who can sign?" she demanded.

The woman winced. "I'm not sure. Let me find out for you." She bustled away on soft-soled shoes which gave a tiny squeak with each step.

Hana tutted and looked at her husband for support. "I bet they don't," she hissed. "They'll wake him up with poking and prodding and terrify him without thinking about it."

Logan glanced at Mac and then back at his wife. "They won't," he assured her. "The surgeon said he can leave tomorrow, so it's only one night." He whirled away towards the wide desk along the corridor and returned with a black marker pen clutched in his left hand. Lifting the medical notes from the end of Mac's bed, he scrawled something across the bottom of the page. He replaced the clipboard and sidestepped Hana to deface the whiteboard above Mac's head. "There you go," he said, snapping the lid onto the pen.

Hana's lips parted in horror and she gaped at her husband. "You can't do that!" Her voice rose and the elderly man in the bed opposite grunted. The sling containing his extended leg vibrated, and she pressed her fingers over her mouth. Logan shrugged. He jabbed the pen at Mac. "I'm proud of who my boy is. If this stops him getting shoddy treatment, then I don't care who it offends." His jaw clenched, and he eye-balled his son. "Unless it's McGillivray. I don't want to upset you, mate."

Mac screwed his head back to read the board behind him. The words appeared upside down as he read them.

'Please use BSL or face me when speaking,' Logan had written.

Hana bristled with distress, her hands fluttering towards Logan. "Why did you do that?" she demanded. "Now everyone can see."

Logan shrugged. "And they can communicate appropriately with my son." He dropped his chin and narrowed his eyes, his grey irises sparkling with an unnatural glint.

Bodie cleared his throat, uncomfortable with the argument. He lifted his hand to wave to Mac. "See you tomorrow, bro," he said. "I have a week's leave, but I'll keep abreast of things and make sure I'm available if you need me." His lips lifted in a genuine smile, which intensified the lead weight of guilt in Mac's chest.

Mac swallowed and chewed the inside of his cheek until the metallic taste of blood tainted his tongue. He ached to call Bodie back and throw himself on his mercy. He could still pass off his possession of the phone as an accident compounded by a lie. But not once he let Bodie walk away without telling the truth.

His brother's heels clicked against the floor as he left the ward. Hana bickered with Logan about defacing hospital property when she really just wanted a reason to stay with her son. Mac popped off his speech processors and kept them in his right hand. Despite the silence from his eardrums, his head filled with the shrillness of Layla's scream and the click of Bodie's departing heels.

15

SWEEPER

Mac couldn't sleep. The painkillers worked, but the sedative didn't. He stared at the ceiling as it glinted with the reflection of passing car headlights. The fingers of his right hand smoothed the nails of his left, an abstract, subconscious movement which dwelled on the baby finger which peeked from the edge of the new cast. A male nurse appeared every few hours, using a pen torch to find his way around. He spent a while reading Logan's scrawled footnote on the doctor's chart at the bottom of the bed. Raising one eyebrow, he placed his torch on the mattress and checked Mac's blood pressure, pulse, and temperature.

"You okay?" he mouthed, noticing Mac watching him. The light from below gave him an eerie appearance.

Mac nodded, afraid of replying with too much volume and waking the old man. He glanced sideways at the processors laid on the side table. The nurse raised his hand. "It's fine," he reassured him. "Good idea whoever wrote that on the bottom of your notes." He sounded out the words with clarity, and Mac appreciated his added effort. Hana had become even more upset at Logan's flagrant disregard for hospital etiquette when she tried to rub his scrawl off the whiteboard behind the bed and couldn't. His father had stolen a permanent marker and wasn't in the least bothered.

Mac wasn't sensitive about his deafness, but hated the conspicuousness of his processors. He'd always hidden them beneath his red curls and his hair often verged on the borderline of rule breaking at school. Neither he nor Deacon had made the cut for a prefect's role in Year 13. Deacon figured it was due to his father's incarceration and the cruel tag which clung to Mac as the Disabled Du Rose.

It bothered Mac at first. The school didn't offer rejection letters. Boys receiving no offer to become a prefect by the end of the summer holidays assumed they weren't good enough. But when the term started, he watched the other boys in their pristine white shirts jump through hoops to please their masters and smiled to himself. He could coach the Year 10 girls' soccer team for his own enjoyment, while his classmates supervised detentions and doled out punishment for trivial infractions.

He thanked the nurse with a soundless forming of the word and closed his eyes, hopeful of sleep. The man left the bay and took his tiny ray of light with him. But sleep still evaded the teenager as thoughts and worries flooded his mind. The plastic bag containing his belongings occupied the visitor's chair. It occurred to him he could wipe the texts between him and Marie and uninstall the app he'd added at her request. Then he could hand it over to Bodie.

But as he lay in the hard bed and walked through his options, he found flaws in the plan. The police sought the phone, which meant they were probably already tracking the number and searching for the signal. Sweat beaded Mac's brow as the evidence stacked against him. His fingerprints covered the phone. The police had perhaps already remotely screened the texts between Marie's number and his and jumped to the wrong conclusion. They would know it was somewhere in the hospital and arrive to search his belongings. He wracked his brain, trying to remember if he'd noticed anything about the device as he retrieved it from the crime scene. Was it still turned on? The action had been an innocent one, but it would twist into a noose around his neck.

His heart rate rose and caused the blood to thud in his ears. The last nurse of the evening shift had disconnected all the monitors during her visit, otherwise the crash team might have come running. Mac knew without a doubt he needed to get the phone and turn it off.

He tested the pain in his wrist by moving his arm. An ache spread out from the site of the surgery to encompass his elbow. Fortifying himself with the reminder he was a Du Rose, Mac supported the cast in the palm of his right hand and edged across the mattress. As his feet hit the cool floor, he had second thoughts. Leaning across, he snagged his processors from the side table. He fitted them into position one at a time as an insurance policy against accidentally making too much noise. The cast weighed against his thigh like a concrete block. Mac studied how the dim moonlight turned the white fibreglass to a dull grey. He would have chosen grey instead of white if anyone had asked him.

It took a superhuman effort to stand and take the few steps around the bed to the visitor's chair. Mac loosened the neck of the bag and supported his cast against his hip as he reached inside the rustling plastic. Movement sounded from across the room, and Mac's hand froze. The elderly man released a loud snore, and the processors relayed his accompanying grunt.

The thick plastic made extracting Mac's blazer difficult. Retrieving his processors meant it rested on top of the pile of clothing, but the bag made sounds like thunderclaps as Mac struggled to slip the garment free. He seized the collar and dragged it with exaggerated slowness, unable to use his left hand to stop the bag from moving and creating a din which would summon curious nursing staff. It slithered out in a rush, the school logo speckled by moonlight. Mac laid it on the bed and searched the pockets one handed. Nothing.

Panic set up a pulse beating in his temples as he sought his own phone and Marie's. None of his pockets contained the device. Exhausted from his foray, Mac sank onto the bed, his mind whirling through possibilities. Logic forced him back through a motion picture of the day's events until he came to his interaction with Bodie.

His brother gave him the speech processors and discovered the phones. Mac didn't remember him bagging Sammy's device, but Hana had arrived and distracted him. He pushed himself upright and risked another look at the man opposite him. His fingers closed over the folds of the curtain and he tugged it around the overhead runner to form a screen.

Light flared from a reading lamp as he found the switch on the remote hanging from the bed rail. Mac took deep breaths in and out to calm himself. He spun on the spot as he searched the tiny area. Nothing. The elderly man grunted and Mac snapped out the light with shaking fingers. A flickering blue glow drew his attention, reflecting off the thin plastic curtain on the far side. Desperate to get back into bed and rest his arm on a pillow, Mac padded around the cubicle to investigate.

He moved a box of tissues aside and exhaled with relief. Adrenaline pulsed through his veins and caused his wrist to throb. Two devices rested on the bedside cupboard. The tissues had hidden them. Mac supported his wrist against his hip and used his right hand to lift the phones one at a time. The faint blue light designated a missed text on his device, and he unlocked the screen to peer at it.

Wiremu had typed out a long list of expletives before finishing with, *'WTF, man! Why do I always miss the action?'*

Mac allowed himself a smile before blowing out a breath filled with agitation. The phone vibrated in his loose grip and he dipped to prevent it clattering to the tiled floor. Another text strobed on the screen.

'So, you're a superhero are you? Then act like it and muster my boys you soft idiot!!!'

Mac's shoulders slumped and he sank onto the mattress, the light from the screen casting an eerie blue glow around his cubicle. Darian responded to pressure from the executive team by paying it forward. He chased glory like a heat seeking missile, hooking onto the promise before detonating it. The First XV coach from previous years had left the school after Darian inserted himself into the team's management. The constant undermining of his authority proved too much for him and he bowed out gracefully, leaving Darian with the role he desired most of all.

Mac closed his eyes and bowed his head. The sports teacher would make his life a living hell until he complied. Slippery and somehow protected by the headmaster, he operated within his own framework. Not for the first time, Mac wished to leave education in his rear-view mirror for good.

Laying his phone on the bed. He turned his attention to the other one. He pressed the side button to activate the screen and used the keypad to enter the code. The numbers formed a strange shudder before turning red and disappearing.

Mac jerked his chin back in surprise. He knew the code because Marie gave it to him. He entered the numbers again with the same result. Left with no other choice, Mac shuffled around his bed to the remote and clicked the switch for the overhead light. It blinded him for a moment and he turned the device over in his fingers as his vision settled.

The iPhone wasn't the latest model, but not defunct by any means. Mac cast his mind back to Marie's plea for help and the day she'd left her device with him. He closed his eyes and searched for something definitive. He'd worked fast, plugging the phone into the Mac he'd borrowed from Deacon. The application he'd saved from the illegal cache on the grey web and recoded took seconds to load onto Marie's phone. Then he'd deleted it from the laptop, removed the dark web browser and hidden any trace of his nefarious task.

"It's Marie's phone," he mouthed to himself in confusion, his lips moving without sound. He laid it on the mattress amid his rumpled bedding and used the corner of a sheet to wipe the screen. Self-preservation dictated he remove all the evidence leading back to him and dispose of it somewhere. His mind worked fast, wondering if the hospital sluice room might contain an incinerator and working out his odds of accessing it without discovery. But as he smoothed the sheet across the back cover and flipped the phone one handed to wipe the screen, he noticed something. The phone bounced as a thread caught at the top left-hand corner.

The curtain swished and the male nurse stared at him through the gap. "You okay?" he asked, spreading his hands to emphasise the question.

Mac gulped and nodded. "Bathroom," he whispered.

The nurse smiled and held the curtain aside. "Come," he said and beckoned with his fingers.

Mac followed him on leaden footsteps, his heart a ball of fear in his stomach. The overhead light picked out the chip glinting from the iPhone screen and the trailing thread of the sheet.

The phone from the crime scene did not belong to Marie Andrews.

16

Volley

Mac left the hospital after seeing the surgeon. He remained silent as Logan drove the truck down the expressway towards Rangiriri. Hana kept turning around to observe her son, her features drawn and displaying her exhaustion.

A vibration from Mac's pocket drew his attention. He tugged his phone free, noting the depleted battery icon flashing at him. A text added itself beneath the alert. Wiremu wrote,

'You're a superstar dude. But the girl who posted the image is talking up a big story. I need the skinny from you asap!'

Mac leaned his head back against the seat and closed his eyes. He'd made several attempts to unlock the other phone, which remained in his blazer pocket. Its battery died just before his parents arrived to collect him from the bustling ward. He squinted sideways at the navy jacket next to him on the rear seat. Hana had blinked in surprise as he'd stopped her from slipping the blazer back into the bag. She hadn't argued with him, but he sensed her confusion over such a trivial issue. Edin owned an iPhone. Mac wondered how much he'd need to divulge in order to borrow her charger.

The sleepless night caught up with him, and Mac dozed. He didn't stir until the truck crunched across the gravel driveway and stopped alongside the covered porch of the house in the mountains. The sunlight hurt Mac's eyes as Logan pulled open the truck's rear door and offered a helping hand. "I'm good," Mac muttered, sliding his feet sideways onto the runner board. He'd dragged the expensive speech processor from his right ear in his sleep and it slithered from his fingers and bounced onto the gravel. Logan bent to retrieve it and the sun's rays kissed the grey streaks speckling his black hair. A wave of guilt flooded Mac's chest. He experienced the childish urge to throw himself on his father's mercy and ask him to fix the mess he'd made. More guilt followed the silent assurance that Logan would do it, no matter the cost to himself. "Thanks," Mac whispered as his father placed the processor into his palm with a smile. He swallowed as Logan's gaze settled on his face. "Sorry for all the trouble."

"Egg." Logan lifted his fingers to ruffle Mac's hair before offering his hand again. This time, Mac accepted his help.

"TV?" Hana asked verbally, as well as with her fingers.

Mac shook his head. "No thanks. I'm tired. Think I'll go to bed." His genuine yawn emphasised the wisdom of his decision.

"Okay." She clasped his good arm beneath the elbow and walked with him into the house. It frustrated Mac how much help he required with everything. Shoelaces. Trouser zip. Shirt buttons. Logan assisted him, making no comment in response to Mac's continual grunts of irritation at his feebleness. His father tugged back the bedspread and plumped the pillows ready for him. Crockery clattered from the kitchen as a distant echo as Hana dealt with the dishwasher.

"Thanks." Mac sank onto the mattress in his boxer shorts. He rubbed his eyes with the back of his right hand. "Is Edin at school?"

"Yeah." His father tugged the curtains closed and turned to face him. He dug his thumbs into the back pockets of his jeans and surveyed his son's bowed head. "What's wrong, McGillivray?"

Mac kept his gaze on the patterned rug and avoided his father's perceptive scrutiny. "Just tired," he admitted. Lifting his hand, he disconnected the other processor and placed it on the bedside cupboard alongside its mate. But not hearing Logan didn't exempt him from sensing his father's concern. He tucked his feet beneath the bedspread and supported the cast as he lay back against the pillows.

Dimples flashed on Logan's chin as he flattened his lips. "I'll check on your mare," he signed, and Mac nodded with gratitude.

"Tomorrow," he promised, fortifying the fake image of himself as indestructible. He'd visit the mare before school the next day to make sure she didn't forget him. Mac clamped his eyelids shut and felt the waft of warm air coast across his bare limbs as Logan left the room and pulled the door closed behind him.

He didn't mean to sleep again, but woke with a start as a cool hand covered his forehead.

"Sorry," Hana signed. "You're too hot. I worried you might have a temperature." She indicated a glass of clear liquid on his bedside cabinet. Two different painkillers sat next to it. The water sparkled and fizzed, bubbles rising to the surface in a crazy dance. She waited for him to sit up and settle before passing them to him.

"Thanks," Mac replied, his tongue working to form the word but his eardrums not relaying their echo to his brain. He contemplated spewing everything to his mother in a guilty vomit of damning information. But his nerve failed him as the words formulated themselves in a semblance of coherence. His parents proved united in most issues, but this one would polarise them. Hana would strategise but ultimately arrive at telling the truth and call Bodie. His father would ask a few pertinent questions before helping him bury the bodies.

Mac drank the water and swallowed the pills. He excused himself to use the bathroom and cringed as his mother paused in the hallway. Conflict budded in her eyes and he sensed her wanting to ask if he needed help. His chest caved with relief as she thought better of it and wandered away to the kitchen. He used the bathroom, cursing when he soaked the cast, washing his hands. Splashing cool water on his forehead removed the sweat and helped him collect his thoughts.

As he walked back to his bedroom next to Edin's, he poked his head through her open door. The room held her essence through the residual cloud of perfume hanging around the dressing table. Mac located the charger cable for her phone, his nose wrinkling at her flagrant disregard of house rules.

Logan refused to allow electronics to remain in his children's bedrooms overnight. They charged on a docking station in the lounge. Though he no longer enforced the rule with only two of them still living at home, he expected Mac and Edin to obey, regardless. Unable to follow regulations of any kind, Edin made up her own behind the scenes. The presence of the iPhone charger indicated as much. Sadness prickled at the back of Mac's mind as he recognised signs of his parents relinquishing the reins. Edin's mother resided at a half-way house following her release from prison. Technically, Edin could live with her despite more than a decade of Hana and Logan's care.

Mac unplugged the charger one handed and padded back to his room. He used a socket at the bottom of his walk-in-wardrobe to charge the iPhone and closed the door to avoid detection. Taking his own phone to the lounge, he sat it on the docking station and collected his laptop under his arm. He found his mother in the kitchen. The scents of baking filled the air, and his stomach growled.

"Tāne!" Leslie rose to greet him. A mug of coffee wobbled in front of her as she knocked against the table in her haste. "I made my special scones for you." She emphasised the words so he could read her lips, her eyes slits of pleasure in her wide face.

"Thank you." He offered her a reassuring smile and devoured the two Hana laid before him. His open laptop vibrated the table as it completed an update. Mac sat with his back to the wall, ensuring no one caught sight of his screen as he downloaded a Mac-in-cloud app. If he wanted to learn anything from the iPhone, he needed his tech to mimic Macintosh technology.

He wolfed a third buttered scone and drank a mug of coffee before feeling more like his old self. The painkillers irritated his stomach and caused the sugary food to curdle and groan. Mac closed his laptop and tucked it beneath his right arm before bending to kiss the top of Leslie's fluffy head. He dipped his body to perform the sign for thanks to his mother and she waved away his one-handed efforts. Mac retreated to his bedroom and sequestered himself beneath the sheets, ready to unmask the owner of the phone.

He prayed it didn't belong to Marie's killer. For his own sake, as much as theirs.

17

INSIDE TOUCH

The iPhone had charged enough to sustain Mac's ministrations. He returned the cable to Edin's room before she missed it. A fossick through a box in the garage disgorged a jack which looked similar. Mac tugged it from beneath an old laptop charger with Tama's name scrawled across the power pack in white correction tape. He debated the risks of damaging the phone alongside the need to reveal its secrets. It trailed beneath his arm with a kink in its centre as he carried it back to his room.

Using the wisdom of anonymous searches on the grey web, Mac unlocked the phone with some considerable effort. He switched from Microsoft commands to Apple with only a few missteps with the keypad. His tired brain cranked through years of classes taken on the school's Macintosh devices.

Mac's fingers grew tired as he scrolled through the icons on the screen one-handed. He sifted through gaming apps which indicated a teenage owner. His father would have gone straight for the text and email folders but a sense of foreboding delayed

Mac. Once he'd revealed the phone's owner, there would be no return to ignorance.

When the screen flashed a warning of a low battery, Mac connected it to his laptop using Tama's old cable and powered up the Mac-in-cloud application. A lightning bolt bisected the battery icon and a warning appeared on the phone screen. "I know it's not the correct charger," Mac whispered. "It's this or nothing."

The emails yielded little information. They comprised of a week's worth of newsletters from gaming sites Mac recognised. Anything of interest either didn't exist or had been deleted. He scrolled through the trash bin, surprised to find nothing in it. It took time to work out how to search the recycle bin using the Mac-in-cloud, but he drew another blank. The phone's owner got rid of anything useful. Only a seasoned forensics analyst would be able to dredge it back up from the ether. Mac's mind flicked to Bodie again and he gnawed his lower lip. Perhaps it wasn't too late to come clean. He half rose to fetch his device from the lounge and then pushed the thought away. If only he hadn't lied.

Mac didn't find a single photograph in any of the folders. He synced the phone with its anonymous cloud storage and checked there, seeing the thumbnail for a lone jpeg file buried deep within a Documents tab. Holding his breath, he dragged his index finger across the mouse pad and right clicked to copy it. Leaving the integrity of the original, he pasted it to his desktop and opened it.

An image bloomed onto the computer screen. It looked pixelated as though shot from a distance using the phone's limited zoom options. Mac tipped forward, his nose almost touching the screen as he searched for recognisable landmarks. Scrubby grass formed the lower planes of the picture and squinting assisted him in identifying the soccer fields at the high school. Mac blew out his breath as the pieces slotted into place. A darker smudge on the edge of the photo showed the equipment shed.

Twenty-two blurred dots spread across the middle distance made him squint and cock his head. Some looked much bigger than their smaller counterparts. "A soccer team," he breathed out loud. He zoomed in as much as he dared before the elements of the image lost their structure, scrolling left to right to inspect the details. A group of spectators lined the far side, their bodies merging as grey blobs as though an artist smudged them out with a dissatisfied finger.

His fingers froze as he surveyed the far left of the photograph. A slender figure straddled the white line at the side of the pitch. With one arm lifted to shield her eyes from the sun, she studied the players. Mac bit down hard on the inside of his lip. "Marie," he whispered.

A lump rose into his chest and limited his airway. She appeared little more than a smudge on a screen, yet the photograph depicted her aliveness in the soft curves of her body. His heart clenched and he scrubbed at his eyes with the knuckles of his right hand. His fingers came away damp. The owner of the phone had deleted every photograph except this one of Marie Andrews. Now, she was dead.

Mac combed the photograph, looking for other defining features. Without a time or date stamp, he found it difficult to identify the day or the hour. He checked the stamp on the uploaded file and shook his head at the generic numbers on the screen. The line of zeroes told him nothing.

Lengthening shadows behind Marie indicated late afternoon. The absence of goalposts suggested an after-school practice session rather than a serious match. He'd attended all of those since the start of term and yet he wasn't in the picture.

Mac snatched up his own phone and opened his calendar app. Overlaid with his academic timetable, it offered a snapshot of his average week. He tapped his teeth with his thumbnail and pondered the dilemma. His analytical mind sifted through dates and times. Term started six weeks earlier, and Marie Andrews approached him about coaching the girls during the third week. He'd assisted with the muster the following Saturday and formulated the training schedule for the girls who'd made the cut. Mac stared at the photograph without understanding. When had she run a practice without him?

"Never." The answer was never.

Mac's colour heightened as a memory returned. A rosy hue shrouded it. He'd left early the previous Thursday for a hearing appointment. His eyes misted as he squinted at the screen. He'd detoured to the equipment shed to search for the cones he'd seen there just the week before the team muster. He hadn't found them. As he turned to leave, he'd clattered against a freestanding metal shelving unit. A cricket bat plunged from its precarious resting place and smacked him in the forehead. Marie had rushed forward, clutching his face in her hands. He hadn't realised she'd followed him into the shed.

So, he kissed her.

Irrational.

Momentary madness.

Mac stared at the photo and lifted his hand to his forehead. The discolouration had faded, but the lump remained beneath the skin. Thursday. The phone's owner had snapped the picture after he left to meet Logan outside the school gates. Before he broke his arm and before Marie Andrews died.

Mac swallowed and flung the phone onto the bed. It bounced twice and stretched the power cable taut. His brain spun through cul-de-sacs of doom where sinister spectres studied his movements. He reached again for the edge of the cast and ran his thumb over his baby fingernail. A shake of his shoulders stopped him making it into a prevalent habit which would later prove difficult to break. He focused on the current dilemma.

Was the picture a message meant for him? Did they know what he'd done?

Mac dipped forward as sickness gripped his stomach. He held his breath and fought the retch threatening to break apart his remaining resolve and soil his bedding with nothing but bile.

"Think! Think!" He knocked on the side of his head with the knuckles of his right hand, leaning into the pain which overwhelmed the numbing fear. "Who knew you wanted to see Marie yesterday? Did they intend you to find the phone?"

He flopped back against the pillows and closed his eyes. No one knew. He hadn't known himself until he slammed his locker door and the thought popped into his head. His fingers scrabbled against the sheets, reluctant to touch the offending phone but willing to smash it into smithereens. Destroy the evidence. But evidence of what?

Mac relied on his natural reason to drag him from the pit of despair. If no one knew he intended to see Marie, then the phone was left for someone else. It had been wiped of anything able to track back to the owner, which suggested it wasn't the result of carelessness. Someone wanted it found.

"The police."

There seemed no other conclusion as Mac formed the words with his lips. He'd accidentally taken something planted for the cops to scoop up in their forensic evidence gathering process. A clue, or a misdirection?

Mac set about covering his tracks, realising his error the further he moved through the process. He'd masked his IP address using an app but failed to disable the location signal until too late. If it ever became relevant, an expert would track the phone to the hospital and then to his home. The notion of destroying the device vied with every shred of decency in his psyche and he turned it over in his fingers while he considered its fate.

He rubbed his eyes in defeat. If the phone's owner had planted it at the crime scene and intended it for the evidence locker, then it seemed likely they tracked its progress. Only, he'd taken it instead. That meant they knew he had it.

Would they come for it?

Should he start worrying for his parents' safety?

Fatigue and the residual chemicals from the anaesthetic tugged at his energy and muddied his ability to think with clarity. He performed the only logical task remaining and turned off the phone. It took a moment of fumbling to place the laptop and phone on his desk, where he left both charging. His tired brain wouldn't let him plan further than a few hours ahead and he promised himself he'd make it into school the next day. He retrieved his own device from the lounge and a quick text to Deacon begged his friend to front up to help him. But he didn't wait for a reply.

The bed creaked beneath him as he collapsed face down onto the soft mattress. His wrist complained and he stretched out his arm and turned his head to the side. His eyes fluttered closed, and he slept.

But not the sleep of the just.

Not anymore.

18

Scissor Kick

"Hey, dude. Give me an intro to your sister." The powerful aroma of cheese and onion flavoured crisps filled the air around Mac's head. He pursed his lips and held his breath. Leaning backwards, he glared at the owner of the voice and the smell. He'd positioned himself in the school dining room to observe rather than partake of the mayhem. Bunched up against the wall, he'd thought hard about his location. Disappointment prickled in his chest at Deacon's uncharacteristic silence. He hadn't replied to Mac's SOS and hadn't shown up at school.

All for nothing.

He'd upset his mother by refusing to stay home as per the surgeon's orders.

And early that morning, after dragging himself from a foggy sleep, his mare had shown affection to Logan while ignoring him.

Only a confrontation with the school's best dressed thug could make his day go any worse. Mac sighed.

Oblivious, the teenager stood over him, already in the process of dumping his rucksack onto the table. "I want her phone number." Syd Ross wore the maroon sweater of a prefect alongside a matching swagger. He made an art form out of being a chameleon, the kind of thug who fooled adults with an air of maturity while terrorising his cohort. "She's hot," he added, slumping into the seat next to Mac. He withdrew a battered phone from his trouser pocket and activated the screen, turning to face Mac with his eyebrows raised in expectation. Teenagers milled around them like seawater, carrying trays laden with food or empty plates. The dining room formed the hub of the school during lunchtime. Mac lifted his right hand to his speech processor and contemplated switching it off. Pressing the button down for five seconds was all it would take to disconnect him from Syd Ross' demands.

Mac sighed and dropped his hand. Isolation seemed somehow worse at that moment. Perhaps Syd Ross was better than no one. But he'd endured several scenarios relating to Edin during his school career. Her stunning Du Rose features and sassy attitude acted as catnip to his horny classmates. A usual week saw at least three teenagers demanding an audience with her. Some asked and others demanded. Mac frowned at today's amorous suitor. Giving a slow blink, he turned to face the dining room's chaos and dug in his bag for his sandwiches.

"Hey." The boy jabbed his knuckles into Mac's shoulder. Pain sensors fired along his arm and nudged the healing bones beneath his cast. Mac gritted his teeth together and rose with painful slowness. He faced the boy before him, a wall of muscle contemplating a bug. The fingers of his right hand bunched at his thigh and moved through a slow arc towards their destination.

Pain and sadness stretched Mac's patience beyond its breaking point. His mind slowed time as he strategised, causing maximum outcome for the least amount of effort. The foolish boy kept talking, looking up at him with his lips moving in an endless diatribe of hormonal immaturity. Mac heard none of it, his fist moving through the air towards the contact.

He gasped as a solid palm met the blow. He hadn't stabilised himself or planted his feet and he groaned as the impact knocked him off balance. The fist unfurled, and he braced himself with his right elbow against the wall.

Syd Ross finally closed his mouth and the droning via Mac's processors ceased. Then, "Hey!" he protested. He dipped sideways to retrieve the rucksack which disappeared onto the floor. A heavy boot knocked it into the aisle beneath the marauding feet, forcing him to exit his seat to chase it.

A girl plonked into the chair next to Mac's and a purple rucksack slammed onto the table. She glared at Syd Ross as he rose, clutching the straps of his rucksack.

"I'm a prefect!" he growled, invoking his right to ownership of the seat next to Mac.

The girl's nose wrinkled. "Yeah. And you stink," she retorted. A flap of her delicate left hand stirred the air in front of her face. "Take your cheese and onion breath somewhere else. I'm sitting here."

"Tilly!" He issued her name as a snarl, his fingers already dipping into his pocket to withdraw a pad of detention slips.

She released a sarcastic laugh and shook her head. "Try it Ross," she retorted. "And I'll shove that pad so far up your ass you can write my name in spit."

Mac sat in his seat with a bump, his heart thrumming in his chest. He unclenched his fist and stared at it. He'd prided himself on being different. Knowing how to flatten someone was a far cry from following through and doing it. Ross would never know how close he'd come to eating his own teeth.

Mac let his mind wander through the probable consequences, toying with the idea that expulsion might not be such a terrible thing. He didn't want to go to university or work in an office. But self-sabotage seemed an extreme way of avoiding a future which filled him with a bone aching misery.

Syd Ross grumbled to himself, but he abandoned a fight he couldn't win. Serving Tilly with a detention slip presented a variety of bigger problems he wasn't equipped to face. He melded into the crowd of moving bodies and disappeared. A knot of his henchmen trailed behind him like a tributary.

Tilly waggled a pierced black eyebrow at Mac and grinned. "Guess he's supervising the Saturday detention this week. And he doesn't want me in it."

Mac snorted and forced his muscles to relax. They ached as though he'd carried a burden for longer than he realised. He shivered with the insight of having left his treasured sense of peace and equilibrium on the floor of the round pen. His problems began with the fall from the mare. "He wanted Edin's phone number." Mac resumed digging in his bag for his sandwiches, locating them beneath a heavy science text book. He extracted them, the wrapper hanging loose and a crease through the centre of the bread.

Tilly wrinkled her nose. "Is that your gran's plum jam?" She leaned sideways to inspect the red stain seeping along the seam where the crusts met.

Mac nodded. "Yeah. Want one?"

Tilly held out her hand and accepted the offered sandwich. Her magenta fingernails contrasted with the red jam and the black sesame seeds in Hana's home-made bread. Violet lips nudged the sandwich between her teeth. Mac settled back against his seat with a sigh. He pushed the wrapper containing the other one towards her. "I'm not hungry," he stated, his tone lacking energy.

"Thanks." Tilly collected it with eagerness, her blue irises sparkling with delight. "You have wonderful lunches."

Mac nodded, acknowledging what she didn't say beneath the compliment. The girl had raised herself since kindergarten, surviving in a home equipped with revolving doors for her mother's stream of drug dealing boyfriends. She bounced from foster care to living with her family, and then back to a children's' home. "You sold your lunch token?" He bent to retrieve a bag of crisps and a chocolate bar from the bottom of his rucksack, pushing them across to her without discussion.

Tilly nodded. "Yeah. Smitty gave me five dollars for it. He likes the custard."

Mac blew out a ragged breath and ran his right hand through his hair. "So, you just wanted my lunch?" A smile curved his lips and lightened his mood.

"Of course!" Tilly joked. But the reply didn't match her serious expression. "Actually, I saw you squaring off with Ross and figured you're more use to me here than expelled. Who would feed me if you left?"

Mac swallowed and stared at a point in the distance. His vision blurred. He didn't have an answer for her. It took a moment for him to realise Tilly had leaned forward to stare at him. He offered her a conciliatory smile and bit back the stream of confessions screaming behind his eyes for release. "I'm okay," he said in a whisper.

Her black eyelashes swished twice as though to call out his lie. The dark make-up she used to disguise her fragility bore a frightening resemblance to his own mask of indifference. Mac cleared his throat and looked away from her, staring at the ceiling, the walls, anywhere but her perceptive gaze. The heel of his left foot bounced against the concrete floor, jogging his wrist as it rested across his thigh. He used the pain to ground himself, seeking something real to banish his secret grief over Marie's death. No one would understand and so he buried his sadness beneath a blank expression. But it built like a tsunami in his chest, threatening to expose his duplicity and sully Marie's memory. The iPhone nestled in an inside pocket in his bag. He'd craved Deacon's help, placing all his hope in their shared dynamic, which usually meant they could solve anything. His aloneness carved a channel in his soul like a giant with an apple corer.

A sudden pressure above his knee halted the frantic, pointless bouncing. Mac started and stared down at the hand resting on his leg. Every finger bore a silver ring. The metal glinted beneath the glow of the overhead strip lights. Tilly's slender fingers curved over his thigh, fitting as though made to measure. He glanced sideways at her, but she ignored him, munching the sandwich and watching a fight break out in the opposite corner of the dining room. White shirted prefects surged towards it like surf on a rough sea. She turned to him then, lifting a black brow and rolling her eyes. "Dinner and a show," she said with a smirk.

Mac blinked and nodded, no suitable retort relieving the flush which spread up his neck and into his cheeks. Sorrow filled the empty space when Tilly removed her fingers. She rose, crumpling the sandwich wrapper and stuffing it with the chocolate bar and crisps into her purple bag. Her heavy right boot nudged the chair out of her way. "See you in Biology," she said. "Save me a seat." Jerking her head towards his blazer pocket, she squinted at him. "And answer your bloody phone."

She merged into the crowd, glaring at anyone who got in her way. Mac watched her leave, admiring her resolve. Smaller than most of their year group, she battled through like a snow plough. He hated to admit it, but once again, she'd rescued him from himself.

Tugging his phone from his top pocket, he released an audible groan. Missed calls from Arthur Darian racked up to eleven and Mac's toes curled inside his shoes. The moment of reckoning approached and he possessed neither the energy or the inclination for a battle he couldn't win.

19

DIAGONAL CRUYFF

Mac saved a seat for Tilly in the biology class, hedging his bets and picking the centre of the room. Dan Masters tried to sit next to him, but Mac shook his head and stretched his leg across the stool. He wasn't in the mood to allow the routine copying of his work. The other boy's lips moved and Mac wrinkled his nose and flapped his right hand next to his ear. "Sorry, can't hear you," he lied.

Masters moved away and Mac ignored the dribble of filthy words which he took with him to the back of the room.

Tilly arrived late, as usual. A haze of cherry bubble gum surrounded her like pink fumes. "Sorry sir," she said without sincerity, slamming her purple rucksack onto the workbench and grinning at Mac. The teacher ignored her apology and postured at the front of the class. His white laboratory coat bore a dubious pink stain on the breast pocket.

"We're starting a new subject today," he trilled, a lisp marring every 's' in his sentence. Spit flew from between his lips and spattered the students unlucky enough to choose the front row.

Tilly turned to Mac and crossed her eyes and turned down her mouth in a comical clown face. Despite the lead weight occupying his chest, he felt his lips part in a smile. She leaned sideways until their shoulders bumped. "Blood or ketchup?" she whispered, jerking her head towards the stain.

Mac raised his shoulders to his ears and shook his head. The smile faded from his lips at the thought of Marie's grizzly death. A crease appeared between Tilly's eyebrows and her mouth flattened into a line as though she'd read his mind.

The lesson passed at speed. Mac's cast put the experiment portion of the requirements out of reach, so Tilly dissected the petals and stamen of a lily while he recorded the results. As the rest of the class threw the floral remains into the dustbin, Tilly collected the petals with care and pushed them into her blazer pocket. "Can't waste them," she said, her long lashes shielding the diamond hardness of her irises. She patted the bump showing through the fabric and raised her gaze to Mac's face. "Sorry," she said, "about before. I forgot you found Miss Andrews' body."

Mac winced and his head dipped. The ache in his wrist seemed to multiply to create a ringing in his brain. He couldn't look up at her, fearful of what she may discern from his eyes. He swallowed as she dipped sideways and collected his rucksack, hefting it over her shoulder with her own. "You have a free period now, don't you?" she said.

The bell rang and the other students bolted for the open door. They took their hum of conversation with them. Mac couldn't think of a plausible reason to lie and so he nodded. With a grunt of satisfaction, Tilly navigated the bench and set off towards the exit. She paused to wait for Mac as he forced his feet to follow her. "You look wrecked," she threw over her shoulder. "You should have stayed at home."

Mac followed Tilly to the Year 13 common room. He waited as she bumped their rucksacks over the heads of other complaining students to get to the window seats. She responded with narrowed eyes and flashing azure pupils at anyone who challenged her progress. Mac winced as two girls stood and left, clearing a decent arc around him and Tilly.

"Why do you do that?" Mac ran a hand over his eyelids, blinking against the scratchiness and the blurring of his vision.

Tilly shrugged and slumped onto the padded bench. "It's easier than asking people to move. I worked out years ago that it's better to apologise than ask permission."

Mac snuffed through his nose and sat next to her. The red faux leather squeaked beneath him. "You sound like my father."

She leaned sideways and bumped her shoulder against his. "You say that a lot. I liked your dad." She blew a shiny pink bubble from between her lips. "Not that I'll ever meet him again."

Tiredness allowed the sarcasm to leak from Mac's psyche and pollute the airwaves. "Because you're not good enough for people like us? You used to come to our house heaps in primary school."

Tilly jerked her head back and peered at him in surprise. "Yeah, you egg. Because my mum lived in the township. Now, I don't have a car and the bus doesn't run as far as your place." Her mouth curved into a wide grin. "And because grown up plebs like me don't get invited to big, rich houses like yours." She dug her elbow into his ribs and he grunted.

"Sorry." He floundered. The cast appeared precarious balanced on his thigh, as though any slight knock could snap his arm at the elbow. "I've been rude not to ask you back again." He sighed and shrugged. "I just assumed you wouldn't come. You started refusing, so I stopped asking."

Conflict budded in her eyes and the hard mask slipped for long enough for Mac to detect her uncertainty. She pursed her lips and frowned. He turned sideways, supporting his wrist and holding his breath. "Would you like to spend time at my house?" he asked, his voice wavering. "I can sort out a ride there and back if you want?"

"No thanks." Tilly's grin spread across her lips to display even white teeth. The mask fixed back in place with a snap. It froze Mac out of her tight circle of one and left him adrift on a tide of confusion. He pressed his lips together, no ready retort springing into his brain. His mind spun in circles, second guessing her motives for rejecting his offer.

Her whisper jerked him back to attention. "Sorry," she said. Sadness infused the curve of her neck as she bowed her head until her fringe touched his cheek. "It's a defence mechanism. People pick me up when their friends are away and drop me when they come back. It always happens. I'm the spare. But you've been nice to me and you didn't deserve that."

Mac gave a slow nod. His voice croaked as he replied, "Okay."

Tilly turned sideways and her knee bumped his through his trouser leg. A run in the delicate stocking material started at a pinprick hole at her skirt hem and snaked beneath the tartan fabric. Mac swallowed and forced himself not to trace its progress further than appropriateness dictated. He fixed his gaze on a hardened blob of chewing gum welded to the carpet beyond the bench. "I don't think of you as a spare," he said, his voice low and gravelly. "But I didn't realise you felt like one." His gaze slid up to meet hers. "I'm sorry. You know you're welcome to hang with me and Deacon, even after he comes back." He breathed out a long breath. "If he comes back, but it's not looking likely."

Tilly tilted her head. "Thanks, Mac. You and Deacon are cool." She pushed out her bottom lip and her attention shifted to a knot of girls sitting in a tight circle in the centre of the room. Mac followed her gaze and gnawed at the inside of his cheek. The unspoken pain in her eyes seemed to wake him from the safety of oblivion. He'd never considered her struggle for acceptance as he drifted through life safely cosseted by his alliance with Deacon. His friend's absence gave him a stark view of what it was like on the outer fringes of their insular community.

He shrugged. "I guess I never cared what they thought of me," he admitted. The fingers of his right hand snaked towards the processor above his ear. His lips lifted at the corners. "I switch them off."

Tilly's bark of laughter drew attention from the groups scattered around the room. Mac's chin lifted, and he ignored them. He adjusted his cast over his thigh and leaned back against the wall, stretching his legs out across the stained carpet. "So, do you wanna?" he asked, glancing at Tilly through the corner of his left eye.

"Do I wanna come to your house again after all these years?" She closed her eyes and let her head fall back against her shoulders as she matched his casual stance. A light sniff preceded her answer. "Yeah. I think I'd like that very much." She turned her head to face him, her long lashes shuttering her blue irises. "But I need to warn you, it's a whole heap of hassle now that I live in the group home. Your parents will have to sign a form for the social workers and talk to them on the phone. They don't make it easy."

"All good." A jolt of electricity snaked through Mac's chest and a sense of rightness settled over him. "I'll give you my ma's number. They can call her. She won't mind." His thoughts turned to Wiremu, Edin and Ryan, plus the other strays his mother had sustained over her lifetime. His Uncle Marcus had been grafted into her family long before he married Isobel. He sighed and grunted with contentment. "You'll fit right into my whānau. My ma will love you just as much now you're pierced and tattooed."

20

CHEST TRAP

"Don't ignore me!" Arthur Darian doorstepped Mac as he exited the common room. The fat little man didn't possess quiet enough courage to enter the adolescent haven and confront him in the confined space. He waited for him outside, raising his voice as though Mac had committed some horrible infringement and causing everyone in the corridor to stare at him. Colour blazed in the teenager's cheeks and a heady rage built up steam in his chest.

"What?" Mac's soles ground against the wooden floor as he dragged his feet. Tilly left minutes earlier and gratitude took the edge off his embarrassment. Her opinion of him mattered. He didn't want her to witness his humiliation.

"Don't you '*what*' me!" Darian slid from the shadow behind the door and jabbed his finger against Mac's wide chest. His lips curved into a spiteful smile as a group of younger boys whooped with mischief at Mac's obvious discomfort. "You're ignoring my texts. When's my muster, Du Rose?" Spittle landed on Mac's white shirt, leaving damp spots of grey fabric. He recoiled, his stomach knotting into a pretzel behind his belt.

Taking a step away achieved nothing as Darian moved with him, reinforcing his superiority in every spark of his muddy irises. "Have you dumped that stupid girls' team yet?"

"The cops took my phone as evidence. And no, I'm still coaching them." Mac spoke through gritted teeth.

"No, sir!" Darian raised his voice to a shout. "Who do you think you're speaking to?"

Mac swallowed. His tongue locked at the same time as his right fist bunched around the strap of his rucksack. One hit. Having grown up in the bosom of the Du Rose's he'd learned to abhor violence. It achieved nothing in his family's long and painful history. But Darian's proximity made him desire the crunch of the man's nose cartilage more than oxygen.

"Hi, Mr Darian." Tilly's bright voice issued from beyond Mac's right shoulder. Her light energy infused the shadowy corner of the corridor, exposing the adult's behaviour in all its ugliness. She tapped Mac's elbow and tugged his sleeve. "Hef needs to see you now, Mac," she urged. "Sorry, Mr Darian. He said right now, not next week."

Slade Hefner outranked Darian in the revolving door of authority within the school's cascading management structure. He eyed Tilly with a predatory smile as he considered the situation, dragging out the painful moment for as long as he dared. Then he whirled away along the corridor, barking orders to a knot of Year 9s waiting outside a locked classroom.

Mac heaved a sigh of relief.

"He got spit on your shirt." Tilly waved a cautious index finger at the splotches to the left of Mac's tie. "Couldn't he get any closer?"

Mac shuddered and ran a shaking hand across his eyes. An unknown sensation prickled behind his eyeballs and he struggled to name it.

"He's revolting, isn't he?" Tilly hauled his hand away from his face and flattened her lips into a line of disgust.

Mac nodded, testing the word against the emotion bubbling at the forefront of his understanding. Revulsion. It fitted both the teacher and his effect on Mac. "Yeah," he agreed with a sigh. "I can't captain a team with that guy coaching it."

"I don't blame you." She turned her feet towards the stairs and flung sentences over her shoulder. "Remember when he took us for Health Science in Year 9? He always picked Deacon to demonstrate stuff to the class. Deacon swore the dude felt him up every time."

Mac nodded. Regret surged through his veins. He should have done something to help his friend. The same sense of powerlessness returned to convict him of his former complacency. They'd hated the class, a dislike of Thursdays leaving a scar on each child's psyche. The torture had continued for a whole semester until the class switched places with another. Mac disliked cookery with similar levels of disdain, his incompetence in the kitchen producing horrors unfit for human consumption. But the teacher had neither ridiculed nor molested them. The stories filtered through from the other Year 9 class as the semester progressed, carried in hushed voices and whispered behind hands. Darian's seemingly accidental and inappropriate touches became a thing of legend. Unproven rumours. Tales lacking physical evidence. Never quite enough for anyone to make a complaint. Arthur Darian had mastered the art of gaslighting and built an empire on its foundation.

Tilly excused herself to use the bathroom before class. She didn't say why she'd returned to rescue Mac from Darian's clutches and he didn't ask. He lined up outside the English classroom with the rest of his group, deactivating his processors and leaning into the temporary peace.

A jab to his elbow produced a groan which rattled his chest. The goalkeeper from his previous team stood before him, an apology already tumbling from his lips. Mac registered the silent sorry as he supported his cast in his other hand. It took a moment for him to collect his wits and press the button on his right processor. Mono sound flooded back to destroy his peace.

"Sorry, man." Ewan MacClay winced and jerked his head at the empty sleeve of Mac's blazer. "I forgot." He frowned and lifted his hand to scratch at a sore blooming from behind his shirt collar. "The coach said you're organising the muster for this season. The boys are worrying. It's getting late. If we don't make the cut for the First team, we're screwed. The Seconds already picked their squad, so we'll have nowhere left to go."

As the boy's concerns spilled into the air between them, Mac clamped his teeth together hard enough to catch his tongue. It hurt, adding another injury to his growing list. Ewan stared at him as his complaint ran aground without a response. Pinned between the proverbial rock and a hard place, Mac registered the return of the awful powerlessness. He struggled to reply with civility, reminding himself of Ewan's innocence in Darian's game of manipulation.

He took a deep breath and made yet another denial. "I'm coaching a girls' team this season." He lifted the cast and rested it across his chest. "This is buggered, mate. I'm out this year."

Ewan gnawed at a corner of his lip. "Sorry about your arm and all that, brother. But the lads hoped you might still coach us like last year. You could do it. Just don't play as well. We hate Darian. You're the only kid he never touches. We reckon he's afraid of your dad." He leaned forward and pushed his weight into one hip. "The lads need you as a buffer. Please?"

Stillness occupied an arc around them as other boys hoping to make the First Eleven gathered to listen. Mac's heart rate sped up until his processors relayed little more than the swoosh of rushing blood. "I can't. "The words stammered free to the backdrop of groans. A scream built like pressure in Mac's sinuses.

Darian had known better than to draw the attention of Logan Du Rose by aggravating his son, but something had changed. The pursuit of glory and sporting accolades had made the teacher careless. Mac didn't fear the flaccid lips or pudgy fingers. No, he feared his own reaction. A lifetime of suppressing the violence lurking in the pit of his stomach would end with Darian's wonky teeth embedded in his knuckles. It would mark a monumental failure to be different to the other Du Roses who let their fury destroy them. Mac's shoulders slumped lower. His existence already marked him as a failure. The Disabled Du Rose. His fists balled against the cruel nickname and his left wrist responded with a stab of pain. The pinkie finger stuck out from the end of the cast, alone and isolated.

"No." The harshness of Mac's tone caused Ewan to take a cautionary step backwards. "I already told him I'm not doing it. And now I'm telling you."

A hush followed the force of his resolution. The soccer hopefuls turned away to huddle as a group and consider their next move. Fed up with being a round peg forced into a square hole, Mac closed his eyes. He reached up to deactivate his right processor and plunged himself into safety once again. When he'd gained enough control to glance up again, he saw a movement through the corner of his eye.

Arthur Darian observed him from the top of the stairs, having watched the altercation. Mac doubted he'd heard the conversation, but the snarling lips and bared teeth betrayed his understanding. His gaze flicked to the knot of bowed heads as the team-less players debated. When he looked back at Mac, the venom in his expression caused a shudder of dread to run through the boy's bones.

21

ELASTICO

Tilly plonked herself next to Mac in English. A vacant chair remained where Deacon usually sat and someone from another table stole it before he could protest. Tilly grunted with irritation and dumped their rucksacks under the desk in the empty space. "They'd take your last breath, wouldn't they?" she hissed, and he nodded. He read her lips and it reminded him to switch on his processors and attempt to engage. But as the lesson started, her comment sent his mind to the memory of the equipment shed and Marie's hideous death. He wondered about her last breath. Was she awake and terrified? He hoped not. Tears pricked behind his eyelids and he gulped in distress.

"Du Rose!" The teacher barked at him from centimetres away and Mac jumped. A knotty finger reached down and jabbed at his closed book. "Is it too much to ask you to join us today?" The hard cover flicked open, and the man flipped pages until a new chapter appeared. "Chapter Two. Start reading and I'll tell you when to stop." He paused until Mac placed his index finger over the first line and cleared his throat. Then, he moved away on soft-soled shoes to haunt the students near the back of the class.

Portly and sour, Slade Hefner possessed an aggressive manner and a frightening lack of empathy. He was the last person Mac wished to cross. But he began reading in an ill-advised faltering tone, forming the words with enough difficulty to ensure he didn't need to carry on for too long. Tilly leaned forward and shook her head, telling him not to exaggerate too much. She glanced at the bald spot at the back of Hefner's head and winced. The man's rigid stance conveyed his burgeoning irritation. Mac sighed and continued at a normal speed, resigning himself to his fate.

Hefner forced him to read a whole chapter of *To Kill a Mocking Bird* to the entire class before choosing someone else. Mac heaved a sigh of relief and tried not to cough as his stint ended. Dryness irritated his throat and pain from his wrist licked the edges of his consciousness. He chanced a look at his plastered wrist before remembering he'd left his watch at home. A sigh escaped from between his teeth.

Tilly nudged his side and jerked her head towards her blazer's breast pocket. She used the fingers of her other hand to push her phone over the cuff so Mac could read the time. He smiled and nodded. Ten more minutes before the bell sounded for the end of school.

His eyes narrowed as he realised what he'd just seen. He shot a gaze back towards the device as it disappeared into the folds of Tilly's pocket. He recognised the scuffed edges and the dent at the bottom left-hand corner of the screen. Deacon's old phone. Realisation bloomed from a spark in his memory. Tilly swapped it for fifty dollars when Deacon's father bought him a new one. None of them had realised at the time that the shiny gold iPhone was purchased with cash stolen by his father from his employer. The old one had become surplus to requirement and Tilly wanted it despite the damage. But it was an iPhone. Like the one at the bottom of Mac's rucksack.

Mac lifted his right eyebrow and his tired mind fired into gear. A girl at the front of the class struggled to pronounce Calpurnia's name with the student next to her, still sniggering over Dill Harris. Hefner raised his voice to a shrill shout and Mac dipped sideways to hiss at Tilly. "I need to talk to you." The urgency in his tone caused her to frown, but she nodded.

Hope tapped a beat in Mac's chest.

But fear brought up the rear alongside guilt and recrimination.

What if she didn't understand?

What if she wouldn't help him?

Circumstance prevented Mac from confiding in Tilly at the end of the class. As the bell pealed its freedom cry, Hefner summoned her to his desk.

"I'll wait for you," Mac whispered, but she shook her head. Her pointed black fingernails waved him off in dismissal.

"Na. I haven't done any homework since the start of the term. This is gonna take a while."

"I need to give you my ma's phone number." A jittering sensation crawled through Mac's chest and into his empty stomach. All hope of her assistance trickled down a plug hole of misery. His hand trembled as he hefted his rucksack.

"All good." Tilly scraped the sleeve higher on her left wrist and handed him a permanent marker. She shook her head at his horror. "It's fine. Just do it. Quick."

The pen squeaked across her smooth skin to leave a phone number in Mac's slanted hand. He struggled to plug the glossy nib into the cap she held in her fingers. "Do you have my number?" he hissed. Slade Hefner blew his bulbous nose on a stained handkerchief, inadvertently providing a few more precious seconds.

Tilly grinned up at him and nodded. "I've had it for years," she admitted, her irises sparkling.

Mac glanced sideways at the teacher as the man stuffed the hanky into his trouser pocket and rose. His gimlet eyes bore into the back of Tilly's head. "Today, please!" he barked.

"Text me!" Mac hissed. "I don't have yours." He forced his rigid legs to carry him through the confusion of skewed desks and chairs to the door. Once in the corridor, he leaned back against the wall and closed his eyes. A sense of doom settled on his shoulders, bowing his spine into an unhealthy arc.

The wall clock mounted over the doorway to the administration corridor counted down the minutes until the school bus left without him. The girls' soccer team didn't meet on a Thursday, even when they'd had a living, breathing manager. Mac took a deep breath and righted himself, moving the rucksack's strap so it didn't cut into his shoulder. A last glance through the partially open classroom revealed Tilly laughing at something Hefner said to her. Mac frowned and made a show of bending to check his shoelace, seizing the opportunity to peer into the room.

She sat in the front row of the classroom, her attention on the teacher as he demonstrated something on the board. Not English, but maths calculations spewed from the nib of his pen. A plate from the canteen sat in front of Tilly, the wrapper rumpled on the desk next to her. She raised her index finger to ask a question and Hefner used a board rubber to erase part of his equation. Tilly's other hand clutched a pie, and she bit down into it while still speaking. Crumbs spattered the desk in front of her.

Mac rose, his cheeks growing rosy with shame as he speed-walked to the bus stop. Edin fell into step beside him but didn't speak, perhaps sensing the growing tempest in his mind.

How had he missed so much of the world around him?

When did he get so selfish?

He shook his head and slumped into his usual place on the bus, allowing Edin to take the aisle seat and chat to a girl in the other row. It struck Mac that his limited knowledge accrued over seventeen years of life just wasn't enough. Things weren't as they seemed.

He realised he'd questioned nothing, when he should have interrogated everything.

22

V-Pull

"You're quiet." Hana nudged Mac's shoulder as she cleared away the dinner plates. Logan stood over Edin while she loaded the dishwasher. She grumbled about the injustice of family life and he ignored her. He leaned against the pantry door and glared at the back of her head, his expression blank. Hana frowned at Mac's plate, at the baked potato collapsed like a broken tent and yellow butter creating a pond next to it. "Do you need painkillers?" Her voice held a softness. She blinked and checked he wore his processors before lifting her hands to repeat the question in sign language.

"I heard you. Sorry." Mac sighed. He rose and lifted his plate. The butter surged to the nearest edge and encroached onto the lip.

Hana took it from him, her forehead furrowed into lines of concern. "Can I get you something else? Some soup, maybe?"

Edin released a snort. "Charming! Why does he get offered something different when I had to eat that horrible mince?"

Hana's shoulders tensed, but she didn't acknowledge Edin's rant. Logan answered for her. "That horrible mince was expensive Charolais, which other people pay a lot of money to enjoy." His tone held warning, though his timbre remained even. Hana's lower lip trembled as though she anticipated the coming storm. They all felt it of late. Everyone except Edin. He'd had enough and each petty stab at the hornet's nest took him one step closer to washing his hands of her. Mac swallowed and wished she had the sense to see it for herself. Perhaps she did, and this was her route to freedom and autonomy.

"Soup?" Hana repeated her question, and he forced a smile and shook his head.

"Just tired," he replied, and faked a yawn. "Painkillers would be good, please."

Relief strode across Hana's elfin features and her shoulders lost their tension. She focussed on her son in order to avoid the conflict brewing in front of the dishwasher. "I'll make you some hot chocolate and bring it to your room," she said, her head nodding like a soft toy. "The stronger tablets make you sleepy."

Mac shuffled to his bedroom and closed the door behind him. He struggled out of his school clothes and contemplated the hassle of a shower with the cast. Pretending to himself that he didn't care about cleanliness, he gave himself a night off and slipped into his pyjama bottoms.

Hana delivered the drink and the tablets but seemed keen to hang around. She slumped into his armchair and lifted his trousers from the arm. Her busy fingers folded them and inspected a pull in the fabric. "Mac?" Her left eyebrow rose as she said his name and he paused in the task of removing his left processor. It magnetised back onto his head with a dull click.

"Yeah?" He sat on the mattress and rested his cast across his thigh.

"Did you take some of the powerful painkillers to school with you?" Her tone held a deceptive lightness.

He shook his head and frowned. "Not the strong ones, no." He jerked his head towards the trousers in her lap. "Just the ordinary ones you gave me this morning. They're still in my pocket." Something about her question jarred, and he sensed her tension roil from the other side of the room. "Check."

Hana pushed her fingers over the folded bundle until the foil wrapper crackled beneath them. She didn't investigate further, but her brow knitted. "The strong ones are opiates, Mac. I put them in the medicine cupboard yesterday, but some are missing."

"Missing?" He blinked as his mind calculated an appropriate response. "How many did the doctor prescribe? I took two when I got home yesterday and two last night." He wrinkled his nose, remembering the strange fog which had descended over him and clouded his vision and judgement. "I don't like them, but they dulled the pain enough to sleep."

"Yes, I gave you those. Don't worry about it." Hana's forced smile alerted him to a wider issue. Her reluctance to press further made him wonder if she didn't believe him. His mouth hung open, and he failed to restart the conversation before she left the room. The door closed behind her with a click.

Mac leaned against the pillows with a groan. He glared at the wrist cast with its greying edges, as though blaming it for all his recent ills. The woman at the round pen had a lot to answer for when he worked out her identity.

His phone chirped on the desk and he forced himself upright and collected it. The charger cable pulled taut as he lifted it and unlocked the screen. A text from Tilly sent a smile spreading across his face, and his mood improved.

'This is my number.'

He texted an acknowledgement in return, an inane winky face in place of words.

She replied, *'So, what's up?'* and he blew out a breath and ordered his thoughts.

'Can we talk?'

He jumped as his phone vibrated, almost dropping it in his haste. Edin's voice rose in the hallway as she continued riling Logan. He texted back to Tilly, begging for a five-minute window and promising to return her call. Dropping to his knees, he dug in his rucksack for the wireless phone clip he'd purchased with the device. He rarely used it, preferring to text rather than speak to callers, but he needed to leave no written trace of his conversation with Tilly.

Edin stomped past his bedroom, anger thudding from the stamp of her heels against the floorboards. Mac cringed and hoped she kept walking, bending double with relief when he heard the bathroom door click and the glass rattle on the shower cubicle. She continued to chunter to herself, her fury evident. Mac stared at the device in his hand and shook his head. He needed more privacy than the house afforded.

The ranch slider hissed on its tracks as he opened it wide enough to pass through and stand on the path, which ran around the building. He paused for a second to close the door behind him, the wireless clip and the bulky phone making it difficult one-handed.

Mac stepped over the border containing the bobbing heads of late marigolds and sighed as his soles contacted the soft grass. He took a moment to ground himself in the earth's solidity and sensing the stress trickle out through his toes. Logan raised his children with a healthy respect for their ancestors, especially for Papatuanuku, the earth mother. Mac got it, more than all the others. His father delighted in their shared connection. But he still wouldn't let him leave school and work on the land with him.

Mac squatted in his pyjamas and rested the fingers of his injured hand against the grass. His phone and the clip dug into his right palm. The cast's weight tugged on his elbow and the earth absorbed his pain. Feeling better, he blew out a ragged breath and rose, fisting the devices and holding them tight against his bare chest.

With his parents busy in the back of the house, he anticipated some safety in heading to the bush line beyond the boundary fence. Cameras kept watch from the corners of the building, but didn't stretch as far as the canopy and undergrowth which shaded the far edge of the lawn. Mac stole across the grass and hopped over the fence, cursing when the clip tipped from his hand and landed in the dirt. He bobbed down and scrabbled for it, wiping the flakes of punga from its surface on his pyjama bottoms. His phone vibrated in his hand and he juggled both devices until sinking into his secret hiding place beneath the waving leaves of a silver fern.

Tilly's text bore a single question mark, chiding him for the delay in returning her call. Mac laid his phone on the ground in front of him and activated it, lifting the wireless device in front of his face.

Tilly's joviality burst into the peace like a bush fire. "What's with you, Du Rose?" she demanded. "You'd better not be yanking my chain."

"I'm not," he promised. "I've come outside to speak to you. Edin's causing trouble and I don't want her to hear."

"She'll tell your parents?" Mac closed his eyes and imagined Tilly cocking her head in question.

"No. That would be the least of my worries." He swallowed and struggled to work out how he could begin the damning conversation. "I need your help but I don't know how to ask." Honesty seemed the best approach. Mac sensed his cheeks flaring with embarrassment. He rubbed his good wrist along the line of stubble sprouting across his cheekbone, accidentally hitting the wireless clip against his nose.

"What are you doing?" Traffic sounded in Tilly's background and he realised she wasn't at home. Wherever Tilly called home, anyway.

"Sorry. Bloody cast." Mac sighed. "I'm in the bush, wearing pyjamas and juggling two devices just to get some privacy." He swallowed, licking his lips and wishing he hadn't just given her all that information.

"What a delightful picture." She giggled, and he blushed to the roots of his hair, his violent cringe involving every nerve ending. "Tell me what's up, anyway," she demanded. "I'm on the roof and I have exactly five minutes before the social worker finds me. It's a new guy, so he'll take a little longer to realise."

"The roof?" A mental image of Tilly standing on a narrow lip sprung into Mac's mind and he held his breath. A car horn sounded, and he gripped the device hard enough to make the plastic creak in protest. "Why?"

He imagined her shrugging as she answered. "Same reason as you. It's hard to find peace in a house full of other kids. A new one arrived at the weekend and it won't stop crying."

"Oh." A memory resurfaced from the annals of his mind and his shoulders tensed. He saw Hana soothing a tiny Edin as the child thrashed and howled for her incarcerated mother. His next breath seemed to scratch his lungs. "That's sad."

"You can't help them all." Tilly's detachment cut him; the throwaway comment a symptom of wisdom earned through tribulation.

"I've got a massive problem." Mac's voice faltered. A myna bird squawked at him from a nearby kauri tree and he jumped, guilt heightening his response.

"Okay." Resignation filled Tilly's tone, backed by a streetwise alertness. "You have four minutes. Go."

23

STOP AND GO

A nauseating case of verbal diarrhoea seized Mac's tongue and his usual reticence disappeared. His mind blocked out the angry chatter of the myna bird, which echoed through his processors as he told Tilly everything. His chest loosened as though a magician tugged a series of knotted handkerchiefs from his lungs. Each revelation brought an increase in catharsis and allowed the next secret to spill from his lips. Even the kiss.

Mac had decided before the call that he would keep that to himself. His brain had other ideas.

The conversation ended with alarming abruptness. As Mac ran out of words and secrets to spill, the wireless device crackled and the connection died. He heaved in a snort of dismay and checked the battery indicator. Still fully charged.

The inspection continued to his phone, finding nothing wrong there either.

Mac released a groan of agony, his hands trembling in anguish at the only other explanation. Tilly hung up on him. And now she knew everything.

"Idiot!" Mac thumped the ground with his good hand and his phone bounced onto the dirt. Dust puffed from beneath its landing place, motes shimmering beneath the sun's filtered rays as they made their escape. Sickness roiled in his gut as Mac berated himself for his stupidity. He missed his friendship with Deacon with every fibre of his being, acknowledging his desperation in confiding in an unworthy substitute.

Damp earth stained the back of his pyjama pants and he brushed at it with futile slaps as he rose. His wrist set up a bone-deep ache in protest of its rough treatment as he hopped the fence with less vigour than his outward journey. He approached the house with less caution, his shoulders bowed and the devices jostling in his right hand.

"Son." His father's voice came from nowhere. Mac halted on the spot, his eyelashes shuttering his expression as he bought himself a second's grace to manufacture a suitable excuse.

"Yep." He reached the ranch slider into his bedroom and eased it open enough to throw his phone and the clip under the curtain. Tugging it closed, he turned his bare feet towards the back of the house.

Logan sat on the deck, his stance casual and relaxed. The sunset reflected off his sunglasses, throwing an arc of refracted colour across his white tee shirt. A tan cowboy boot rested over his knee, the sole dusty and the leather scuffed. Logan stretched his arms backwards far enough to touch the weathered brick of the house, and he groaned in satisfaction. Mac judged his mood, sensing more soulfulness than tension. He sank into the deckchair next to his father. There seemed no point in asking how his father knew he was there, despite appearing as though he hadn't moved. Logan Du Rose saw and heard everything. The stockmen theorised that the earth whispered their secrets to him with every purposeful step he took over its treasured surface. Mac wondered if it had a more technological source. His fingers twitched to activate the phone screen lying blank on the table in front of him. There was a reason he dodged the security cameras wherever possible.

"You wanted me?" He dipped forward in his chair and inspected a green stain on his left knee. His lips twisted as he wondered if chemicals would remove the fern's crushed remnants.

Logan nodded. He jerked his head towards Mac's cast. "Your ma thought you'd appreciate an evening away from the stables. The mare is fine. How's your arm? You ate little for dinner."

Mac screwed up one eye and considered the sunset with his head tilted. His information dump to Tilly had left his brain feeling strange. Empty. Confused. Afraid. He viewed his father's solid shape from beneath his lashes and considered telling him everything, too. If Tilly proved untrustworthy, he'd know soon enough, anyway.

Logan considered him through eyes the colour of slate. Mac knew he wouldn't interrupt or fill the silence. It was his father's special skill; giving people enough rope to hang themselves. He sighed and shook his head. "My arm hurts. I'm fed up."

Logan blinked at the surprise response. Mac never complained. Silent and stoic, he'd battled through deafness, surgeries, and a world which made little effort at inclusion. He nodded in acknowledgement and set his boot on the wooden deck with a thud. "You want to know who the woman is." He presented it as a statement rather than a question.

Mac cocked his head and nodded. "Yes."

Logan blew out his lips and remained still. But the fingers of his left hand strummed guitar notes on an imaginary fretboard on his thigh. Dark stubble coated his cheeks and chin, adding the finishing touches to the devastating good looks which still made women falter. Black curls flecked with grey peeked from beneath the cowboy hat which had rested on his head forever. Toby said it once belonged to Logan's grandfather, but not to mention that fact to Hana. Never. "Right." Logan's chest heaved, and he turned in his seat to face Mac. If he thought the bush-stained pyjamas a weird attire, he kept it to himself. "I owe you that much," he conceded.

"Is she your mistress?" The words popped free before Mac could stop them and he pressed the fingers of his right hand over his mouth to prevent anything else from escaping against his will. He hadn't realised the root of the worry chipping away at his sense of fairness.

Logan's sharp laugh gave him even more cause for alarm. But his father cocked his head as though studying his son for the first time. "You're serious?

"Yes. No. Sorry." Mac floundered, the situation spiralling out of control against his powerlessness. He ached to rip off his processors and plunge himself into the safety of silence. His feet scrabbled against the worn deck as he rose. "It's okay. It's none of my business."

"Sit." Logan's command held authority.

Mac bent his knees and perched his bottom on the edge of the deckchair. It seemed ridiculous, posing ready to run before a man who'd never used violence to exert his dominance. Logan's disappointment would always trump the most vicious of physical attacks. "Yes, sir." Mac rested his cast across his thigh, masking a groan at the dart of pain firing through the joint. He'd taxed his energy beyond his stores, and his eyelashes fluttered as he fought for concentration. His father's willingness to draw him into his confidence made him realise he'd rather not know the woman's identity. He didn't want to share this burden, besides the others piling up behind his green irises.

"She's Edin's mother."

Mac breathed out a sigh of understanding. If he'd thought it through properly, he would have realised. He nodded. "Right. You don't want her to see Edin."

Logan shook his head and flattened his lips into a severe line. "Not at all. Edin doesn't want to see Caroline. We gave her the choice, and she made it. Unfortunately, I'm the enforcer." He didn't add *'as usual'*, but Mac sensed the words lurking within the statement.

He cocked his head on one side and studied his father with renewed interest. "If you're doing what Edin wants, then why is she being so difficult? She's punishing us all."

"I know." Logan reached out his left hand and rested it on Mac's shoulder. The connection fired between them and offered a soothing confidence. He sighed and tiredness drew dark circles beneath his eye sockets. "She's confused and pushing the boundaries again. We'll get through it."

Mac's lips twitched. His ill-advised confession to Tilly tightened the knot in his stomach. It prevented him from complaining to his father about Edin's persecution of any girl who got close enough to smile at him. But the mention of Caroline presented a different opening, and he attempted to capitalise on it. "Caroline made trouble for you and Ma, didn't she?" He regretted the question when Logan withdrew his hand and laid it in his lap, where it fidgeted with its mate. Still, he pushed on regardless, not waiting for confirmation. "How did you handle it, Pa? What do you do when you don't feel the same way about them and they won't leave you alone?"

"Ah." Logan raised a hand and tilted the brim of his hat with his crooked middle finger. "You mean when kindness doesn't work?"

"Yes." Mac leaned forward. "When they just won't listen."

Logan lifted his arms above his head and clasped his hands behind his neck. He leaned back in the chair as though buying time to present his answer. His tee shirt rose above the waistband of his jeans to display a brown stomach still taut and muscled. He didn't look at Mac as he spoke. "You run, son. Far and as fast as possible. And you never look back."

Mac's lips parted in surprise. He swallowed, not able to process the implications. He couldn't run from Edin because that meant leaving home. The reply left him in a state of heightened confusion. Would the answer remain the same if he'd confessed that Edin was the problem? He didn't know.

"Is that what you did?" Mac dipped forward in the chair. He spotted his dirty toes peeking from beneath his pyjama bottoms and crossed the big toes over each other. "Are you answering through hindsight or experience?"

Logan's eyelashes fluttered, and his lips curved into a smile of appreciation. He and Mac connected often through ruminating over complicated problems and thrashing around ideas. "Good question," he replied. "Hindsight is the only truth, so I guess that's the root of my answer. Caroline's behaviour never deviated from childhood to adult. I should have stayed well away from her and not acted surprised when she hurt me, and later killed my brother. There aren't many changes I'd make if I had my time again, but that's one of them."

Mac nodded. "Are you saying you knew you'd get your fingers burned, but you still put them in the fire?"

Logan's grey-eyed gaze settled on his son's face and he gave a slow dip of his chin. "That's exactly what I'm saying. No means no, MacGillivray. For the wāhine and for us. Be clear if you're not interested. Leave no room for doubt."

"And what about Caroline?" Mac lowered his voice to a whisper. He glanced behind him at the closed ranch slider leading into the dining room. His father's jaw flexed, but truth-seeking forced Mac to box on for conclusions. "She dressed smart. For you. She came for Edin, but also for you." He didn't explain how he knew, but she'd oozed desperation. Enough for him to believe his father was capable of an illicit affair.

Logan's Adam's apple bobbed in his throat and he used the backs of his fingers to rub at the stubble beneath his chin. "You want to see me walk the walk?" His irises glittered like storm water.

Mac's throat dried, leaving his tongue sticking to the roof of his mouth and his nerve gone. A dimple appeared in Logan's chin, creating a cleft as a reminder of a past injury. He gave a single nod.

"You're right, son. I always give that woman far too much rope, and all she does is wrap it around Hana's neck and pull." Another nod and he reached for his phone, still balanced on the edge of the table. "Good talk, MacGillivray. I should ask for your advice more often." His eyelashes flickered as he called up a number on the screen and dialled, putting it on speaker for Mac to hear. The familiar voice of his father's lawyer burst into the peace.

"Hey, Logan. Is this about the lease renewal for the hotel? I don't have the paperwork at home with me." Children's laughter sounded in the background and a small dog yapped.

"No." Logan paused a beat before issuing his command. He didn't apologise for calling the man out of hours. "It's about Caroline Marsh. Please can you write to her at the address I'll text to you? Her daughter isn't interested in contact with her right now. I'd like her to stay away from my property and my family."

"We could issue a trespass notice. That gets lodged with the local police station."

Logan considered the suggestion with his brows furrowed and his head on one side. "That would breach her bail conditions though, wouldn't it? She'd go back to prison."

The lawyer made a humming sound. "That's debatable, but it would hurt her with the probation service."

Logan inhaled, his jawbone showing through his cheek. "Then threaten it. Trespass, injunction, whatever it takes. If she persists, we'll make it official and contact her probation officer."

"All good." The lawyer smacked his lips. "I'll get on it tomorrow. Give my regards to the family." He hung up without waiting for a reply, his exorbitant clock ticking and adding up the dollar value of the call. Logan pulled up an email and squinted at an address which Mac couldn't read. He copied and pasted it into a text box and sent it spinning into the ether.

Satisfaction shrouded Logan in a cloak of peace. He leaned back in the deckchair and rested his clasped hands over his stomach. "You have a good head on your shoulders, kid," he mused, sending a smile of approval Mac's way.

Gladness bubbled in Mac's chest at having attained a level of equality he'd dreamed about possessing. He pushed away the hollowness which followed it. Logan had indeed answered his pressing question, but Mac didn't know how he could put any of it into play. He'd given more help than he'd received.

Wooden framework and particle board separated him from Edin. He wished his solution was as easy as trespass notices and court injunctions.

24

MARADONA

Mac spent a restless night thrashing around in his bed. The heavy weight of guilt and fear bore down on his muscular shoulders until he dreaded the new day. The sheets tangled with his legs as he turned fruitless arcs in search of a comfortable position, which didn't cause his wrist to throb.

He rose and took a shower in the early hours of the morning. The plastic sleeve didn't fasten to the correct tightness and allowed water to dampen the edges of the cast. Mac's one-handed efforts caused frustration to build in his chest like a bomb. He switched the temperature to cold and held his breath under the freezing stream, shocking his body in revenge for its failure. Towelling dry without care created red welts across his stomach and pectoral muscles. Mac glared at his reflection in the mirror, his resolutions less clear through the fog of exhaustion and pain.

The suggestion began as a nagging thought in the back of his mind, growing in influence as he stopped shoving it aside. He patted the edges of the cast with a hand towel and allowed the awful thread to sneak forward and announce itself.

Edin could have done it.

Mac blew out a ragged breath and gnawed the inside of his cheek. She'd accepted a ride from her dodgy friend but left the group soon after arriving on the site. It gave her an opportunity to kill Marie, and he didn't need to look too hard for a motive. Whoever took the covert photo of the sports teacher on the side-line the previous week would have watched him leave. Perhaps they observed his fumbled kiss and assumed Marie shared his passion. Edin needed little more than a whisper of attraction to see off Mac's potential suitors.

Sickness threaded through Mac's gut and he sank onto the side of the bath. Droplets from his red curls trickled along his shoulder and into the cast. He lost track of time as his mind wrestled with the real possibility that Edin had murdered Marie Andrews.

Mac crawled into bed, still wearing a towel around his hips. An emptiness filled his chest at the prospect of telling his parents what he'd discovered. He pushed away the thought with distaste, knowing he couldn't do it. Not to her and not to them.

Just before dawn, he rose and reached for his phone. Bodie would know what to do. The message icon on the screen showed a missed text, and he opened it, dreading what it might reveal.

'*Sorry,*' Tilly had typed, sometime after midnight. '*Social worker isn't as dumb as he looks. Found me in record time. Also, confiscated my phone. Had to break into the office after everyone went to bed. I'll find you at school tomorrow and we'll talk then.*'

Relief gripped Mac's head in a rush of heat and he sank into the nearby armchair. A waft of his mother's perfume rose to shroud him in safety, left over from her earlier visit. He shelved the need to text Bodie for a while, hoping that Tilly's logical thought processes could provide an alternative to destroying his family from the inside.

Edin coughed next door, the sound sharp as it filtered through the thin wall between them. Mac ran his right hand over his face and blinked against the burgeoning sense of constriction. She hedged in every facet of his world, at school and at home. He'd allowed her silent creep into his existence with passivity and good grace. Until now.

Mac swallowed the lump in his throat at the memory of Marie's charred remains. She hadn't deserved to die, or to be left like a piece of meat in a dirty shed surrounded by the tools of her trade. He readied himself for school despite the ridiculous hour and filled his rucksack with everything he needed for school. Then he left the house in silence and walked down the mountain in the stillness of the pale pink sunrise.

The mare nuzzled his fingers as Mac stroked the knotty ridge of bone along her nose. "Sassy," he murmured, enjoying the word on his tongue. She dropped her head and rubbed her poll against his bent knee, almost pitching him backwards off the fence.

Sharp fingers pressed against his spine. "You're up early." Toby paused for long enough for Mac to retrieve his dignity and settle his bottom on the thin rung. Then he removed his protective hand. A pine scent followed him, underwritten by the minty tang of chewing gum.

"Yeah." Mac frowned and inspected his useless left hand. Hay dust from Sassy's inquisitive lips accompanied a line of slobber. "I couldn't sleep. This thing gets hot, and it's started itching."

Toby nodded in sympathy. His relaxed muscles radiated peace despite their earlier fraught conversation. "Borrow a knitting needle and shove it down the opening. Leslie lent me a thin one when I busted my ankle." He closed his eyes as though memorising the moment of excruciating satisfaction as he reached the offending spot with the sharp point. Mac glanced at the cast and shuddered.

"It's still swollen and I have stitches." He winced. "I might do more damage."

"Yup." Toby tilted the brim of his cowboy hat with his left index finger. "You might. Or you might not." He winked at Mac, humour twinkling in his blue irises. "God loves a trier."

Mac blew out a snort. "Yeah, but not an idiot."

The mare jerked at the sudden sound but settled with her lids half closed and her head lowered. Her thick lips twitched and a fleck of hay bounced against her whiskers. Mac reached out with his right hand and twisted her forelock into a loose coil along her dappled brow.

"She's going great." Toby rested his chin on his forearms and regarded her with interest. "I saw your pa working with her last night. I figured she had too much of the wild one in her, but she's responding better than I expected."

"Thanks." Mac accepted the rare compliment. His father's favourite mare had produced two amazing male offspring. Logan had used the first, Le Prochain, to sire three foals after the stallion retired from the jumping circuit. But Sacha's genes had filtered through in the blue wall eyes and unpredictable tempers. Two of them kicked their way through the stable gate and fled back to their dams on the mountain. Only Sassy remained as Mac's lone project. It galled him that the broken wrist meant he needed his father's help to train her. "I'll get on her again at the weekend." He asserted his ownership and competence while stealing a glance at Toby.

The stockman nodded without contesting the wisdom of his plan. "Yeah," he agreed. "Probably best." He tapped the top rung of the fence and swung away, his mind already on the long list of jobs in his head.

Mac started at the sound of footsteps crossing the stable yard's rough concrete. He turned to find his father striding towards him. "Hey son." He smiled and Mac's shoulders relaxed. Smart suit trousers and an expensive jacket hugged his father's powerful frame. The toes of polished black cowboy boots peeked from beneath the pressed hems. "I have a meeting in Auckland." He qualified his appearance at the same time as glancing at his wristwatch. "I can give you a ride to the bus stop or to school, but we'll need to leave now."

"Okay." Mac leaned over the fence as his mare lifted her muzzle to his shoulder. He rubbed her hairy cheek, feeling the hard plate of bone beneath it. His father turned and stalked back towards the car park, and Mac used the opportunity to plant a spontaneous kiss on the soft dent above her muzzle. Her ears flicked back and forth in response and his heart gave the first tiny skip of pleasure since before his fall. "See you later, Sassy," he promised.

Mac lifted his rucksack onto his right shoulder and hurried to the waiting truck. Edin's frowning face stared at him through the rear window. He blinked in surprise to discover his mother sitting in the passenger seat and waved to her as Logan waited with the boot open. Strong fingers seized his rucksack and slung it into the cavernous space before slamming the lid. He paused while Mac settled himself and then closed the rear door. Hana turned to smile at her son. "I didn't hear you leave. I appreciated the text." She held out her hand to reveal a blister pack containing two painkillers.

He nodded his acceptance of her thoughtfulness and pocketed them. The belt clicked into place between him and Edin, and he grunted as he unfurled his body to sit straight in his seat. If she was incapacitated, he would have helped her. It amazed him how he'd never catalogued the moments when she should have returned the favour, but didn't bother. Their relationship spread before him as a litany of one-sided graces. "I couldn't sleep," he admitted. Hana's face still turned to observe him, and he sensed her needing reassurance. "I groomed Sassy and fed her some hay. The walk down the mountain helped to clear my head." He blinked and forced a smile onto his lips, knowing his heightened blush betrayed him.

Hana laughed and pointed to his blazer. "I can see you groomed her, sweetheart. You're wearing most of her dirt."

Mac stared down at the grey and white flecked hairs dotting the fabric. He wrinkled his nose. "But I took my blazer off and left it in the tack room."

His father's stone-coloured irises flickered in the rear-view mirror. Clattering issued from the driver's seat as he grappled for something in the door pocket. A lint roller appeared from between the seats, and Mac leaned forward and snagged it. "Thanks," he murmured.

It took him most of the journey to separate the annoying layers of sticky paper in search of a suitable length to clean his uniform. Edin faced away from him and ignored his quiet request for her assistance.

Logan stopped the truck along the street from the school entrance and turned in his seat. The slam of Edin's door and the accompanying breeze ruffled his fringe. "Bye, Edin," he murmured. "Have a nice day." He grinned at Mac. "We'll be heading back this way around home time. Would you like a ride, or do you have soccer practice?"

Mac's shoulders slumped. "I don't know. Can I text you when I find out? We don't know what's happening now that Miss Andrews isn't here. Mr Darian wants me back in the boys' team, so he'll make sure he disperses the girls through lower groups."

"What do you want?" Hana twisted in her seat and folded her right leg beneath her. A sumptuous floral fabric covered her knee and ended in a delicate lace edging.

Mac blew out a breath and leaned back in his seat. He shifted the cast across his stomach. "I enjoy coaching, but Darian won't let me manage them alone without a school adult." He set his jaw and made the first of many decisions for that day. "I'm not going back to the boys' team, anyway. Not now he's coaching."

"Fair enough." Logan tapped his fingers on the steering wheel, his body still turned to watch his son. He'd met Arthur

Darian during a semester of relief teaching at the high school and labelled him a jerk after a single meeting. A vein twitched in his neck at the memory. "You and I work well together, don't we?" He cocked his head and waited for the reply with good grace. Mac's torso relaxed.

"Yeah, Pa. We're a great team." His response oozed sincerity, although the question appeared strange and out of place. "Why?"

Logan pursed his lips and seemed to stall, his gaze searching Hana's face for something he needed, permission perhaps. She spoke for him, dipping her body and smiling at her son. Her right hand stretched across the gap to rest on her husband's knee. "Pa and I wondered if you'd like help with the team. We could be the adult representatives for this season. You coach and we'll act as managers. Pa can drive to the games and I'll stand in for him when he's unavailable. We'd like to support you, and this is one solution." She flapped her free hand between the seats. "Don't answer right now. Think about it and let us know tonight. Then, I'll contact the school if it's what you want. It's fine if you don't like the idea."

Mac's mouth opened and closed. He imagined relaying their kind offer to the girls and knew they'd squeal with collective delight. Nothing good could come from Marie's death, but perhaps they could salvage her team.

He gave an abrupt nod, embarrassed by the tears of gratitude which sprang into his eyes. "Thanks," he managed, the lump in his throat choking him. "I don't need to think about it. The girls will love it."

"Okay then." Hana's bright reply gave him confidence. He wiped his nose on the cuff of his sleeve and paused as his father exited the vehicle and lifted the boot to retrieve his rucksack. "Ma." He edged forward in his seat. "I invited my friend Tilly to visit. Do you remember her from primary school? The thing is, she lives in a group home now and apparently the social worker needs to speak to you. I gave her your phone number. Is that okay?"

"Yeah, sure." Hana's eyes glittered with a curious spark. "I remember her. Tell her it's fine. I'll do whatever's necessary. It's not like Oranga Tamariki doesn't already know us. We shouldn't need to start from the beginning again."

Mac nodded. Hana had endured protracted involvement with the social services department since Edin arrived in their home. He adored her willingness to put herself through the extra demands of legal checks and balances levered into place to protect the nation's disenfranchised young. "I love you, Ma," he added, embarrassment causing a flush to rise into the roots of his hair. He pushed the door open and glanced back at her. "You're a great person."

The door clicked behind him, and he accepted the rucksack from Logan's outstretched hand. He didn't resist it when his father ruffled his red curls and gave him a nod of approval. "Let us know if you want a ride home," Logan said, and Mac nodded.

"Thanks, Pa, for everything."

Logan's momentary frown of confusion ruined the sentiment. Mac saw the flash of alarm in his grey irises and punished himself for worrying him with the backhanded gratitude. The words were common before a lengthy absence and not for thanks. He sensed Logan watching him as he hefted his rucksack and stalked towards the school gate. He ached to run back and wrap his arms around his father and tell him how much he loved him. But the notion of his cohort laughing at him prevented it. He couldn't get more like Jacob D'Arcy if he tried.

The thrum of multiple heartbeats surrounded him in the throng of bodies surging through the wrought iron sentries.

Overwhelmed by life and circumstance, Mac lifted his right hand and turned off his processors, proceeding to his locker in a blessed silence.

25

ADVANTAGE RULE

Tilly sat on the wooden floor, her back pressed against a wall bearing a past generation's graffiti. She blew out a bubble and grinned as it popped against her lips in a wrinkled pink mask. A boy stepped over her outstretched legs without care, scuffing his sole against her tights. Tilly lifted her foot and kicked the inside of his knee, ignoring his shout of pain. The boy raised his shoe, ready to stamp on her leg before noticing Mac's bulk moving between them. He licked his lips and thought better of it after reading the unpredictability on Mac's creased forehead.

"Hey." Tilly used her stomach muscles and legs to slide herself up the wall. She licked her finger and thumb before hauling the spent bubble gum from between her lips and dumping it in a nearby dustbin.

Mac reactivated his processors and noise filled his head. "Hey, yourself," he replied. His locker closed with a bang and he leaned his shoulder against it. "Where and when? I've realised something."

"Now." Tilly glanced around her. "But not here." Her purple rucksack clung to her shoulder at a lopsided angle, the strap frayed and hanging by a thread. She turned against the moving bodies, pressing into the flow without concern. Mac blew out a breath and braced himself, lifting his cast above the heads of the other students and supporting its weight at the elbow. Tilly looked back at his progress and winced. She jabbed her finger at a nearby janitor's cupboard and ducked inside. Mac followed, and she shut them in, jamming a mop handle between the wall and the door. It cut the tiny room in half and forced them together. Mac's shoe sent a metal bucket clanking onto its rounded edge.

The pungency of disinfectant, dust, and damp filled his nostrils, and he held his breath. Tilly activated her phone torch and held it up between them. She tilted her head back to observe him, dwarfed by his height in such proximity. "What's happened?" she whispered.

Mac closed his eyes and concentrated on the sentence he'd rehearsed. Despite his earlier efforts, it emerged as a stilted, fractured mismatch of words. "Maybe, I think Edin... No, well, she could have done it."

Tilly cocked her head, black coils bouncing against her shoulders and glinting like raven feathers in the phone's blue light. "What do you think she did? Killed Miss Andrews?" Her expression remained blank and Mac raised his right hand and scrubbed at his eyes. It sounded foolish when spoken aloud by another voice.

"No. It's stupid. Forget it."

"Can't." Tilly's curls bounced. Her teeth flashed an odd blue above the phone's thin beam. "You've said it now. Let's work it through." She lifted her free hand and clasped Mac's fingers, dragging them away from his face. He waited for her to release them, not sorry when she didn't. Her grip infused him with warmth.

"She got a ride to school that day. I didn't see her with the other girls. The photo I found on the cloud storage for the phone shows Miss Andrews alone on the side-line of a practice. I left early for an appointment, but I don't remember if Edin rode on the bus, or if Ma fetched her. She didn't come with us." He shrugged. "I didn't realise she had access to lifts with the other girls. That gives her heaps more freedom than I accounted for."

"True." Tilly paused and considered his theory. "But why would she kill a sports teacher? Did Miss Andrews teach her?"

"No." Mac shivered, the tremor running through his body. "But the photo shows the evening when I tried to kiss her in the equipment shed." The words stuck in his throat. "If Edin saw that, it gives her a motive. She texted some girls from the soccer team and threatened them to stay away from me."

"I know she's possessive." Tilly turned her face and the beam of light softened her profile. "I've also heard she's violent and the younger girls are afraid of her." Her curls bounced again. "But murder? I'm not buying it. Sorry, mate, but I think you're wrong. Last time I saw her hanging out by the hockey turf, she was getting cosy with a boy from our year." Her gaze darted to his face, and she paused as his brows furrowed into a single line.

"Who?" he demanded. His hands clenched into fists and he groaned at the pain generated by his left wrist.

"Just flirting. Nothing serious." Tilly squeezed his right hand until the fist released. She wormed her thumb into his palm and forced his fingers to open. "She plays games with people. That can't come as a surprise to you. You're not blind, Mac."

He gave a shallow nod. "I know." He winced. "But I didn't think she'd pick someone in our year to mess with. It's too close to home."

Tilly's eyes grew round. "Let's find out where she went after school last Thursday. But keep it discreet. I feel certain you're on the wrong track, but let's eliminate her." She bowed her head and pursed her lips. Her next sentence dragged from her with reluctance. "You and Miss Andrews." She shook her head. "I didn't realise."

Mac groaned and tilted his gaze to stare at the ceiling. "I've never done anything so dumb as to kiss a teacher." He squeezed his eyes closed against his discomfort. "She didn't feel the same way. I'd misunderstood. We got close when I helped to install the app on her phone. Her ex-boyfriend made her life a living hell. He turned up here at school once and the secretary threatened to call the cops if he didn't leave. I installed a piece of software which allowed her to press random buttons and generate an alert." He tutted. "It didn't help her, did it?"

"Who received the alert?" Tilly demanded.

"Her sister." Mac gave a series of rapid blinks as he imagined the poor woman receiving the news of Marie's death. "I don't know if she tried to send a message to her. The police didn't find Marie's phone."

"You need to speak to them," Tilly concluded. "And soon. We both know they don't need her phone to track all her calls and messages. They can do it through the telecom company using her number. Did she ever text you from that phone?"

Mac's head drooped. "Yes. Lots. Most of the messages related to the team, but a few talked about me helping her to sort out her phone. And she called and messaged me the night before she died. She thanked me because the app made her feel safer. It's the reason I didn't ping her phone once I realised I'd picked up the wrong one. I didn't want the cops to see me do it if they'd set up a watch."

"Why haven't you told your brother all of this? Her ex might have killed her. He could have bolted by now."

Mac released an agonised sigh. "Because I thought I had her phone. It's only when I hacked into it I realised I didn't. The killer left it there for someone to find it. The photo contains a message, but I don't know what that is. If I hand it over now, I need to admit that I took evidence from a crime scene. I'll get into heaps of trouble. I can't risk disappointing my parents."

He dropped his hand to his side and the force of the movement broke Tilly's grasp. "Ma says you can give her number to the social worker. You're welcome to visit."

Her smile seemed to light up the room. "Really? That's awesome." She gave a snort, which sounded like exasperation. The metal bucket clattered again as she moved her foot. "I need to tell you something." Her voice wavered.

"Yeah?" Mac tensed as the bell sounded, muffled by the heavy door behind him.

Urgency entered Tilly's eyes and the phone torch dropped to light up the bucket on its side and a puddle forming around its rim. He had a moment to rue his rotten luck before Tilly's palms rested against his chest. His eyes widened in shock as she planted her lips over his in the darkness and her cherry flavoured lipstick filled his senses.

Tilly's unexpected passion woke Mac from an emotional slumber. His fumble in the darkness of the equipment shed with Marie paled in comparison. The kiss left him breathless, but one certainty emerged from the fog. He liked it. Very much.

Mac lost count of the minutes as Tilly led the dance, her tongue pressing between the seam of his lips to invade his mouth. He forgot to breathe, his chest aching as every nerve ending jarred in a timeworn rhythm he hadn't known existed. He tasted her essence, their intimacy raw and urgent. All too soon, her palms dragged along his pectorals as she dropped on her heels. Mac ached for her to rise onto her tiptoes and resume the kiss, disappointed when she didn't. Language escaped him and he pushed many sentences around his fuddled brain before abandoning them. Instead, he wrapped his right arm around her shoulders and mashed her cheek against his shirt. She sighed but didn't pull away from him.

The bell tolled again as a final warning. All students should have reached their registration class. Mac released a groan of dread deep in his throat. "I'm in so much trouble," he whispered, his voice ragged.

"I don't think so." Her tone held a lazy, contented drawl. "You need to speak to the cops. I have an idea, but you might not like it."

Mac took time to swallow before replying. "Why mightn't I like it?"

Tilly tilted her head, and he sensed her gaze on him in the darkness. He lifted his right hand and smoothed his fingers across her cheek until he found her lips. Bowing his head, he took aim and his kiss landed with clumsy accuracy. A fire ignited in his belly, driving him to satiate himself by possessing every part of her. The addiction started, a manic, woken need for sensations he hadn't known he lacked. Her kisses provided an education and her hands roved to the waistband of his trousers.

The door handle rattled, catching Mac's hip as someone outside rived on it. "Oh," a muffled voice complained, "He said he left it unlocked." Footsteps thudded against the floorboards as two adolescent males moved away from the tiny room. Their voices echoed in the empty corridor.

Mac released the held breath and his gulp sounded loud in the silent room. "Shit!" he hissed.

Tilly giggled. "Probably for the best." She lifted her phone, and the torch performed a lighted arc, grazing the walls packed with toilet rolls until it rested on her face. A lazy wink suggested she wouldn't have held out on him. He swallowed. Fear and anticipation prickled in his chest. A million buzzing voices in his head demanded to know if he'd have stepped over the point of no return, their accusation like the sting of wasps. He didn't know the answer.

"I'll leave first," Tilly whispered. "Hefner won't care if I'm late." She rose onto her toes and planted a soft kiss over Mac's lips. His body twitched as though electrified and he willed himself not to seize her shoulders and vent the pent-up lust building in the back of his brain. It took every fragment of his self-control to respond to the chaste kiss without the Stygian passion, which demanded a different ending.

"Okay," he managed. His body spasmed as he gave a jerky nod. "What should I tell my tutor teacher?" He heard his own question and gaped in surprise, wondering when he abdicated all his strategising to the beguiling teenager for the price of a knee trembling kiss.

"Take this with you." Her ear brushed his chest as she dipped and retrieved something from the floor. She levelled the phone torch at it so he could recognise a plastic dustpan and brush. He had enough time to register the useless bristles bent out of shape before she pressed it into his good hand. She dropped the fingers containing the phone and the hard case brushed his groin before she tucked the device into her blazer pocket. The sense of urgency built again from the accidental contact and Mac held his breath to stop her from hearing the ragged action of his lungs. The wasps filled his head again and he willed them to silence just long enough for him to produce a coherent thought.

Tilly pulled away the mop handle, and it gave a pitiful thud as she leaned it against the equipment cluttered along the wall. "See ya later," she whispered and tugged on the door. A vent of light bathed her as she created a gap and she shot Mac a wordless grin. She left a waft of air in her wake and the door clicked closed behind her.

Mac soaked up the heady scent of floral perfume and cherry bubble gum, which remained in her place. He'd lost the ability to think in full threads. Gripping the sticky handle of the dustpan and brush in his right hand, he took a deep breath and levered open the door.

26

DRIBBLE

"What are you doing?" The janitor glared at him from beneath hooded lids and set his hands on his hips. Two boys waited behind him, their brows furrowed in identical confusion.

"Getting this." Mac waved the utensils between him and the older man, his cheeks still flushed from his unexpected tryst. "I'm taking it to tutor group. Hope that's okay?"

The janitor grunted. "And you found the door unlocked?" he demanded.

"Yeah." Mac exhaled in relief at the fresh taste of the truth on his tongue. He detested liars and yet, he'd become one in a matter of days. Since Marie.

He trudged along the corridor with a heavy heart. Tilly's floral-fruity scent preceded him.

The door to Mac's tutor class stood open, chaos running amok inside the airless room. He stood in the gap and stared towards the biggest desk. Syd Ross occupied the teacher's chair, his colour high and his hair on end. "Sit down!" he yelled and

Mac turned his gaze on a group of Year 9s shifting desks and chairs into a massive table at the rear of the classroom.

"Where's Mr Simms?" Mac set the dustpan and brush on the wide desk and stared at the prefect.

Syd swore and shrugged his skinny shoulders. "Don't know." He waved a slender hand toward the younger students. A girl with her uniform skirt folded over at the waist displayed too much thigh as she danced on a desk. "I need to take the register. They won't behave."

Mac turned his body towards the back of the classroom and raised his voice. His father's mana and power emanated from his lips as an echo of the past schoolteacher. Mac sensed their combined will rise in defence and reacted as Logan taught him. He puffed out his chest and relaxed his shoulders, making the decision that his will was stronger. They would behave. No doubt occupied a hidden corner of his mind. "Sit down!" he bellowed. His voice cut through the chatter and the room silenced as though someone flicked a switch.

Everyone followed his gaze to the foolish girl dancing on a row of desks closest to the rear wall and her colour rose. The joke lost its effect as her audience turned away from her.

"Come here." Mac crooked the index finger of his right hand, his expression severe. The girl paused as though set to refuse. The air molecules in the room zapped together in a curious ringing tone as the world halted on its axis. Mac cocked his head and raised an eyebrow, daring her to defy him. With an awkward descent which displayed her knickers, the girl clambered from the desk and dragged her feet to the front of the class. "Sit there." Mac jerked his head towards an empty chair at the front and the girl slid into it. She chanced a half-turn and a grin at her compatriots, but blank stares met her. A flush rose into the roots of her blonde hair and Mac experienced a moment of sympathy for her. "Take the register now," he ordered Syd.

The bell sounded to dismiss all students to their first class and Mac slammed the classroom door. As feet shuffled and bag zippers whooshed, he rose an eyebrow in warning. Syd Ross finished scribbling names onto a notepad and nodded to Mac. "Finished," he said, his tone rushed as though he'd held his breath. "They can go now." He sat back in the teacher's chair and blew out a sigh. "Little shits. I hate this vertical streaming. Why can't they keep the year groups together for tutor class? I'm sick of those Year 9s."

Mac pulled open the door and after a stuttering start, the students filed out. The dancing girl went with them, perhaps convincing herself he'd forgotten about her. He hadn't, but no longer cared about her punishment. It amused him to watch her sidle past and blend into the cohort to avoid his glittering green eyes.

Mac grunted and nudged the dustpan and brush on the table. Syd didn't comment on it, rising and folding the paper into quarters and stuffing it into his top pocket. "I'll run this to the office. They'll need to enter it on the computer system. Thanks for your help."

Mac jerked his head upward to acknowledge his appreciation. As Syd Ross exited, a stream of Grant Simms' Year 11 accounting class filed into the room. Mac loved peace and order in his life, inheriting Logan's high discipline and sense of structure, but he wasn't an idiot. Miss Trenchard, the Year 13 dean, hadn't seen fit to award him with a prefect's badge and so he resisted voluntarily fulfilling any more of the role. Simms had apologised for the perceived oversight. He promised he'd recommended Mac for a prefect role, but as the Year 10 dean, he carried no authority over the position.

Mac took the dustpan and brush back to the janitor's cupboard and, finding it locked, left them leaned against the door.

He retrieved his rucksack from the locker and made it to his English class on time. Tilly patted the seat next to her and he slumped into it. His heart thudded with a heightened beat as his thigh brushed against hers. He sensed his concentration trickling away through his toes. One kiss. That's all it took to detonate his brain. One toe curling, addictive kiss. He thought of nothing else for the next hour, counting down the minutes until interval and the possibility of more kisses, more intimate contact. Just more.

"I can't get used to this," Tilly grumbled as the bell sounded and they remained seated. "Double periods suck!" She laid her forehead on the desk with a groan.

Slade Hefner trod a circuit of the room and tapped her wrist as he passed her. "Come on, Miss Rae. Wakey wakey." He kept moving, his sensible soles squeaking against the floorboards like a trapped mouse. A slam resounded off the whiteboard as he slapped the wooden desk beside Syd Ross' head. "This is ridiculous!" he shouted. "You're adults. The real world won't allow nana naps between tasks. Lab sessions at university run for three hours. Sort yourselves out! This isn't kindergarten."

"I'm having a bad day," Syd complained. He spun his head on his scrawny neck to gain Mac's alliance. "Mr Simms didn't show up for tutor group and the kids were gits. Where is he, anyway?"

Hefner dug in his trouser pocket and Tilly tittered and nudged Mac's thigh beneath the desk. A blaze of heat emanated from her fingers, racing up his legs and into his groin. His body tingled, and he watched the teacher's familiar movements with more intensity than they warranted. Hefner placed a dull coin on the desk in front of Syd Ross. "Here's ten cents," he declared, his tone dripping sarcasm. "That's so you can call someone who gives a shit." He snatched back the coin and stuffed it into his trouser pocket. "Right!" He turned to face the rest of the class. "Let's talk about the overriding purpose of Boo Radley, shall we?"

"I hate Boo Radley," Tilly declared as they escaped the classroom at the end of the two hours. "I read this novel years ago and he's ruined it for me now."

Mac nodded and steered his feet towards the common room. He ached to take her fingers in his, but found himself hampered by his useless wrist and the rucksack dangling from his other hand. "I quite like it," he admitted. "My papa is an English teacher. I enjoy dissecting the thoughts in a writer's head and watching them unravel on the page."

Tilly wrinkled her nose and the silver ring in her right nostril sparkled. She pushed her way through a crowd of younger students who blocked the common room doorway. They grumbled and groaned, listing like flotsam in her wake. The aperture closed before Mac could pass through. He paused, his cast lifted above their heads. "Excuse me," he said, throwing his voice over their din. They parted like the Red Sea before Moses and he stepped through.

"Hey, Mac!" Sammy appeared at his elbow, Layla not far behind her. They followed him to the hallowed entrance of the Year 13 common room but ventured no further. He turned with a frown and pursed his lips. It would take months for the school community to forget Sammy's skilful depiction of him on social media. They skipped from foot to foot, jostling each other like ants transporting a leaf.

"Yeah?" He sensed Tilly pause behind him. The soccer team's allure paled against the promises contained in her kisses. Time marched on without regard, doling precious moments to the silly girls, which he was loath to relinquish. Resentment rose in his chest. "What?"

They spoke over each other, a confusing vomit of information which took a second to sort in his mind. Mac caught Darian's name and got the gist. "He wants to break us up and slot us into different teams." Layla's lips turned down in a pout. "Do you want to see the burn on my foot from where the electricity used me as an earth?" She dipped and began removing her shoe in the crowded corridor. A bottleneck formed behind her, of Year 13s wanting to enter the common room for their free period.

"Are you doing a full strip?" Dan Masters demanded. He lifted an eyebrow and a lascivious smile played across his lips.

Mac fought the urge to smack the grin off his face, halted by the fear that Tilly drew the same lustful thoughts from him. Did his expression reflect such baseness? It worried him.

Mac frowned and stepped sideways, encouraging the girls to move away from the door. He dropped his rucksack at his feet. The loud entry of the Year 13s blocked Tilly from view. "I have an idea," he stated. "Grant Simms didn't show up this morning, but I need to speak to him first."

"What idea?" Layla bounced on the balls of her feet, a sock and a single shoe dangling from her right hand. "Tell us now."

"It's a way to keep the team together," he offered. "But no promises. I need permission from the sports department."

"Yey! Yey!" The girls performed an impromptu jig in the doorway, irritating a group of Year 13 girls wearing heavy makeup. "Thank you, Mac." Sammy wrapped her arms around his waist and pressed her cheek against his shirt. Her giant inhale of his scent caused his cheeks to flush pink. He glanced at the doorway and saw Tilly watching. She'd clasped her full lower lip between her teeth and he couldn't read her expression.

"It's not definite," he warned. He cursed himself for revealing any of the plan.

"We'll tell the other girls." Layla disappeared into the throng, waving her shoe above her head.

"No. Don't." Mac's voice tailed off as he recognised the futility of his request.

Sammy gave his waist a last squeeze before taking a step backwards and folding her hands in front of her. The bulky knot of fabric at her throat showed she'd put her school tie on inside out. "I might get my phone back soon," she declared. Her lips turned down into a sulky pout. "That rude policeman wiped all my videos. My dad banned me from social media." She shrugged and her effervescent mood returned. "I don't care. I've got another phone they don't know about."

Mac's breath halted half way to his lungs. He stepped forward and gripped her shoulder. "Did you take Miss Andrew's phone?" he demanded, his tone harsh.

"No." Sammy shook her head and her ponytail brushed his knuckles. "It's just an old one."

"Okay." Mac swallowed and dropped his hand. His fingers tingled as adrenaline surged through his bloodstream from the false boom of a starting gun. He wished she'd given a different answer. It would have made a better solution. His hand shook as he clasped the frayed strap of his rucksack and lifted it onto his shoulder. "Let's meet tomorrow at lunchtime. Get the girls to come to the practice pitch. I'll know more by then."

Sammy's lips rose into a wide grin. "Awesome!" she hissed.

Mac shook his head. "No promises, remember. Oh, and don't let Mr Darian know anything. He'll stop it from happening."

"Okay." Sammy wrapped her arms around herself as though hugging the secret to her chest. "Thanks Mac." She turned and disappeared into the crowd, resembling a ladybug caught in a cattle stampede.

Mac walked into the common room and found Tilly waiting inside the door. "Should I be worried by your groupies?" she demanded, her tone serious.

"No!" Mac's head jerked back, noticing the faint smile on her lips too late. "Oh, good one," he growled. Tilly slipped a possessive arm around his waist, her fingers warming his spine through the thin fabric of his shirt. His blazer covered her arm and shrouded the way she pushed her fingers beneath his waistband, below his last rib. Her gentle stroke sent his pulse into orbit.

A wolf whistle disturbed the general chatter in the room as they strode across the stained carpet towards the window seats. Every face turned towards them and for once, Mac's cheeks flushed bright red against his orange freckles. He ignored the heckling and the jibes about erotic positions he'd never heard of. He plunged his heart and soul into his connection with the alluring girl who played his ribs with gentle strums like a harp. It cost him everything to keep his processors active to absorb the comments from his classmates. He ached to switch them off and retreat into oblivion.

But every moment spent staring into the glittering pools of Tilly's irises offered one more second without recrimination. He'd become a spider in a sticky web, caught between his usual behaviour and the addiction of lust. It stopped him thinking. And Mac Du Rose needed to stop thinking.

Coulda, woulda, shoulda.

He wasn't sure if he could have stopped Marie dying but would have done anything to prevent the tragedy. But he should have told Bodie the truth about the help he gave her and the phone he retrieved from the crime scene. The responsibility weighed him down until Tilly kissed him and then it dissipated in the wind. She offered him a reprieve containing soft murmurs as they whispered behind heavy text books. And Mac's heart lightened, right until the moment his name blared over the intercom in the secretary's wavering voice.

"MacGillivray Du Rose to the Headmaster's office, please. Immediately."

27

AGGREGATE SCORE

Coulda, woulda, shoulda.

Mac could have anticipated the uncomfortable hour spent in the headmaster's office. He would also have known his half-brother's disgust at him merited the painful conversation with Logan, which Bo forced him to listen to. He blamed his new infatuation with Tilly for the failed shoulda. The Mac Du Rose of last week showed more promise than the pale effigy which endured threats of prosecution from the detective who'd attended the murder scene.

"We're now days behind because of you!" the man raged. "Who is this ex-boyfriend she needed protecting from?"

Mac cleared his throat and cradled his aching wrist in his right hand. "She said she'd followed the official route." An uncustomary edge of insolence entered his tone. Sal Richard raised a warning authoritative eyebrow and dipped his chin at Mac. Conceding, he moderated his tone into one containing less aggravation. The headmaster had insisted on supporting him through the interview. Gratitude vied with Mac's nausea as the scent of Marie's burning flesh returned to haunt him. "She got a trespass notice issued after he visited the school looking for her. There was some issue with getting an injunction, but I don't remember what that was or whether she ever managed it." Mac lifted his gaze to Bodie's angry face. His voice wavered. "Did she use the app?" he whispered. A lump grew in the back of his throat. He'd done nothing to absolve Edin from the crime and, despite his desire to throw everything he knew at the policemen and run, he couldn't.

"She did." The detective's tone softened. "I should commend you for trying to help her, MacGillivray. Why did she ask you when the school has an IT department with its own expertise?"

Mac slid his gaze to Sal Richard and back to the detective. An expression of his mother's rose into the forefront of his brain and he tested it as a distraction. *Better to be hung for stealing a sheep than for a lamb.* Is it though? His mind seized the phrase and began its systematic dissection.

What made it better?

Which act formed the bigger crime?

"Mac?" Bodie's bark of irritation made him jump.

He licked his lips and plunged into the truth like a sweating runner leaping into a frozen lake. "The IT teacher is ancient," he whispered.

Sal Richard straightened his spine and sat up in his seat. His fingers rested on the polished arms of the original Victorian chair where other headmasters had worn a groove in the grain. Mac gulped and understood they would hang him for both the sheep and the lamb.

"And?" The detective rose and paced the floor, following the patterned motif depicting the school logo until he ended up back in his chair. "She didn't ask him for help because he's ancient?"

"Her," Mac corrected. "She's ancient. She hasn't kept up with technology. Mrs Paterson is a biology teacher who knew a little about using computers when everyone else still feared them." Mac's need to produce evidence won out over his common sense. "She once demanded a whole ream of paper from Deacon's dad because he printed a document without realising someone leaned on the return key. It printed blank paper for the rest of the afternoon. She phoned Deacon's dad in a temper and demanded a new ream by the next day. He asked her why she didn't right click the mouse and then cancel the print job." Mac glanced up at Bodie and caught his brother smirking. It emboldened him to continue. "That's why, anyway. The real geeky teacher left at the start of term. He kinda took all the knowledge with him."

Sal Richard's eyes flashed as Mac highlighted the reason behind the IT department's diminishing numbers. He reached for a calligraphy pen and scratched something onto a pad. "Yes, Ian Fraser left on the first day of the new year. Very sudden." His bushy brows knitted into a whiskery fringe over his eyes. "Very odd," he murmured to himself.

Mac blazed on, truth yanked from his lungs in a heady catharsis. "So, I coached Miss Andrews with a program she used for sport assessments, and she asked for my help afterwards." He ran aground with nothing else to add. Last week's sensible Mac begged him to tell them about the phone left at the crime scene. He batted its urging away, knowing the photo incriminated both Edin and him. She could have been there. He'd definitely left just moments before the shot, after making a complete fool of himself.

"Mac, did you remove Miss Andrews' phone from the equipment shed?"

Mac breathed out with relief, a giant gush of air which caused Bodie to raise his eyebrows. "No, sir." Confidence infused his tone. He would have struggled with the lie had the detective left out the name of the owner. But he hadn't taken Miss Andrews' phone. He'd just believed so at the time.

"You didn't take any phone?" His sharp minded brother rephrased the question and dread snaked a cool hand around Mac's throat.

A rap on the door made the headmaster jump in his seat and he half rose. His glare at the widening gap involved his entire face and his colour heightened. "I'm in a meeting!" he barked, bristling with irritation. The detective's body blocked any view of the newcomer, but Mac sensed his father's mana enter the room like a power surge.

Logan made no comment as he strode across the patterned carpet. The pressure of his cowboy boots left steps of the crushed pile in his wake. The door slammed behind him. He arrived at his son's side and jerked his head upward in greeting. Mac read nothing in his blank expression or the flashing grey irises, but rubbed his eyes with his right hand to avoid catching the full force of his gaze. "You don't question my son without my presence," Logan growled.

A picture of a former headmaster increased its precarious lean behind Sal Richard's chair. Mac pursed his lips into a tight line and clamped his teeth together to prevent the bubble of hysteria from escaping. The oil canvas slipped by degrees as though the esteemed principal and former Auckland mayor tipped his painted head for a better view of the offender. A whimper seeped from Mac's chest and Logan frowned down at him. The patriarch's glare burned his adolescent cheeks like a wildfire. "You had no right to do this." Logan levelled the accusation at the three men hedging his son into the visitor's chair. He saved the sum of his fury for Bodie. "Why didn't you call me before you ambushed my tamāroa instead of half way through your little interrogation?"

First-born son. Mac's heart shrivelled like a wilting leaf. The label formed both a compliment and a jibe. Tama and then Wiremu had preceded his birth, but the awful moment marked the first time Logan had acknowledged his own blood-son's importance.

Mac's shoulders drooped. He'd blown it. Emotion welled into his throat and his mouth, causing his eyes to water. He clutched his broken wrist in its clunky cast until the bones ached, keeping it as a barrier between himself and the room's occupants.

"We're leaving." The fingers of Logan's right hand made a beckoning motion, telling Mac to stand. He rose on wobbly legs, his confidence a mere shadow on the cushion of the uncomfortable chair.

"Logan, don't do this." Bodie's jaw worked to maintain control of his own temper and of the situation. "He withheld evidence from us. We need to catch a killer."

Logan snorted in response. His body dipped at the waist to emphasise his disgust. "He went straight into surgery!" he snarled. "But you know where we live. Why do it somewhere he's outnumbered and without support?"

"Well!" the headmaster blustered. "Well!" If he intended his exclamations to deny Logan's accusation, they burst into the atmosphere as wasted breath.

"I'm his brother!" Bodie protested. He parted his arms in a placation. "I'm supporting him."

Logan made a sound low in his throat. His distrust of the police force stretched back to another time and place to create a habit of resistance. "Pick a lane, Bo," he hissed. "Pick a lane."

Bodie jerked backwards as though slapped. The cracks beneath their opposing tectonic plates widened and a decade's worth of pretence spewed free like liquefaction. Even Hana's gentle nature couldn't repair the threatening gulf.

"It's okay," Mac blurted. He raised his right hand like an oath taker. "I'm good." He gulped and edged closer to Logan, drawing strength from the waves of power rolling off his father's shoulders. "Pa's right. I went into surgery and the pills made me forget stuff. You've tracked Miss Andrew's phone and know she texted me. I helped her with the app and I can tell you she acted real scared of someone. But she never told me who." He drew his phone from his blazer pocket and held it out with a shaking hand. Bodie's lips pursed, but he didn't mention the iPhone he'd noticed at the hospital.

Mac used his thumb to unlock the screen. He handed it to Bodie. "Just look at it. I listed her contact as 'M' to stop my cousin from getting jealous."

Logan's head turned, and Mac felt the weight of his stare as his father joined the random dots in their frank conversation about Caroline Marsh. And realised he'd missed something important.

28

IN PLAY

Despite Logan's brooding presence, Bodie checked both Facebook messages and texts. He took his time scrolling through them and photographed Marie's last text to Mac. He showed no interest in the ones between him and Tilly, or the unanswered ones to Deacon. His thumb moved at speed, sifting through past texts about the team and practice drills. He paused a few times and blinked. "Edin's threatening other girls?" He sounded surprised, but not shocked. Logan said nothing in response to Mac's mute nod.

Detective Elliot sidled next to Bodie and peered over his shoulder. Bodie outranked him, but the case still belonged to his subordinate. He couldn't work on a case involving a family member. Mac swallowed a ball of regret, realising his brother's presence indicated he had come to support him after all.

Bodie tilted the screen to show something to Elliot. The other man grunted. "What does this mean?" he demanded. His eyebrows flattened into a line as he screwed up his forehead. "She writes, *'Thanks so much for your help. I feel safer knowing it's there. See you tomorrow.'* Does that relate to the app you installed on her phone?"

"Yes." Mac nodded. "If you can access her online data, it'll show her location at any point. I turned it on in case she needed it."

Elliot tutted. "She expected to see you the next day? Yet, you told us she didn't."

"No." Exasperation filled Mac's voice as he acknowledged the twisting of his former statement. "I didn't make a formal arrangement. I already told you that. We'd see each other around the school." He shrugged. "And the girls wanted extra practice at lunchtimes. We'd meet then. All together." He stared down at the fingers of his left hand. They poked from the greying edges of the cast, the skin already becoming white and lined from lack of use. He flexed them and the ache intensified in his wrist, inflammation still causing tightness within the fibreglass.

"MacGillivray." Logan squatted next to him, resting his forearm along the wooden side of the chair. "Are you okay?"

Mac sighed and shook his head. "No, Pa. I'm tired and sore. I liked Miss Andrews and I can't get the smell of burning out of my nose."

Logan tutted and slipped an arm around his son. His biceps strained the fabric of his fitted shirt as he glared up at the police officers. "We're leaving," he stated. He nodded at his stepson. "Thanks for calling me."

"We haven't finished." Elliot spread his hands and his waggling eyebrows appealed to his senior.

"It's fine." Bodie cleared his throat and ran a hand across his chin. The headmaster's stuffy office muted the scratchy sound. "Just one more thing, Mac. You said Miss Andrews took legal action after her ex-boyfriend showed up here? We can't find a record of it." He turned to Sal Richard. "Does your staff have a written process for incidents such as this?"

Sal grunted and grumbled as he rose. The chair cushion sighed as it inflated in the absence of his skeletal frame. "I'll check with the front office," he said, his sensible soles shuffling against the plush carpet as he exited the room.

Bodie offered Mac a tight smile. A sideways glance at Elliot's bowed head induced a wince of discomfort. His tongue made a curious click as he turned to his subordinate. "Go with him," he ordered. "I'll meet you outside."

Elliot's brows met on his forehead, the resulting line not quite symmetrical above his nose. He shot a glare at Mac and Logan before leaving the room with a huff of irritation.

"You all right, bro?" Bodie crossed the distance and took the chair next to Mac's. "I came to help you, but there's only so much I can do."

Logan smoothed his fingers across Mac's spine. "I know, mate." He released a faint snuff through his nostrils. "We put on a reasonable show, though, didn't we?"

Curiosity drove Mac's chin up and he gazed from his father to his brother. They'd fooled even him. Guilt prickled beneath his sternum at the proximity of the iPhone hidden at the bottom of his rucksack, mere centimetres from the toe of Bodie's smart shoe. He promised himself he'd confess everything, but only after he'd interrogated Edin's involvement to a definitive conclusion.

"Where's Ma?" Mac managed, his scratchy throat making the words disjointed. The Mac of last week convinced him a hug from his mother could still make his world whole again.

"I left her at the shopping mall," Logan confessed. "She doesn't know Bo called." The men glanced at each other and shared a millisecond of confidence.

"Like you needed more cushions." Bodie snorted, but Logan didn't bite. Their alliance ceased at the point where Hana became the source of combined hilarity.

"You want to come with me?" Logan pushed his wrist free of his shirt cuff and examined his watch.

"No, thanks." Mac hefted his rucksack onto his shoulder. "I have stuff to do here." His mind shot to Tilly and the possibility of more kisses. Shame drove a heightened colour, flaming into the tips of his ears.

"Ah, yeah." Logan nodded. "You need to organise the soccer team." His lips curved into a smile. "Let us know what you need."

"Thanks." Mac pointed his shoes towards the door and the prospect of escape. "Grant Simms didn't show this morning. I need to start with him. He'll know how to make it happen."

"Say hi to him from me." Logan dragged his phone from his tight trouser pocket and squinted at the screen. "Hana's ready to get lunch." A frown dogged his expression, and he reached out and rested a hand on Mac's shoulder. "You sure you're okay?"

"I promise." Mac detached his brain from the invisible pull of Tilly's allure. A hysterical bubble popped in his chest and he fought it back beneath his ribs. He sensed himself losing control and nodded to his brother as he tramped across the carpet to the doorway.

Sal Richard barrelled inside, almost flattening Mac in his haste. His breath stank of orange peel and tobacco. "Ah, MacGillivray," he boomed, his tone formal. "Do you recall the date and time of this alleged visit? Our school office has no record of such an incident." His gaze slid to Logan, and his eyes flared beneath his hooded lids.

A heavy frame behind his head displayed a reflection of Logan's expression as he cocked his head. Mac sensed the truth of his story fading. His lips parted, and he gulped for air like a fish. "But Miss Andrews said it happened." His tone held a plea. Confusion dulled the lust in his chest and thoughts of Tilly washed out as anxiety replaced them. "That's why she needed the app." He glanced back at Bodie, a mute appeal for assistance in his frightened eyes.

Bodie winced. The expression of doubt proved enough to send a tremor through Mac's torso. His fingers gripped the strap of his rucksack like a lifeline. "She asked for my help. I put the app on her phone and she added her sister's number." He shrugged. "My involvement ended there. Why are you looking at me like that?"

As though caught out by jumping ahead in his mind, Bodie stared down at his shiny shoes. Logan took a step towards his son. "Nobody doubts you, tāne." His eyes narrowed, and he jerked his head towards Mac's pocket. "Give them your phone, son. Let them take it away with them."

Mac's teeth clenched hard until his jaw ached, and he glared at Logan. His father took a step towards him and his tone softened. "They'll want to check for the app on your phone and make sure you're not the one tracking her. That's all."

That's all. It sounded such a small thing on Logan's lips, and yet it proved massive. The device contained Mac's world. His calendar, timetable, homework assignments, contact numbers. Everything. He doubted his ability to function without it.

"Just do it," Logan urged. He held his hand out and a moment of mental tussling stretched the distance between them.

"When can I have it back again?" Mac's voice sounded almost faint enough for the processors to miss it. He only knew he'd spoken because Bodie licked his lips and drew a clear evidence bag from his pocket.

"Sorry, mate," he breathed. He held it out to Mac, his dark eyes unreadable as he waited. The bag's slender mouth closed around the device, which Mac dropped into it. It resembled a clam closing around its diamond. Anger surged in his breast, a beast unleashed by Marie's death and Tilly's kisses. A fog closed around Mac's head and he stormed from the headmaster's office. He didn't wait for a reply and ignored the calls from the old man.

"MacGillivray!" He raised his voice to a shout. "I need a date and a time."

Mac kept walking, his back straight and his shoulders locked hard enough to make his neck ache. He strode to the unlocked janitor's cupboard where he found Tilly waiting for him. She slipped into his arms, her lips already parted and her eyes glittering with mischief.

29

BOOTER

Tilly Rae bounced into Mac's life at the age of seven. Alone in his silent world and always one step behind, he'd watched life as though glass separated him from his classmates. Few people knew sign language or took the trouble to speak slowly enough for him to comprehend. Stoic and well behaved, he'd accepted his lot in life and paddled behind the academic stars and the sporty kids.

And then Tilly showed up one rainy Friday and introduced a sparkle into his world.

She arrived at registration and went straight into a lunchtime detention, turning everything into a fight. And she shrugged off trauma and hardship as though shedding an unwanted coat. Mac had craved the special smile she kept only for him, welcoming her into his safe friendship with Deacon and donating many lunches to her worthy cause. But he'd kept her at arm's length and as he brushed soft kisses over her earlobe in the solace of the cupboard, he wondered why.

"Am I your first girlfriend?" Tilly kissed the underside of his chin and her breath sent a feather light warmth across his neck.

"Yeah." Mac swallowed and his Adam's apple bobbed in his throat. "I always figured nobody wanted me. The Disabled Du Rose." He deepened his voice into a spooky tone to repeat the label given to him in high school.

Tilly snorted. "I've liked you since my first day in primary school. I fell off my chair trying to impress you."

Mac pressed a kiss against her soft forehead. Her floral scent embraced him through a haze of comfort. "I remember that." His frown remained hidden in the darkness. "Please don't think I'm only doing this because Deacon is away. I won't drop you when he comes back to school."

"I know." Tilly smoothed her palm across the sensitive ridges of his spine. She sighed and pressed her fingers beneath the waistband of his trousers and caressed the soft rise of his buttock. "It never seemed the right time."

"It is now?" Worry infused Mac's voice. He sensed himself washed away in a tsunami he hadn't seen coming. It occurred to him she might drop him when the mood took her, casting him off like an old shoe. His arms wrapped around her and he crushed her slender frame against his chest. She grunted against the force of it.

"Yes, I think now is the right time. Don't you?" She slid her other hand behind his neck and tugged his head forward. Her lips met his in the darkness. "I know it seems sudden to everyone else, but to us, it's right. It feels easy with you. Like it was always meant to be this way."

Mac's neck ached with the effort of bending to meet her kisses. It added to the mix of sensations driving him. A curious bewitchment shrouded him and nothing else mattered but submitting to Tilly's gentle caresses and the intoxication of her nearness. His breath caught in his chest as he satiated the well of emotion with a smouldering kiss. His tongue explored the soft seam of her lips and his fingers closed around the clip at the back of her bra. Heat rolled off them as the tsunami carried them away to unknown lands.

The insistent peal of the bell forced them from the cupboard. Mac's loose tie screamed of his illicit activities, echoed by Tilly's meticulous retying of her ponytail. She bent down and retrieved the dustpan and brush in a familiar ruse. But Mac sensed her stiffen beside him as they slipped, dishevelled, into the corridor.

Arthur Darian leaned from the window opposite, yelling something unintelligible to someone outside in the courtyard. He turned, catching them in the act of skulking past him.

"Hey, you!" He jabbed a pudgy finger at Mac. "How did the little girlies take your bad news?" Darian hauled his trousers above his protruding stomach and stared at Tilly. He missed the deflation of Mac's chest as he realised he hadn't escaped the demands. "This is your new girlfriend, then?" His pink tongue poked from between his lips and Mac's skin crawled at the way the older man directed his gaze to her chest. She'd mismatched her buttons in the darkness and a soft, rounded breast peeked from between an accidental gap. Hatred burgeoned in Mac's heart, budding and blooming like a toxic flower. The unfurling of its leaves filled his head with the distraction of crackling and organic sighs. He balled his fists and took a step towards the object of his disgust. His left wrist complained in a series of darting jabs, which set up an ache in his elbow. But the latent warrior gene, given to him by his father, sparked to life.

A sixth sense caused Tilly to snatch at him, catching his cast with the end of the dustpan. Her blue eyes flared in mortification at his grunt of pain. Mac kept his ire on the teacher, but focussed his right hand on supporting his broken wrist instead of smacking the man head first through the open window behind him.

"No bad news," he spat. "I'm coaching the team. My parents will manage them." His warning to Layla and Sammy echoed in the background. He knew in his heart that Darian would do everything in his power to nix the fledgeling scheme before it took its first breath.

Mac's green irises flashed like emeralds and he projected pure rage towards the lecherous, incompetent teacher. "It doesn't matter what you do about it. I'll never play for your team again. Not if you're the coach." Spittle issued from between his lips as he threw the last salvo. He spun his body and forced his legs to carry him along the corridor in jerky steps.

Tilly jogged behind him after a second's pause. "Wait up!" she demanded. "What are you doing? Crossing that dude is like pulling the pin from a grenade. He'll go after you for sure now."

"Let him!" Mac growled. He stopped dead in the middle of the corridor, his shoes squealing against the floorboards. A groan spewed from his lips. "Shit! Why did I just hand him all the cards? I'm an idiot."

Tilly herded him to the edge of the corridor to allow the bottleneck behind them to pass. She wrapped her arm around his waist and peered up into his face. "Because he's slimy, and you caught him staring at my breasts." She used the cover of his height to refasten the buttons into a neat line one-handed. Her eyelashes flickered and her expression of acceptance sent sadness like a dart through Mac's ribs. "He does that to all the girls. We have an unspoken rule that no one gets left alone with him. Nobody cares about us. We don't matter alongside academic ranking and sports trophies."

"I care!" Mac growled. "Who does he think he is?"

Tilly leaned against the wall but didn't relinquish her hold on his waist. The warmth of her body heat thawed Mac's confusion. "So, I guess you do like me after all." Her irises sparkled like diamonds. "I'm enjoying your possessive streak, Mac Du Rose." Pleasure flushed her cheeks pink beneath the layer of foundation.

Mac's mouth fell open. "Of course, I like you!" he hissed. "I just spent ten minutes kissing you!"

"And the rest." Her ready laugh rose above the clatter of feet and voices in the narrow corridor.

Shame coursed through Mac's blood as his eyes opened to the obvious misery around him. He'd drifted along in his isolation, his world narrowed to just him and Deacon and sometimes Tilly. His stomach roiled around Arthur Darian, but he'd never considered the emotional collateral of the man's unhindered abuse of his authority. He'd accepted it just like everyone else.

Mac floundered. "I've heard the rumours about Darian." He gulped. "Why has nobody stopped him? We can tell someone. He can't do this anymore."

Tilly sighed. "Who do we tell? No one wants to listen. It's about scandal and reputation versus a little child abuse within the patriarchy. Darian's protected and we aren't." She snaked her fingers through his, waiting until his hand closed around hers. "I love that you care." She raised a black eyebrow and winked at him. "But one task at a time. Let's round up the soccer girls and you can break the news to them. Their enthusiasm will kill any moves he makes to stop you from coaching their team."

Mac's shoulders slumped. "The cops took my phone," he growled. "I can't contact anyone."

Tilly stood on tiptoes and placed a gentle kiss on his cheek. "Then it's a good job I can," she replied, her tone light.

30

BICYCLE KICK

"All done. The girls will meet us on the practice pitch at lunchtime." Tilly grinned up at Mac with sparkling eyes and slipped the battered phone into her blazer pocket.

"You know Sammy?" Mac wrinkled his nose and dragged an exercise book from the depths of his rucksack. He set it between them and flipped it open to the correct page.

Tilly nodded and turned her attention to the teacher glaring at them from the front of the classroom. She waited until the woman turned back to the whiteboard before closing the gap between her lips and Mac's ear. "She lived in the group home until last year. A couple adopted her and her sister."

He jerked back in surprise and his pen plunged to the floor. Its loud clatter disturbed those around him and the teacher. "Sorry, sorry," he muttered. His useless left hand meant he needed to get up, turn his body, and bend to retrieve the pen. Thirty-two pairs of eyes watched his movements with lacklustre interest.

"Where's Deacon today?" Mrs Lansdown placed her chunky blue pen on her desk and peered at the computer screen. She'd launched into her scintillating description of Auckland's volcanic structure without taking the register. The empty seat next to Mac recalled her to her duties, and she tapped the mouse to unlock the app.

"Don't know, miss." Mac's jaw tightened at the taste of absolute truth.

"Liar!" Dan Masters sneered at him from the table next to his. "He's not coming back. Everyone knows that."

Mac gaped at him, studying the way his index finger dug into his left nostril without shame. Tilly's blazer brushed his arm as she reached around him to engage in a debate. "You don't know that!" she jeered. "Stop making stuff up, you loser."

"That's enough!" Mrs Lansdown cast her eye over the rows of students. Each desk housed three, and only Mac's held an empty space. She blinked as she jabbed the mouse and clicked on the names of those present.

Masters leaned forward, his gaze roving across Tilly as though she lay like a tasty morsel on a butcher's slab. "Deacon isn't coming back!" If she didn't understand the first time, he repeated the sentence at a slower speed. "I saw him last night! He's working at the supermarket."

Mac jerked backwards hard enough to catch his cast on the desk. He hissed in pain and white light filled his vision.

"I saw him too." One of the nicer girls in the year group gave Mac an apologetic smile. "The one in Parnell near the railway station." Her lips flattened into a line. "I'll ask him to call you, if you like."

Mac's lips moved, but he said nothing. His head emptied of all the useful information. Tilly worked on their shared map of the fifty-three volcanic centres scattered across Auckland city, her coloured pencils producing a key for the landmarks. She left him alone, not commenting when his right hand snaked up and switched off both his processors. Her thigh touched his beneath the table, providing an earthing effect. She forced him to remain physically present while his mind wandered elsewhere.

Mac rested his right palm on the table and dropped his head until his cheek lay against the back of his hand. His knuckles dug into his jaw. Blessed silence offered room for him to process Deacon's rejection.

It took time for the lump in his throat to dissipate and allow him to swallow again. His gaze fell on Tilly as she gnawed on the end of a yellow pencil. He imagined the sounds her lips made as she thought through the series of instructions written on the whiteboard. Gratitude budded in his chest. She understood him. She let him be himself in a way no other girl ever would.

A tap on his right shoulder forced him to sit up straight. The sudden movement made his vision swim. Mrs Lansdown stood next to him, her lips moving. He caught the gist of her sentence through instinct, but reached up and turned on his right processor. "I asked if you're okay?" Her lips flattened into a line of sympathy. "You've had a rotten few days." Her gaze moved to Tilly's inspiring depiction of the reasons humans shouldn't inhabit New Zealand. She brightened and her painted lips split into a wide beam. "Oh, that's wonderful!" She spun and clapped her hands to get the attention of the other students. Mac dodged her jacket sleeve as she reached across him and snatched up the A3 page. "This!" she exclaimed. "This is what I'm looking for from you all." Mac heard the groan of protest even through one working processor. Pages rustled and chatter resumed.

Mrs Lansdown patted Mac's shoulder again. "Very good work," she said with a definitive nod. "Merit points to both of you."

"But," Mac began. He squeaked as Tilly pinched his thigh.

"But thank you so much." She leaned across him and jabbed the end of her yellow pencil into his stomach. "We love geography."

Mrs Lansdown's steps held the spring of success as she launched herself back to her whiteboard. Mac snorted. "You suck up!" he hissed to Tilly. His brow puckered, and he activated his left processor with difficulty. "I did none of that. You should have both merit points."

Tilly shrugged and grinned up at him. Her gaze moved from his emerald irises to his lips and back again. "Don't worry. I'll offend another teacher and lose it by home time."

"No!" Mac breathed. "Behave."

"Or what?" Her eyes glittered, the glow of her skin suggestive of a blush beneath her heavy makeup.

"Or no more kisses." Mac raised an eyebrow, and she sniggered.

"I think that'll hurt you more than me." She pressed her palm over his thigh. "Have you finished in your cone of silence now? I need help colouring Maungawhau Mount Eden."

"Sorry." Mac's shoulders slumped. "I just needed a minute." His own immaturity reflected at him like a condemnation. He couldn't continue to abdicate from the world when he didn't like something. Self-reflection pointed a knotty finger at his lack of courage.

Tilly shrugged. "It's no different to me climbing onto the roof. Sometimes you just gotta be by yourself." A dark curl slid into her left eye and blinked with the motion of her long lashes. A warmth blazed behind Mac's ribs and her comprehension left him without suitable recourse. She got him.

He sighed and fingered a blue pencil with a blunted point, rolling it back and forth in thought. "You said you had an idea about clearing Edin. I don't want to believe she killed a teacher. What do you suggest?" He picked up the pencil and brushed it across a crater beneath a neat label. Tilly's slanted hand identified it as Lake Pupuke, a volcano presenting as a deep lake.

"I said you wouldn't like it." Tilly's yellow pencil whispered across the paper as she shaded Maungakiekie or One Tree Hill as a Tūpuna Maunga or ancestral mountain.

"Oh-kay." Mac stretched out the word. "What's your idea?"

Tilly's red lips curved into a wicked smile. Her jaw shifted beneath her soft cheek as she shifted her bubble gum to the other side of her mouth. "Just ask her, idiot," she said.

31

Box

J ust ask her.

Three simple words with no understanding of the levels of explosion such a question might cause in the Du Rose household.

Mac met the soccer girls at lunchtime. They whooped and hollered, squealed and celebrated. Three more of them munched on raw baby carrots, proving the health kick had spread beyond Layla. He admired their commitment but hoped they didn't expect him to join them. "It's not definite!" He raised his voice to cover their excitement. "I need to run it past Mr Simms. He's the teacher in charge of soccer."

"Let's ask him now!" Layla limped around the group, her burned foot causing her discomfort. She tripped over Sammy's legs as her friend sprawled on the grass. A sandwich pinged from her fingers and landed on a patch of clover. Already moving, Layla attempted to avoid it and tripped over Mac's rucksack. "Sorry, sorry!" she called, whirling around to survey the damage.

Mac's pencil case lay on its side, the zipper open and pens and a protractor spewing from its interior. His lunchbox disgorged an uneaten banana and a sandwich Tilly didn't want. He bent to retrieve his belongings, his useless left arm braced against his bent knee. "It doesn't matter," he grumbled.

Sammy placed her fallen sandwich on her lunchbox and scrambled to help him. The other girls chatted as she picked up the pens and protractor. She giggled and tugged the sharp point of a set square from the folds of a daisy patch.

Mac retrieved his laptop free and opened the lid to check the screen for cracks. Sammy's fingers froze around the set square and she stared at him with darkness in her vivid blue eyes. It tumbled from her hand and she rose on jerky legs. The plastic crunched beneath her shoe as she turned in haste and hurried back to her bag.

"Sammy?" Mac's lips parted, and he shot a glance at Layla. "What's wrong with her?"

"Dunno." Layla bent to retrieve the set square, the broken point of its triangular edge lost in the grass. She gazed after her friend with knitted brows. "The cops took her phone. She's been miserable ever since." Her lower lip protruded in a pout. "You could go out with her. That might cheer her up for a few days."

"Gee, thanks. A few days. Wow." Mac rose, his sarcasm lost on the younger girl. "The cops took my phone, too. It contained my calendar and all my homework assignments."

Layla gazed up at him, blinking into the bright lunchtime sun. She lifted her right hand to shield her eyes. "But you still have that other one, right?"

"What?" Mac held his breath. His mind moved at speed through a memory of the awful discovery in the equipment shed. He wondered for a moment if Layla had seen him pocket the mystery phone.

"That one." She jabbed her finger at the ground and Mac followed her direction. The iPhone rested against a tuft of burned, ochre grass. Its jaunty angle mocked him, the chipped corner uppermost. His lips parted in the ready lie of denial, but he stopped himself. He bent to retrieve it, affecting a nonchalant air. Layla dipped forward, her nose almost touching the edge of his hand. "Lots of people have that phone, don't they?" she asked.

Mac nodded. "Yeah. The iPhone is a popular make." He covered his discomfort by bending to shove the phone into his rucksack with the laptop.

Layla's mouth opened again, but another girl cut off her thought. "Let's find Mr Simms. We'll beg him to let Mac coach us."

"Okay." Her face broke into a wide grin and she limped back to the last rucksack sitting in the grass. "Bye Mac," she called over her shoulder. "See you at practice."

❧

"Didn't it go well?" Tilly took Mac's hand as he strode from the soccer field. "Don't they want to stay as a team?"

Mac frowned and held the door open for her. He struggled with its weight against his rucksack and she ducked beneath his arm and danced into the lobby. Without speaking, she took the bag from his shoulder and hefted it with her own. "It's not that," he replied, licking his lips. "They seemed excited."

"What then?" She walked ahead of him, up the wide staircase and onto the landing. Turning left, she followed a well-worn route towards their common room.

"I don't know." Mac ran his right hand under his chin. The bristles protruded to the point of earning him a rebuke. The school rules forbade full beards, especially bright red ones. He shrugged off Sammy's odd behaviour and broke the bad news instead. "Layla saw the iPhone."

Tilly groaned. She held the common room door open for him. "That's not good. Why are you walking around with it?"

"You have Deacon's old iPhone, so you understand all the subtle differences with Apple products. I thought you could look at this one and see if there's something I'm missing. The grey web contains apps and caches I don't understand. I used one to unlock the screen, but I'm not familiar with the commands."

Tilly held out her hand and waited as Mac unzipped his rucksack and dug inside it. He retrieved the phone and the banana. "I found this at the bottom," he said, pointing the yellow fruit like a revolver. "Want it?"

She nodded, and he set it over her thigh, shifting with discomfort as his brain turned its curve against her leg into something lewd. He unlocked the phone, and she took it.

A few minutes of scrolling and poking around in its apps brought her to the same conclusion as his. "There's nothing on it. Just that photo on the cloud storage. Its owner wiped it." She leaned back in the squashy chair, her features screwed up in concentration.

Mac blew out a breath and reached for his maths homework. He thudded the exercise book onto his knee and unearthed a pen from beneath its folds. He started on a series of complicated equations before Tilly interrupted him. "You're in this photo, Mac." She spun the screen to face him and displayed the pixelated image. "Look." She zoomed in even closer and pointed to the open door of the equipment shed.

Mac squinted and peered at it, unable to discern anything different from his previous inspections. His fingers brushed hers as he cupped her hand to bring it closer. "Nope," he concluded, dropping his arm. "I'm not there."

"Look again." Tilly zeroed in on a dark shape in front of the shed door. "Isn't that your bag?"

Mac made a sigh in his throat and narrowed his eyes to slits. He shook his head from side to side. "Maybe. It's too hard to tell. But it could be. What does that mean?"

Tilly cocked her head and her brow furrowed. The silver stud in her left eyebrow sparkled beneath the light from the window next to her. "I think it means someone watched you and Miss Andrews in the equipment shed."

"When I kissed her?" The colour faded from Mac's cheeks to leave heightened orange freckles across his nose like a starburst. He jerked back in his chair, causing it to rock backwards onto two legs. "Oh, my gosh!" he breathed. His calves twitched with the urge to run and hide as mortification seized his nerve endings and lit them on fire. The maths book tumbled to the dirty carpet, the open pages forming a wonky tent. He half turned in his seat to see if anyone had overheard his exclamation. Tilly rested a steadying palm over his left thigh.

"Don't make me hurt you." She spoke without emotion, the sentence lacking threat. She raised her pierced eyebrow and gave him a lopsided smile. "We don't run from each other, okay? Nothing is so terrible we can't work through it?" Her blue irises glittered with vulnerability and she gave a visible swallow. She dropped her chin and hid the soft curve of her neck from him.

Mac gulped, his brain empty of reply. He remained half turned in the seat, his cheeks flaming red as though slapped. "I'm so embarrassed!" he whispered. "It felt bad enough telling you without knowing someone else watched the actual moment."

Tilly dipped forward, reaching her other hand around his body and drawing him back to face her. "Mac," she soothed, her voice trembling. "I have far worse things in my past. Some of them are so awful, I'm not sure I can even share them. But when I'm ready, you'll be the first person I tell. Fumbling a dodgy pass at a teacher wasn't your finest hour, but your honesty made me kiss you. Confessing something like that to me meant I knew I could trust you."

His shoulders slumped, and the seat creaked beneath him. "You should cut your losses," he breathed. "This gets worse every second." He glanced around the common room, eager to scrutinise his classmates for signs of overt interest. Nobody looked up, too busy with exercise books and sheaves of lined paper. A group debated in the far corner, a wooden structure teetering on the coffee table between them. Mac sighed as the sense of violation settled as a leaden weight in his chest.

Tilly brushed a finger down the side of her nose. She touched the silver ring as though checking it still hugged her nostril as a mark of rebellion. Her lips pursed, but she didn't remove her right hand from Mac's thigh. He sensed her strengthening her resolve and sending it through the tentative connection.

"You two screwing, or what?" Dan Masters appeared at Mac's elbow, a yellow stain speckling his tie. "Couldn't you find a whole Du Rose to meet your needs?" He cackled and crumbs flew from his open mouth. "You had to pick the disabled one." The sandwich in his left hand bore a giant bite from its centre and mustard seeped from beneath an escaping pickle. Mac cringed, detesting the scrutiny and judgement of his peers.

"Get lost." Tilly wasted little effort on her reply. But Mac noticed how her gritted jaw showed through her cheek. She slid the phone between the pleats of her skirt and closed her knees, hiding it from view. Her lips pursed to release an exasperated sigh and glared at the teenager. "Go perv on someone else, loser."

"I need help with this." His other hand raised an exercise book, and he flapped it in front of Mac's face. "I'll get a detention again if I don't finish it."

"Try paying attention in class," Tilly growled. "It helps."

Dan took a step forward, his heavy shoe crushing the cover of Mac's fallen maths book. He waved his sandwich in Tilly's direction and the pickle seized its moment. It plunged to the carpet and rolled beneath a nearby armchair. He raised his voice, and the air crackled. "Tell the Goth to shut her face!"

Mac rose, his movements slow and calculated. Rage built behind his sternum like a music note readying itself to detonate an audience. He glared down at the other boy's upturned face, his right hand already balling into a fist.

"What's going on here?" Syd Ross entered the fray, a pad of flapping green detention slips in his right hand as a weapon. He stepped inside the closed circle of bodies without fear, his prefect's uniform gaining him instant entry. Only in his own head did it make him invincible.

A wry smile spread across Mac's lips and he glared at Dan. Leaning close to him, he whispered, "Call her names again and you'll pick your teeth out of that sandwich." He jerked back in a recoil of disgust. "Go away and stay away!"

Syd's flattened hand rose between them as a barrier. He wafted it back and forth as though believing his spindly presence would make a difference if the dispute became physical. Dan backed away first, his sandwich haemorrhaging more of its contents onto his school tie. "We're not friends anymore, Du Rose," he barked, throwing the comment over his shoulder.

Mac snorted at the removal of a label he hadn't known existed. They'd never been friends. Dan Masters allied himself according to the needs of the moment. He coasted through life as an academic parasite. Mac regretted ever helping him.

"That's a warning," Syd barked. "To both of you." He flapped his ever-present detention slips, a satisfied smile on his lips. He turned towards Mac, his tone confidential. "I don't need to make a big thing of it, though." His eyes glinted. "Not if you give me Edin's phone number."

Mac sighed and slumped into his seat. The ache in his arm sapped his energy and left him without reserves. Tilly spoke for him. "She doesn't date losers, so you're wasting your time." She barked out a laugh as Syd tore off a fluttering slip the colour of stale bogey and flung it at her.

"Saturday detention for you!" he shouted. Whirling on his shiny shoes, he stamped across the carpet, the empty blazer pockets lifting the fabric like wings on either side of him.

Tilly dipped to retrieve the slip. She smiled with satisfaction and pushed it beneath Mac's nose. "Guess who doesn't know he's meant to write names on them?" she whispered, before tucking it into her blazer pocket. "That's why you should never pick good kids to do unpleasant jobs."

"What?" Mac blinked and turned towards her. "What do you mean?"

Tilly shrugged and retrieved the phone from between her thighs. "Have you ever seen him get a detention slip?"

Mac's mind refused to probe into his memory banks, and so the answer eluded him. Tilly stared at the phone in her hand and her tone sounded wistful. "The answer is no, Mac. He's never had one. He's also not mixed with kids likely to get one, either." She lowered the phone and turned her body towards him. "Which means he doesn't know how it works."

"Right." Mac offered the response to placate her. He still didn't understand. Her warm palm on his thigh seemed to sear the skin through his trousers.

"It takes a thief to catch a thief," she breathed.

Mac nodded and cradled his arm. His ego smarted from the realisation that someone else had witnessed his humiliation. Marie had treated the incident with such extreme kindness that he'd liked her even more, despite his embarrassment. Mac sighed. His first kiss with Tilly had woken him from his childish stupor and exploded his foolish crush to smithereens. He'd never felt more alive.

"Do you know any thieves?" His tone lacked commitment, but he congratulated himself for forcing his attention back on her. He wanted to deactivate his processors and hunker down in his mental cave for a while, but she deserved better than his indifference. His wrist protested as he turned his body to face her. He balanced it across his thigh, brushing her fingers with his elbow. Tilly turned the phone over and over in her fingers.

"Maybe," she mused. The detention slip poked from her pocket and Mac frowned.

"Why did you keep that?" he asked.

Tilly's serene smile held a predatory flatness. She blew out a pink bubble while she considered her reply. "There's a boy on my bus who picks on the kids from the group home. He doesn't respond to threats. It made him sneaky and harder to catch doing it." She patted her pocket. "I'll fill his name in and make sure he gets it. See how cocky he feels when his parents need to drive him to school on Saturday morning to sweep floors and clean windows for Slade Hefner?" She chuckled. "I just need to think of the wording for the infringement section."

"Wow. You're devious." Mac rubbed his right eye with his fingers. He leaned sideways to pick up the maths book and smoothed out the creases from Dan's shoe.

"Yep." Tilly's eyes sparkled as she faced him. "See, it takes a thief to catch a thief. We need to think like them."

"Like who? Marie's killer?" Mac realised his mistake as he used the teacher's first name. He chided himself and overwrote his error. "The owner of the phone might have no connection to Miss Andrew's death. What then?"

Tilly wrinkled her nose. "No such thing as coincidence, Mac." She raised the device between her thumb and fingers. "We could take another photo and sync it to the cloud. Then whoever owns the phone will see it there and know it's in circulation."

"What? Set ourselves up as bait?" Mac shook his head. "I hate that idea. It puts other people at risk as well as us." He swallowed and removed her presence from the danger. "As well as me, I meant."

Tilly's hair flicked into her eyes as she shook her head. "Nope. We're in this together now, Du Rose." She shook the phone at him. "The cloud storage is an account set up by someone with an email address and a password, right?" She dipped her torso as she spoke, her brow furrowed beneath her black fringe. Her silver rings tinkled against the phone's metal casing. "How did you get into it and view the photo?"

"I used coding from the grey web." A pink blush flared at Mac's throat, hidden beneath the red stubble which abutted his shirt collar. His eyes widened, and he sat up straight. "Oh no! Do you think they got a notification when I hacked into it?"

"I don't know. Maybe." She flattened her lips into a cherry line. "Perhaps that only happens if someone sets up two-step-authentication." She shrugged. "But then they would have locked their account or changed the password, so I doubt that's the case."

Mac winced, his mind moving through the disturbing tangents. "I'd hate to think of someone trying to track me." He swallowed and eyed the phone as it nestled in the folds of Tilly's tartan skirt. "We should turn it off for now."

"Okay." Deft fingers pressed a button, and the screen powered down. She dug in her pocket for a paper clip and released the SIM card. "But you're without a phone, so you may as well use it." She poked out her tongue as she worked. "I'll get you a new card and a case to disguise the phone. At least then you'll have a way to communicate. And the phone's owner can't track you anymore if you log into your own account instead of theirs."

The bell sounded for their next lesson, and Mac sighed. Exhaustion nipped at the edges of his psyche. He pushed the unfinished maths homework into his rucksack and wondered what the Mac of last week would think of his failures.

Tilly's smile, accompanied by a touch of her hand, wiped all recriminations from his mind.

32

OUT OF PLAY

"Hey, Macky! Wait up!" Tilly appeared from the art room as he strode towards the exit and his waiting bus. She jogged to catch him, her black ponytail swinging behind her like a pendulum. Edin walked beside him, and her shoulders stiffened. She turned to face Tilly with her lips pulled back from her teeth in an inaudible snarl.

"Hey." Mac's face creased into a smile and he righted Tilly as she collided with his chest. He moved his cast aside to avoid her bumping it.

"Just wanted to say goodbye." Tilly rose on tiptoes and pressed her lips against his. Students flowed around them like flotsam bumping against an island. Mac heard Edin's grunt of disgust at the same moment he felt a pressure against his blazer. Something slipped inside in a reverse pick-pocketing move. He frowned as Tilly stepped backwards. Curiosity outweighed his mortification at the public display. She folded her lower lip beneath her teeth. "See you tomorrow," she said and turned away. The crowd swallowed her, moving towards the row of waiting buses in an eager rush.

Mac cleared his throat and schooled his expression into blankness. He'd left his processors switched on, hoping to speak to Edin on the bus. Worry nagged at the back of his mind as he forecast her predictable explosion in a crowded space.

By the time they'd queued and clambered aboard the bus, Mac's nerve had failed him. The vehicle set off before he'd finished settling, and the jolt threw him half across Edin's lap. His cast contacted her knee and nausea rose into his throat, along with the familiar bloom of pain. He eased himself upright and leaned forward, fighting the overwhelming urge to vomit. His height made it impossible for him to put his head between his knees, and the cacophony from the younger students didn't help. Their noise filled his head with a noxious buzzing and stopped him from summoning coherent thoughts. He reached up to disconnect his processors, the fingers of his right-hand scrabbling to reach the one over his left ear. Cool fingers covered his to halt the movement.

"Don't," Edin said, her tone soft. "Don't shut me out, Mac."

He blew out a ragged breath and forced himself upright, careful to keep his gaze away from the windows and the blur of trees and hedges whizzing past at speed. He stared at the back of the seat in front of him, studying a rip in the gaudy fabric. A knot in his chest warned that the danger hadn't passed, but the ache in his wrist lessened.

"Okay," he managed. Sweat beaded on his forehead and across his upper lip. The growing moustache absorbed it and gave the red bristles a slick appearance. Mac used his blazer cuff to wipe his forehead.

Edin turned sideways in her seat and leaned closer, her expression pensive. A dark curl snaked between her eyes in a single act of rebellion. "Why did the cops want to speak to you today?" she whispered. Her perceptive gaze raked his face for unspoken clues.

This was his moment.

And it found him wanting.

Mac hadn't yet planned his sentences or anticipated the routes the conversation could take. He felt like a swimmer equipped with all the gear, jumping into the deep end moments before their first lesson. He fumbled with his answer, his words interspersed with a series of grunts. "Bodie came with a detective. He, well, he erm, Pa came, and it was a setup." Mac cleared his throat. "I didn't do it, Edin. I didn't kill Miss Andrews."

She jerked back as though he'd slapped her. "Geez Mac! I never thought you did!" Her eyes bugged and for a moment, concern shone through her glittering grey irises. She raised a hand and rested her palm against his sweating cheek. Comfort vied with confusion in his heart as he glimpsed the Edin she kept for him. Generous, compassionate, understanding.

"And you didn't." Verbal diarrhoea seized his tongue. "You didn't kill her either?" He framed it as a statement, but the rise in tone on the last word turned it into a question. She dropped her hand and her forehead furrowed into a deep line. The escaped curl snaked between her eyebrows like an exclamation mark.

A sensation of vertigo distorted Mac's vision. The buzz in his ears came from stress, not requiring the amplification of the processors. In a millisecond of stillness, Edin's mood changed. Rage crashed over her as a breaking wave and she rose despite the precarious swaying of the bus. Her rucksack hit him around the head as she shoved her way past him and strode to the back of the vehicle. His left processor pinged onto the seat where it slipped towards the window and disappeared over the edge of the cushion. Mac imagined uncaring feet stomping it into oblivion as it journeyed beneath the benches to the exit steps. Their value exceeded a dollar measure. They were his ears and his connection to life, and she'd taken it from him without a backward glance.

The nausea returned and Mac became afraid to close his eyes. The pitch and roll of the heavy vehicle competed with the yelling of overenthusiastic teenagers. Mac looked under his seat but couldn't see the floor because of the bags and rucksacks crammed into the narrow gap. He disconnected the right one in defeat and tucked it into his blazer behind the school logo. His fingers contacted a hard shape beneath and he pulled open his blazer and reached into the inside pocket. Tilly's seamless manoeuvre had replaced the phone. It slipped free, its metallic body shrouded in a new navy case. When he turned on the screen, it flared to life without requiring a code.

A quick scroll through the contacts list revealed the level of Tilly's care. She'd added her number, Deacon's, Sammy's, and his mother's. Gratitude bloomed in Mac's chest and drove away the misery for long enough to raise a small smile.

The bus stopped many times on its journey through the mountains and students disembarked at each point. Mac watched their lips moving but didn't concern himself with deciphering their words. When it halted at its final destination, Mac rose with the last of the teenagers bound for the tiny township nestled in the mountains. He pushed the phone back into his blazer pocket, before sighing and hefting his rucksack onto his right shoulder. A faint tapping in the centre of his spine forced him to make an awkward turn in the narrow space.

A Year 9 girl stared at him, her eyes magnified from behind her spectacle lenses. "Is this yours?" she asked. She mouthed the sentence with extreme care to ensure clarity. When she lifted her palm, it held Mac's processor sitting against her pale skin.

"Thanks," he breathed. He collected it from her, embarrassment flushing his cheeks a livid red. She didn't justify her decision to help him, but he recognised her as a student he'd assisted a few weeks earlier. The Year 10 boys had refused her entry onto the bus and he'd intervened. She offered a single nod and a smile before glancing behind her at Edin. The other girl observed the interaction with her flashing grey irises. Mac recognised jealousy and something else akin to sadness in Edin's expression.

He smiled at the younger student and waited for her to pass before following her down the steps to the street. The mountain's balmy scent shrouded him in its comforting haze. His mood lifted at the thought of his mare and the safety of the stable yard. Squaring his shoulders and not attempting to communicate with Edin, he walked towards his mother's waiting truck.

33

CLEAR

Mac stripped off his school uniform in the tack room over the stables. Toby breezed in and disturbed him as he tugged an old tee shirt over his stomach. He'd fastened his zipper, but the cumbersome cast had stalled at closing the metal button gracing the top of his fly. Toby jabbed a finger at it and shook his head. "No way!" he mouthed. "I'm not grovelling around with your crotch. So, don't even ask."

Mac dropped the tee shirt over his half-fastened fly and shook his head. He gave a nonchalant shrug and stuffed his feet into tatty brown cowboy boots. "Getting Sassy," he mumbled, reluctant to engage in conversation without his processors. The left one seemed undamaged, but he'd put them both in his rucksack for safety.

Toby tapped him on the arm as he passed, their height almost equal. "Logan," he mouthed and jerked his thumb towards the rear window of the upstairs room.

"Thanks," Mac managed, disappointment wrinkling his nose. He'd wanted to fetch her in from the paddock himself, but Toby's single word inferred his father had done it for him. Sure enough, Logan stood in the centre of the round pen, Sassy's lunge rope in his right hand. His left arm opened out wide and a lunge whip extended his reach, its trailing tail touching the sandy ground.

Mac strode towards the pen and leaned his right forearm on the top rail. The mare kept her concentration on Logan and ignored him. His thoughts clamoured in his brain, reminding him of her status. Horses followed the food and reacted to the pressure. As he possessed neither, her ignorance of him seemed reasonable.

Logan continued to push her into a circle, using the whip to indicate her direction. He didn't use it on her, but stirred the air beneath it to form a barrier. The lunge rope enclosed her into a triangle of obedience. Instead of watching his father's progress, Mac used the iPhone to send a quick text to Tilly.

'Didn't go well. Edin now mad. Thanks for cover and SIM card. I've logged into my own accounts now.' He frowned with the realisation he no longer knew his own phone number.

Mac blew out an exasperated breath and pushed the phone into his pocket. He looked up to find his father staring at him. Logan narrowed his eyes and dipped his chin, his gaze dropping to Mac's front pocket. When his right eyebrow quirked upward, Mac sensed him demanding an explanation.

"Borrowed it," he said. Logan's blink indicated he'd said it too loud. His father nodded and held out the rope and the whip.

Gratified, Mac clambered over the fence and accepted the tools with eagerness.

He worked the mare until his stomach growled, putting her through her gaits in the manageable space and delighting in her fast responses. He struggled with the lunge whip in his left hand, balancing the cast over his stomach to take the weight. Logan helped him to reintroduce the saddle and gave him a leg up onto her back. Mac tried to protect his wrist in the manoeuvre but failed. His father's frown led him to believe he'd cried out in pain. But the ready victory of sitting astride his own mare dismissed the ache of protest from his healing bones and tendon. His heart stirred with elation as she tolerated his weight without complaint, her head low and her hooves square in the sand.

Logan's grin split his face and stripped years from his appearance. He shared in the achievement and pride glittered in his grey irises. He embraced Mac as he dismounted, pressing a jubilant kiss to his son's forehead and slapping his back with enthusiasm.

Mac led Sassy to the stable yard, a lightness in his chest which served to chase away the recent cloud of doom. He forced his fingers through a one-handed half-hitch knot before patting her neck. Her ears flicked back and forth as she sensed his pleasure with her performance. They'd arrived back at the point where it all went wrong. Relief bubbled in Mac's chest.

Logan tapped Mac's shoulder as he bent to loosen the mare's girth. He jerked his head towards Mac's jeans and mouthed something he didn't catch. It took a moment for him to realise the iPhone vibrated in his pocket. "Sorry," he blurted, realising he'd forgotten to mute the sound. He slid it free and stared at it, seeing an icon for Tilly strobing on the screen. With his processors in his rucksack, he couldn't answer and hear anything she said. Sand and dust formed a line in his furrowed brow as he killed the call and typed a quick message, promising he'd call her later. He looked up to find Logan watching him, a strange expression on his face. Mac forced himself to control any external sounds of exasperation or guilt, busying himself with Sassy's tack. He breathed a sigh of relief as Logan took the heavy Western saddle over his forearm and strode up the wooden staircase to the tack room.

Sassy blew out a warm breath as he rested his forehead against the solid plate of bone forming her cheek. He fondled her ear with his right hand, closing his eyes and relaxing into the sensation of soft fur, pulsing blood and strong cartilage. She turned her muzzle to sniff his jeans, and the skin twitched across her withers and shoulders like a wave of subliminal disturbance. Mac felt, in that moment, the essence of true love. He couldn't imagine life without the feisty mare. His other worries paled in comparison.

He haltered her and agitated her dusty coat with a rough, dandy brush. A stream of cool mountain water hosed off the foamy sweat beneath her forelegs and across her chest. She tolerated his repeat of the one-armed and awkward hoof picking exercise.

Logan returned from the tack room with Toby, and they conducted a conversation at the bottom of the stairs. Mac used the hosepipe to wash Sassy's metal bit and hung the bridle from its headband on a nearby hook to dry in the sun. He rinsed out a clean cloth from the box containing the grooming equipment and used it to spread a mixture of water and citronella oil over her damp body. Sassy lifted her near hind leg into a threatening hook as he smoothed it across her stomach. "The flies will get you," he soothed, aiming to keep his voice low and gentle. The hoof remained raised and bobbed near his right hand as he finished the process and rose. Her coat gleamed beneath the sun, dazzling white with patches of grey across her rump to denote her Appaloosa heritage. She reminded him of Sacha and he sensed his father felt it, too. Logan's gaze drifted from Toby to the mare as they continued their discussion.

Mac freed Sassy's rope from the hook with a flick of the quick-release knot. Some innate instinct caused him to focus on his father's lips as he clicked his tongue to the mare. She moved with deliberate slowness, reluctant to leave the salt block held by a loop near her nose. Mac tugged the rope and waited for her to respond. His father dipped his head towards Toby and said something Mac couldn't see. Less devious of nature, Toby looked straight at Mac and his lips moved in a series of staccato beats. "Edin?" he mouthed and his head jerked back on his neck. "You think she'd do that?"

Mac spun to face his mare, the hairs rising on the back of his neck. Cool fingers slipped around his heart and squeezed until his vision blurred. As Logan's cousin and manager of the bloodstock side of the business, it made sense to include Toby in family issues. Despite his unrequited affection for Hana, he remained on the inside of Logan's close-knit circle. Family first.

It pained Mac to realise his father suspected Edin of killing Miss Andrews. He corrected himself as his mind steered him back to her Christian name. Marie. His breaths came in quick gasps and he pulled Sassy into a tight turn with a jerk on her rope. Her hooves dragged against the concrete, but she picked up speed as he headed towards the gate and her freedom. Mac caught his fingers in the metal gate catch as he closed it behind him, wanting to scream at the top of his lungs but knowing it would achieve nothing. He sucked at the bleeding cut to his index finger and ground his teeth in his jaw.

Sassy drank at the trough before satiating herself and displaying her trust in Mac with a game of splash, which he didn't appreciate. He patted her neck and, after unclipping the rope from the halter, dug in his back pocket for pony nuts to reward her. Her rough lips left droplets of water in his palm as she took the treat and searched his jeans for more. Finding nothing, she dropped her muzzle to the earth and ambled away in search of tasty shoots she hadn't already hoovered up.

Mac clambered over the gate on the return journey, finding it easier than fighting with the catch again and damaging another of his remaining functional digits. But a heaviness dogged each step as he dragged himself upstairs to retrieve his rucksack from the tack room.

If his father found him uncommunicative on the drive up the mountain, he kept his opinions to himself.

34

DEAD BALL

Mac's appetite failed him, despite his mother's preparation of his favourite dinner. He twirled the softened spaghetti on the end of his fork and stared at it.

"Mac." Hana leaned across the table and touched his wrist. Mac blinked as his father and Edin rose from the table. He'd missed the customary request to be excused and pursed his lips. Hana frowned. "Sorry," she continued, using her fingers to communicate. "Spaghetti isn't the easiest to eat one-handed." She raised both hands and used her pinkie fingers to create the looping sign for noodle. He nodded and dropped his fork onto the plate. Tiredness caused him to fumble while adding the spoon and it splashed into the red sauce. Mac tutted as droplets spattered the front of his tee shirt. He glanced up in time to catch Hana, asking if he felt okay.

"Yes. Thanks," he replied, speaking the words out loud. "Tired." Her chin jerked downward, and he guessed he'd misjudged his pitch again. She tapped the centre of her palm with the middle finger of her right hand, asking if he needed painkillers. He nodded, not because he needed them, but because it excused his misery.

Hana jerked her head towards his shirt and wrinkled her nose. Mac sensed her wanting to take possession of it and expunge the stain. He nodded and lifted his cast in the air. She read his mind with her supreme maternal perception and rose from the table. "I'll fetch the cover for your cast," she signed, before turning away.

Mac escaped to his bedroom and withdrew his phone from where it charged in the wardrobe. An icon strobed on the screen, warning him about the inferior charging cable. He'd also missed a text from Tilly in response to the one he'd sent before dinner.

'Your parents think she did it???!!!' She'd overdone it with the question and exclamation marks and sadness lodged itself in Mac's chest. He didn't want to believe it either, but his father had an innate instinct for people's behaviour and wasn't often wrong.

'Yes.' His one-word reply zinged into the ether as Hana entered his room with the plastic cover over her forearm.

"Ready?" she asked.

Mac followed her to the bathroom and paused outside the door. He hauled his tee shirt over his head, getting the bulky cast caught in the sleeve. Hana helped him to free himself before fitting the cover over his cast. Her lips moved as she prattled to herself about something. He cocked his head, and she glanced up and repeated it. "I know the cast is waterproof," she mouthed. "But this stops your stitches from becoming wet inside and getting infected. Or worse." She frowned and didn't elaborate on what might prove worse than itchy stitches he couldn't reach.

So, he nodded, retreated into the bathroom, and closed the door.

The hot water pounding on his neck and back helped to clear Mac's mind. He knew he'd gone past his allotted three minutes when he cleared condensation from the glass and peered at the timer on the vanity. It already showed zero, and he didn't know when it had stopped counting. Cool air greeted his steaming skin as he emerged from the cubicle. Sick of fighting a towel, he tugged his robe from a peg on the back of the door and shrugged it around his shoulders. He shoved his right arm through the sleeve but didn't bother with the cast or its plastic shroud. Then he sat on the side of the bath to continue his uninterrupted stream of thought.

Someone killed Miss Andrews, but why?

He suspected he had their phone, and they had taken hers. Again, why?

The police seemed certain she'd died elsewhere, and the killer moved her to the equipment shed. Mac brushed his right hand under his nose at the memory of her burned flesh. He shivered and allowed the remnant of the floral shower gel to heal his thoughts. Who moved her, when, and how?

Mac didn't hear the persistent knocking on the bathroom door, and jumped in shock as he stepped into the hallway and fell over Edin. "About time!" she snapped, her lips forming the words in a jerky motion. Anger rolled from her in waves.

"Sorry," Mac blurted and stepped away from her. She retreated into the bathroom and slammed the door in his face. The cord of his robe caught between the frame and the door. She ignored his frantic knocking. In defeat, he unhooked the cord with difficulty from the loops on the robe and abandoned it, holding the folds together one-handed to protect his modesty. For the longest time, he hadn't cared about his nakedness, happy to frolic outside in the nude. He didn't recall when it stopped being okay, just that it had. A dusting of body hair and defined muscle tone heralded the end of his naturist tendencies, coupled with the way Edin stared at him.

Mac pushed his bedroom door closed with his heel and shed the robe. He hauled his pyjama pants on one handed and hoisted them to his waist. Snatching the phone from its charging cable, he flung himself onto his mattress. He smoothed his thumb across the chip in the top left corner, which created a diamond effect over the battery icon. The damp from his curls caused his scalp to prickle against the pillow, but he concentrated on forcing the iPhone to meet his needs. The fingers of his right hand both supported the device while interrogating the keypad as he downloaded the apps most urgent to him. He logged into his Google calendar, although the Apple suite protested the superiority of its own apps. Mac retrieved three homework assignments and his Gmail from the Drive. Abandoning the desire to text and suspecting Deacon would ignore him again, Mac sent him an email with a list of assignments he'd missed. He added a question about one they'd intended to do together.

When he downloaded the Facebook app, he discovered a direct message in his inbox. He'd checked on his laptop earlier and hadn't seen it back then. A friend request flashed up in the notifications and he held his breath at the sight of the profile picture.

'Marie Andrews would like to connect with you.'

Mac glanced at his bedroom door and then at his phone. His index finger hovered over the button to grant the request. He should call Bodie, but curiosity trumped his sense of duty. Abdicating his need to make an urgent decision, he opened the message first. His brow furrowed as he read its contents.

'Hi, my name is Susan Andrews. Marie was my sister. I understand you helped her to set up the system which sent the emergency alert. Unfortunately, I'm a nurse and didn't have my phone with me at the time. I'm coming to terms with having let her down so badly.'

Mac's teeth ground in his jaw, causing a bloom of pain to shoot behind his left ear. He forced himself to relax and typed a reply. *'Why are you using her Facebook profile?'*

He jumped as three dots appeared below his message. It showed as *Marie is typing* and a tremor ran through Mac's body.

The burning scent returned to him and the little he'd eaten for dinner roiled in his stomach.

The reply popped onto his screen. *'Marie must have added me as a legacy contact. It gives me permission to take over her account now she's gone. I'm private messaging her contacts so they don't just read a post about her death and feel shocked. Then I'll download her photos and shut down the profile.'*

Mac considered his answer with care. The three dots flashed again, but no message appeared. He imagined Susan typing her sad missive to multiple strangers and wondered if he'd bother individually communicating such a tragedy. He shivered and prayed he never needed to.

'You'll have to back the photos up somehow if you want to keep them forever,' he suggested, the tech in him unable to let her make a single download to a fallible device.

'That's why I sent you the friend request. I hoped you could do it for me.'

Mac groaned at how easily he'd stepped into the trap. The police had possession of his phone and therefore, access to every app stored on it. Including Facebook. A police officer at that very moment might be watching the messages play out. His brain whirred with the need to extract himself from the conversation without sounding rude or dismissive. He considered changing his password but realised the futility of such a move. The police would just hack it and then he'd look even more guilty when his account revealed the conversation. He decided to play it safe.

'I'm sure Victim Support can help you do it properly. I don't have her password or access to her account.' He lied. If he accepted the friend request, he could download every photograph from Marie's profile. But he didn't want to get caught in a crossfire without understanding the stakes. And even then, his answer would probably remain unchanged.

And then another thought occurred to him, one so horrible it caused him to fumble the phone and it dropped into his lap.

Whoever had possession of Marie's phone could also see the conversation on her Facebook app. Which placed him in the firing line of her killer.

Mac cursed his stupidity. No one had known about the favour he'd done for her. Thanks to her sister, the killer knew his identity and what he'd done to protect Marie from them. He realised far too late that the killer may also assume Mac knew their identity.

He wasn't just in the firing line now. The foolish conversation had placed him on the target board with an 'X' over his heart.

35

KICKER

"It's not Edin." After an uneventful weekend, Tilly met Mac at school the following Monday. She waited for him by the bus stop and lowered her voice as the other passengers trooped past them.

Mac's pulse pounded in his eardrums, a nauseating vibration belying his stress. Sassy had misbehaved in the grey light of dawn, sensing his unease and reacting to it. She'd stepped on his right foot and crushed it, leaving a dent in his cowboy boot and bruising his toes. Deaf, with a broken wrist and a limp, he had very few body parts left undamaged. Self-pity and disillusion shrouded him like a knitted cardigan.

"The killer knows I helped Miss Andrews." Mac sank onto the low wall of the courtyard and watched Tilly's eyes grow wide. He recounted the Facebook messages of the previous evening.

"Remove them!" she hissed. "You can delete them." Her body dipped as though his news pained her. The blueness of her irises dulled with angst.

Mac shrugged. "I can remove them for myself, but not for someone else. Once the recipient sees them, that's it. Marie's sister saw them straight away, so I'm screwed. I almost wish Edin had done it. At least she might show me some mercy."

"Oh, Mac!" Tilly slipped her hand through the crook of his good arm. She nudged his rucksack aside with her shoe to make room next to him. He experienced a surge of gratitude when she fell silent and didn't waste words on empty platitudes. She dropped her chin and appeared to find something engaging in the cracks between the paving slabs at their feet.

Mac's sudden groan roused her. "I forgot to do my biology homework." Loose grit shuffled beneath his shoes as he leaned down to poke inside his rucksack. Reluctant fingers drew out a textbook. A pad of lined paper came with it.

Tilly held out her hand without speaking, taking the textbook from him. She drew a pen from her top pocket and retrieved a tick sheet from between the book's tattered pages. "It's just multiple choice," she said, already busy with the ink. In less than a minute, she'd completed the task and pressed the paper back into its slot midway through a chapter on genome sequencing. "Easy," she announced with a smile, though Mac knew the initial research and trawling through endless pages proved neither easy nor pleasant. Her black lashes flickered as she narrowed her eyes in a devious expression, her red lips tilting upward on one side. "I marked one wrong on purpose, to make it less suspect."

"Thanks," Mac replied. His nose wrinkled at her motives, but she'd done him a massive favour and so he let it pass.

A rush of air brought Layla to his feet in a flurry of excitement. Tilly jerked sideways to avoid a clattering with the girl's flying rucksack. Sammy brought up the rear, her manner quieter than usual, and she hung back from Layla's enthusiastic arm waving. "Mr Simms said yes!" she gushed. Mac saw Tilly smirk and bite her lower lip as Layla dipped forward and wrapped her arms around his neck. He hissed and withdrew his painful foot from beneath her stampeding shoes. A haze of cloying perfume doused the oxygen around his head and she only released him as he started coughing. He covered his mouth with his hand and turned sideways, surprised to find Sammy perched on the wall next to Tilly. She'd slipped her hand through Tilly's elbow and clung on as though afraid of being sucked away in a passing wave of students.

Irritation found a foothold in Mac's chest. "I wanted to talk to Simms about it first," he replied, a bite in his tone. Oblivious, Layla danced on the spot.

"My foot is heaps better," she enthused. "Can I play a winger? I want to play a winger." She paused and yanked a green slip from her blazer jacket. "Oh, Mr Darian asked me to give this to you." It fluttered in the breeze as she held it out to him.

"Why?" Mac snatched the detention slip and read the reason scrawled onto the lined paper. "Insubordination." He ground his teeth and stuffed it into his side pocket. The campaign of intimidation appeared set to continue.

"Can I then?" Layla demanded. "Can I play a winger?"

"I'm not sure yet." Mac rose and pushed the fingers of his left hand into his blazer pocket. They brushed against the detention slip. The cast stretched the fabric but took the weight off his elbow. "I'm glad your foot's improving," he commented, staring down at it. Tilly snorted as though reading his mind, having watched Layla stamp all over him. The upper of his black left shoe contained a dusty imprint of her sole.

"Lunchtime." Layla clicked the fingers and thumbs of both hands. "Let's meet on the practice pitch. I'll be captain." She pursed her lips and challenged him from beneath her fluttering lashes. Sammy gasped in protest, and she qualified her usurped authority. "Just for today."

The girls twittered away, although Sammy's steps held reluctance. Tilly watched them leave, her brow furrowed. The bell pealed, negating Mac's need to sit back down on the wall. "What's wrong?" he asked, offering Tilly his hand.

"Not sure." Her brow furrowed, and she still stared at the space where the marauding crowd swallowed the girls. "Sammy's lost her sparkle."

"And her phone." Mac fixed a wry smile on his lips. "And probably her social media influence. Temporary but devastating."

Tilly nodded and accepted his hand to stand. "I guess so. Finding your dead teacher didn't help." She shrugged. "I thought she'd got past it all, but maybe finding Miss Andrews set her back a little."

"Past what?" Mac turned his attention to the main building and the location of his tutor class. He'd asked the question with no interest in the answer.

Tilly dipped and lifted both their rucksacks onto her shoulder. She waved away Mac's protestations. "She got into something dodgy last year. It happened before the nice family adopted her."

Mac cocked his head. He frowned, his curiosity piqued. "What?"

Tilly waggled her eyebrows. "I don't know, but she got very sneaky. I tried to find out what she was up to but got nowhere. She asked me an odd question once about Mr Darian and if I thought spying on people was wrong. Then the family adopted her, and she stopped doing whatever made her miserable. I forgot about it until now."

"Spying on people?" Mac blinked as his mind ran through a series of harmless possibilities to something more sinister. He stared down at Tilly. "You think she spied on Darian?" He blew out a breath. "What if she saw him doing something awful? You know his reputation."

Tilly shrugged. "That's a massive leap, Mac. I just said she'd lost her sparkle."

"True." Mac followed her through the crush at the main door. He held his cast above the shoulders of smaller students as they filtered into the corridor. They deviated to the side as the throng continued, pausing for a quick kiss before they parted. It felt natural to press his lips to Tilly's and a bloom of happiness cut through the multiple worries dogging Mac's mind. "Oh." His brow furrowed as he remembered something. "You said it wasn't Edin." The second bell rang and Mac's pulse sped up, needing the answer but not wishing to show up late to his tutor class. "How do you know?"

"Tilly Rae, get your backside into that classroom!" Slade Hefner tapped her on the shoulder and glared at Mac. Spittle hung in the dust motes between them and Mac took a hasty step backwards. Hefner focussed on Tilly. "Do the register and sort out the Year 9s for me. I left a careers questionnaire on my desk for them to fill in and don't let the little shits leave before they've finished." He didn't wait for her to respond. "Come on! Hop to it! The headmaster wants to see me about nothing again." He leaned sideways like a listing building, cutting Mac from their discussion. "Sandwiches are in the top drawer. Wife thought you might like cheese and homemade pickle today." He shot Mac another glare before leaving.

"Wow." Mac watched Hefner slide through the dwindling crowd of latecomers, rounding them up like a collie. "Are you head of your tutor group? Why didn't I know this?"

Tilly turned her body and lifted her lips in a coquettish smirk. "Gosh, Mr Du Rose. Did you think me so utterly delinquent?" She blinked, her eyes filled with laughter and the corners crinkled beneath dark eyeshadow.

Mac shrugged. "Sorry. You're a woman with hidden depths." He bent and kissed her again, seized by a wave of insurmountable need and longing. The urge to retire to the janitor's cupboard for the morning whispered promises in his ears, and he heard nothing else. His heart ached as she turned away from him and he covered the bulge in his pants with his rucksack as he limped to his tutor class. Deaf, a broken wrist, a sore foot, and a curious sense of separation in his chest.

36

FIELD

Mac didn't see Tilly again until lunchtime. Syd Ross tried to sit next to him in the dining hall and he sighed, lacking the energy to protest. But Tilly's appearance made the prefect remember a forgotten duty, and she spared Mac from the familiar demands for access to Edin's phone number. She stood over the boy until he vacated the seat. "What did Simms say about the soccer girls?" she asked.

Mac shrugged. "Blah blah blah. He ranted about Layla accosting him and asked why he didn't hear it from me."

Tilly bugged her eyes. "Well, that's what happens when you spend the whole day on the toilet. You miss all the good news." She curled her upper lip. "I thought everyone knew you needed to soak kidney beans before cooking with them. Didn't we learn that in Year 9 cooking classes?"

Mac smiled. "Yeah. We did. And Simms looked like he'd lost half his body weight into the sewer. What did you mean earlier?" He accepted her chaste kiss to his cheek, not trusting himself to present his lips to her. A monster had awakened in his chest and it wanted full possession of her body and mind.

He sensed himself losing control of it with every passing minute in her intoxicating presence. Tilly dumped her purple rucksack beneath the table. Its many frayed straps and buckles whacked the metal legs as she stuffed it there without care. She bent her right knee under her and sank onto the chair with the elegance of a cat folding its limbs beneath it.

"What are we talking about?" She withdrew a sandwich from her blazer pocket and stared at it. Grated cheese mingled with a sticky brown liquid and stained the bread. Eager fingers set about tugging the wrapper free, and Tilly closed her eyes as she sampled the first bite. "Yum," she concluded. "Hef's wife makes a cracking sarnie."

"You said Edin didn't do it." Mac lowered his voice and leaned closer. "How do you know?"

"I asked around." Tilly spoke with her mouth full and crumbs dotted her lips and chin. "She arrived at school with that rich girl from her class. They drove here. She left them and disappeared into the main building and nobody saw her until tutor class."

"So?" Mac frowned. "That's not an alibi."

"It is." Tilly narrowed her eyes and observed him with curiosity. "Nobody saw her, Mac. Which means she didn't leave the main building. There are two doors and I spoke to people who sat near both. She didn't come outside again until the bell rang for tutor class."

Mac sighed, but his dissatisfaction with Tilly's conclusion refused to leave him. "Where did she go then?"

Tilly shrugged. A crusty right angle of bread tumbled into her lap and remained there. Mac stared at a smear of margarine ridged by a bite mark. He imagined her teeth grazing his neck, and a shiver ran through him. Oblivious, she continued. "It doesn't matter as long as she stayed inside that building. Besides, the cops said Miss Andrews died somewhere else, didn't they?"

Mac's lips parted in surprise. A vein throbbed, a nervous tick in his neck. He hadn't told her that. Had he? He sifted through a mishmash of conversations, but remembered only the sensation of her kisses.

His appetite fled, and he turned his body in the seat. "Where did you get the cover and the SIM card from?" He reached for his rucksack and dug into its folds one-handed for his wallet. "How much do I owe you?"

"Nothing." She flapped her right hand at him. "I called in a favour. It's free to you."

Misgiving grew like a snowball in his stomach, accumulating mass with every lurching roll. He watched her, unsure how to continue. Her red lips curved around the sandwich as she devoured another bite, a pink tongue shooting free to lick escaped crumbs. His body rebelled against the screamed warnings in his mind, overwriting any wisdom with a hunger to kiss her lips, her hair and her neck. His right hand twitched before dropping into his lap. Clearing his throat and shifting in discomfort did nothing to clear the fog of lust from his brain. "Do you want to go to the cupboard?" he whispered, his voice husky.

Tilly shrugged. "Yeah, but it's locked. I checked on the way here."

"Right." He squirmed in his chair, unable to control the surge of hormones seizing his body in an uncontrollable palsy.

Tilly smacked her lips around the remnants of the sandwich and closed her eyes in pleasure. "That tasted good." Her right hand snaked across the gap between them to smooth her palm across Mac's muscular thigh. An electric shock passed through him with a dangerous mixture of pleasure and pain. "I'm sure I can snag a key from somewhere soon," she breathed. "One of my contacts will have a master key." A contented sigh escaped her as the sandwich satiated an inner need which seemed more powerful than hunger. "About Edin," she said, squeezing her fingers against his leg and causing him further torture. "Why don't you hack her phone and look at her location's history?"

Mac frowned as he considered such an unlikely feat of daring. "How?"

Tilly shrugged and turned to face him. "I don't know. You'll think of something. If she walked anywhere near the equipment shed, her location will switch to the tower on Alexandra Street." Her lips curved into a grin. "Remember the time Deacon pretended he met a married woman for a lunchtime quickie? He used his phone's location history to prove it."

Mac closed his eyes at a memory of happier times. Life seemed so much simpler in hindsight. "Yeah," he breathed with a sad sigh. "He left his bag at the side of the rugby field and his phone location switched to the Alexandra tower." He pursed his lips. "It looked like he'd spent a happy hour at the motel."

Tilly dipped her head and observed him through the tops of her eyes. Fake lashes added a black frame to her sparkling irises. "Yeah. So, if Edin went as far as the equipment shed, it'll show her location as the motel. You need to get her phone and double check." She shrugged her shoulders in a nonchalant wave of dismissal. "She didn't do it though, Mac."

He wanted to test her certainty and sensed not doing so would cause him regret later. But her scent washed over him to produce irritating clouds of mind fog, which left him bewildered. The monster in his chest wriggled with discomfort at the sight of her black bra peeking from between the gaps in her shirt buttons. He tensed every muscle in his body to stem the lewd thoughts and hissed as his wrist protested. "Let's go for a walk," he begged, but a glance at his watch raised a groan. "Oh, no! It's twelve thirty. I need to meet the soccer team."

GUARD

Tilly turned on her location and shared it with Mac before he left. He cocked his head and hesitated before returning the trust. "I keep mine turned off," he said with a grimace. His finger hovered over the setting in his Google account.

Tilly shrugged. Disappointment tugged down her lips. "It's up to you," she said. "I'm not stalking you. It's just an experiment. Walking across the soccer field should throw your location to the Alexandra Street tower." She shrugged again. "You wanted to know."

Mac nodded and blew out a breath. He stabbed at the screen and the button flicked from grey to blue. "Okay." He fiddled with another setting. "I'm only sharing it with you. I've left everything else turned off." He smiled down at her and the twinkle returned to her irises. She reached up and kissed him.

"See you later," she said. She lifted her phone in her right hand. "I think you'll find the midpoint is at the centre circle of the pitch used by the First Eleven. There's always a second's delay before it clicks over."

"Thanks." Mac checked his watch again and picked up speed towards the exit. His rucksack cut into his right shoulder and a biology text book dug through the lining and pummelled his spine as he ran.

The soccer girls practiced with enough flare to stop him from regretting his decision.

He avoided using equipment from the shed, unable to face the gloom and the memories of the sports teacher's charred body. Instead, the girls used their school jumpers and rucksacks as markers for an obstacle course and obeyed his instructions on dribbling and passing. It occupied the rest of the lunch hour as Mac paced in a circle shouting orders and blowing on an old whistle liberated from the junk drawer at home.

"That was amaze-balls!" Layla gushed as the school bell pealed from the distant main building. "We're gonna rock the junior girls' league this season. She punched the air with a fist and hopped on one leg. "My foot hurts a bit. Mac, please, can you look at it for me?" Her eyelashes fluttered and Mac noticed Sammy frown and purse her lips.

He shook his head. "No chance. I hate feet." He stuffed the whistle into his pocket. "That reminds me, do any of your parents know first aid? It'd be good to have someone on the side-line to take care of minor injuries each week."

"My dad's a doctor." An elfin child with auburn hair raised a nervous hand. "But he might not come every week."

Mac offered a reassuring smile. "A doctor is fantastic. I'm grateful for whenever he can make it." The complimented child flushed red to the roots of her hair, pleasure in her sparkling eyes. He paused, remembering Miss Andrews' desire to demote the girl before pushing away the notion. Gratitude infused him that she'd provided something useful, even if only on the sidelines. Mac cast around at the gathered girls as they guzzled water from plastic bottles. He supported his cast with his right hand, his thumb automatically tapping each of his injured fingers in turn like a muted drumbeat as he contemplated the task ahead. "I'll need a lot of help to keep the team running, but let's make it simple. Which social media platform do you use?"

A cacophony broke out loud and muddled enough to make Mac wince and touch his right processor. He changed the movement at the last second and raised his hand to get their attention. The nearest girls shushed the others, Layla providing the prominent lead.

Mac ran through the different platforms and asked for a show of hands. Facebook won out, and he promised to create a private group and communicate the link. "I want adults to join the group too," he stated. "So, your mums, dads and carers will see your comments." He raised an eyebrow as he followed his mother's advice about maintaining transparency. It also meant he didn't need to take individual girls' phone numbers, which she'd counselled against. The team members chittered with excitement and filtered away as the warning bell sounded. Layla remained behind to collect the practice balls into a net, and Sammy helped her bear it away to the temporary cupboard at the back of the gym.

Within seconds, Mac stood alone on the white line bordering the soccer pitches set aside for the better teams. He squinted down at the fresh paint and the coarse tufts and marvelled at how different they'd look in a few short months. Lime green shoots would soak up the winter rain and then endure ripping and trampling by studs and sliding tackles. His gaze moved to the cast over his left wrist and he sighed. The greyed edges of the fibre glass gave it a dirty appearance, but he recognised the convenience of the break. He wouldn't play for Arthur Darian, and the broken wrist provided his ready excuse. Mac sighed, knowing he'd still miss the stress and exhilaration of competing in the senior league.

He dug his cast into his blazer pocket and hefted his rucksack onto his shoulder, noticing a stray soccer ball sitting in the centre circle unattended. His feet carried him across the grass towards it with eagerness, and he dribbled it a few paces before chipping it into the air and bouncing it against his right knee. "You've still got it, Du Rose," he murmured to himself.

Layla's ponytail bounced against her shoulders in the distance. The bulging net hung between her and Sammy like a bulbous hammock. Mac inhaled before realising they'd already gone too far to call back to him. It seemed pointless to make them late for class on account of a single football.

Mac bent to retrieve it with his hands and his rucksack plunged from his shoulder and landed on the grass. It caused his body to list, and the ball rolled away to land in a patch of bobbing daisies. He glanced up to see if his accidental clowning had drawn attention, but saw no one. The last of the students cleared from the playing fields and filtered through classroom doors.

Mac jumped as a voice spoke from behind him. "You okay buddy?" The gravelly timbre heralded the older of the two groundsmen who managed the exterior work on the school site. He turned to find the grey-haired man walking towards him.

"I'm good, thanks," Mac replied. "The girls left this behind." He frowned, wondering how they'd failed in the simple task of counting to twenty.

"Ah yep." The man raised his chin and smiled at Mac. He lifted a dirty baseball cap from his head and scratched the damp grey curls stuck to his scalp. "You're the dude who's coaching my granddaughter's team, aren't you?" Luckily for Mac, he didn't wait for him to name her or offer encouraging comments about her skill level. The man ploughed on regardless. "She's stoked. It's great that Grant Simms is letting you keep them together. Kiera didn't want to play for another team." He stuck out his hand to Mac. "I'm Foggy."

"Kiera." Mac took his hand and pictured the slender child with auburn hair. "She's my striker. Dad's a doctor."

"That's right." The groundsman beamed. "She needs something good in her life after her mum dying last Christmas an all." He bent to retrieve the ball at Mac's feet and his eyes sparkled as he rose again. He kept his gaze from Mac's until he'd collected his emotions back into his chest. "What are you doing with this?"

Mac blew out a breath, but words abandoned him. He fought the urge to switch off his processors and disconnect from the man's sad news. It pained his conscience to know that while he'd taken on the team for selfish reasons, someone else had needed it more. He just hadn't known it. Mac shelved Miss Andrews' opinion of her lack of skill. He couldn't tell the doting grandfather she hadn't rated the girl. "I have a free period now," he said instead, his voice husky. "I'll walk it over to the gym."

Foggy slapped his cap onto his head and twisted it into place. "That's miles away," he observed, squinting into the sunlight. "Opposite direction to your common room." He bounced it once in his hands. "I'll shove it in the equipment shed for now."

Mac's body turned in a slow circle without his bidding. He cringed as he faced the wooden shed. Memories flooded back into his mind. Layla collapsing, his wrist snapping, the awful burning smell. He shivered and his teeth clacked together. Foggy frowned. "Sorry, mate. Kiera showed me that picture of you carrying her friend from the building. You were lucky not to take a whack from that wire, too." His lips curved up on one side and he dipped his head so the cap's wide brim shadowed his smirk. "Nice cape, Superman."

Mac groaned. "Don't remind me. I thought the cops removed all those pictures from the internet."

Foggy shrugged. "Screenshots, mate. The kids snatch everything nowadays, like they're in a candy store."

Mac nodded in agreement. He aimed for humour to cover his embarrassment. "It got me a girlfriend, so I can't complain." He jerked in surprise as Foggy threw his head back and laughed.

"Good one!" he chortled and aimed a soft punch at Mac's upper arm. "Right," he commanded, "you get going and I'll shove this in the shed."

"But isn't it still a crime scene?" Mac narrowed his eyes at the police tape flapping from the door handle. He forced his steps to trace Foggy's through the grass towards the shed, though every nerve ending screamed in protest.

"Na." Foggy shook his head. He reached the building first and tugged open the door. "I've got orders to clear it out and store the equipment at the back of the gym. The rugby coaches are livid, but there's nowhere else for it." He reached into the darkness and pulled out a padded black bag, which he used as a doorstop. A set of weights clanked inside it as he leaned it up against the wooden door. "They built that gym for everyone, but the rugby guys monopolised it from the get-go. The board of trustees decommissioned this old place as soon as the mayor cut the ribbon on the new building." He aimed a kick at a loose board next to the door frame. "Heads are rolling now, for sure. I'm staying here out of their way."

"Whose way?" Mac took a step closer. He inhaled and then released the breath, relieved not to smell burning flesh in the building's vicinity anymore. "What do you mean by rolling heads?"

Keen to chat rather than enter the dark bowels of the shed, the groundsman leaned against the rickety siding. He crossed his legs at the ankles and tapped the football with the steel toecap of his uppermost boot. "Well, it's like this," he began. "The school site underwent a massive upgrade of the electrical wiring five years ago. Nobody thought to include the equipment shed in the scope because the architect created storage at the back of the new gym for everything inside here. But then the rugby boys hired rowing machines and took over that cupboard as a store room. So, nothing changed out here." He waved towards the darkness. "This place takes its power from an old junction box in a forgotten cupboard in the main building. The forensics guys found rubber wires and original fuses." He waggled his bushy eyebrows. "That's what fried her and the little girl."

Mac blinked and considered the man's tale. He cast his mind back to physics lessons before he'd dropped the subject in favour of biology. "But surely an RCD covers the school site. The fuse would blow as soon as it detected a fault in the circuit."

Foggy's head shook from side to side as he enjoyed his superior authority. "Not if someone years ago removed the fuse wire and fixed a screw into the gap to stop the power tripping." He shuddered. "Before my time, thank goodness, or they'd blame me. The cops found it rusted into place, but enough metal still showed to keep the power running through it. They think someone put it there in the seventies by the make of the screw and the state of it. It wasn't a recent thing."

"Oh." Mac's lips flattened into thin lines. "So those wires carried the full amperage available to the school site?"

"Yep. All 2400 watts of it." He ran a hand over his grizzled chin. "The forensics guys couldn't find an earth either."

"Wow!" Mac mustered the expected response and eyed the dark interior.

"Yup." Foggy galvanised himself and reached inside the door, dragging out the first of many wire baskets filled with balls. He dipped and retrieved the football and dumped it on the top.

Mac watched him as a question formulated in his mind. It took time for him to shape it into something which sounded casual. "Do you know why we found Miss Andrews here?" The words emerged with the wrong intonation and he rushed to clarify them. "I mean, why here? Did she meet someone here or come to check on something? Why here?"

Foggy dropped his hands by his sides and stared at a point in the distance, his eyes unseeing. He considered Mac's question with care. "The headmaster said she didn't die here," he replied. He closed one eye and observed Mac through the other. "But you didn't hear that from me. The cops think the killer brought her body here to burn it on purpose."

Mac clenched his teeth as the singed flesh filled his nostrils and his mind with its noxious scent. "But how?" he demanded, looking around him. A group of Year 10s hurried in a diagonal beeline towards a gap in the far hedge. Their jerky movements and furtive glances betrayed their illegal mission. Sensing their discomfort and reminded of riskier escapades with Deacon, Mac dragged his attention back to Foggy and left them to their lesson wagging. "This is a rat-run to the shops on Alexandra Street," he stated. "Everyone walks across this paddock. You'd need to be half asleep to miss someone carrying a woman's body to the sports shed."

"They might have done it in the dark," Foggy offered. He frowned and touched the side of his nose with a dirty index finger. "I shouldn't tell you this, but they found an extra crate that didn't belong here. So, maybe the killer shoved her in there, buried her in equipment, and wheeled her across the field in front of everyone." He shrugged. "It's the most terrible thing I've seen happen at the school and I'm in my tenth year." His lips released an audible tut of pity. "Poor wee girl. My Kiera liked her a lot. Terrible thing to happen."

Foggy frowned and then, in a momentary lapse of judgement, forgot the age and maturity of his audience. "I found her crying in here one night last week. She said she'd be okay, but she looked real upset. Didn't want to tell me at first but then admitted someone made a pass at her and she had to play nice." His eyes blinked wide to display rheumy brown irises. "People don't realise what women have to put up with in schools, do they?" Foggy shook his head in a slow arc. "I wish I'd stopped to listen to her for longer now. The kids are always making sloppy advances to the young ones, so I don't know why it upset her so much." He turned back towards the shed's yawning doorway with a sigh. "Told the cops, anyway. I guess they'll sort it out and we'll read all about it in the papers."

"Yeah," Mac managed. "Yeah." His shoes dragged against the dirt and kicked dust around his trouser legs. It settled on the fabric as a loose grey haze. Fear lit a fire beneath him as he hurried towards the main building, eager to leave Foggy's surmising far behind him. He saw nothing of the familiar landmarks or the students wearing the school's sports gear as they piled onto the hockey turf. His mind went into freefall as an invisible net closed around his head. Bodie couldn't shield him forever. One day soon, Detective Elliot would come for him.

Despite his own internal voice, which promised him justice, Mac knew his watery defence couldn't save him.

38

HAND BALL

The rest of the day passed in a blur. Mac's mind whirred with the new information and his head ached from the relentless pounding of his blood in his veins. He waited for the police to come for him, wondering if he should confess before the inevitable happened. But too many lies already dotted his story. The prospect of the task spun his stomach into a tight knot.

Tilly sat next to him in biology, but he remained uncommunicative. She told him his phone had pinged off the Alexandra Street tower during his lunch hour but he no longer cared. His world had collapsed around his ears and he couldn't bear to tell her what he'd discovered. Shame prickled his skin, allied with bitter regret. His fumbled pass had brought Marie to tears. What had it cost her to pretend it didn't affect her and continue with business as usual?

By the end of the day, Mac hated himself.

Tilly frowned in concern as they parted company at the bus stop. She stood on tiptoes for a kiss, but his reluctance meant she only dotted one on his chin. Mac forced a smile and trudged towards his waiting bus, not stopping to see if Edin followed. She didn't, and his mother made no comment about her absence when she fetched him from the township.

Once in his bedroom, Mac tested Tilly's theory with the location app. He opened his Google account and saw a jagged purple line from the school's main building to the motel on Alexandra Street just after half-past twelve. His lips tightened into a thin line as he traced his return journey from the soccer pitch to the common room fifty minutes later. He couldn't save himself, but he could at least absolve Edin of suspicion.

His mother appeared in his doorway before dinner, bringing the heavy scent of chicken with her. She beckoned to him with her fingers and he rose with reluctance. Hana disappeared through the front door without waiting for him. She lifted a pile of metal waratahs from beside the porch and carried them across the lawn. A reel of electrical tape trailed from beneath her right arm. Mac rued his absent processors and contemplated returning for them, but Hana shook her head and jerked her chin towards the far edge of the garden.

She set about pressing the sharp prongs of the waratahs into the baked earth and winding the tape through the loops. Mac understood she wanted him to help her set up a pen. He spread his hands in question, but she ignored his request, hurrying to finish the task ahead of an unspoken deadline. She fetched a water bucket from the garage and filled it from the tap, setting it inside the pen. Another trip found her hefting a car battery, and the unit needed to set up an electric boundary.

"Let me," Mac said, taking the heavy items from her. He followed her lead, tightening the tape into a decent barrier. When she emerged again, she carried an empty bucket from the garage and upturned it over the battery. Holes drilled into the side allowed the wires to protrude and connect to the tape. The bucket acted as an umbrella, and its plastic base sagged as Mac sat a paving slab over it to prevent it blowing away in a strong wind.

"Is everything okay?" Hana's red curls lifted in the breeze as she worked alongside him. They moved in a well-worn pattern of cooperation.

"Yeah?" Mac's forehead knitted into thin lines. "Why?"

Hana paused with a waratah in her left hand. "The school phoned, love. A guy with a squeaky voice. He said your behaviour had slipped in the last week and he wanted to flag it with me and your father." She cocked her head and frowned. "Thing is, he said he worked in the sports department, but it made no sense." She pointed towards Mac's arm. "You haven't done PE since before the accident. How would he know anything about your behaviour? Anyway, when I questioned him, he said he'd called on behalf of your tutor teacher." Hana gave a visible shudder. "There's something hinky about it. I thought I'd ask you before I tell your father."

Mac sighed. The tape fluttered in his fingers as he struggled to fit it beneath the metal pigtail one-handed. "Mr Darian," he told her. "He wants me to coach the First Eleven team. It's clear if I don't, he'll make my life a misery."

"He can't do that!" She exhaled. "Would you like me to call the headmaster and complain? You know I will if it's what you want."

"I know, Ma," he murmured. "Thank you." He reached out and touched her shoulder in a gentle movement. "Hopefully he'll get bored when he realises I'm not interested. I'll organise the girls to start training next week. That should send a clear message." He forced a convincing smile onto his lips. "I've got this, Ma. Don't worry."

Hana studied him for a moment before answering. "If you're sure," she replied, doubt in her voice.

It seemed only seconds later that Logan appeared at the top of the hill, riding his sturdy gelding and towing another horse behind him. Mac frowned at the sight of Sassy tossing her head and bumping her chin against Sonny's rump. Logan's horse kept his ears flat to his head in a silent protest, but he kept moving in obedience to his rider.

Logan dismounted and slipped Sonny's reins over his ears. He beckoned Mac across the grass to stand next to him. "I know you're finding it hard," he mouthed to his son. "Let's keep her up here for a few days while you have your wrist in the cast."

Mac nodded and a strange knot collected in his throat. Having the mare outside his bedroom window negated his need for early morning visits to the stable yard. It meant he could continue building their relationship just by hanging around with her. He dug his bare toes into the grass and nodded, unable to summon anything other than thanks.

Logan turned his gaze towards the gate and pushed his cowboy hat back on his head. His lips moved, but Mac didn't catch his words. His father's forehead crinkled into lines of concern and he stood as though waiting for something. Hana fixed her hands over her hips and shook her head. Her yellow skirt blew in a light breeze and Sassy reached out to nip the fluttering fabric.

Logan's truck eased through the gate at a painfully slow pace. Light reflected off the windscreen to hide the identity of the driver. Mac held his breath as the truck jerked to a stop in the centre of the driveway. Logan pointed and shouted something Mac didn't hear. Edin emerged from the driver's seat, her face alight with enjoyment. She laughed and clapped her hands, her grey irises dancing and glittering in the evening sun. She held the truck keys out to Logan before rising onto her toes and pressing a kiss to his cheek. He'd let her drive his expensive wagon up the narrow track to the house despite only having a learner's licence.

Jealousy and injustice filled Mac's breast. He'd never driven Logan's truck. An ugly wave of red rage snaked through his chest and, sensing it, Sonny took a step away from him.

Edin ignored him, flouncing back to the truck to retrieve her school bag before disappearing through the front door. Mac ground his teeth in his jaw, catching his tongue as he forced a ragged breath into his lungs. A sensible voice in his head reminded him they'd done it for his benefit, wanting to make his life easier. But his world had already tipped and he couldn't accept the voice's gentle reasoning. He unhooked Sassy's lead rope from the rigging dee at the back of Logan's saddle and led her into the enclosure.

Logan untacked Sonny and let him loose on the lawn, closing the main gate and trusting him not to stray. He completed the fence's circuit by hooking a plastic loop over the last waratah to form a gate. Connecting one wire to the fence and the other to the exposed metal provided an earth. Mac glanced up to find his father pointing to the battery, telling him to turn it on before leaving. He jabbed a finger at Sonny as the gelding munched through Hana's ornamental daisies and then back at the pen. His father wished him to put his horse into the enclosure when he'd finished with the mare. The horses would spend their time together. Company would soothe Sassy's nerves in a new environment and Sonny would waste his time believing he could impregnate her. Logan must have reasoned they'd either become friends or kick each other to death.

Mac collected a spare grooming kit from the garage and passed a dandy brush over Sassy's coat. She ignored him, grazing the springy grass from around his feet. Her hooves and frogs proved clear, and Mac released the last foot and pressed his forehead against her flank. So many emotions flew through his body, he found it difficult to isolate one from another. Jealousy, lust, misery and fear vied for prominence. If Sassy had been less green, he'd have taken her into the bush and fled where no one could find him.

Sonny allowed Mac to lead him into the temporary pen, trailing chunks of late apple stolen from the tree. Twigs protruded from his mane where he'd reached for the choicest fruit, and Mac groomed him as the gelding circled the mare with a glint in his eyes.

After a lazy attempt at running his muzzle along her backside, Sonny got the message as Sassy squealed and kicked out at him. He reared backwards in haste and clattered Mac's broken wrist. The air whooshed from the teenager's lungs to leave him breathless and hating his life. The brush fell to the baked earth with a thud.

He connected the battery and watched as Sassy tested the boundary. When a nonchalant barging of the tape earned her a shock, she avoided it. The horses settled into a peaceful rhythm, grazing the untouched grass with steady enthusiasm. Mac used the hosepipe to top up the bucket after they'd both drunk and he turned the tap off at the wall. Horse hair covered his school trousers, and he brushed it loose outside the front door. He glared at Logan's truck, still sitting at a jaunty angle in the middle of the driveway. Life seemed suddenly so unfair.

39

Own Goal

Edin buzzed throughout the dinner. She appeared more animated than she had since her mother stepped through the gates of the prison and began her campaign of recognition. Mac forced himself to eat the tasty casserole and completed his chores without complaint.

He seized his moment for vindicating Edin as she chatted with Logan about the intricacies of getting clutch-bite on the heavy truck. "Please, can I borrow your iPhone charger?" he asked, his tone contrite. "Someone at school lent me a phone, but the battery is low."

Edin's lips pursed tight, and she widened her eyes at him, unable to confirm the charger's location as her bedroom in front of an audience. She cleared her throat and faltered, so Mac filled in the blank for her. "I'll look for it, if that's okay?"

Relief loosened the muscles in her face as she offered a tight nod. A speck of custard stained her cheek, accompanied by a light dusting of sugar from their dessert. Edin worked over hard to earn Logan's approval, and she seemed keen not to lose ground. She returned to their discussion with eagerness as

Logan used pencil and paper to explain the workings of the truck's mechanics. Released to search, Mac strode first into the lounge to keep up appearances, and then to Edin's bedroom.

Her iPhone charged under her bed and he knelt to retrieve it. She'd never altered the code for the lockscreen and he used 1234 to activate it. The foolish girl took no protective measures, and he logged into her location history with a few wrong turns. The tower on Alexandra Street recorded no visits to that side of the school site in the last month. Edin's sports lessons corresponded with her phone remaining stationary and locked in the changing shed near the main building. Mac backtracked to the morning of his ghoulish discovery and traced Edin's ill-advised trip in the overloaded vehicle. They'd driven to a fast-food restaurant and stayed for twenty minutes. She'd arrived at school before him, walked to the main building and remained there. Mac pulled up her calendar app and ran a cursory eye across it. His shoulders sank with a mixture of surprise and relief. At the moment he discovered Marie Andrews' body, Edin's diary put her halfway through a counselling session in the guidance rooms at the end of the administration corridor. The police still hadn't released a time of death, but Edin had travelled home on the bus and remained there the night before the disastrous find.

"What are you doing?" Her tone held a warning as she closed her bedroom door with a click. Mac pulled the charger free of the phone and pressed the power button to dim the screen.

"It just needs a few seconds more to finish," he said. He rose and sank onto her mattress. "I don't want to leave you with no charge. But Tama's cable is too old and I'm scared it might screw up the phone. I can't give it back knackered."

"Right." Edin remained by the door, but her gaze didn't shift from his face. Mac ached to snatch up the cable and bolt. He ran a nervous hand over the cast and wished he could reverse time and begin the last week fresh. A sigh escaped from his lips. Not just the last week, but the one before as well. He'd go back to the moments before he kissed Miss Andrews and give anything not to make her cry. Edin folded her legs into the armchair by the door. She continued to stare at him. "Is Tilly Rae your girlfriend?" she demanded.

Mac closed his eyes and waited for the repercussions, his muscles constricting at the force of her expected outburst. It didn't come. He opened his left eye and squinted at her. "You have nothing to say?"

Edin shrugged. Her grey irises flashed like storm water. "Just be careful, Macky." Her tone softened. "You are being careful, aren't you?"

Her insinuation drove straight into his heart and guilt turned the tips of his ears pink. He bristled and squirmed on the bed. Clearing his throat, he bent and snatched the cable from the phone's charging port. "It's none of your business," he growled. His jaw worked hard enough to show beneath his cheek. He spoke through gritted teeth. "Would you like her number so you can send her hate mail like you did to the soccer girls?"

Edin snorted. Mac's processors didn't pick up the sound, but he saw it in her expression and the deflation of her torso. She shook her head. "Not soccer *girls*, Macky, you've got that wrong. You've walked into a hornets' nest, cousin. I don't know how to help you."

"The only help I need is this, thanks." Mac dangled the cable from shaking fingers and stormed from the bedroom, his heels aching as they struck the floorboards with force.

Edin's voice fizzed through his processors as she threw her judgement at his retreating spine. "You hate the limelight, Mac. That's why it suits you not to play in the First Eleven anymore. And now you've picked a girl who craves a grand gesture. She needs a white knight, not a phantom. She's your worst nightmare."

Mac finished his homework while the phone charged. It made no complaint about inferior cables and the battery filled faster than on previous occasions.

His eyes ached from peering at mathematics formulae, and he sat up and rubbed them with his right hand. Setting a biology textbook aside, he reached for the phone. It took mere minutes to set up a Facebook group for the soccer girls. He attached it to his personal profile but altered the privacy settings to create a unique entity. Tilly had included Sammy's number in the contacts of the iPhone and he texted her the link to the group and asked her to pass it to the team members. She didn't reply, but the phone vibrated as the girls asked to connect one by one. Within an hour, most of the team chatted in long comment threads as they competed to choose a name for the group.

Mac left them to it and concentrated on an English assignment. He silenced the notifications for the constant chatter and didn't return to it for another hour. The infamous photo of him carrying Layla from the equipment shed flashed up as a banner, along with an unbroken stream of name suggestions related to super-men and women. Mac groaned and deleted the image from the group. He changed the settings to ensure he vetted every post from then on. But they foxed him by continuing the post, advising *Mac Du Rose set up this group*. He scrolled through, speed reading the silly suggestions until he saw one from Kiera Kohu-Parker. Her grandfather's nickname of Foggy made sense considering the Māori surname meaning mist or haze. Mac read her suggestion with sadness prickling his chest.

'What about Miss Andrews' Angels?' The girls had ignored her as always.

Mac added a thumb's up to the comment and, without consultation, filled in the group name as *Andrews' Angels*.

The girls accepted it, and Mac took time to update the group rules. He didn't want to spend his days policing bitchy comments or sorting out online drama. He listed the expectations for their conduct and reiterated the appeal for parents to join. Within the next half an hour, he accepted requests from mothers, fathers and adults linked to the girls. He also deleted a series of requests to join from other teenagers with no relevance to the group. Irritated by the time already consumed by social media, he made the group secret and posted a URL to its location in a pinned post.

Hana knocked on his bedroom door before going to bed. "You okay?" she signed.

Mac nodded and reached for his right processor, attaching it to his head to avoid signing one-handed. "I sent you a link for the Facebook group I've set up for the soccer team." He winced. "Would you have time to act as an administrator?"

"Okay." Hana shrugged. "Pointless asking Papa, so yes, if it helps. I'll sort it out in the morning."

"Thanks." Mac heaved out a heavy sigh. "I've had to make the group a secret to stop all their friends from joining." He patted the air between them with his hand. "I took your advice about transparency, so I've asked the girls to invite their parents to the group. A few already joined, so it's not just me and the girls." He shook his head. "I had to stop them posting without admin approval." Pique entered his tone. "They're so stupid, Mama. They'll run rings around me if I'm not careful."

Hana padded across the room and pressed a kiss to the top of his head. "Girls are all puffy hair and attitude," she said with a smile in her voice. "I'll help you, son. Don't go to bed too late tonight or you won't cope tomorrow." She walked across his rug and paused at the door. "Do you need painkillers?"

"Na thanks." Mac shook his head. "You found them?"

Hana made a non-committal sound and jerked her chin towards his phone. "Don't forget to take that to the lounge until morning." She left the room, closing the door behind her and trusting him to obey his father's rules.

Mac finished his homework and padded to the lounge. He discovered Edin's phone was already there and plugged it into her charger. As he turned to leave, his device vibrated, and he frowned and lifted it to his face. The blue glow of the message formed the only light in the darkened room, and his heart sank. Marie's sister had messaged him again.

'Did you think any more about helping me?' she asked.

Mac sank onto the sofa with a groan. He didn't doubt the police watched his social media for signs of guilt, especially after Foggy's statement about Miss Andrews' tears. And whoever took the teacher's phone also had access to his interactions through her Facebook messages. But Susan would see that he'd read her question, and it left him with little option. He needed to reply or block her. The latter would raise too many red flags with the police and set them on a path of wondering which he didn't wish them to pursue.

Mac considered his response, keen not to act in haste or throw even more shade his way. The conclusion held an element of genius, even to his tired brain. His right thumb sped across the digital keypad on the screen as he typed his answer.

'I've kept Miss Andrews' soccer team going. They want to call themselves Andrews' Angels. Is that okay?' Not waiting for a reaction, he ploughed on with his rehearsed sentences. *'It's keeping me busy now, but my girlfriend does Computer Science. I'll ask her for suggestions if that's fine with you?'*

He'd managed to do two important things. The first part conveyed compassion, while offering a reason he couldn't help. The second pointed to his safe involvement in a relationship, which threw off suspicion of him making a sloppy pass at the teacher just days before her murder.

'I'd appreciate that,' Susan Andrews replied. She added an email address at the hospital, perhaps as sickened as Mac by her use of Marie's Facebook account. Mac added a thumb's up and turned off the phone.

Leaden steps took him to the bathroom and then to bed. Tilly hadn't contacted him and he couldn't say he blamed her after his afternoon of sullenness. He hated that he'd used his relationship with her to wriggle free of trouble and promised himself he'd show her more kindness the next day.

As he lay down to sleep, Edin's words returned to him and created confusion. She'd said she only threatened one girl on the team. She'd advised him to be careful, and he assumed she referred to his relationship with Tilly and their risky sexual exploits in the janitor's cupboard. But in the inky blackness of his bedroom, her words took on a different meaning. He lay awake and wondered which of the soccer girls she'd threatened and why.

He also tried to remember what Tilly had done with the old SIM card from the iPhone and realised she'd never mentioned it again.

40

PROMOTION

Mac yawned as he filled the water bucket for the horses and added another from the shed. His processors relayed the sound as a crackle. He couldn't lunge Sassy on the front lawn, but he fixed the lead rope to her halter and took her for a walk. Perhaps picking up on his exhaustion and the slew of emotions rolling off him, she spooked at loose leaves and the cackle of a tui bird in the old kauri tree near the front gate.

Logan leaned against the pillar of the porch and watched him, his expression hidden beneath the brim of his cowboy hat. As Mac led the dancing mare alongside him, he lifted his hand. "She'll settle," he promised. He pushed the hat further back on his head and revealed irises glittering like diamonds in the light of the watery sun. "I'll leave Sonny up here with her for now. There's enough grass for at least four days, and then we'll ride them back down the mountain." He reached out and laid his hand on Sassy's muzzle, not concerned when her lips curved upwards to grab his fingers. His natural state of peace infused her with a calming solidity and she sighed and let her head dip towards the ground. The lead rope hung slack, casting a looping shadow on the flags of the porch. Mac rolled his tense shoulders and forced them to loosen.

Logan smiled at him, his expression kind but his grey eyes perceptive. For a moment, Mac sensed his charade being flayed from him and his lies and sins laid bare at his father's feet. He gulped, and a confession rose into his chest and caused a blockage in the back of his throat.

The front door opened and Logan broke the connection with his son. He turned to listen to Hana as she stepped from the house. The fabric of a pale green skirt fluttered around her thighs and she tugged a cardigan over her shoulders. The sage hues exaggerated the emerald of her eyes and set her hair on fire. Mac heard Logan's sigh of appreciation.

"I'm leading a school party around the museum this morning," she said, standing on tiptoes to press a kiss over Logan's lips. He raised his arms and clasped her elbows in his palms, his expression both gentle and awestruck. Mac recognised in that split second how the strength of their union rested in pure adoration. His mind strayed to Tilly, and he struggled to compare their lust filled fumbling with his parents' devotion. Would she die for him? He ground his teeth in his jaw as the other question plagued him. Would he die for her?

Logan walked Hana to her truck, eager for another kiss. They shared a whispered conversation which Mac's processors failed to relay to him. His shoulders bowed as he led Sassy back to the makeshift pen. Sonny greeted her with enthusiasm as though she'd left the planet months ago and not just taken a stroll around the garden. He sighed as the gelding followed Sassy to the water bucket and then grazed in her stead. She reached her neck over the charged tape to nibble shoots on the other side, but wise to the potential shock, Sonny tugged a dandelion from next to her off-front hoof. Mac wrinkled his nose and acknowledged that even the horse drew limits on his devotion.

Hana left and Logan tapped his wrist, warning Mac of the time. He nodded and collected his rucksack from the foyer. As he re-emerged, he saw Logan lifting a bale of hay from the truck bed. His biceps bulged as he dropped it over the tape and used a pen knife to slit the orange twine from around it. He gathered the snaking string into a ball and stuffed it into his jeans pocket. Sassy snorted and dived towards the hay, Sonny bringing up the rear.

Edin claimed the front seat on the way to the bus stop and Mac didn't complain. His mother rotated the chores and privileges alike, but Logan didn't bother with such minutiae. The bus arrived early, forcing them to run to catch it. The other boy had reclaimed the front seat. Mac made no comment as Edin took her usual spot next to him. She checked her phone on the bumpy ride through the mountains and Mac saw her in his peripheral view as she switched the colour of her counselling appointments from blue to yellow. Sadness enveloped him. He'd misjudged her in too many ways to list. It didn't escape his notice that he'd changed. He wasn't sure he liked the result.

Tilly met him at the school gate. He reactivated his processors in response to her moving lips and the furtive glances she took at the other students filing past them. "Come on!" she hissed. Taking his hand, she speed walked into the main building, not stopping until they reached the locked janitor's cupboard. Her blue irises sparkled like gems. A pink flush crept as far as her jaw line as she pulled a rounded mortice key from her blazer pocket. "I got a master," she whispered, leaning sideways as she twisted it in the lock.

Mac held his breath. This wasn't how he planned for the morning to go. He needed answers to his questions, not to lose himself yet more in her kisses.

But as his feet shuffled into the cupboard and the lock clicked behind him, he found himself powerless to resist her. He couldn't name the thing between them any more than he could bear to lose it.

If Mac believed the sum of his sins beyond redemption in the quiet of his tortured night, the darkness of the janitor's cupboard watched him cross another significant line.

In procuring her illicit key, Tilly had one object in mind. No questions. No discussion. Mac offered neither objection nor complaint as she wedged the broom handle between the door and the wall and lifted her skirt to reveal she wore no underwear.

The tiny space, which smelled of dust and disinfectant, resounded with the muted cries of teenagers at the height of mischief. For Mac, sex proved ten times as amazing as he ever imagined and fifty times more addictive. He fell into a pit of endless wonder and pleasure, marvelling at the softness of her skin, the heady scent of her arousal, and the heightened sensation of every nerve ending tingling at the pinnacle of his climax.

He groaned as Tilly tightened her arms behind his neck and released the grip of her thighs around his hips. His legs trembled with the aftermath and sweat beaded his forehead. A strange fire occupied the pit of his stomach, arcing outward in every direction as she slid down the front of his body. Her shoes made a delicate thud as she stood upright. Mac heard the swish of fabric as she tugged her tartan skirt to cover her thighs. A hazy red spot of light from a nearby shelf gave her a ghoulish glow. The outline of a cordless vacuum stood like a sentry beneath it, storing power for future cleaning. A new addition to the already limited space, it promised the end of the cupboard's long-term availability.

The bell pealed as a distant echo and Mac jumped. He grappled for his zipper with his right hand, his fingers trembling and making a meal of the action. His breath still rang out as stuttered gasps and his heart yammered in his chest.

"We need to go," Tilly hissed, her voice eerie in the darkness. "I'll return the key."

"Where did you get it?" Mac tugged his shirt over his open button and hoped no one noticed. The useless fingers of his left hand fluttered within their fibre glass prison. He felt at his neck and found his tie askew. Running his hand through his hair made his scalp tingle from the sweat of exertion.

"A contact in the lower school. It doesn't matter." Tilly lifted their bags onto her shoulder and removed the key to peer through the lock. "Are you ready? The corridor is clear."

"Wait." Mac felt for her shoulder in the dim glow. "I needed to talk to you."

He heard her low snort as she replaced the key in the lock and ground it into an open position. "Wasn't this better?" she whispered.

"Okay." But he didn't sound certain. Light flooded the room as Tilly hauled open the door and stuck her head outside. She stood on one leg and tilted her whole body through the gap. "Quick!" she hissed. "Darian's coming!" She barrelled into the corridor and dragged Mac behind her. They merged with a passing group of prefects heading to a meeting in the common room, their blazers blending with seamless efficiency.

"You didn't lock the cupboard!" Mac leaned sideways and addressed Tilly in lowered tones. He glanced back to find Arthur Darian taking up a position opposite it. The teacher paused with his arms folded and a curious expression on his face. He glanced up and down the corridor before pulling a bunch of keys from his trouser pocket and dipping to press one into the lock. The group swept Mac and Tilly around the corner to the common room, surprised to discover them among their number.

"You're not allowed in here," Syd Ross announced, barring the doorway. "It's a prefects' meeting. You have your tutor group now."

"Our mistake." Tilly yanked Mac's arm and turned them at a right angle towards the registration classes.

"Did you see that?" Mac's teeth chattered together as adrenaline flooded his veins. "Darian almost caught us."

Tilly frowned and pushed her bottom lip upward in denial. "I told you to hurry."

"But why would he go into the cupboard?" Mac's eyes narrowed as he analysed the odd behaviour. "Teachers never go in there."

Tilly shrugged. She rose onto tiptoes to press a kiss over his lips. "Are we okay?" she asked, tilting her head in concern at Mac's distraction. "I really like you, Mac. Did I make a mistake?"

"No." He shook his head and forced a smile onto his lips. He gave a negative answer even though his brain yelled, its cautions proving the opposite. It occurred to him too late that he'd taken no responsibility for using protection against pregnancy, while losing his virginity without romance, in the stinky darkness of a janitor's cupboard. He clamped his teeth over his lower lip while acknowledging he'd do it again if she asked. When she asked. "Can we meet again at lunchtime?"

Tilly's countenance relaxed, her eyes losing their hunger. "Not in there," she whispered. "I paid ten dollars to borrow the key."

A chill slithered through Mac's body and banished the last remnants of his afterglow. "What?"

Tilly nodded. Her expression showed no concern. "Yeah, you can borrow the key for fifteen dollars. I got it for ten. We kept finding it open because people forgot to lock it. Like we did." She winked at him. "It's safe there, not like the other places."

"Other places?" he stammered. A shiver ran through him. "What do you mean by that? How are they not safe?"

Tilly clamped a hand over his mouth. "I'll explain later," she promised. The bell pealed its final warning and her lips flattened into a line. "You can't arrive late again," she hissed. "Hef lets me get away with murder, but Simms will lose patience with you." She dropped his rucksack at his feet and spun towards the direction they'd already come from, her pigtails bouncing in a haphazard rhythm against her shoulders. Mac watched her leave, the misgiving worming its way through his psyche like an unseen infection. Something was wrong.

No. Something was very wrong.

41

RELEGATION

Mac searched for Tilly at the morning interval, but she didn't appear in the common room. He drifted past the janitor's cupboard with mixed emotions. His true motives evaded him, and he hated not knowing this new version of himself. Did he want Tilly, or crave more of the addictive highs she fostered in the dark recesses of his basest nature?

Seeking fresh air and a clear head, he strode outside into the sunshine for a walk. The soccer girls found him wandering across the first team's pristine pitch with his hands in his blazer pockets. The cast tugged on his elbow and a dull thud hammered in his forehead.

"Hey Mac!" Their joyous shouts filled him with dread and a grim humour settled over him.

"Yeah." His lacklustre reply did nothing to discourage them. Sammy, Layla, and Keira bounced alongside him as he walked.

"Where are ya going?" Layla demanded. She turned her jogging into a skip to keep up with his long stride.

"Clearing my head," he replied, his tone gruff. He stared at the grassy stripes and imagined quitting school with the flick of a pen. A world of possibility opened before him. Leave school, abandon Tilly, rid himself of the adoring crowd, and distance himself from Miss Andrews' murder.

"Andrews' Angels, Andrews' Angels." Keira and Sammy giggled as they danced alongside him with their arms linked. The irritating chant grated on Mac's nerves. His mind strayed to the heat and emotion of the janitor's cupboard and he sensed arousal begin in his stomach and shoot down his thighs.

"Wait for me!" Layla halted as though shot and dug in her blazer pocket. She pulled out a phone and lifted it. Jamming her finger in the other ear, she grumbled at the caller. "It's interval, Gran. Yes, I'll ask him to let you in the group. Gotta go!" She disconnected the call with a jab of her index finger. "Mac?" She began speaking without looking up, keeping the phone in her hand as she caught up to him. "Can you let my granny into the secret group, please? She wants to bake cakes for us."

"Yey! Cakes!" Keira punched the air with her fist and added an extra skip on the spot. "Can she make chocolate ones? I love them best."

Mac watched in horror as Layla skidded to a halt in front of him. "What the hell?" he exclaimed. His gaze fixed on the phone in her hand.

Layla's cheeks reddened at the ferocity in Mac's expression. "What?" she demanded. "The cops took my phone just after they confiscated Sammy's. I'm borrowing this one."

"Who from?" Sickness swirled in Mac's gut at the sight of the distinctive crack splaying like a hand across the top right corner and the glitzy pink protective case. Marie Andrews had dropped her phone onto the floor of the equipment shed after their first muster. Mac had witnessed the unfortunate moment and inspected the damage. He also remembered the placement of the crack from helping the teacher to block her violent partner from her contacts and social media. The distinctive cover would contain the dead teacher's DNA. "Where did you get it?" He took a step forward as Layla slipped the device into her pocket. "I know who owns it."

Layla's irises flickered, and a guardedness entered her manner. Jerky movements conveyed her discomfort. "I'm just borrowing it," she persisted, a whine entering her voice. "You asked us all to join the Facebook group and I don't own a computer. I use the ones in the IT lab." She cocked her head and frowned. "Do you think the cops will keep our phones forever? Sammy's really upset about hers, aren't you, Sammy?" She looked to her friend for corroboration. "She borrowed her new mum's and her new dad banned her from TikTok and Instagram."

"I don't know." Mac flicked off her attempt to divert the conversation. "Where did you get that phone?" His voice held a dangerous edge, and Layla blinked up at him. Her pullover trailed from around her waist, the sleeve dragging in the dust. It flared the panels of her blazer into a disembodied skirt. Her shoulders tightened and lifted towards her ears.

"Tilly got it for me," she said in a whisper. "She's amazing at getting things for people." She shot a sideways look at Keira and the other girl's lips flattened into a line.

"Tilly?" Mac's voice wavered. "Tilly Rae?" Dread fingers snaked around his heart and squeezed. A buzzing echoed in his head and he couldn't locate its origin. As he paused, Layla hurried away as though afraid Mac might confiscate the phone.

"Bye Mac." Like tributaries, the other girls turned and followed her, still skipping and still singing the hideous chant. Mac watched as they caught up to Layla. But she kept her neck stiff to prevent her from looking back at him. Keira slipped her arm through Layla's and bounced along next to her.

He recognised the buzz as his processors amplifying the throb of his pulse and relaying it to his eardrums. His chest tightened and pain shot into his left arm. For a moment, he panicked, convinced of a heart attack, until he glanced down and saw his balled fists. He blew out a ragged breath and forced his left fingers to release, easing the pain and numbness rampaging through his wrist. But the awful facts remained.

Tilly had given Layla Miss Andrews' phone.

Tilly, who'd also procured a new SIM card and a case for the one found at the crime scene. The same Tilly who'd encouraged him to use it.

The memory of the satisfied flush from their tryst washed from his system like broken glass. Instead, a bitter aftertaste filled his mouth.

Mac didn't see Tilly until the next free period. He strode towards the common room door with his head bowed and his mind whirring. He jumped as she dragged on his hand and pulled him to a halt.

"Careful!" Syd Ross admonished them as he tripped over her trailing rucksack. Her threatening look made him think better of picking a fight he couldn't win.

"We need to talk." Mac's green eyes flashed as he leaned close to hiss at her. His breath mussed her black fringe with its force.

"Do you have any cash?" Tilly lowered her voice and glanced over his shoulder. Her gaze flickered as though she struggled to concentrate.

Mac shook his head, his jaw hanging slack. "Why?" A series of nasty possibilities ran through his addled mind. Was she asking him to pay for what he thought she'd freely given? He swallowed and Tilly snatched his right hand again and dragged him away from the fresh stream of classmates heading to the common room.

"I need cash. Quick!" A frenzied quality entered her tone. "Please. I'll explain everything once I've fixed things."

"Fixed what?" Mac pulled his hand away from her and shifted his rucksack from his shoulder to the floor. He dipped and retrieved his wallet from a hidden pocket inside the front seam. "I have ten dollars for emergencies." He lifted the note from the folds of the leather, blinking as Tilly snatched it from between his fingers. "What's happened?" He straightened and studied her with a fresh view. Terror backlit her flashing blue irises and her lower lip trembled. "Is it about the janitor's key?" He fell on the most logical explanation, offering her a lifeline.

She inhaled a ragged breath and her blouse buttons gaped across her chest. Mac caught sight of the black lacy bra beneath it and all sensible thought fled. "We could go to the cupboard," he whispered, his lips curving up in a smile. "You said it cost ten dollars." His suggestion provided a shock to his system as he heard the craving in his tone. One taste and he'd already become an addict.

"No. No." Tilly backed away from him. "You don't understand. I didn't know about it." She beat her temple with a balled fist, the ten dollar note fluttering with the motion. "That's not true. I knew about it, but I didn't realise it was there." Her chest hitched. "I'll fix it, I promise."

"Fix what?" Mac's brow knitted. He tucked his wallet back into his rucksack and closed the zipper. In all their shared schooling, he'd never witnessed her so lacking in composure. Lipstick seeped over one corner of her mouth and created a red stain against her cheek. Black curls tumbled from her usually immaculate pigtails. She backed away from him, her skirt swishing around her thighs. Mac's eyes widened as he worried about her lack of underwear.

Tilly blended into the surge of bodies, carried away from the common room like a speck on the tide. A spark flickered in the back of Mac's mind, banishing the insidious lust with a litany of unanswered questions.

He snatched up the only lifeline remaining to him.

He followed her, hanging back and lowering his head to avoid detection.

But it didn't matter, anyway. Tilly didn't once turn to look behind her. She left the main building and picked up speed, deviating left around the changing sheds and skirting the row of garages hugging the rugby field. Mac took care to follow at a distance, exercising caution at each junction and letting her get far enough ahead not to notice him.

He paused at the last corner with dread lodging like a brick in his stomach. Gulping air instead of swallowing caused him to smother a cough with his forearm. He pressed his lips against the cast, keeping his rucksack balanced over his other shoulder. Fearing he may lose Tilly, he pushed his head sideways to peer around the last building. Exaggerated care heightened his anxiety.

Their friendship stretched years behind him like a golden thread, a bright spot in his often silent world. Tilly paused by the equipment shed before rapping twice on the wooden door with her knuckles. A familiar click sounded, and the door opened outward.

Mac's heart shattered into a million tiny shards.

42

Relegation

"You feel sick?" Grant Simms waggled his eyebrows and rubbed his belly with his right hand. "I sympathise after spending a whole day with my face down the shitter." His eyes widened, and he wrinkled his nose. "Is it vomiting, or do you need to do a toilet swivel? I hated that part the most, the moment where you can't decide which one you'd rather clean off the walls."

"Just sick." Mac glanced through the window at Simms' waiting class. He chewed his lower lip and resented his need to run as far away from the school as possible. Tilly tilted her head sideways and stared at him through the glass, confused by his presence outside the lesson instead of in the seat beside her.

Grant Simms cast his eye over Mac's appearance, noting the clammy skin and the paleness of his complexion. He relented with a nod. "You look like crap, boy," he concluded. "I'll mark you absent. Go to the front office and get them to phone your mother. Tell them to call me if they don't believe you."

"Thanks." Mac's shoes dragged against the floor as he turned away. He hunched his shoulders as though in self-defence. His elbow ached from the dragging sensation caused by the cast, and he wished he'd accepted the cloth sling offered to him at the hospital. The safe world of MacGillivray Du Rose collapsed inwards as a vortex stripped away everything he knew about life.

The receptionist didn't believe him and forced him to wait while she phoned Simms. Mac sank into a hard chair and supported his cast across his thigh. Laughter issued from the headmaster's office, accompanied by the chink of glass. Genuine nausea roiled his guts as he pictured Tilly's interaction with the dark-haired boy at the equipment shed.

Mac hadn't heard his conversation with Tilly. He'd leaned down to listen to her, his brows knitted into a black line. One side of his mouth curved up in a sneer. Mac pressed himself against the wall and watched the unexpected transaction take place. He'd seen the boy before, but not for a long time. Two years younger, he'd disappeared into a young offender's institution a while ago. He plucked the ten-dollar note from Tilly's hand with ease and offered her a shallow nod in response. She'd continued speaking, her voice infused with the jerky timbre of panic.

Then, to Mac's horror, Tilly pressed herself against the boy's chest and wrapped her arms around his back. The tension in his spine slackened, and he kissed the top of her head and patted her shoulder in an awkward motion. She released him and took a step back, and he seemed relieved. He glanced to his left and Mac withdrew his head before the boy repeated the motion to his right.

Mac swore to himself and retreated, feeling he'd seen more than enough to create a disparaging picture of his relationship with Tilly. "Idiot!" he hissed to himself.

He'd retraced his footsteps as the bell rang, hiding in the toilets until the school grew quiet. But as he'd approached Simms' lesson, his nerve failed him and he bent double outside the door. A chance glance through the window had alerted the teacher and set them both on a convenient excuse for Mac's ready escape.

"I've phoned your mother." The receptionist called to Mac from behind the counter, her tone dismissive. "She's sending someone to fetch you. Do you need a bucket?"

Mac shook his head and closed his eyes. He remembered Hana saying she had a busy morning at the museum and prayed she didn't send his father. Hana would shower him with love and sympathy, but Logan could see straight through him. A few pointed questions would unpick him at the seams and he wasn't ready for the crushing of their sparkling illusion of him yet.

Mac dipped forward in the uncomfortable chair and gazed at his dusty shoes. He ached to turn off his processors but feared missing the arrival of his ride and appearing a fool in front of the receptionists. Laughter issued from the women in the office. Their joviality distracted them enough to make them miss Tilly's entrance into the foyer. She hoisted her purple rucksack on her shoulder and ducked into a crouch. A peculiar jutting stride carried her across the space and below the level of the counter. She knelt in front of Mac and peered up into his face. "I fixed it," she whispered. "You don't need to leave."

Mac snorted. He lifted his heels but didn't look at her. "Go away," he growled.

Tilly jerked as though she'd slapped him. Her lower lip folded beneath her teeth. "Why?" she pleaded. "Please, Macky. I got it wrong and I'm sorry." She balanced herself by resting a hand over his left knee, but her body still rocked with emotion. "I didn't know they'd added a camera to that cupboard too. I swear I wouldn't have taken you there if I'd known."

"Camera?" Mac inhaled, but the breath kept on filling his lungs. His chest locked and he couldn't release the air. Bright spots swam in front of his vision as panic sent a flare of heat to his head while an eerie chill engulfed his feet. "Camera?" he repeated. A memory of the winking red light in the corner completed the picture. Someone had filmed them.

Genuine sickness bit into Mac's gut and he groaned. Tilly paled and stared up at him. Her cheek indented as she gnawed on its tender insides until blood speckled on her tongue. "I'm so sorry," she repeated. "But I fixed it. I paid them to remove the footage, and he promised he'd do it right then." Her chest hitched and her soft skin flushed with a rash fuelled by anxiety.

"Who?" Mac ground out the question from between gritted teeth. "Your boyfriend?"

Tilly blinked up at him, her brows knitted into a V of confusion. "My boyfriend?" She shook her head and frowned. The rash pressed along her jawline and into her cheeks. "You followed me?" Her lips drew back to reveal her even teeth. A snort of disdain issued from between them. "Right." She rose, listing to one side as she let go of his knee. Mac watched her rub her fingers on her tartan skirt as though ridding them of a contamination. She took a step back from him and he quailed against the fury backlighting her blue irises. "I really got this wrong, didn't I?" she snarled. "You'll never trust me, and I'll never be good enough for someone like you." She shrugged and hoisted her rucksack higher on her shoulder. A pencil protruded from a frayed edge and threatened to make its escape as she half turned from Mac. Her parting arrow drove a path through his hardening heart, burying itself as far as the fletching. "I guess you've had what you wanted," she spat. "See you around."

Mac rose, his right hand lifted in protest. She'd called him out as an asshole and it pained him how neatly the label fitted his behaviour. But as Tilly flounced from the lobby, Toby blasted through the front doors and made a beeline for Mac. "Sorry," he growled. "Your ma sent me. Accident on the expressway stopped me arriving earlier."

The receptionist rose and waved a tatty exercise book towards him. Toby winced, and his eyes narrowed. "Can you do that?" he hissed at Mac, a groan in his throat.

"Yeah." Mac walked towards the counter, but his body remained turned to the internal door through which Tilly exited. He knew he should go after her, but couldn't summon the right words to correct her awful impression of him. She thought he'd used her for sex. It left him questioning his motives and hating himself more.

Mac signed himself out of school, but the receptionist kicked up a fuss at Toby's reluctance to touch the well-used biro. "We need the adult's signature," she maintained, glaring at the stockman from behind lenses like milk bottle bottoms. "It's the rules."

Toby grimaced, but obeyed. He seized the pen and added a squiggle in the box, which Mac indicated for him. His lips puckered with concentration and he laboured over his mark. Hana had taught many of the farm workers basic literacy, but Toby had declined. He'd spent too many years faking an understanding of Logan's handwritten lists. Mac also wondered if he feared that spending large tracts of time in Hana's company would only fuel his crush even more.

Toby laid the pen on the counter with painstaking reverence. Then he turned to Mac. "What's up with you then?" he demanded, reasserting his superiority through smack talk. "You look a bit shite."

Mac ignored him and returned to his seat for his rucksack. His pulse had slowed enough to allow him thinking time. Toby shrugged and strode out to the car park, and Mac followed. Too many questions required answers he didn't possess. At the back of everything lay Miss Andrews' burned body. He'd distressed her with his unwanted advances, and now he'd screwed up his budding relationship with Tilly. Mac leaned his temple against the side window and closed his eyes, balancing his cast across his thigh. After a few attempts at conversation, Toby realised Mac had deactivated his processors.

They made the journey to the mountain in blessed silence.

43

TACKLE

Toby dropped Mac at home and returned to his work. The teenager mooched around the empty house, feeling more lost than ever. The kitchen counter looked a mess, which surprised him. Logan's neat freak tendencies called for order and calm. Mac lifted a tin of peaches which lay on its side. The label clung to one ridged side, the glue dried and useless. "Out of date," he murmured. Closer inspection indicated a clear-out of old food from the back of the pantry, and he lost interest. His mother would deal with it. Pulling out the rubbish drawer he saw what had halted her. Full. A packet of broken biscuits balanced on top of a bag of dusty looking oats. White dots seethed behind the plastic wrapper, which explained why she hadn't opened it or added the contents to the compost. He pushed the drawer closed, reluctant to be the one to carry the sack to the wheely bin outside and mess around replacing it.

Mac changed into jeans and a tee shirt before going into the makeshift paddock to see Sassy. She grazed without concern as he braced his arms across her spine and rested his forehead against her ribs. Remembering Edin's criticism of his preferred silence, he activated his processors and allowed the bush sounds to percolate his brain. She'd accused him of shutting her out and he forced himself to acknowledge his tendency to do exactly that. He missed things. Too many things. Perhaps if he'd disconnected less, he'd have seen Tilly's mischief making before he fell for it.

"I hate this cast," he murmured to no one. The cackle of a tui bird provided the only response. He topped up their water and added two more slices of hay. Sonny shuffled through the strands as though each one might hold a unique taste.

The trilling of the landline in the hallway dragged him back to reality. Mac hated answering it, but when the caller persisted, he relented. He held the handset to his ear. "Ma?" he said, expecting to hear Hana's voice. Instead, Alfie's coarse tones grated across the short distance from the hotel.

"I need you to fetch me," he growled.

"Sorry, what?" Mac frowned in confusion, imagining he'd misheard.

"Get me!" Alfie barked. "I want to go somewhere."

Mac squeezed his eyes closed and gave his head a shake. "Poppa, I've come home because I'm sick. And I have a broken wrist. How am I supposed to get you?"

Swearing issued from Alfie's side of the call. "Bloody hell!" he cursed. "Do I need to do everything myself?"

"I don't understand what you want." Mac sank onto the low bench containing his school shoes. Edin would add hers later when she returned home, lifting the squeaky lid and dropping them onto his without care.

Alfred humphed and released a heavy breath into the phone. Mac jerked and pulled the receiver away from his ear. "Fine!" the old man grumbled. "I'll grab whatever I can find and meet you at the fork in half an hour. Be ready."

"No! Poppa, you can't drive. And Ma's not home yet. I'm sick." He finished his sentence with the realisation Alfie had ended the call.

Mac contemplated phoning his mother at the museum. Failing health and terrible eyesight made Alfie's potential journey hazardous. But Tilly's ringing endorsement of his poor character still carved a wound in his chest. He foresaw an early confession of everything to his mother while he felt so vulnerable and dreaded it with all his being. Avoiding the inevitable, he pushed his feet into cowboy boots, locked up the house and cut through the bush to the fork in the road. A glance at his watch highlighted his need to hurry. He clutched his cast to his ribs and picked up speed to a steady downhill jog. The guttural rumble of a quad bike echoed through the canopy. He cursed his inability to move any faster.

A narrow ledge worn bare by bush creatures took Mac along a treacherous ridge to meet the lane. He arrived with sweat beading his forehead and curling the auburn hair at his nape. A damp circle under his armpits joined a line along his spine. He clasped his cast in his right hand and burst from the tree line in a foul mood. "What the hell?" he demanded.

Alfie baulked at the sight of him and flattened his lips into a line. "Your ma told Leslie you were at home. And she's out at the supermarket, so we need to go now."

"Go where?" Mac demanded. He concentrated to avoid misunderstanding Alfred's reply. As he dropped his right hand to his side, it contacted the outline of the phone in his jeans pocket. "I should call Nonie Leslie," he grumbled. "She'll talk some sense into you." He fingered the rectangular edge and realised he didn't have her number on the borrowed device.

"Help me off this." Alfred turned his body in the seat and pitched forward, only just waiting for Mac to dash around the bike to assist. His fragile frame clattered against the teenager's chest, and Mac grunted as his wrist protested.

He braced himself for Alfie's weight, shocked at the delicacy of his bones and the lightness of a man who'd once mustered cattle. The old man's clothes hung off him and a musty scent issued from between his lips. Mac only needed his right arm to set his grandfather on the sloping lane and help him around the vehicle. "Where are we going?" he asked, keeping his tone light. A moment's thought painted an adventure with Alfie with the colours of light relief. Someone had filmed at school, having sex with a classmate in a janitor's cupboard. If Tilly had failed to get it wiped for the price of a measly ten dollars, he'd need to confess to his parents before they found out for themselves. But the temporary distraction with his poppa promised a fortifying delay.

"Reuben's place." Alfie grunted as he settled in the passenger seat. "You're driving. I can't see the edge of the road."

Mac's eyes widened, and he gulped. A mental picture of the old man careening off a cliff silenced him for a moment. "Where did you get the key to the bike?" he asked.

Alfie raised his chin and used a crabbed hand to push his battered cowboy hat further back on his egg-shaped head. "It had the keys in it. Toby hopped off to go into the hotel, so I stole it."

Mac groaned. "Poppa! You'll get us both into trouble."

Alfie cackled like a hyena. "Come on, boy! I've asked everyone to take me up here, but they won't. This is my last chance to pay my respects to my brother. Do this one thing for me?" His rheumy grey irises sparkled as he gazed at Mac.

The teenager shrugged. "It won't be pretty or safe." He raised his left arm to display the grungy cast.

Alfie winked at him. "You'll do better with one arm and two eyes than I did with arthritis and cataracts." His expression fell. "I scratched your pa's truck." His lips twisted. "So, at least now he has something to remember me."

Mac's eyes bugged. "You drove the quad into Pa's truck?"

He glanced at the wheel arch in front of Alfie's feet and winced at the streak of red paint interspersed with the bike's factory green. Slippers covered his poppa's feet, and he shook his head. The afternoon got stranger with each passing minute.

But a tide of worry chased him like an inevitable tsunami and Mac's courage failed him. He hopped into the driver's seat and drove one handed, pointing the quad bike and its jittery passenger towards the fork in the road.

44

TEAM

Mac's hasty exit from the house meant he rode hatless. The sun took full advantage of his auburn curls to heat his scalp and give him a headache. It forced him to release the handlebar at intervals and wipe his arm across his sweating brow. At those moments, he used his knees to keep the quad bike on its correct trajectory.

Alfie leaned back against the seat and observed his surroundings from beneath his bushy brows. His fingers fidgeted in his lap. "Your pa did a great job paving this," he commented, as Mac steered the bike up the steep slope. He grunted in reply, knowing the context but not connected to the emotion fused with the popular tourist attraction. Alfie sighed and wrinkled his nose. "I loved Logan like my own boy," he mused. "But it's a wicked thing I did to Reuben." He leaned sideways and patted Mac's strong thigh. "Take care of your seed, son. You don't want some angry tāne like me denying you access to your own blood." He hawked and spat from the moving vehicle as though the misery filled his toothless mouth. "Look what I ended up with." His head shook from side to side, his skull shrunken beneath a hat which once fitted his broadness with ease. "Serves me right, too. The whatura will gather when I'm gone, Macky."

"Vultures?" Mac's brows knitted, and he turned the quad onto the last portion of the track. The maze flooded their view, a viridescent block of conifers. The verdant wall stood out against the lime and emerald of the bush to form both a blight and a thing of beauty. "What vultures?" Mac glanced at Alfie, but he'd lost the old man's attention. A curious light filled his eyes as he gazed on the monument to his failure as a husband and a brother. A single tear trickled over the crevices of his sunken cheeks.

"I haven't come up here for too long," he admitted. His shoulders slumped. "I miss them all, Mama and Miriam. But most of all, Reuben." Mac's lips parted at his grandfather's distress. He realised in that instant that he'd made yet another grave error of judgement. He should have refused Alfred's command and instead called Logan.

Coulda, woulda, shoulda. It formed the painful theme tune for his life.

"Let's go back now, Poppa," he urged. The quad bike's motor rumbled beneath them, but Alfie shook his head.

"Kāore." Alfie provided an instant refusal. His insubstantial slippers shuffled in the footwell of his seat. "I need to make peace with my family. Reuben took my wife, but I kept his son. I left her no option but to choose me." He stared down at his writhing fingers. "I've had a long while to think about my behaviour, Macky. And there's no doubt now that I committed the greater crime. Logan deserved what I took away from him." Alfred's eyelashes fluttered over his sparkling irises and Mac swallowed in fear. He leaned forward and touched his grandfather's knee.

"Pa loves you, Poppa. You raised him and he's grateful."

Alfie shook his head, and the tears streamed with more constancy. His sallow skin shone with the wetness of his regrets.

"I failed him years before Reuben's boys blurted the truth, Macky. He watched his mother die in the fire, but to discover he'd lost his father, too. It's more than any soul can bear." Alfred rested his right hand over his heart, the twisted fingers forming a reluctant fist. "Oh, he tried, son." Mac's lips and tongue formed denials which emerged as a series of tuts and a futile shake of his head. Alfie waved them away. "When did you ever hear him call me Pa?"

Mac's shoulders slumped. He didn't speak aloud the answer. Never. Not in his lifetime.

Alfie's chest hitched. "Your ma anchored Logan," he sobbed. "She saved us all. Never underestimate the value of a good woman, Macky. His anger would have taken over. I saw it in his eyes. He wanted to burn the lot to the ground, carve it up and sell our legacy to the highest bidder. She stopped him. She made him fight." He edged sideways in his seat, his slippers dangling over the edge of the bike. He threw his next comment over his shoulder. "I love my wāhine. Make sure she knows that, won't you, boy?"

"Yes sir," Mac whispered. He picked at the frayed edge of his cast and observed the old man's bowed head. The precious hat brim lifted and fell in a light breeze, as if wishing to escape Alfred's wispy skull. Mac shivered and forced himself to banish the heaviness which clothed them in sadness. He leapt from the bike and strode to Alfred's side, offering his hand to assist him.

His poppa wobbled next to him, all his energy expended on the unwise mission. Mac gathered his elbow into his good arm and led him to the shadowy entrance of the maze. The old man reached out and stroked the information board, which tourists stopped to read before dashing into the passages and cul de sacs. They culminated in a central courtyard bearing a statue of a woman releasing a dove in her raised hands. Miriam Du Rose. "Read it to me," Alfie commanded. He used his free hand to scratch at his watering eyes.

If he'd expected some outing of his mistakes in a written form, he found himself without cause for the rebuke of strangers. The words, crafted by Hana almost two decades earlier, showed restraint and compassion. Mac cleared his throat and read the gentle sentences, imagining his mother pouring over and second guessing each word.

'The planting of this maze commemorates the fire which took the lives of Miriam Du Rose and her brother-in-law on Christmas Eve of 2004. Reuben Henare Jacob D'Arcy Du Rose built the original rimu homestead in 1971. Parts of the exposed foundations are evident within the structure of the maze, which was designed to embrace the memory of our lost family. We constructed benches throughout the maze from the remaining roof timbers collected after the fire.

Our whānau love and eternally miss both Miriam and Reuben.'

A Māori translation occupied the left column and Mac wondered why he'd reached automatically for the English version. He started to read it in Alfred's preferred language, but the old man waved a hand to silence him. "I heard it the first time," he whispered. He turned his feet towards the yawning mouth of the maze and Mac locked his knees in fear.

"It takes half an hour to walk to the centre." His voice wobbled with the thoughts he managed to suppress. Though he knew the twists and turns by heart, he sensed Alfred wouldn't manage both the walk to and from the statue commemorating his wife. Flustered and filled with misgiving, Mac floundered as Alfred's slippers took him nearer the entrance. "Please, Poppa," he begged. "I'll bring you again another day. Toby can drive us in one of the Jeeps and I'll push you anywhere you want to go in your wheelchair." The stupidity of the promise returned to bite him as he glanced down at his useless left arm.

It struck him then how silent and deserted the maze seemed. With the campground filled with families snatching the last rays of summer, the grassy area should have teamed with parents chasing toddlers as they crowded to read Hana's careful description. A convention of Catholic priests on a retreat filled the rooms of the hotel. Mac had seen them moving in silent groups or sitting in deep contemplation in Miriam's rose garden. Their stark clerical uniform jarred against the unruly, natural surroundings, like smooth pebbles teetering at the edge of a waterfall. Intrepid hotel guests always walked up to the maze. "Where is everyone?" he demanded, spinning on the scrubby grass until he left divots.

Alfie stroked the fringed edges of the nearest conifer, his fingers clamped into a clubbed fist by the arthritis which twisted his frame into a reluctant pretzel. "They're not coming," he croaked. The sentence ended in a cough. "I shut the bottom gate and hung the sign. They think it's closed." His slippered toes edged towards the threshold of the first of many passages. One more step and Mac would lose the battle.

"No." He reached Alfred's side and clamped his good hand over the thin shoulder. "I can't manage it today." He lifted his cast and shook his head. "Ma will go nuts. Anyway, it's after lunch and I need my painkillers."

To Mac's great relief, Alfred nodded and shuffled a half step backward to meet him. The old man dropped his hands as though in defeat and the steepled conifer fronds pinged back into place. "I'll wait for him here then," he said. His body dipped as his knees buckled and the suddenness of it took Mac by surprise. His reactions weren't fast enough, and Alfred hit the baked earth with a sickening thud.

45

Cross-Over

"Poppa! You need to let me get help!" The awful tightness in Mac's throat caused his sentence to end in a strangled squeak. He fell to his knees and the hand he laid on Alfie's shoulder trembled, the fingers splayed and rigid. Mac gulped for air, but the old man reached out and patted his forearm.

"Nobody else," he breathed with a sigh. "Just you, son. Let me be, will ya?" His battered cowboy hat slithered from his wispy head as he lay in the grass. It rolled behind him and cast a shadow over a patch of crumpled daisies. They swayed as though drunk, their petals bobbing and confused.

Alfie closed his eyes and a single tear rolled down his cheek. "No tarawewehi," he whispered. "I'm not scared. You mustn't be either." The clawed fingers of his left hand scrabbled in the dust beneath him. "I needed to come. My brother breathed his last here and I owe him this much. Apart from besting him as the elder son, I always followed in his stead, Macky." A smile parted his lips and despite the bare gums from missing teeth, his countenance held the spark of a much younger man. "Reuben Du Rose," he said with a sigh. "He even beat me to Hawaiki, the bugger. Couldn't let me die first and have just one more victory over him." His chin wobbled, and a moan escaped his chest. Rigid veins stood out on his neck as the palsy subsided. "He took my wife, but I forgive him, see? She belonged to him first and I shouldn't have done it. I need to make my peace."

Mac shuffled beneath him so that he cradled the old man's head in his lap. Alfie's eyelashes fluttered as he searched for his borrowed grandson and then gave a weak smile on seeing him in his peripheral vision. His vibrant irises seemed to shift and change in a kaleidoscope of stormy grey and glittering diamonds. His gaze moved in and out of focus.

"I need to call for help," Mac whimpered. He leaned over Alfie's face, rounding his shoulders into a protective arc of misery. "Please, Poppa. Let me call my pa."

Alfie inhaled a long breath, which stuttered into his lungs. "I don't need him," he croaked. "Just you. It's how I wanted it."

Mac closed his eyes and tipped his head to face the sun. It warmed his freckled cheeks as though offering consolation. He recognised too late his own naivety. Alfie had engineered the final visit to the maze. Mac's absence from school had played into it with unintended perfection. A tremulous voice in his head dismissed the notion, ridiculing the possibility of Alfred knowing with certainty the time and date of his exit from life. Mac overruled the logic, acknowledging the truth in his heart. "I don't know what to do," he confessed. Tears issued from his eyes with the ferocity of sparks.

Alfred murmured deep in his throat. "Just sit with me a while, boy," he asked. "I'd like for you to meet Reuben." His words trailed into a whisper. The processor in Mac's right ear set up a high-pitched whistle which cut through his brain as a distraction. He ached to switch it off, but dare not shift a muscle. The gravity of the moment wrapped itself around his shoulders like an iron jacket, restricting his movements and trapping him in place. Alfie's round head nestled in the cradle between Mac's left calf and right knee, his breathing laboured.

The boy kept one hand on his poppa's shoulder, the cast solid against the fragility of the old man's bones. He dug in his jeans for his phone, unable to free it without straightening his right leg. Any attempt at movement raised a gasp of discomfort from Alfred's lips.

"My pa's hat," Alfie whispered. His right hand patted the earth without effect.

Mac reached behind him and dragged the cowboy hat through the daisies by its brim. "It's here," he said, his voice ragged. His wrist protested as he lifted it and held it before Alfie's face.

"Yours." Alfred reached up and batted it away, giving the precious heirloom without fuss. "For you."

Mac shook his head from side to side. His teeth chattered in his jaw. "No, Poppa. It's yours. You'll wear it again."

Alfie smiled and sighed. The look of contentment remained as his parting expression, disturbed only by the rise of his bushy eyebrows. "Miriam's wedding ring is hidden in the blue pot on the roof. I want you to have it. And tell your pa I'm sorry. For everything." He lowered his chin and stared into the distance. His irises glittered like a calm lake. Then, "You came," he said, his watery gaze fixing on a point near the entrance of the maze. "I hoped you would. I couldn't get to her statue."

"Poppa!" Hysteria laced Mac's voice. "Who are you talking to?" He squinted through the dappled rays of sunlight which kissed the fringes of the shorn conifers. He saw no one.

A bark of laughter broke from Alfie's chest. It rocked his frail body and sent a shiver through Mac's legs. He cackled as though at a joke only he'd heard, and his chin rose and fell in an enthusiastic nod. "Āe!" His tone held jubilation. "And you brought Mama!"

Delirious. The word popped into Mac's mind and offered comfort alongside recrimination. He'd let his poppa become overheated and dehydrated. A glance at the old man's crinkled brown forehead showed no sign of sweat. Mac turned his torso to take in the idle quad bike containing Toby's familiar drink bottle.

His brain busied itself with strategies. "I'll fetch the water, Poppa," he promised. He stripped off his tee shirt and bunched it into a hasty pillow. "Let me put this under you. I'll call Papa. He'll help."

Mac eased his legs from beneath Alfie's head, hissing as the old man's skull bumped against his cradling palm. His wrist protested as he used his left hand to push the wadded garment under Alfie's neck and lowered the man's head onto it. Free, he scrambled backwards and onto his knees. Alfred's lips moved as though in response, and Mac pushed himself upright and ran to the quad bike. As his feet punched the dry earth, he dug in his pocket for his phone. He transferred it into his left hand and skidded next to the quad. With his right hand, he hefted Toby's water bottle. It clattered against the bike's chassis, releasing a metallic clang at the same moment his wrist gave a zap of pain. The phone flew from his fingers and landed in the dirt.

Mac dropped the bottle and concentrated his energy on calling for help. He wiped the dusty phone on his knees and peered at the screen.

"One bar!" His wail of dismay vied with a lack of surprise. Parts of the mountain fell in the lee of the mobile phone mast and attracted little signal. It felt like Fate's twist of the knife in his gut, though nothing had changed in the signal's weak boost since yesterday or the day before that. And worse, Tilly had only entered the numbers she knew into his contacts. She didn't know Logan's.

Mac dialled his mother's number and activated the speaker, tapping his boot against the earth with every passing second as he prayed for a connection. The phone didn't echo a ring tone and returned an error message as the call dropped. Rationalising the futility of labouring over it, Mac jabbed his thumb over the keypad and typed out a message. It comprised two words. He prayed the only bar of reception would carry his stunted plea.

'*Help. Maze.*'

Then he carted the bottle to his stricken poppa and fought the catch to release the precious liquid.

Though the greyness of Alfred Du Rose's complexion betrayed the truth, Mac's mind dismissed it. He knelt on the ground next to him and fumbled with the bottle's shiny lid. Droplets sputtered from it as he yanked it free and tossed it onto the grass. Knowing he didn't have enough control to deliver the water with his left hand, he faced the more painful option. He used the weak fingers to raise Alfie's head, a burning sensation searing the healing joint with every centimetre gained. His breath emerged in quick gasps until the old man's head rose enough to allow Mac to fold his legs once again beneath him.

Alfie's head lolled in his lap and Mac struggled to angle the bottle. Water pooled behind the old man's lips and ran down his cheek and into his fluffy ears. But Alfred's mouth remained immobile. He made no attempt to swallow or choke.

Still not wanting to acknowledge the reality of his situation, Mac contemplated performing the kiss of life. He knew how to do it, but doubted his broken wrist would provide the required pressure against the thin chest. An echo of Alfred's words played on a loop in his mind. He'd wanted no one else, just Mac. Anger vied with dismay. Why would he condemn his grandson to this horror?

Still refusing to admit defeat, Mac shuffled from beneath Alfred's head. It rolled like a bowling ball, heavier without life. He knelt over the prone body, his brain sifting past instructions about administering CPR. "Remove the shirt from under his head," he told himself in a hiss. Shaking fingers tugged it free. Alfred's head lolled to the side and faced him, the eyes half open to betray their lifelessness. Mac knew it was futile, but still needed to try. He positioned himself and tilted Alfred's chin high enough to reveal the bristles he'd missed that morning when shaving. His chest hitched and tears coursed unacknowledged down Mac's cheeks as he began the revival process. To his own cost.

46

SHUTOUT

They found him that way an hour later.

Mac crouched over the old man's body, the edge of his cast stained with his own blood. He'd lost all feeling in his left hand, imagining the stitches long since bursting within their fibreglass covering. The sun beat down on his bare back, infusing his skin with the blush of its eager kisses. And Alfie slept, his lips a bluish circle against his waxen grey complexion.

Mac didn't hear them. His processors lay in the dirt where he'd thrown them, unable to cope with the peaceful sounds of birdsong and rustling grass as his world collapsed.

"Leave him, son." Logan dismounted from David Allen's horse and pressed a hand against Mac's shoulder. Mac started and read his lips, but ignored him. Hana slipped from her borrowed mare, her steps cautious as she eyed her son in his distress. She still wore the pretty dress but had added jodhpur boots. Her gaze flicked to her husband as he tried to persuade their son to cease his futile ministrations.

Dirt and sweat streaked Mac's torso and face. He'd bestowed every spare breath on Alfred and kept only just enough for himself. Exhaustion dulled his eyes, and he moved with a heavy, laboured action. He used his left hand to tilt Alfie's slack neck for the millionth time and prepared to fill the old man's lungs again.

"Stop!" Logan's right hand performed a chopping action over his left palm. Mac shook him off and continued to shuffle towards Alfred's face, dust coughing up from beneath his knees. His thighs ached, his calves past the point of numbness, and he listed to one side, clattering against Logan's shins. Strong fingers slipped beneath Mac's armpits and hauled him away.

"No!" he managed, his protest weak. His heels gouged ruts in the dry grass as Logan dragged him. Mac glanced up in time to witness his mother's first grief. She knelt next to Alfred and lifted her fingers to stroke the old man's brow. When she dipped her face to his, Mac experienced a sense of relief that she'd pick up the fight where he no longer could. He expected her to continue his efforts to revive his poppa.

Rage replaced the fragile hope when he saw her lips contact the old man's cheek in a silent kiss goodbye. Her body shook, and she smoothed her fingers over Alfred's crabbed hands and lifted them to rest across his stomach. She didn't even try to save him.

Mac wrestled in Logan's grip. He dug his heels into the ground and halted their backward movement. Vibration reached him through the earth, the steady beat of more hooves arriving to witness his failure. Mac twisted his body until the action forced Logan to release him. Still, his father did it with gentleness, holding him until he'd found stability on his backside. Mac's body ached as he pushed himself to his feet. The numbness of his mind spread over him like an infection. "You can't stop!" he yelled at his father. Spit flew from between his lips, though his mouth felt dry. "Help him!"

Logan shook his head and lifted his arms towards his son. "He's gone," he mouthed and Mac didn't need his processors to feel the pain in the words. "Let him be." An eerie calm shrouded

Logan, and Mac mistook it for a lack of caring. The rage built into a force he'd never experienced. Though he listed and aimed wrong, no stability in his stance or power in his fist, he punched his father square in the face.

Logan recoiled, the mask of control falling just long enough for Mac to register his father's dismay and disappointment. Other hands clasped Mac's shoulders from behind and held him upright after the mistimed lurch. He expected Logan to knock him out cold, wishing for the nothingness with all his heart. But his father raised the back of his right hand to his lip and inspected the blood which trickled across his knuckles. Then he stepped up close to his son's face, his eyes narrowed and the mask back in place. He mouthed the words, ensuring no error in Mac's understanding. "I'll give you that one," he said through clenched teeth. "But that's your best and final." He jerked his head to whoever stood behind Mac, and they moved him away from the scene. Rough fingers dug into the centre of his spine and forced him to walk.

Mac glanced back only once at Alfred. He caught his mother's eye and recoiled. Tears snaked down her cheeks and her fingers still rested over his poppa's hands. But horror at his actions faced him from her emerald irises and, despite the heat, it chilled him to the bone.

Mac spotted his processors in the grass and dipped to collect them. He jammed them into his jeans pocket before retrieving Alfred's hat from the ground next to them. "It's mine!" he growled at his father. "He gave it to me." He swallowed, unable to tell his father Alfie had also bequeathed Miriam's wedding ring to him. The notion seemed too ridiculous. He couldn't picture himself on one knee in a crowd, holding the ring in his fingers and readying himself for rejection. Even if he turned off his processors, his lip-reading skills would relay the murmurs of hilarity from anyone watching. Alfie had wasted the gift on him.

So he sat the battered cowboy hat over his auburn hair and forced his feet to carry him, staggering, away from his family.

47

Pitch

Toby shoved Mac towards the quad bike and waited until he'd settled on the passenger side. With an upward jerk of his chin at Logan, he jumped into the driver's seat and fired the engine. Numbness infused Mac's blood as the stockman bore him away from the tragic scene. Toby left his horse standing with the others, her mane lifting in the light breeze as she tore at scrubby shoots.

At the first fork in the narrow lane, Mac leaned across and tugged Toby's sleeve. "Take me home," he ordered.

The stockman's lips flattened into a disapproving line and he shook his head. "No," he mouthed. He jerked his head towards Mac and lifted his left index finger to touch his own ear. "Put your things in," he said.

Mac resisted. Inviting sound into the situation would wake a flood of other senses he couldn't deal with right then. The silence helped him to stay one step from the edge of misery. He knew it would come, but fought to hold it at arm's length. He closed his eyes. One more minute's peace.

But the image of Alfie's prone body seemed imprinted on the inside of his lids, as clear and hopeless as if he still knelt beside him in the dirt. "Home!" he shouted. A craving for Sassy's warm, grassy scent called like an invitation in the back of his brain.

Toby's involuntary jerk indicated the accidental pitch and hysteria contained in Mac's command. Again, he shook his head and jabbed a finger at his ear.

Twisted ferns and leaning punga trees flashed past on the dangerous downhill slalom. Mac's mind sought to distract him with the familiar spelling. *Punga*. A bastardisation of the Māori word ponga, it had become endemic to the nation's vocabulary. He hated it. He hated everything, and the realisation closed around his head like a knitted balaclava. Most of all, he hated himself.

Toby kept the quad bike moving at speed, familiar enough with the landscape to make the journey with his eyes closed. Mac sensed he knew if he slowed even a little, he'd lose his passenger in a dangerous leap from within his control. As the first of the farm gates appeared, Mac glanced down at the cast laid in his lap, his eyes widening at the sight of the blood soaking into his jeans. Toby drew the bike to a skidding stop and lifted his index finger, warning Mac not to move. Sympathy flooded his expression and his face lost its customary hardness as he pointed at the blood. "Yeah," he mouthed. "That's why."

"What happens now?" Mac demanded. The vibration of his voice through his chest betrayed its lacklustre note.

Toby pointed again to his ears and turned to unlatch the gate. A knot of dappled mares lifted their heads at the jangle of the chain and squeak of the hinges. They turned their bodies as one, stomachs rounded with late foals. Curiosity pricked their ears, and hooves dragged across the ground as they trudged to investigate the disturbance.

Toby drove the quad bike through the gap and leapt off to close the gate behind him. Mac pressed his processors back into place behind his ears, alarmed by the crimson hue of the blood and the threat of more surgery. Patting his pockets, he realised he'd left his phone somewhere on the mountain in his haste. The horror seeped through his bones and chilled his marrow.

He let Toby take his arm after stopping the quad bike at the bottom of the hotel steps, his mute acceptance sudden and alarming. The stockman frowned at the shiver which rocketed through Mac's body. He slipped an arm around his waist for support as they trudged through the main doors and turned right towards Logan's office.

48

GOALKEEPER

David Allen appeared moments later, the local medic trailing behind him. Dr Seuli's heavy black bag preceded him into the room, his rotund body negotiating the door and then David's statuesque frame. "I'm very busy this morning," he chirruped. "What's this all about?" His eyes widened at the sight of Mac seated on Logan's couch. "Oh," he said, eyeing the blood staining the teenager's jeans. "I think you need an ambulance."

Toby's features set into spiky ridges as he reacted to the doctor's attitude. "Just look at him," he growled.

The doctor fluttered his eyelids, clearly reluctant to find himself back in Du Rose territory after suggesting its mistress had mental issues almost two decades earlier.

"Why him?" David jerked his thumb at the doctor's profile. "Isn't there someone else?"

"The hotel receptionist called the medical centre," Toby replied. He moved across the rug to station himself beside Mac, his arms folded and his stance threatening. "You're a doctor," he stated. "So do some doctoring."

Dr Seuli sighed and accepted his fate. He knelt before Mac and released the catch, which held his bag shut. "I saw in your notes you'd broken your wrist. The discharge notice came through from the hospital." With both hands, he turned the cast over with exaggerated care. "Did you fall again?"

"Poppa's dead." Mac's tongue tripped over the words. "You should take care of him first."

"They're bringing him off the mountain." Toby tilted his head to observe the doctor's shiny brogues and immaculate trousers. The crease appeared as sharp as a knife's edge. "Take care of Mac." He raised an eyebrow at David and the other man shrugged.

Dr Seuli became all business as he tended to Mac. "Let's work out where the blood is coming from." He peered into the end of the cast and frowned. "I need to get this off. Do you have a multi-tool handy? Something with an oscillating blade." A click sounded as David left the room. Toby remained, arms folded and his expression serious.

Mac closed his eyes and concentrated on the hiss of air molecules and the blood rushing through his eardrums. The doctor cleared his throat a few times as he wiped blood from Mac's fingers and tutted.

Within minutes, David returned, his breathing fast enough to suggest he'd run to the equipment shed and back again. Strands of hay cascaded from his boots and littered the rug. He leaned across to give the tool to the doctor, his work-roughened fingers a stark contrast to the doctor's soft hand. The machine's whirring fizzed through Mac's processors, and he winced. Dr Seuli's hand shook as he lifted the spinning blade to meet the cast.

"Give it here!" Toby snapped. He snatched it and knelt beside Mac. In seconds, the cast lay splayed like the hull of a ship. He'd made two cuts in the fibreglass and cracked it open like an egg before lifting out the loose portion. Mac gazed down at his ruined wrist and his lower lip folded beneath his teeth. "Shit!" Toby hissed. "Not keyhole surgery, then."

Mac held his breath at the sight of the long, ragged scar which began on his palm and snaked as far as the fading mark where his wristwatch should sit. Pink and raised, it appeared stark against his pale complexion.

"Emergency surgery is practical, not pretty," the doctor huffed. He swivelled on his heels and reached into his bag for more cleaning wipes. He set about expunging the blood from Mac's palm and wrist, the alcohol causing a painful, stinging sensation. "Ah," he sighed, relief in the single note. "The wounds are undamaged. Thank goodness. The cast rubbed on the tops of your fingers and excised the skin." He turned Mac's hand over without disturbing his wrist. "And look, it's done the same with your palm. You've grazed through to the fatty layers." His brown eyes blinked up at the teenager as he asked him, "How did it happen?"

"The kid did CPR on Mr Alfred." Toby answered for him, his lashes fluttering. "He didn't know."

Mac shifted his gaze from the wadded and bloody wipes littering the carpet, to rest on Toby's face. "Know what?" His voice croaked as he spoke. The memory of his futile efforts and resulting exhaustion returned as a floating image in his vision. It merged with the burning scent of Miss Andrews and caused a knot to form in his chest.

Dr Seuli's expression softened to one of kindness. He placed Mac's hand on his stained jeans with care. "DNR," he said, his tone gentle. "Mr Alfred didn't want anyone to resuscitate him."

Mac gulped and his chest hitched. His head shook from side to side in denial. Toby's firm hand landed on his shoulder as though to steady a helium balloon before it floated skyward. "We thought everyone knew, kid. Sorry." His voice held a soothing edge. "You keep turning off those hearing devices and we assume you know stuff. But in your mama's defence, she never expected you'd be the one with him when he passed."

Mac raised his free hand and dragged the battered cowboy hat from his head. It tumbled to the seat cushion next to him and he stared at its worn interior. The faded name, *H. Du Rose,* stared up at him from the seam, placed there by a shaky hand. Toby's fingers squeezed the ball of his shoulder in a comforting motion. "So, he gave you Henri's hat then, did he?"

Mac's slow nod involved his chin and little else. But he looked up at the gravity in Toby's voice. "You need to hide that when they all descend for his tangihanga. Michael Du Rose will snatch that off your head. That's for certain and make no mistake."

Mac's right hand closed around the brim and he dragged the battered offering against his ribs as though his uncle had appeared and lunged for it. A recriminating voice in his head told him it belonged to Tama as Alfred's first grandson. Mac adored Tama, but the thought of giving up the trophy pained him.

They'd come soon, as his poppa foretold. All the vultures descending for the slim pickings of an old man who lived on Logan Du Rose's benevolence. Mac shuddered and distracted himself by watching the doctor's ministrations. He placed antiseptic cream over the deep grazes on Mac's fingers and palm before covering them with gauze. Producing a metal splint from his bag, he used it to support the still healing break and wrapped Mac's forearm and wrist in a tight bandage. "Don't get this wet," he warned. "And you need to contact your orthopaedic surgeon soon." He raised a fluffy brown eyebrow at Mac and lowered his voice. "When did you lose the feeling in your little finger?"

Mac blinked as though slapped. The familiar fear reared behind him to wrap its smothering arms around his head again. His lips moved, but no sound emerged. He saw Toby shift in his peripheral vision, his keen ears missing nothing. The doctor continued to wait, balanced on the toes of his shiny shoes. Mac needed to answer, and he cleared his throat first. "After the surgery," he murmured. "The little finger and the end of the next one." His chest locked. "Will they chop them off?"

"No, son." The doctor inhaled. "The circulation looks fine, but you have nerve damage. You could have more surgery?" His voice rose at the end of the sentence, his chin lowering at Mac's shake of his head. "Probably best. It might not work."

Mac closed his eyes against the terrible thing's release. It hung in the air after its accidental escape, and he sensed Toby's shock. He'd known since the moment he woke up after the surgery and allowed the fear to flex and grow within his chest. Miss Andrews' death had left more than an emotional mark on his soul. He'd lost the full use of his left hand. He'd done many things to distract himself, none of them good.

"You're a grand boy." The doctor surprised him by squeezing his shoulder as he heaved himself to his feet. He looked up to find the man smiling down at him. "You're a credit to your father. I'll phone the hospital and speak to the surgeon this afternoon." He tipped his wrist to peer at his watch. "Oh. Tomorrow. I'll do it first thing. He'll call for you, I'm sure."

With a last glance at Mac, he lifted his bag and turned towards David. "Can you take me to see Mr Alfred now, please?"

Their exit seemed to leave the air molecules clanging together in the silence which ensued. Mac ached to switch off his processors and plunge him back into the silence he craved. But Toby's loud ringtone stopped him and he watched as the stockman turned away to answer the call. "Yeah?"

Mac recognised his father's gravelly tones and winced. News of what he'd done would rip through the workforce like a wildfire. No one hit Logan Du Rose and walked away without consequences. He imagined the stockmen scorning his stupidity, sitting in their saddles and placing bets on what Logan would do next.

Mac shivered, his bare torso prickling with coolness in the dim office. The sunburn across his deltoid and trapezius muscles sapped his remaining energy and left him with a painful emptiness. He rose with trembling knees, taking Alfie's hat with him to the bathroom attached to the office. The latch clicked, the sound offering privacy to release the emotions bunching behind his eyes and tongue.

Mac found clean towels and flannels in the cupboard beneath the sink. He ran warm water and pumped hand soap into the basin, studying the bubbles as they formed beneath the tap. His one-handed wash expelled the blood and dust from his right hand and torso. His jeans sickened him and he stripped them off, adding his boxer shorts and socks to the filthy pile at his feet. He sponged his whole body, recoiling against the pain of his sunburn. The grime peeled from his cheeks and neck, offering satisfaction as he banished the misery of the day. Using the last squirt of soap, he washed his hair and dried it with a fresh towel. The auburn curls stood to attention across his head, damp red spikes giving the appearance of prickles. He dug in the cupboard over the toilet and found a clean set of clothes belonging to his father. He took it all, socks, boxers, jeans, and a tee shirt. Surprise flooded him at the realisation they fitted. The hem of the jeans hung a centimetre lower on him than on his father, but everything else matched his tall frame with perfection. His mind swept him back to the moment of impact as his knuckles contacted his father's jaw. They'd stood nose to nose. He didn't recall ever noticing he'd grown to match Logan's formidable height.

Toby knocked on the door as Mac finished the laborious task of dressing one-handed. "Edin's here," he called, his voice muffled. "David fetched her from the bus stop. She knows."

Mac braced himself before releasing the catch on the door. He eased himself through the gap like a man approaching the gallows. Edin had replaced him on Logan's sofa. She stared at her shoes, her arms wrapped around her like a straitjacket. Her eyes swam with a lake of tears, held back by the shallowest of watersheds. At the sight of Mac, she rose, and with all animosity forgotten, ran to him.

"Careful, careful." Toby held her back with his fingers clamped over her shoulder, and it forced her to look at her cousin. She took in the altered state of his arm, his flushed cheeks, and the overpowering scent of floral soap. When she wrapped her arms around his waist and pressed her cheek to his chest, the action held more care than he'd braced himself for.

"I can't believe he's gone." Her chest hitched and her tears soaked Mac's borrowed tee shirt. Her familiar presence offered him an unexpected lifeline. He buried his face in her hair and wrapped his right arm around her shoulders.

"Will you two be okay here?" Toby asked, his tone filled with hushed reverence. "I want to welcome Mr Du Rose home." The unmistakable strains of an impassioned haka echoed off the mountainside and drifted through the open windows. Toby's feet shuffled at the call, aching to add his voice and his grief to the ages old sound of uncontainable joy, pride or sadness. Edin tensed as Mac nodded. At the tiniest sign of Mac's acquiescence, Toby's boots pounded across the rug. The open door allowed the haka to permeate the narrow corridor outside the office. The mingled male shouts ricocheted around the room. A lone kuia lifted her voice to join theirs, and Edin released a heart-rending sob.

"Nonie." Her body shook as Leslie called her sweetheart home to the place of his birth. "Her karanga."

Mac nodded, unable to speak. Alfred's body had become tapu in death, sacred, and set apart under God's protection. The carving above the hotel's front door depicted a female chief, legs splayed and eyes wide in challenge. He couldn't enter beneath her, and Mac imagined the haka leading him through the side door and upstairs to his apartment. Heavy footsteps shook the hotel's structure around them, the shouts increasing in volume as male soles hammered out their grief on the front steps. His heart raged with them, though his body remained still. "E karanga ana i nga tama o te Waikato," the men cried in their guttural tones. *Calling the sons of the Waikato.*

"It's begun," Edin whispered. She turned her blotchy face up to his and voiced his thoughts. "Let's get out of here."

49

TRANSFER

"We shouldn't do this." Mac rested the splint across his thigh in the passenger seat as Edin took the bends with exaggerated care. Alfie's hat nestled in his lap. "Poppa stole Toby's quad bike from under his nose and we just took his truck. We can't keep nicking his stuff."

Edin shrugged and checked her rear-view mirror. "He should stop leaving the keys in his vehicles then, shouldn't he? It's an invitation."

Mac winced and closed his eyes against the growing nausea in his gut. "You're on your learner's and I don't have a full licence. If the cops stop us, we're both in big trouble. And you know Pa can track all the farm vehicles. He'll come and find us."

She shrugged again and her lips closed into a thin line. "I'm Caroline's daughter. I've spent my life proving I'm not the same as her. Maybe he'll give me this one blot on my copybook. Anyway, did you really smack him in the face?"

Mac quailed in his seat. "I don't want to talk about it," he muttered.

"I bet you don't." Edin's lips pulled back from her teeth to reveal her grin. "Where do you want to go?" She glanced at the diesel indicator and smiled. "Toby just filled the tank. He's the gift that keeps on giving."

"I don't know." Mac leaned his head back against the seat and groaned. "My life is a complete mess, Edie. I don't think I can fix any of it."

She reached across the gear lever and rested her cool fingers over his thigh. "Two heads are better than one." Her chin dipped, and she lowered her voice. "I can't believe Poppa's gone, can you? Hearing Nonie call him home almost broke my heart."

Mac gulped and words failed him. He managed a nod and stared at her slender fingers. She promised safety and familiarity, two things he needed right then, like the satiating of a physical ache. Despite his previous misgivings, he laid his hand over hers, gathering it into his wide palm. He lifted it and turned her wrist, placing her palm against his warm cheek. Then he kissed it and closed his eyes, ashamed of the tears which crashed against her fingers and soaked her blazer sleeve.

⁂

The busy fast-food restaurant provided a backdrop for anonymity. Edin drove with extreme care, parking the heavy vehicle at the furthest edge of the car park to avoid an accidental ding. Mac slumped into a booth and stared at his left arm, the useless fingers protruding from the bandage in silent condemnation. Edin's tartan skirt tapped the backs of her knees as she waited in line to buy coffee. Mac observed her through a different lens, witnessing a beauty he'd never allowed himself to acknowledge.

She could have been sisters with Phoenix, their identical black curls tumbling from unruly ponytails. The Du Rose genetics coursed through Edin's veins, marking her as stunning and special. She turned to smile at him and her grey eyes sought his approval as they always had. Something clicked inside his chest and he wondered why he fought it so hard. She was his best friend on the planet, and he'd hated the last few weeks of animosity. His shoulders slumped, and he dipped his head, resting his elbow on the laminated table and balancing his forehead against his fingers. A sense of weightlessness entered his soul. He realised he no longer cared about anything. Poppa had used him as his springboard into the afterlife and then left him there to live with the consequences. He squeezed the bridge of his nose between his finger and thumb, knowing that another waterfall of tears collected behind his closed lids.

"I got you a latte." A tray clattered onto the table and Mac jumped. He reached for his right processor and Edin grabbed his wrist. "No. Don't leave me here alone," she demanded. "You can't avoid life forever." She slipped into the seat opposite him but didn't release her grip on his wrist. "My counsellor says we need to feel things to their fullest extent and not stint on kindness to ourselves. That means staying present and not avoiding the pain." Mac dipped his chin, and she loosened her hold. A smile of satisfaction crossed her lips, and she busied herself with her purchases, setting two mugs of coffee and a portion of fries between them. She lifted a golden chip to her lips and then dropped it back onto the tray. "I don't know why I bought these. I'm not hungry." She reached for her coffee instead.

"What next?" Mac stared at the bubbles bursting on the top of his drink, but made no move to claim it. The open-ended question held too many probabilities for her to answer and he knew that, asking it anyway.

Edin sipped her drink and wrinkled her pretty nose. "In terms of what? Let's take things one at a time."

Despite himself, Mac smiled. She sounded just like his father, sifting and analysing facts and figures without jumping into poor decisions. The shadow of her mother had hung over her for far too long. She beat him hands' down as the better child. He shrugged. "Me and you." The loaded words hung between them. He couldn't look up at her, not wanting to read her righteous indignation or satisfaction. He fiddled with the cowboy hat instead, feeding the brim between his index finger and thumb in a continuous motion.

"What about us?"

Her reply gave him no comfort. She would make him say it out loud, and he cringed against submitting to her manipulation in public. "About our relationship." He hazarded a glance at her and blinked at the expression of surprise, which drew her brows into a neat black line.

"Relationship?" Her chin jerked backward against the collar of her blouse. "Mac, I love you more than anyone else in the world. Isn't that our relationship? Best mates, cousins. Like brother and sister?"

Mac gulped, already wrongfooted in this uncomfortable conversation. His fingers strayed to his ear again and Edin's eyes widened in warning, her lips forming a tight line of unspoken rebuke. She leaned forward and clasped his hand, slopping a line of coffee over the rim of her mug. Alfie's hat slid into Mac's lap. "I want that relationship back so bad. Is that what you mean? Or something else?"

"I thought, I thought you..." Mac pursed his lips. "I thought you wanted more. You threatened the soccer girls and didn't like the idea of me getting close to Tilly." His jaw ached and his brain throbbed with the effort of explaining himself. He dug into the depths of his memory, trying to work out when it all went wrong. He'd misunderstood. Perhaps he'd projected his own confusing emotions onto her by accident. But then Miss Andrews' face floated before his inner vision, joined by his poppa's slack lips and staring eyes. Mac shivered, and Edin stroked his fingers with tenderness. She didn't let go of them but leaned forward, her breasts crushed against the table.

"Mac," she breathed. "You're such a wally."

His lips parted with indignation. He'd poured out his heart, and she'd ridiculed him. Her curls bounced against her shoulder as she shook her head. "Rude!" he managed. His fingers twitched with the need to disconnect his processors and absent himself from the conversation. It had become his only weapon against myriad situations which taxed his ability to express himself.

Edin increased her pressure on his fingers until it hurt. The bruised knuckles where he hit his father stung against her grip. He looked up at her, terror mingling with regret in his emerald irises. "Macky," she whispered, lowering her voice and forcing him to lipread. "I already have a boyfriend."

50

REFEREE

"What?" Colour flushed up Mac's neck and into his cheeks. "Since when? Who?" He blinked as his mind sifted through a mental image of the spotty, immature boys in her year group. She'd rejected them all at some point.

Edin twisted her lips into a bow and her grey-eyed gaze held him with frightening intensity. "Since the end of last year. And you'll freak out when I tell you his name."

Mac tilted his head to the side and glared at her. "Why? Who is it?"

Edin dropped his hand and lifted the rejected chip in her fingers. She twirled it and her gaze lost focus. "Deacon is my boyfriend."

Mac jerked backwards until his spine hit the booth. A couple in the one abutting his bench seat turned to stare at him. "My friend Deacon?" he hissed.

Edin nodded, forcing her expression into a blank mask. "Yes. Your Deacon."

Tilly's comment about Edin and a boy from their year returned to bite him. He'd dismissed it to his cost. His teeth ground in his jaw until the bone ached. "Well, I hope he's returning your messages, because he's ignored me since his father's sentencing."

"Because he's ashamed!" Edin leaned forward. "It's not about you, Mac. He and his mother lost everything. The state is liquidating all their assets to pay back the creditors. His father didn't just steal from his employer. He shafted a long list of clients. Deacon is fortunate his mother didn't get convicted as an accessory, but it's bad enough as it is. They've lost their house and vehicles. He's living with his grandparents and cycling to a supermarket job. His mother applied for bankruptcy, but it's likely the court will refuse and force her to pay back everything her husband stole. They had all their bank accounts frozen and they've both undergone long interviews with the police. His father hid money in accounts all over the world and the police think they're protecting it."

Mac dipped his chin to his chest. "I tried to support him, Edie. I really did."

"He understands." She dropped the chip back onto the tray. "We bonded over having a parent in prison while his dad was on remand. I always liked him, but it grew into a relationship when he stayed with us over the summer holidays. We wanted to tell you, eventually."

Mac lifted one eyebrow but remained silent. Their deception felt like a knife wound to his throat, no matter which way he studied it. He rested his palm on Alfie's dented hat and searched his soul for a reaction. The tentative threads of consciousness returned with the bitter taste of numbness.

"Anyway." Edin reached again for the fries and jabbed one between her lips. She spoke while chewing. "What's this about me warning off the soccer girls?"

Mac snorted. "You threatened them over text. It upset them."

Edin shook her head and reached for another chip. Having started eating, she'd discovered a hunger blooming beneath her sadness. "I warned one girl. That's all."

Mac swallowed. "So, you interfered in my life while concealing something much bigger? Nice. Well played, Edin." His tone held an uncharacteristic bite. An unexpected jealousy crowded out the surprise. He realised he disliked thoughts of her with another boy. And Deacon of all people. A strange sickness roiled in Mac's gut, as though Edin had rejected him for a brother. Like Logan and Caroline. He slammed the lid hard on the awful revelation. His brain continued analysing, sifting and picking through the data. Nothing made sense anymore but Edin's lips continued to move.

"No. It's not interfering when I'm looking out for you. It's different." She chewed a chip, her gaze switching to the car park and Logan's truck. "Like I always do."

"Which girl did you threaten?" He plucked a chip from the mouth of the cardboard packet and pushed it between his lips. The salt hit his tongue and brought comfort.

Edin closed her eyes and clicked her fingers, as though she struggled to remember. "The little one. Blonde hair, always squealing."

"You just described all but two of them." Mac heaved out a sigh. "So, Deacon." He shook his head in a slow arc of disappointment.

Edin dragged her phone from her blazer pocket and sifted through her contacts. She scrolled for a while before turning the screen to face him. "That's her number. I can't remember her name, but she's trouble. I'm surprised your girlfriend didn't tell you all about her."

"Are you talking about Sammy?" Mac narrowed his eyes, the number offering no clarity but the reference to Tilly jarring loose a connection. "She lived in the group home with Tilly until last year. A family adopted her." He leaned forward. "Why would you warn her off? She's years younger than me."

Edin's eyes widened, and she gave a decisive nod. "That's her. Sammy. And that's the point, Mac. She's jail bait. It proved a nice little scam while it lasted. She'd get the older boys interested in making out, take them to an isolated spot on the school site, and engage in a bit of foreplay. The bell goes, they leave and then footage appears of some stupid idiot with his pants around his ankles. He either pays up or his photo goes on the internet."

Mac blew out a tortured breath and swore. Tilly's demand for cash and her promise of getting footage deleted rose to the forefront of his mind. Edin stilled and her jaw tightened. "You didn't. Please, tell me you didn't fall for it?"

Mac shook his head. "Not with Sammy." His lips flapped like a fish yanked out of water. "Oh, crap! I'm such an idiot." The fear which had plagued him in the school's reception returned like a tsunami. "I had sex with Tilly in the janitor's cupboard on the second floor. I saw a flashing red light in the darkness but linked it to a cordless vacuum cleaner." He swallowed. "Tilly paid ten dollars to rent the room. Later, she panicked and said she didn't know about the camera. She gave more money to a younger kid in the equipment shed where Miss Andrews died." He closed his eyes and slumped against his seat. "She said he'd delete it." He swallowed. "But then she hugged him." Dryness affected his mouth and tongue. "Do you think Tilly is in on the scam?"

"No." Edin's ready denial surprised him. "She dresses weird, but she plays a straight game. She's not my first choice for you but that's because of the bad actors she orbits and nothing more. I think I know the kid she paid, and it's not what you think."

Mac inhaled, the breath painful against his straining lungs. "Yeah. What do I think? I'm no longer sure." He rubbed his hand over his swollen eyes. "I can't believe Poppa is gone."

Edin's expression softened, her lips parting and her gaze dropping to her lap. "Did he suffer?" she whispered.

"I don't believe so. It looked like he fell down and went to sleep." Mac swallowed at the memory of his futile efforts to save a man who'd expressly forbidden it. "Did you realise he didn't want us to resuscitate him?"

Edin frowned. "Yeah. We all did. Pa met with Poppa Alfie in the summer and we had that big family meeting after they'd spoken. Pa helped him to make his will. Don't you remember?" Then she sighed and her ponytail swung with the motion of her head. "You didn't listen, did you?" She jabbed a finger at his right ear. "I bet you turned off your processors. Or took them out." She huffed through her nose. "Don't you realise how bloody annoying it is when you do that?"

Mac gave a slow nod. "I'm starting to." He lifted the hat above the edge of the table. "Poppa gave this to me. He wanted me to have it. Do you think he wrote it down? Toby said Uncle Michael will demand it for himself. Henri Du Rose wasn't even our great grandfather. We came from Jacob's line, didn't we?"

A curious yearning filled Edin's eyes. She held out her hand. "Please, can I just hold it for a minute?"

Mac nodded and passed it to her. Grief rose like a leviathan in his chest as silent tears trickled down Edin's cheeks. She lifted the hat with reverence and closed her eyes, resting the brim against her forehead. "It smells of him," she whispered, her voice muffled. "Coal-tar soap and horses." She kissed the knotted leather band above the brim before returning it. Her fingers smoothed the wetness from beneath her eyes as she collected herself. "Will you keep it safe somewhere? Or give it to Mama for the museum?"

Mac shook his head. He lifted the battered antique and sat it over his auburn curls. "I'll clean the leather and wear it. Does it suit me?"

Edin gave a sad smile. "It kinda does. The tan matches your hair. He adored you more than any of us. Did you know that?"

Mac made a sound in his throat like a strangled groan. "No," he whispered. "He treated us all the same."

Edin scoffed and widened her eyes. "Are you kidding? Girls terrified him. Phoenix and I never stood a chance. He loved you best." She jerked her head towards him. "And he left you his hat to prove it."

"We should go home." He turned his attention to their surroundings. The restaurant had filled almost to capacity with the demands of the approaching dinner hour. "I'll take the blame for making you drive Toby's truck. I'm already in trouble. A bit more can't make Pa much crosser than he already is with me."

Edin glanced at her phone before sliding it into her pocket. "I'm surprised nobody called yet. Maybe they're too busy getting Poppa to the undertakers and then the marae."

"The marae?" Mac jerked in surprise. "He'll go home, won't he?"

Edin rolled her eyes, her lips pursing with exasperation. She fished the truck keys from the tray. "No, Mac! During the same family meeting you zoned out of, Papa explained that Poppa Alfie asked to lie in at the marae. They'd never get a coffin up the stairs to the apartment. And can you imagine the disruption to the hotel with the whānau descending en masse? They'll take him to the marae. He'll go in through the window while he's noho tapu and out through the door after the tangi. Like Pastor Sam's father. Remember?"

Mac gave a slow nod. "Right. If we take the truck back, they might not realise we borrowed it without permission."

"True." Edin tilted her head to one side and observed her cousin. "If we go straight back. But we won't." She slipped her phone from her pocket and her fingers jabbed across the screen at speed. With a nod of satisfaction, she replaced it and faced Mac. "We both have some place else to go first." She rose and held out her hand to him. "Come on. It's always better to apologise than to ask permission."

51

BALL WATCHING

E din drove through south Auckland with enough care to avoid either accident or detection. She stopped outside a narrow townhouse and lifted her phone from her pocket. "They're coming," she announced.

"Who?" Mac tipped back the brim of his hat and peered through the window. "It looks nice."

"It looks small!" Edin scoffed. "Two bedrooms and four occupants." After another glance at her phone, she gave a decisive nod. "Right, let's get this over."

Deacon answered the door and Mac took a step backwards, almost pitching off the second step. Oblivious, Edin kicked off her shoes and reached up to kiss him on the mouth. He smiled down at her and then his gaze flicked to Mac. "You told him?" His left eyebrow lifted into a blond arch.

"Yep." Edin slipped her fingers through his and turned to face Mac. "He's okay with it."

Relief flooded Deacon's face, softening the tense features and removing the line from between his brows. Familiar crow's feet creased the corners of his eyes as he grinned. "Thank goodness!" he breathed.

Mac's expression remained blank. Edin claimed an acceptance which she'd pre-empted without evidence to the contrary. But he doubted he'd ever be okay with it. She gripped her boyfriend's fingers and Mac breathed through a tearing sensation in his chest. The wretched day seemed capable of stripping him of everyone who mattered. Poppa. Now his best friend.

"Come in." Deacon waited as Mac stepped over the threshold. The door clicked behind him. The fingers of his right hand twitched, wanting to absent himself from the moment. But they clutched Alfie's hat and forced Mac to choose between one comfort or the other. He gripped the hat harder and made his choice.

"The olds are on holiday." Deacon urged them along a thin corridor and into an open-plan kitchen. A dining table nestled against the far wall, two of the chairs trapped against the patterned wallpaper.

"What about your Mum?" Edin's voice sounded lighter and Mac envied her.

Deacon opened a tall fridge and pulled out a bottle of water. Air hissed from its neck as he released the lid. "She cleans at night and works at the aluminium factory during the day." His gaze slid to Mac's stony expression as he set four glasses on the counter and dribbled fizzy water into the first one. "We're paying off the lawyers and then the court fees. The house sold this afternoon, so that will make a dent in some of the other debts." His brows knitted into a line and he licked his lips. "You told him about that too?" He directed his question to Edin, and she nodded.

"Yeah."

Mac set up a vibration in his jaw, grinding his teeth together in a regular beat. It drowned out some of Deacon's reply, but not all of it. He wondered why his friend miscounted as he poured water into the fourth glass, but a sound behind him caused him to turn.

"Hey." Tilly slouched into the room and edged past Mac's rigid body. "You left the front door unlocked. Anyone could just walk in off the street." She wore a pinstriped pinafore which ended in frayed pleats just above her knees. Heavy Doc Marten boots topped off the harshness of her look and she'd fixed her hair into two small buns above her ears. Mac slid his gaze sideways and eyed her with curiosity. She resembled a gangster with punk overtones and he discovered he approved. His lips twitched, and he shifted Alfie's hat into his other hand. The splint offered his thumb more motion and it curled around the brim and held it fast. Mac turned his right hand over and fixed his gaze on his palm. The short groove representing his lifeline always freaked out Nonie Leslie. He curled his fingers around to protect it. Tilly slumped onto a tartan sofa and fought her shoelaces into submission. Painted black toenails slid into view and she pushed her boots to the side.

Deacon retrieved the glass and handed it to her. "Sorry, it's just water from the Soda Stream," he said, pinching his lips tight.

Tilly shrugged and took a sip. "Thanks. It's better than the water in the group home." She wrinkled her nose. "Sometimes, it's the colour of chocolate and tastes of mud."

Mac remained sentry-still by the kitchen door. He shot covert glances at her as she worked hard to ignore him.

"Their poppa just died." Deacon folded his long legs beneath him on a rug in front of the ranch slider. Beyond the window, a narrow-paved space held plant pots filled with colourful blooms. A wooden fence and the next-door house rose to block any view of the sky. Mac sighed, finding nothing to earth himself in this suburban jungle.

Tilly groaned and dipped forward, hugging her knees with her arms. She set the glass on the floor and bubbles broke the surface. "That makes me so sad for you both." Her voice wobbled, and Mac pursed his lips. The sentence contained her own pain, laid out for them to trample or accept. His heart softened, and a tut issued from his throat. The black war-paint and clothing slipped enough to reveal the child hidden within her soul, and a flush of compassion prickled his warm skin. He counted his steps to her side and imagined himself covering her vulnerability with his body. His feet took more persuasion than he'd anticipated and he tripped over the edge of the rug. Tilly jumped at his abrupt arrival on the sofa and pushed herself up straight. The moment slithered away and left Mac apologising for his clumsiness.

Edin sank onto the floor next to Deacon. She rested her head on his shoulder and silenced. Their fingers linked like dancers performing a well-rehearsed adagio on the patterned weave. Mac fidgeted as his mind whirled. He should have guessed. How did he not guess?

"Why are we here?" he demanded. His tone held an unintended harshness. The image of his poppa lying on the hard ground sent his mind into freefall and he held his breath. He needed to return to the mountain and take his place in the vigil. Wiremu and Phoenix would hear the news from someone else and he regretted that more than anything.

"I invited Tilly." Edin's chin raised in defiance. "You both have things to discuss."

"We should go." Mac shivered at his stupidity. She'd taken control, and he'd allowed it. It couldn't end well.

"We will." Edin patted her blazer pocket and Toby's keys jangled. She braced her fingers against Deacon's shoulder and rose before offering her hand to help him stand. They matched. Her darkness and his white-blond hair like opposing forces in union. He'd missed it. Blind *and* deaf. They looked right together. She said, "You two sort your crap out and then we'll go."

They left the room and silence created a steady hiss in Mac's processors. Floor boards creaked, and a TV woke in another room. Tilly exhaled and dipped forward, resting her fingers over her bare toes. Black polish on her finger and toenails sparkled with a silver sheen. The bun above her left ear sagged, but she didn't speak.

Mac's head emptied of all sense. He'd accused her of deception, and she'd replied with a salvo of equal weight. She believed he'd used her for sex. Edin seemed better informed when she denied Tilly's inclination to cheat, which left Mac with a nasty alternative. His mind whirled with the possibility he had used her for sex. "I'm an asshole," he concluded, his words tumbling into the void.

Tilly turned her face to study him. Her irises sparkled like gems. Tears collected along her lower lids and her long lashes caused them to ripple. He'd hurt her more than he realised. A gulp escaped from his throat and it proved enough for her. His body rocked as she launched at him. He flung his injured arm out sideways to avoid her clattering it and she arrived in his lap. Alfie's hat flew over the sofa arm and pattered onto the floor. Soft kisses covered his nose and lips, her weight settling across his thighs. The fingers of his right hand stroked her silky thigh, her pinafore rough against his knuckles. A flare of temptation in his breast told him to seek further and answer the unspoken question about her underwear, or lack of it. He resisted, wrapping his arm around her waist and hauling her against him. In that fragile moment, he realised it was more than just risky teenage experimentation in a janitor's cupboard. He liked her. He liked her so much. Alfie's words whispered through his processors, his poppa's voice as clear as if he stood behind them. *She saved us all. Never underestimate the value of a good woman, Macky.*

Tilly tilted her head and rested her cheek on his shoulder. Her soft breath caressed his earlobes before dissipating along his neck like kisses. They stayed that way, their silent companionship backed by the muted, digital strains of a war game in the next room. Edin whooped as she killed Deacon's soldier and Mac closed his eyes and let their laughter wash over him.

Tilly released a disgusting sniff, which destroyed the vibe as fast as it began. Mac snorted and jerked his head back to stare at her. "Don't snot on my pa's tee shirt," he warned, his tone light. Then he groaned at the memory of his embarrassing punch. "On second thoughts, have at it. I'm racking up the offenses today. What's one more?"

"What did you do?" Tilly collapsed to his side and curled her legs beneath her. She rested her chin on his shoulder and stared up at him.

"This." Mac lifted the bruised knuckles of his right hand. A split over the middle finger showed the force of his anger. "I smacked my pa right in the chops."

"Did he do that to you?" She ran her an index finger along his bandaged forearm. Her question held the casual acceptance of someone expecting an affirmative answer and finding family violence normal.

"No!" Mac turned and pushed his weight into his left hip. He cupped her cheek in his palm. "He's never hit me. I have no memory of him ever raising a hand to any of us." He closed his eyes and wrinkled his nose. "Not that we didn't give him lots of reasons to slap us into next week." Logan appeared before him in his mind's eye. He saw him towing Sassy up the mountain, defending his son against the police detective, feeding, clothing and housing an old man who'd lied to him for forty years. A surge of love filled his chest until he couldn't speak.

As though sensing him disconnecting from her, Tilly placed her hand over his thigh. The fake stones in her rings twisted on her slender fingers and they dug into his leg. "I haven't cheated on you," she whispered. Her eyes narrowed to slits of rebuke as she glared up at him. "I resent you following me, but you saw me speaking to my brother. He told me they'd added the camera after he read my name against the booking. I needed the cash for him to pay another kid to delete the footage." Her gaze fell and her irises glazed. "This is all much bigger than you imagine, Macky. It's huge."

Mac blinked in surprise and canted his head to one side. The processors carried her words, but his brain fumbled over their meaning. He tucked her fingers into his wide palm and licked his lips. "Then explain it to me," he demanded, his tone soft.

52

TIMEOUT

"**W**hen did this start?" An adolescent squeak crept into the end of his sentence and Mac ignored it. His expression held shock and disbelief, his lips pulled back from his teeth and his eyes wide.

Tilly shrugged. "Ages. Forever. Gray spent last year in a school for young offenders', but the court let him come back here to sit his exams. They must have recruited him for BAC fast because he's running the money side already."

"What did you say? BAC? What the hell is that?"

Deacon knocked on the half-open door before entering, and Edin followed close on his heels. He snorted. "How can you not know what BAC is? Even the Year 9s whisper about it." He crossed his legs at the ankles and dropped onto his haunches, an old party trick which displayed an unnatural control over his muscles. Mac rolled his eyes and Deacon smirked.

Edin sank to her knees with less dignity and curled her legs beneath her. "He doesn't listen." She pursed her lips and shrugged her shoulders at Mac's glare. "Well, you don't. Ma agonised over whether to let you have the cochlear implant surgery. Did you know that? She did months of research and had heaps of discussions with Uncle Dean. They wanted you to have the choice of sound or signing. Nonie told me." Her long curls brushed her shoulders as she shook her head. "You reject both. Every time you switch off your processors and opt out, you're choosing not to take part in our family. You could lip read or sign, but you won't." She lifted her arm and jabbed a finger in his direction. "You choose deafness and silence, Mac. You reject us. So don't complain when you miss out on important information." Her teeth snapped shut as she smothered further admonishment. Her chest curved in on itself as she suppressed a deep anger which bubbled inside her soul.

Mac dropped his gaze and considered her accusation. The fingers of his right hand fluttered to his ear and then dropped into his lap. He'd caught himself in a well-worn path of serial avoidance. Not hearing and choosing not to hear separated into two distinct paths. He saw himself stumbling along the latter in a haze of contentment which lacked compassion for those outside his safe, nullifying bubble of peace. "Sorry," he murmured.

Deacon winced and slid his arm around Edin's rigid shoulders. His voice had deepened in the months since Christmas and it jarred with Mac's memory of his best friend. "BAC stands for Book A Cupboard system."

Mac released a disparaging laugh and looked up, finding Deacon's serious gaze in response. "Truly?" He swallowed and his head moved from side to side in denial. "It's an actual thing? With a name and everything?"

Edin licked her lips and focussed on Tilly. "I can understand him falling for it, because he's an idiot. But what's your excuse?"

"I don't have one." Tilly seemed to shrivel in her seat. She engaged her fingers in furious activity, loosening the tie holding her right bun and starting from scratch. Mac watched with fascination as she released her black hair and spun it back into submission. When she turned to face him, the buns had lost their symmetry and resembled wonky Mickey Mouse ears. "I'm just sorry." She exhaled and her chest deflated. "Gray promised to delete the footage of us and I trust him."

"You paid him ten dollars." Mac conjured up a painful memory of the interaction.

Tilly's nose crinkled into a series of fine lines along its bridge. "I told you, another kid does the video downloading. Gray is a small cog in a huge wheel."

Mac's torso collapsed forward, and he clasped his forehead in his right hand. A wall clock displayed the passing time in Roman numerals, its steady tick producing an illusion of futility. "We don't have time for this," he sighed. "The family must have gathered at the marae by now. They'll notice we're missing. We should leave."

Edin nodded and sadness settled over her slumped shoulders. "At least you know Tilly's side of things now," she concluded. She leaned in to press a kiss over Deacon's lips. "You've caught up to the rest of us."

Mac nodded and pushed himself to his feet. He offered his right hand to Tilly. "You need a ride home?" he asked.

"I'm not ready for that yet." Her lips flattened into a line. A stab of pain flicked through Mac's heart. She'd just told him she didn't trust him with her address. He wanted to kiss her with the same ease with which Edin possessed Deacon, but he couldn't. Embarrassment sent its familiar blush creeping up his neck.

"See you tomorrow," he whispered.

"No, you won't." Edin's tone held the harshness of reality. "We need to stay with Poppa for the next few days. It's gonna be heavy." Her feet dragged against the rug as she moved towards the door. Stopping, she turned with her fingers clasping the handle and directed her comment to Deacon and then to Tilly. "You're both welcome to attend the tangihanga if you can make it." Her gaze took in Mac's discomfort and a half-smile lifted her lips as she stepped into the narrow hallway.

Edin drove with care, despite her obvious tiredness. The prospect of home, and the sadness and chaos surrounding it, weighed on them both. Mac tutted as she turned off the expressway and navigated the first of many bends. "I forgot to ask Tilly what she did with the SIM card from the phone." The bush began as an untamed riot of green behind an invisible demarcation line. The unpredictability of Du Rose country contrasted with the neat grey roads and bright signage. Mac snapped the fingers of his right hand. "It went out of my head. And Layla said Tilly lent her the other phone. I recognised it. It belonged to Miss Andrews."

"The SIM from what phone? The one the cops are searching for?" Edin raised her eyebrows but kept her focus on the twisting road. She'd misunderstood his slew of questions and melded the issue of two phones into one problem. "Ouch. What will you do?"

Mac exhaled and leaned his head against the seat. "Wait, I think. I need to avoid any more accusations. Maybe she bought it from her brother. I don't want to jump to conclusions." But his mind whirred the rest of the way to the hotel. A thought occurred to him and he pushed it away several times before it took root and held. By the time Edin finished backing Toby's truck into his space in the car park, Mac knew less than he wished, but more than he could bear about his teacher's death.

53

WAIT–WAIT–SEE

Edin hid the truck key in the glove box and left the vehicle unlocked. Their heavy steps took them through the front doors of the hotel and up the stairs. As though by an unspoken agreement, they used the narrow staircase up to Leslie and Alfie's apartment. The unlocked door suggested they'd find it occupied, but a check of every room returned only emptiness.

Edin lifted Alfred's ratty blue cardigan from the back of the sofa and held it to her nose. She closed her eyes and inhaled his musty scent. She sighed and glanced up at Mac. "They should have let him smoke the weed," she concluded. Her feet turned and her body followed, as if reluctant to sweep her gaze around the room. Mac shrugged. He had no ready answer. Edin narrowed her eyes at him and cocked her head. A pout formed on her lips, the rebuke just behind it.

Mac raised his right hand to halt the promised tirade. "They're on," he reassured her. "I can hear you."

Her expression relaxed, and she sank onto the sofa, the cushions flattened from overuse. "What do you think we should do?" she whispered. "Go home or to the marae?"

"I don't know." He tugged out a dining chair and sat down, his body aching and his left processor fizzing. "It feels wrong, doesn't it?" he said, his voice too loud in the silent space. "It's like he's still lying on the bed buck naked with his goofy smile and using the newspaper as a blanket."

Edin nodded. "Yeah. Or staring through that long window and claiming he saw Miriam."

Mac licked his lips. His voice caught in his throat. "He spoke to his brother at the end." Tears sparkled in his eyes. "And his mother. It's like they came for him."

"But not Miriam?" Edin's lips turned down into a sad arch and she sighed. "Poor Poppa. Nonie loved the bones of him and he never realised, did he?"

Mac cast his mind back to their coffee in the hotel bar and the memory soothed him. "Yeah. I think he did towards the end." His tone grew wistful. "I wish we'd known Reuben, don't you?"

Edin shook her head. "Na." Her eyelashes fluttered, and a tear escaped her right eye and plunged into her blouse. It left a dark track in its wake. "I'm happy with what I've got."

Mac contemplated her words against the backdrop of his recent behaviour. Her conclusion held a wisdom he should borrow for himself. They sat in silence for a while until Edin moved towards the secret doorway leading to the roof. She closed it behind her and he sensed he shouldn't follow, though he wanted to. Alfie said he hid Miriam's wedding ring in a blue flowerpot. Mac ached to search for it, despite knowing it should remain undisturbed. What would he do with it once he'd liberated it?

He heard Edin's footsteps climbing the stairs, the cardigan still tucked under her arm. His fingers ached to turn off the processors, but he didn't. It forced him to endure her piercing scream of rage as she railed at the wide blue sky. He stayed at the dining table and listened to her sobs filter down to him. His fingers crushed a lone crumb missed by the swiping of Leslie's cloth, as she'd unknowingly cleared away the remains of her husband's last lunch. He crushed it into a million micro pieces until it became invisible. And then he cried because his processors continued to relay Edin's grief.

He glanced up in time to watch the cardigan flutter past the French doors leading to the balcony as she threw it off the roof. The dangling arms filled with air and the torso twisted, the buttons flashing as they flew by on their saggy blue bird.

And then he laughed until his sides hurt. Because only Edin Du Rose would dare to do something so public and so utterly ludicrous. He envied her courage with every fibre of his being.

54

SCORELINES

When the landline trilled in the tiny apartment, Mac rose to answer it. His fingers hovered over the old handset, reluctant to overwrite his poppa's last act of calling him. It persisted with its irritating, shrill cry, and he sensed the vibration of Edin walking overhead. She assumed he'd avoid answering it.

"Hello." His voice croaked as he handled the receiver with care and lifted it to his ear. He held it with awkwardness, not wanting to smudge Alfie's precious fingerprints.

David Allen's gruff tones echoed through his right processor. "Oh, there you are. Is Edin with you?"

"Yeah." Mac stared at the ceiling as her footsteps ceased.

"Have you seen Toby's truck?" Exasperation filled his tone. "He can't find it."

Mac pursed his lips, reluctant to add more lies to his growing stack. "Car park?" he suggested.

David grunted. "Probably. Hey, everyone drove to the marae to wait for Mr Alfred. Do you want me to drive you both there?"

Mac closed his eyes. He pictured the weeping and sadness shrouding the meeting house and wished to inoculate himself from its reach. His futile headshake left a silence. "Sorry, no. Not yet." He gulped. "Edin's not ready. She needs time." He glanced again at the ceiling. Streaks of faded paint revealed where Leslie had mopped fly crap from its rippled surface. She'd used bleach. He inhaled. "Please, could you drop us at the house? I'll fetch some things for Ma and Pa. They'll sleep at the marae with Poppa when he arrives, won't they?"

"Yeah." A rustling indicated a rough hand placed over the speaker. David muttered to someone in the background. He breathed into the phone and Mac winced. This was the reason he avoided listening to other people. *Body noises.* "Toby found his truck," he said, accompanied by a loud sigh and a swearword. Mac missed the intonation but got the gist of the curse. "Meet me downstairs in twenty minutes." Mac jerked as a hissing silence filled his auditory nerve. David hung up on him.

He jumped as Edin spoke behind him. "Who was that?" she asked, her tone lacklustre.

"David." He forced his body to turn in a slow arc, like the Titanic avoiding the iceberg. His foot snagged against the rug and exhaustion caught him up in a powerful yawn. "I asked to go home. He'll take us there. We should pack some things for Ma and Papa."

Edin nodded. "Are you okay?" She didn't refer to the cardigan no longer in her arms, but the dullness of her grey irises warned him against mentioning it.

Mac frowned. "Please, can I borrow your phone?"

She nodded and slipped it from her pocket. It leaned towards the floor as she held it with her fingertips and swiped a zig-zag pattern with her thumb. "Who do you want to call?" Her attention wavered as she faced the apartment's emptiness. "I'll collect some clothes for Nonie while we're here. What do you think?"

"Good idea." Mac worried at his lower lip. "I need to phone Tilly. You have her number." He didn't ask how she'd acquired it, or why. He just knew she'd texted her from the truck before driving to Deacon's place.

Edin's fingers stroked the back of the dining chair, which Mac had left at an angle to the table. "I don't dislike Tilly." Her tone held a strange foreboding. She fixed her gaze on his eyes as though searching for some hidden speck of understanding. "Just don't dive into it feet first with her, Macky. She's a straight shooter. You might lose an important body part." Without a backward glance, she drifted to the far end of the apartment and disappeared. The opening of a drawer punctuated her strange warning.

Mac shook himself before inspecting Edin's phone screen. She'd unlocked it for him, and he scrolled through her list of contacts. He frowned at what he'd missed before when he'd hacked into it. Deacon's number drifted past at a swipe of his thumb. She'd added him as *ABoy*. It put him at the top of the list.

He found Tilly's number from memory, pursing his lips at Edin's name for her. *Trouble*. It meant she'd got it from Deacon. The pet name went back as far as primary school. He connected the call and waited.

"Hey?" The whispered reply took Mac by surprise.

"Erm. Hi?"

Tilly blew out a ragged breath. "Oh, it's you," she said, her tone flat. "What's wrong?"

"The other phone got left on the mountain somewhere," he confessed. "I borrowed Edin's to call you."

"I can see that." Just a tiny smidge of humour accompanied the jibe. "I'm on the roof." Another sigh. "They moved a new girl into my room. She doesn't like me."

Mac tutted. "Sorry. That sucks." He couldn't imagine having to share space with a disagreeable roommate. It underlined his sense of privilege with a red pen.

"What do you want?" she asked.

Mac inhaled. He doubted the wisdom of testing her patience again. His mind's eye produced an image of the fluttering cardigan and it stalled him. Tilly wouldn't jump if he upset her. Would she? He swallowed. "I want us to start again," he stammered. "Will you be my girlfriend?" The words slipped from his tongue, not the ones he'd meant to utter. He wished he possessed the courage to ask her in person. He imagined himself doing it in front of an audience and his heart rate rose enough to cause sweat to bead on his forehead. It would require keeping his processors active in a high-density situation, something he'd never managed to do. He always switched them off, keen to avoid the scrutiny and judgement of others.

"Wow." Tilly paused. "I didn't expect that."

Mac glanced towards Alfie and Leslie's bedroom. A zipper sounded as Edin found a bag and packed fresh clothes for Nonie. She'd sleep beside her fallen spouse until they laid his body in the urupā. Māori didn't leave their dead alone. A bubble of pain popped inside Mac's chest, and it rose to block his throat. He'd jumped in feet first, against Edin's advice. But he dreaded the coming storm of the funeral and sought distraction. Distant family members would enfold him into their tight unit, pressing their noses to his and expecting a fealty he didn't understand. He jumped as Tilly spoke again.

"Okay. I'd like that," she whispered. She sniffed. Did she sense his fear? Was he using her again? He struggled to sort out the threads of conviction. But that wasn't why he'd called.

Mac cleared his throat. "Please, can I ask you two questions?"

"Go on." Her guard rose, adding a growl to the end of her short sentence.

"Don't get angry," he couched. His fingers gripped the phone, and he stared at them. Alfie's hat. Last seen clutched in the same fingers. He whirled on the spot and raked the small lounge and dining room with a frantic gaze. Panic made the questions emerge with more roughness than he intended.

"What did you do with the SIM card from the phone I found? And where did you get the other stuff?"

"Oh." Relief flooded Tilly's reply, and Mac stopped spinning to concentrate. "Easy. I hid the SIM card in your locker. It's under the innersole of your right soccer boot. I bought the new SIM and cover from Gray."

"You paid for them?" He didn't qualify his response. She'd never thieved from him or Deacon, but he couldn't presume she didn't appropriate things which weren't hers. He glossed over her covert entry to his locker and handling of his belongings.

"Yeah." A clipped reply. "They're not stolen."

Mac gulped and the scent of burning filled his nostrils. "One thing is," he breathed. "It belonged to Miss Andrews."

55

PUNT

Of course, she freaked out. Mac sensed her panic as the phone vibrated with her cursing.

"It's okay," he pleaded. "Please Tilly. We'll talk tomorrow, I promise."

A knock on the apartment door heralded the arrival of David Allen. His bushy brows drew into a line of irritation. "I asked you to meet me downstairs!" he grumbled.

Edin emerged from the bedroom carrying a leather holdall. It dangled from one strap, the other broken and trailing. A line of tears streaked her cheeks, and she clasped the lower right pocket of her blazer against her hip.

"I'm sorry," Mac hissed. He said it into the phone but David Allen accepted it as meant for him. He killed the call with guilt blossoming across his chest. He'd got it wrong again, dumping a massive problem on Tilly's fragile shoulders and leaving her with it. "One second," he pleaded, turning aside from David's glare. His fingers sent a quick message firing into the ether for Tilly. *Do nothing!* he urged her. *Promise me?*

"Let's go." David took the bag from Edin and turned on the spot. He seemed eager to leave the sombre apartment and it made him careless. Mac narrowed his eyes as he handed back Edin's phone, jerking his head with a pointed glance at her pocket. She pursed her lips and ignored him, but as they paused at the bottom of the narrow staircase for David to lock the door against intruders, Mac recognised the object of her theft. Poppa Alfie's spectacle case peeked over the lip of her blazer pocket. His mind conjured a memory of Edin fondling its furry surface as a smaller girl. She'd liked the way it snapped closed on taut hinges without warning. He nodded at her but said nothing.

"My hat." Her covetousness reminded him of his loss and his chest locked.

"You lost it already?" David's bristly lip curled back in disgust.

"No." Mac widened his eyes at Edin and took a step backwards. "I know where it is."

"He'll catch up with us." She covered for him, a well-worn groove in the floor of childhood conspiracy. She waved him away and turned to David, forcing herself to endure a conversation about minutiae while Mac jogged back to Toby's truck. The stockman leaned against his front bumper, his arms folded across his chest. Alfie's hat sat next to him on the bonnet, its dented crown darker against the white paintwork.

"Looking for something?" he growled. Mac licked his lips and nodded. Toby lifted the hat and held it out to him. "I'm not as green as I am cabbage looking," he said, his tone dull.

Mac pursed his lips at the unintended humour. He imagined Toby dressed in crinkled cabbage leaves and forced the bark of laughter back into his throat. "I know, sir," he managed. He used the deference of respect for an elder, though Toby would one day dance to the teenager's tune. Ash blond lashes swished across Toby's gaze as he accepted the silent apology. "We needed to get away," he murmured and Toby nodded.

"Fair enough," he replied, his voice soft. "So, I shouldn't expect any speeding tickets or fines?"

"No." Mac tapped his breast with his left hand. The clunky splint clattered against his sternum.

Toby's gaze settled on the curled fingers, the pinkie sticking out separate from the rest like a rejected family member. His lips curved upwards in a smile. "Let's leave it at that then, shall we?" He eased himself upright and Mac blinked. When did Toby shrink? As the stockman turned on his heel, Mac noticed the bald spot spreading outward from his crown like an ink blot.

Toby tugged open his driver's door. "You need a ride to the marae?" he asked.

"No, thanks." Mac backed away, the hat clutched in his fingers. He leapt a grass verge and a dangling chain-link fence to arrive next to David's rolling truck. He climbed into the back seat and the stockman bore the teenagers away to the sprawling house at the top of the mountain.

⁜

Edin packed a bag for Hana while Mac fed and watered the resident horses in the front garden. He moved the electric tape to give them access to more grass and topped up their hay and water. Edin waved her hands from the front porch.

"I'm wearing my processors!" Irritation bloomed in Mac's brain and communicated itself to his downturned lips. "I can hear you."

"Oh. Okay." Edin stepped onto the grass in her bare feet. She'd changed into jeans and a tee shirt. Her toes curled against the prickly shoots. "Do you want to pack something for Pa?" She wrinkled her nose and jabbed an index finger at the horses. "Is this permanent now?"

"No!" Mac rolled his eyes behind his closed lids. His psyche ached for the even keel of silence. He forced a slow exhale to deflate his tight chest. "It's temporary. But things have kinda gotten away from us this week. I need Pa's help to take Sassy back down the mountain. It's impossible to lead them both."

Edin twisted her lips but didn't offer to help him. She focussed on the more immediate issue. "Will you pack things for Pa? I don't want to rifle through his drawers."

Mac nodded. Collecting his father's belongings meant handing them over at the marae. He wasn't sure he felt ready to see the cut on Logan's lip or take responsibility for his actions. So, he stalled. Edin's phone rang and she pulled it from her back pocket and lifted it to her ear. Mac frowned as she held it out to him. "What?" he demanded. She widened her eyes with insolence and wagged the phone towards him, not willing to step over the electric tape for his convenience. "Your brother," she said with a sigh. "Supercop."

Mac's shoulders slumped. He strode across the chewed grass and hopped over the tape. His long legs cleared it in a pincer movement without touching it. Edin dropped the phone into his palm and flounced back into the house, her long black curls swinging against her spine. "Hi." A nervous tick tugged at Mac's left cheek and he fought to keep it still.

Bodie's voice contained a weird echo. Putting it on speaker didn't help and Mac held the device to his ear. "Why didn't you tell me the victim's sister contacted you on Messenger?" he demanded.

Mac's lips twisted into a pout. The cops must believe him a serious contender for the murder if they'd trawled through his social media and messages. He didn't know what to say and for once, the truth seemed best. "I said I couldn't help her. Told her to ask Victim Support. You must have seen that."

"Yeah, but still." Bodie sounded tired and irritated. "It would serve you better to come clean about something ahead of us tripping over it."

Mac swallowed hard against the jibe. A black raincloud gathered in the distance like a warning. He'd lost the phone he'd taken from the crime scene and knew the location of the dead teacher's missing device. But he still couldn't tell the police officer any of that. "Sorry." He blew out a breath. "Poppa died this afternoon. I need to go."

Bodie exhaled. "I'm so sorry," he replied. His voice became tight. "It must be chaos there. That's maybe why Mum gave me Edin's phone number. She sounded fraught."

"Yeah. We're just packing some clothes for them."

Edin stepped from the front door wearing a denim jacket and sandals. She dumped a small suitcase onto the pavers and disappeared back inside the house. Mac sensed her readying herself for something and licked his lips with fear. Even with his processors working, he'd still missed something important. Anger leached through the stiffness of her spine.

Bodie had continued speaking and Mac tuned back into the conversation. His world contained an unhinged element and it caused him physical distress. He couldn't keep up with the speed of changing events. "Pardon?" Rapid blinking accompanied his plea. He felt like he'd run a race. And finished long after the organisers and the crowds went home. "Can you go back a bit? There's a lot of distraction here." Mac turned off his left processor and pressed the phone to his right ear. He concentrated his gaze on the horses as they bickered over a nondescript blade of hay. They ate from both ends of it, their muzzles touching as they each tried to win the unspoken battle. Sonny snatched his head back and Sassy released a nasal whinny filled with fury.

"I said we found the complaint the victim made to police about harassment."

"Did you arrest the guy?" Mac's voice rose and his processor communicated the sound back to him out of sync with the vibration.

"Not a guy." Bodie cleared his throat and Mac winced.

"What?"

"A woman. Not a guy. Marie Andrews' ex-partner is female. A fruit loop according to the officers who visited her. But innocent on account of having the perfect alibi."

"What alibi?" he breathed.

Edin appeared again. She tapped her wrist to warn Mac of the time and dropped the bag she'd collected for Leslie next to the one for Hana.

"She got knocked off her bicycle weeks before the teacher died. Hasn't left the hospital since. She'd called her a heap of times looking for a sympathy vote. In the last few days she discovered the victim blocked her number."

"I did that." Mac released a sigh. "I blocked a phone number and a profile on both Facebook and Instagram. She didn't say who they belonged to, but I remember the name looked like Paul."

"You're telling me this now?" Bodie spoke through his teeth. "Geez Mac! Anyone would think you don't want us to catch her killer!"

"I'm sorry! I forgot until you just reminded me." Mac cast his mind back to the two seconds he'd had to perform the actions between soccer practice and class. Marie already had the Facebook profile ready on her screen and he'd shown her how to block unwanted connections. She'd taken back the device to switch to Instagram and the bell sounded. The girls flooded towards the main building and he'd pushed his fingers at speed through the process. She'd brought up the contact for him and he'd shown her how to block the calls. He'd assumed she had issues with a male. He gulped as he remembered his own poor conduct. The only male she'd had a problem with was him. "She asked me to do it right before a geography test." Mac heard the whine in his voice and recoiled. Something hard pinged off his leg and he looked down at a shiny pebble. He looked up at the sky and then spun in a slow, confused circle.

Edin stood in the doorway with her hands on her hips. Her lips moved and Mac dragged the phone from his ear.

"David's almost here!" she shouted. "You still haven't packed for Pa!"

"You lobbed a stone at me." Disbelief clouded his vision. Remembering his half-brother, he raised the phone to his ear again. "Pardon?"

"I said Paulette!" Bodie growled. "Paulette is her ex-partner's name. Not Paul."

"Right. Thanks." Edin disappeared again and Mac's chest tightened. "Did you discover where Miss Andrews died? You said someone moved her to the shed." A fleeting memory zinged past his inner vision and he lost it again. "When will you return my phone?"

"I didn't say anyone moved her to the shed." His tone sounded snippy. "Her handbag, house keys and phone are still missing. She didn't own a car, so that's a bust. But we're done with all the kids' phones," Bodie confirmed. "I can get yours sent to the watch house in the township if you like. It's maybe best if I stay away until after the funeral. I'll only get in the way."

Mac sensed the heavy emotional energy percolating through the speaker. His processors failed at discerning pitch and timbre but the yearning still reached him, settling over his head like a weighted blanket. He cleared his throat. "Yes, please. Send it to the watch house. But you're welcome at the marae. And with Amy and the children. It's my family, so it's yours too. Come to the tangihanga. Don't go with the manuhiri in the guest area, sit with us."

"Oh. Right." Surprise lifted Bodie's voice at the end. "Well, thanks. I'll do that."

"Oh, Bo?" Mac licked his lips. "Whoever moved Miss Andrews' body to the equipment shed knew about its dodgy wiring." He remembered the thing which had illuded him earlier. "The groundsman, Foggy, said he found an extra crate while clearing it out. You need to speak to him. Her killer must be a staff member. There's a weird sports teacher you should look at. His name is Arthur Darian." A dart of anxiety shot through his legs and weakened his knees. He wondered why he'd drawn Bodie back to the school site. Foggy told them about an anonymous boy's fumbled pass at the poor woman and now he'd sent them to go over it all again. He swallowed the lump in his throat. "Talk soon," he blurted and ended the call.

Edin swore at Mac from the doorway. She dropped Logan's gym bag onto the pavers. "I asked you to do one thing!" she shouted. "How am I meant to know what Pa needs?" The front door slammed behind her, locking him outside.

"Open it or I'll keep your phone." He strode across the lawn with her device raised in his right hand. Hysterical laughter bubbled in his chest, tears and fury just a half-step behind it. He reckoned he'd achieved at least six feet and three inches in height to compete with his father, and yet Edin reduced their relationship to that of bickering six-year-olds. But he needed to get into the house and at least fetch a change of clothes for himself.

Edin glared at him before producing her key and fiddling with the lock. The door swung open under her anger and banged against the hall table. Mac placed the device on top of the gym bag and while Edin lunged for it, he shot through the gap and slammed the door behind him. And then everything changed, his priorities reordering like chess pieces moving around a board.

After a moment's pause, Edin hammered on the door. Mac shot the deadlock as her key clattered against the metal. "I'm not coming!" he shouted. "Go without me." The handle rived up and down as she yelled at him, so he deactivated his right processor.

Silence flooded his senses, deadening everything in his frantic world.

MacGillivray Du Rose yanked his bedroom curtains closed against any attempt to get his attention and hurled himself face down on his bed. Avoidance became his only weapon against the fear and grief building behind his eyes.

56

BREAKAWAY

It took time for Mac to gather his wits enough to raise his head from beneath his pillow. If David and Edin had hammered on the window, they'd wasted their time. His processors lay on the rug where he'd thrown them.

Mac wiped his nose on his arm as he sat up, realising David had extended a hidden kindness to him. Logan's trusted property manager had a key to the house. Though Mac had deadlocked the front door, it wouldn't stop someone with a master key from opening numerous other external entrances. Mac stiffened with a sudden, horrible thought. Perhaps they sat in the kitchen even now and waited for him, listening to his roars of anger and the beating of his fist against his mattress. He placed his feet on the rug and dipped forward in anguish.

A cursory search of the house found him alone, as he'd craved. Mac wandered the empty rooms and sat on his parents' four poster bed. Hana's floral scent encircled his head, and he closed his eyes and pictured her. Gentle and sweet, she'd take up her role in the marae kitchen and, despite her personal grief, would feed the ready stream of mourners paying their respects to Alfie.

He'd stayed with her so many times as she served his father's community. As a small boy, he'd orbited her with a swathe of her skirt clutched in his fingers. Always underfoot but never a treated as an irritant. Hana Du Rose occupied a pedestal in his heart, which he doubted any woman could shake.

He stroked a hand across his father's pillow and sighed. "Idiot," he mouthed to the silent room. "I'm an idiot."

Still, the thought of facing his father burned like a brand on his cheek. Embarrassment, humiliation. He succumbed to them both in equal measure. Only shame overtook them, shame that he'd struck his own father after a life of abstinence from violence. He'd hit the one person on the mountain who least deserved to experience the worst of him. Tears prickled behind his eyelids and Mac rose on heavy legs.

He found a completed card in Hana's bureau by the window. She'd cut around a cartoon image of a golfer and decoupaged rolling hills from embossed paper. Mac sifted through the pile of condolence cards and floral tributes she'd created as a hobby, not finding one suitable as a *sorry-I-smacked-you card*. He sighed and lifted the golfer, hoping it didn't compound the insult. Logan had once had a handicap of three, according to mountain-legend, but he hadn't played in years. Lifting a silver pen in shaking fingers, he poured out his guilt onto the handmade card. The ink blotted and spread to create a decorative fringe around his words.

'Pa, I'm sorry,' he wrote. *'I have no excuse.'* The pen hovered over the white surface as Mac's brain stalled. No further contrition dripped from the nib to the page. He'd said it all in two small lines of slanted silver scrawl. Mac glanced at his watch and the digital display showed time sifting through his fingers like sand. David and Edin must have reached the marae and raised the alarm. One of his parents would leave their duties and seek him out. The thought sent his mind into a freefall of panic.

Mac stuffed the card into an ordinary envelope from the first drawer of the bureau. He'd once loved Hana's creative collection and enjoyed sifting through the artistic wonders to bestow handmade birthday cards on classmates. He swallowed the burgeoning sense of loss and choked on it. His hand shook as he scribbled his father's name on the envelope and laid it on the pillow. The green voile, which shrouded the bed, fluttered against his quick movements. He strode from the room and closed the door behind him.

His laptop booted at a press of the power button and Mac went straight into his Messenger account. The police had stopped watching his social media when they dismissed his phone as evidence. So, he took a risk and sent a message to Tilly.

Her profile picture appeared as she read it and three dots strobed beneath the phone number he'd put on the screen.

'K,' she'd typed.

Carrying his laptop with him, Mac strode to the hall and stood next to the house telephone. He groaned and swore, laying his computer on the narrow table next to a wooden bowl containing random keys. The jog to his bedroom caused him to slip on the polished floorboards in his socks. His damaged arm clattered against the door frame. Gasping, he dived for his processors and ran back to the telephone. He settled the right one in place and activated it in time to catch the trilling of the landline.

"Sorry," he puffed, pressing the receiver to his ear. "I have no other way of contacting you. Edin left and took her phone with her."

"That's okay." Tilly's voice held an unfamiliar tightness. "I'm sorry about your poppa. I didn't mean to go nuts before. You shocked me by saying the gear belonged to Miss Andrews."

"Yeah." Mac sighed. His laptop glinted in the dull light, twenty notifications hovering at the top of his Facebook profile page. He sank onto the bench and dipped forward, holding the phone while clicking the mouse with his right pinkie finger. It pained him he'd never again do that with his left one. He groaned with irritation. "Geez. The soccer girls are blowing up that group page. There are eleven posts to approve and nine requests from parents to join. I wish I'd never started this."

"I'll help you." Tilly's tone softened. "Add me as an administrator and I'll share the load." She exhaled. "As long as I'm not locked up first."

"Right." Mac sat up and turned his gaze towards the opposite wall. He focussed on the family pictures mounted there. Hana called it the *Hall of Fame*. His father called it the *Wall of Shame*. A much younger Logan frowned at him from behind a pair of sunglasses. He rode a white mare called Sacha, whose famed ill temper had matched her owner's. Mac forced himself to tune into Tilly's one-sided conversation.

"I bought the SIM and the cover from Gray. This is bad, Mac. It's terrible. He can't go back to juvenile detention. He's freaking out! A staff member is involved in BAC. They oversee it. I only just found out about that!"

"Arthur Darian." Mac ground out the name through gritted teeth. "It makes sense. That's why he checked the cupboard after we left. He downloaded the footage from the camera. Dirty bugger! I wonder if Miss Andrews found a camera in the equipment shed and confronted him. I'll kill him if he touched her!" His guilt reflex flicked to his fumbled kiss with the teacher and he cringed. Arthur Darian knew about it. He wondered why the teacher hadn't threatened him with it yet. Perhaps it would come after his persistent refusal to coach the First Eleven team.

"The BAC system isn't about blackmail." Tilly's voice contained panic. "It relies on the passive income of the bookings. If too many get caught by damning footage, the system doesn't function, does it? Word gets around it's unsafe and kids go back to doing what they did before. They go behind the bike sheds or find an empty classroom. But they don't pay to use the cupboards if it leaves them exposed. Gray says it's quite the money maker just as a booking system."

"So, what are you saying?" Mac squeezed his eyes closed and pressed the bridge of his nose with his thumb. He struggled to hold the phone against his ear and it tilted. "I don't understand."

"Someone else hijacked the system." Tilly gulped and Mac recognised the smacking of her wiping her lips with the back of her hand.

"Gray?" Mac shivered, the implications horrible. The question threatened to detonate the rest of his fragile world if Tilly's brother killed Miss Andrews.

"No!" Her instant objection held certainty. "The camera thing started ages before he came back to school. Some of the younger girls got mixed up in it. Gray only arrived back this term. He took over from another kid, and he says the two systems are separate. He only takes money for the cupboard system. Someone else told him about the footage of us and he paid them to delete it. And he promises he didn't know the new SIM, and the cover came from Miss Andrews' phone."

"What?" Mac pressed the handset closer to his ear. His lobe burned with the pressure. "The SIM we put into the iPhone I found at the crime scene?" His breath emerged as strained gasps. "It's hers? It can't be. Can it?"

Tilly groaned and a hard object hit the wall. "You said it!" Her voice rose into a cry. "You said it earlier when you phoned me. Gray is getting ready to run!"

"No! Not the SIM and the cover. The phone! The one you gave to Layla!"

Tilly's lips made another smacking sound, and she stammered, "I don't know what you're talking about! I only got those things for you. Gray bought them from another kid in his year. The boy's dad works in a tech store reconditioning old phones and computers for resale." She lowered her voice. "So, are they from Miss Andrews or not?"

57

Centre Pass

"I need to speak to Gray. Now! Get him." Mac breathed through his nose, frustration building in his neck.

"He doesn't live here." Tilly's voice held the high notes of fear.

Mac grunted. "Sorry. I'm stuck at home alone by choice. But I should get away from here to avoid a confrontation with my father. We need to talk. I must speak with Gray."

"Start walking and I'll see what I can do."

Mac snorted. "You're planning to borrow Deacon's bicycle?"

"Rude! I have resources."

"I want to see you." He sniffed. His lashes fluttered closed over his glassy irises as he conjured up her patchouli scent in his mind. "Ah, don't worry. I know it's not possible."

"I'm not sure I can get as far as your place without someone challenging me. And you can't come here to the group home. The social worker will call your parents." Tilly turned her mouth from the phone and it became harder for Mac to hear her. "My mother's old place just came up for rent again. It's empty and I still have a key."

"In the township?" Hope blossomed in his heart. The mountain of impossibility shrank just a little.

"I'll grab a ride and set off soon," Tilly promised. "But how will you get there?"

Mac blew out a breath. "Not sure. I'd borrow my pa's horse, but he's keeping mine company and I can't bring them both." The idea sprang into his mind like a starburst. "I know what I'll do. See you in a couple of hours."

Mac had struggled to drive the quad bike with his broken wrist. Its weight and bulk required too much steering on the winding tracks and besides, he needed to travel across country to avoid detection. The echoing rumble of the quad bike would draw attention to him and the old machine moved too slow. And even if he found it in the building behind the stables, he could guarantee Toby wouldn't leave the key in the ignition again.

He sat the receiver in its cradle and strode to his bedroom. It took a few minutes to dump the contents of his school rucksack onto the bed and refill it with clean clothes. He wrapped his laptop in a sweatshirt and pushed it into the depths, along with the charger. Snatching up the case for his processors, he pushed the left one into it and added it to the bag. After pressing Alfie's hat between the laptop and the front pocket, he hefted the heavy rucksack onto his back.

Mac wasted more time searching for the key to the shed. He fretted that perhaps his father had it with him until he unearthed it from the bowl in the lobby. After locking up the house and checking on the horses again, Mac uncovered an old dirt bike from the back of the shed. He hauled off the tarpaulin his father used to cover it. Spider webs hung from it in swathes of white, and he shoved them aside as he unwound the petrol cap. His right processor relayed the gentle hiss of escaping fumes to his auditory nerve. "Damn!" he cursed. "Empty."

Mac leaned against Edin's old bicycle and contemplated his options. The prospect of cycling to town across country on a pink bike filled him with dismay. He could use petrol from the bulk fuel tank in the valley to fill the dirt bike, but then risked someone seeing him. And he didn't know the code for the lock, anyway. Mac tapped his front teeth with a fingernail and his gaze settled on the lawn mower parked in the corner. His mind filled with an image of him lowering the blades and mowing a giveaway stripe like a runway from home to Tilly's rental. "You're hilarious," he chided himself.

A glance at his watch revealed another ten wasted minutes. He half expected to feel the vibration of Logan's truck arriving outside. Or worse, Hana's. While he still couldn't face his father, he dreaded the prospect of encountering his mother so soon. He recalled the disappointment in her eyes as his fist contacted with Logan's jaw. A cringe tensed every muscle in his body.

But the mower gave him an idea, and he covered the concrete pad in four strides. Logan washed and filled the heavy vehicle after every use. Mac couldn't recall ever climbing into its plastic bucket seat and finding it empty. He squeezed between the wall and the mower, leaning sideways to reach the metallic red container nestled behind the vehicle. His eyes fluttered closed as he tested its weight. A sigh escaped his lips. "Full," he breathed. His fall from Sassy had disrupted their routine. Logan had fetched gas, but Mac hadn't cut the grass on schedule.

He utilised another five minutes using the funnel to pour petrol into the bike's fuel tank with only one good hand. A glance at the acceptable oil level brought relief. Breaking down and pushing it half way to town didn't feature in his desperate plan. Mac pushed the bike outside and balanced it against his thigh as he locked the shed behind him. He shoved his right processor into a pocket on the outside of his rucksack before clamping a helmet over his ears. It seemed foolish to startle the horses with the roar of the motor and so he pushed the bike along the driveway and through the gate one-handed. The splint gave him more flexibility with his working fingers and allowed him to at least rest his arm over the left handlebar. It helped to balance and steady his trajectory more than control the bike.

Mac swung his right leg across the saddle and his rucksack dug into his spine. For the first time since breaking his wrist, he cursed his misfortune, needing his left hand for both the hot start lever and the clutch. He managed by leaning across and using his right hand to open the air flow, and then kick started the engine. His grip on the right handlebar meant he accidentally turned the throttle as the bike fired and it shot towards the hedge. Mac grunted and clenched his stomach muscles as he regained control in time for the downhill slalom towards the fork. He'd run out of time and he sensed disaster looming with every borrowed second.

Too late, he remembered the security cameras which had silently recorded his escape. Logan would work it all out and track his errant son. He knew how much gas the bike's tank could contain and he'd run the mileage through his analytical brain. No one in town would cover for him if Mac tried to buy petrol, and the bike wasn't licenced for road use. His shoulders hunched as he met the fork in the road too fast and the wheels slewed against the tight turn. A twinge from his left wrist registered its protest at the rough treatment.

Once off the lane leading from the house, Mac relaxed and slowed to a safer pace. He dropped his left arm onto his thigh to diminish the ache. The sun dipped behind the mountain in its steady pull to the horizon and shadows sprung up around him like waiting spectres. Alfie's laughter cackled in his head, and Mac's concentration wandered. He'd made the same fateful journey just a few short hours ago, its horrific outcome burning into his soul.

He made the journey again, his poppa's ghost riding with him. But this time, a sense of peace shrouded Mac's memory of the old man. Peace and an awakening. Because this time, Reuben Du Rose also hung close, a smile on his handsome, upturned lips.

Vindicated and unleashed.

Because if the township folk believed Logan was a chip off the old block, they'd seen nothing yet.

58

BALL CARRIER

It took longer than two hours for Mac to cover the many kilometres between home and the township. The hard cross-country slog exhausted him in a blur of endless gates and ditches. He pushed the bike into a hedge at the edge of the final paddock and pulled branches over the chassis. Shoving the key into his jeans pocket, he crossed a deep gully. His immobilised arm hindered him as he navigated the last Du Rose bastion. The barbed wire fence tore his borrowed tee shirt and ripped up his fingers as he half-clambered, half-tumbled, over it.

Tilly's mother's former home channelled an eerie darkness as Mac studied it from the road. Memories tugged at his psyche of their primary school years. He'd watched through the truck window after playdates as Hana delivered the elfin child back to her mother. She'd turned back to him with her green eyes troubled and her brow knitted into lines, never comfortable leaving the little girl with the latest uncle to answer the door. Mac had sensed his mother's concern but never questioned it. Another black mark blotted the smooth white copybook in his mind. He punished himself with another incidence of his abstinence of care or responsibility. The path of least resistance seemed a poor choice now as he nipped at adulthood. He resolved to do better.

The flickering of the street lamps heralded the darkness, and Mac shivered. He jogged around the side of the single storey dwelling and arrived on a smart porch overlooking a neat garden. A glance behind him revealed no interest from neighbours. Digging in his rucksack, he blinked in confusion when the tartan case containing his hearing devices disgorged only one processor. He fixed it to his head before remembering the other one in his jeans pocket. A single car rumbled along the street, hiccoughing as its exhaust backfired. The throaty bang echoed, but the silence of the tiny township closed in like a tide to muffle its effect.

Having readied himself, Mac raised his right hand and rapped on the rear door. He took a step backwards as a curtain twitched to his left. Then, a key rattled in a lock and the door swung inward just a crack. Tilly peeked out at him, only her fringe and her eyes visible. Mac froze in place, unable to read her body language with such a small amount showing. "Hi?" he managed, making it sound more of a question than a statement.

Black painted nails protruded from the gap and her fingers snagged the front of his tee shirt. "Get in here, you idiot!" she hissed.

Mac clattered with the door as she yanked him through the small gap. He jerked in surprise as he caught the top of his head on the lintel. Tilly manhandled him into a narrow galley kitchen and closed the door with a definitive click. Then she stood back and observed him. "What the hell happened to you?" she demanded.

Mac licked his lips and considered his answer. He couldn't decide on a reply without searching for the basis of her question. It had taken him longer than he anticipated making the journey and he might have annoyed her with his late arrival. He opened his mouth to speak and then clamped it shut again. The mental wrangling continued behind his eyes. Perhaps something else irritated her, something beyond his reach. It occurred to him he should ask. It seemed easier. "What do you mean?" He pursed his lips and waited. His right processor crackled, warning him it required recharging.

Tilly pointed to the front of his tee shirt, forcing him to cast his eyes downward and observe his broad chest. His eyes widened in surprise at the streaks of blood covering patches of the white fabric. "Oh!" He flicked at a bright streak near his neckline and frowned when another joined it. "My fingers," he said with a sigh. "I got caught on the barbed wire."

"That looks bad." Tilly took his hand in gentle fingers and led him to an aluminium sink near the window. She leaned forward to draw the blinds over the aperture and block out the view for prying eyes. "Run your hands under the water," she said, turning the tap and checking the temperature. She tapped his left one and shook her head. "Not this one. You'll wet the bandage."

Mac obliged by shoving his right hand beneath the flow. Tepid water coursed over his bleeding fingers. He winced as he inspected his left hand, the bandage tattered and dirty from his haphazard cross-country journey. "It didn't work out like I thought," he admitted. "Kinda chaotic, actually."

"No kidding?" Tilly liberated a bar of soap from the cupboard beneath the sink and placed it into Mac's palm. "Do your best with this," she said, her brows drawing into a black line. "It'll sting." She helped to lift his rucksack from his back before she turned away and left him to his one-handed ministrations. Mac pursed his lips and swallowed his smile. Hana would have stayed by his side, hovering, helping and offering reassurance. Tilly's lack of maternalism brought a strange kind of relief. She didn't micromanage him and he appreciated it.

He ignored her advice and used soap and water on his left hand also. It smudged some of the worst stains into the fabric, turning it into a hazy grey. She returned bearing a faded blue towel. Tufts of thread stuck out over it like prickles, and she pushed it into his hands. "I found this at the back of the airing cupboard," she concluded. "The last people left it behind." She leaned her spine against the sink and observed his patting action, making no comment about his damp bandage. "You're more accident prone than usual," she stated, her tone casual.

Mac nodded. "Yep." He sniffed and wrinkled his nose. "Be careful. It's infectious." His thoughts turned to Alfred and tears prickled behind his lids. Embarrassment sent a heady flush into his cheeks and he concentrated on patting the bandage to hide his discomfort. The painful grazes beneath it tingled against the fabric plasters applied by the doctor.

"It isn't." Tilly looped her fingers through his elbow and held it there. She offered no other platitudes but allowed him time to recover. When he glanced up at her with the worst of his grief back under control, he witnessed concern on her down-turned lips. Gratitude infused his chest when again, she didn't comment. "Do you want some food?" she asked instead.

Mac frowned as he made a mental audit of his stomach. He released a slow nod at the realisation he'd gone past the point of peckishness to a raging hunger without realising. Circumstance had robbed him of both lunch and dinner. "I am," he said, surprise in his voice.

"The electricity isn't connected." Tilly led him through an archway into a wide lounge. She walked across a carpet dappled by early moonlight and turned left into a hallway. "We need to stay away from the front of the house in case someone sees us moving around. I've set us up in my old bedroom for tonight."

Tilly drew heavy curtains across the window and activated her phone torch. She shone it onto a double air mattress shrouded in a patterned duvet. Mac's rucksack leaned against the wall on the left side. The torch beam picked up another next to it and Tilly dipped to retrieve the rustling packets. "I grabbed some snacks from the fridge at the group home," she said, her tone matter of fact. She shone the light onto a crinkled wrapper. "Bacon and cheese. This is yours." Her irises glinted as she held the package up to him.

"Thanks." Mac took it and kept it in his hand. He didn't open it, though his stomach growled in protest. Danger and excitement vied for prominence in his mind, the obvious consequences crowding him with advice he didn't want to hear. He swallowed and fingered the rounded edges of the pie through the wrapper. "What will happen now?" he asked, trying to whisper, but hearing his words emerge too loud for the silent house.

"About what?" Tilly set her phone against the skirting so that the glow filled the room. It cast shadows in the empty corners and she sank onto the mattress. It gave a flatulent creak and her eyes widened. "Oh no, I grabbed the farty mattress. Sorry."

A laugh burst from Mac's chest like an explosion. He couldn't seem to contain it. Another followed it and he clapped his right hand over his mouth, crushing the pie against his cheek. He wanted to apologise, but the words couldn't escape over the sound of his laughter. The hysteria bubbled up and out until he wished she'd stop sitting there staring at him and just slap his face instead. She didn't. Sympathy radiated from her sparkling eyes and it proved more than Mac could cope with. He turned and left the bedroom, feeling his way along the hallway until moonlight glinting off a shower cubicle showed him the bathroom. He ran water into the sink and washed his face, losing the crushed pie somewhere in the procedure.

His right processor gave a second warning. Mac turned it off and relied on his left. His tartan case contained the charger but without power, it had added extra ballast to his rucksack for nothing. He braced his right arm against the sink unit and leaned forward as water dripped off the end of his nose. Everything seemed too difficult and he couldn't filter the thoughts galloping through his mind like racehorses.

A hand rested on his back, the fingers gentle but firm. The ratty towel touched his cheek, and he lifted his hand to take it. "Thanks," he muttered. "Sorry."

"I understand." Tilly rested her cheek against his back as he used the towel to dry his face. Her arm slid around his waist. "I can leave if you'd rather stay here alone. It should be fine until the weekend. There's an open home on Sunday. I made a fake enquiry online, but the agent couldn't arrange a viewing until then."

Mac nodded and blew out a long breath. "I don't want you to leave," he replied, his tone harsher than he'd intended. "Stay with me."

"Okay," she whispered, the left processor relaying the sound as a series of crackles and a sigh.

59

CORNER KICK

Mac couldn't get enough of Tilly on the squeaky air mattress. She proved an energetic partner in crime and they wore themselves out. Physical and mental exhaustion emptied Mac's mind of anything but the desire to recover his wits enough to make love again. No other thoughts received attention. For the first time in his life, he loved being able to hear, marvelling at the gasps Tilly made when she orgasmed, and wanting more. Finally satiated and content, they collapsed onto the sagging mattress.

"I didn't think girls liked it like that," Mac said with a sigh.

Tilly snuggled against him, accompanied by a series of complaints from the rubber mattress. She giggled at a particularly vile expulsion of air from the leaking vent. "Who says?"

Mac groaned as his left processor threatened to die. "Damn. I won't be able to hear you soon," he grumbled. "Tama. Tama said it. Well, not to me, but I lipread, remember?"

Tilly snuffed out a contented breath. "I like it," she asserted. "I can't speak for other girls. Is this the same Tama who went back to a hotel room for a quickie and ended up servicing a whole bridal party?"

"Yep." Mac twisted his lips in the darkness. "Including the bride. Apparently. Pa freaked out because he thought he'd get the hotel shut down for prostitution. They left cash at the front desk when they checked out the next morning."

Tilly snuffed. "I don't think I could sleep with a complete stranger." She raised her head and Mac slipped his arm behind it and cradled her against his ribs.

"Me neither," he admitted. He pressed a kiss to her temple and smiled to himself in the darkness.

They slept until dawn the next morning when a grey light filtered through the corrugated gap beneath the curtains. Mac woke and lay for a moment in confusion, smelling the earth through the joins in the floorboards and waiting for recognition to come. He jumped as Tilly's arm snaked across his stomach. Then he remembered.

The heady blush of sex with Tilly set his heart racing, but memories of Marie and his poppa's death crowded them. It came to him in a rush, his excuse for not lying in his own bed and the reasons he'd left the safety of home.

His last processor had died in the night and left silence in its wake. Mac enjoyed the familiar peace before worry flooded in like a waxing tide. The mattress puffed from the vent as he disconnected himself from Tilly's embrace and rose.

A chill had crept into the house overnight and it nipped at Mac's naked buttocks as he padded to the bathroom. Washing his painful hands in the sink, he glanced up at his reflection in the mirror. Grief and turmoil had scored deep lines on his forehead. The dawn shadows coloured them black above his regal nose to create a starkness against his freckled cheeks. Disloyalty burned in his gut as he imagined his poppa's arrival at the marae. Leslie would perform her karanga to welcome him home, her thin voice piping her grief. Mac knew he should be there, helping his father to shoulder the casket as they threaded it through the window of the meeting house. he rested the fingers of his right hand on the smooth porcelain sink as he considered Alfie's words before he died. It explained his father's journey of stoic misery and Mac ached to support him.

But not yet.

He needed to find justice for Marie first. And watch Arthur Darian get what he deserved.

Tilly stumbled into the bathroom, her black fringe obscuring her eyes. She'd pulled Mac's torn and rumpled tee shirt over her head and sank onto the toilet without embarrassment. Her teeth glinted in the dim light as she smiled up at him, her expression lazy. "Come back to bed," she crooned. She mouthed the words so he could read her lips, but the glint in her diamond irises projected her desire without sound.

Mac settled on the side of the bath and ran a hand over his face. Stubble scratched his palm, and he blew out a breath. "I want to," he admitted. "But we should leave before the street gets busy. I've run out of time. My parents will notice I'm not at the marae this morning. If I force my father to search for me, it'll make it so much worse when he finds me." Mac dipped his head and stared at Tilly through the tops of his eyes. "And he will find me. Make no mistake about that. It's just a question of when."

"Will he hurt you?" Tilly's eyes glinted in the semi light. She made sure he'd understood before she rose and flushed the toilet. She washed her hands without looking at the running water, keeping her gaze trained on Mac's expression.

"Never." Mac pursed his lips and considered his reticence to meet Logan just yet. "But Poppa asked me to give him a message. It opens a dark part of my family's past and I'm not ready." He forced a smile onto his lips. "Arthur Darian killed Miss Andrews. And we need to prove it before I go home."

Tilly bent her knees and grimaced. Her whole body constricted into a scrunched, painful arc. "No, Mac!" She shook her head. "Please, let's leave this alone."

"Nope." Mac's lips tightened over his teeth. "How did you get here?" He jabbed his finger at the floor.

Tilly raised her arms and gripped an imaginary steering wheel with her fingers. "Car," she said. "I borrowed it."

"You have your full licence?" Mac cocked his head, surprised when she nodded. He added it to the list of things he didn't know about Tilly. In less than a day, he'd learned the most intimate things about her. He knew where she liked to be touched and where she didn't. He could anticipate the tilt of her head or the flash of her eyes and modify his lovemaking. But he couldn't recite her address at the group home because she'd never given it, and he didn't know the name of her new room mate. Mac sighed and wrapped his good arm around her waist as she edged between his thighs. The tee shirt rose to expose her bare buttocks, and he ran his fingers over the soft, familiar arch. "Edin said you wanted a white knight," he whispered. He tilted his chin so he could look into her eyes, drinking her expression as well as her reply. "Is that true?"

Tilly's lips curved into a grin and she poked her pink tongue into one corner. "No," she replied, mouthing her words for him to read. "I need a black knight."

Mac didn't understand her answer, but he accepted it. She trembled against him as he pushed her tee shirt higher and pressed his lips against the silky curve of her stomach. "Okay," he breathed. He didn't know what a black knight's performance might entail, but he could give her what he had. "One more time. Then we leave."

60

Diagonal Cross

"We need to go somewhere I'm able to charge my processors." Mac studied Tilly's lips for a response as she steered through the chicanes towards the expressway. "For the first time in my life, I'm lost without hearing." He blinked at the strange reversal of his thought patterns.

"Library." Tilly turned her head to speak to him, and waited until he nodded. She winced and tilted her head towards him again. "That text I sent to your mother has unleashed an unbroken string of missed calls from her. What should I do?"

Mac held out his hand, and she fished her phone from her jacket pocket. "I'll block her number," he said, his tone hushed. "Just for today. We'll unblock it when this is over." His fingers worked across the digital keypad to perform the action. Flakes broke off his heart and lodged in his stomach at his disloyalty. He opened the first of many unanswered texts and read Hana's frustration. Tilly's typed message kicked off the frantic exchange, but she hadn't replied to any of his mother's subsequent panicked enquiries. Mac had dictated the message, wanting his family to know he was safe. He'd promised to return once he'd dealt with his pressing issues.

Mac plugged the phone into a charger cable dangling from the cigarette lighter. He checked the battery's depleted status. By the time they joined the busy motorway, he'd relaxed at the sight of the percentage increase on the strobing marker on her screen. He sighed and touched the brim of Alfie's hat. A dint in the leather betrayed its uncomfortable journey down the mountain in his rucksack. But it screened the vibrancy of his auburn hair as they made their escape from Tilly's former home. It didn't fit right. His processors caused the brim to dip, and it wobbled on his head.

The town's loyalty to the Du Roses made staying local too risky. They'd tidied the house and left, locking up behind them. Tilly had hidden the social worker's silver car two streets away, and it started without complaint. "How did you get this?" Mac asked the question and dipped forward to rest his palm over Tilly's thigh. Another tartan skirt left her knees exposed. Heavy boots encased her feet as she rode the brake and gas pedals.

She tilted her head to allow him to read her lips while maintaining her focus on the vehicle in front of them. "He flew to a course in Wellington. Two of them travelled together, and took one car to the airport. They left the other in the garage attached to the group home." Her lips curved upward in victory. "He stashed his keys in the office safe. I've been breaking into that for years."

Mac groaned and leaned his head back against the seat. He closed his eyes to avoid becoming complicit in even more of her crimes. She didn't seem to care, and her unpredictability worried him. A flare of rebuke crushed his selfishness, and he cringed. She'd come to his aid without a moment's protest. Unpredictable but reliable then. He jerked as her hand landed on his thigh. "What?"

"An accident or something up ahead. A cop just sped past on the hard shoulder and the traffic is slowing. What should I do?"

she mouthed. She tilted her chin upward at the passing sign and Mac registered a list of Auckland off ramps. He sat up straighter and squinted as he considered their options.

"Let's go to Pakuranga," he replied. "Find the library. We can probably charge my processors there and use their internet connection for searching. It's near enough to Saint Kentigern College for students not to cause too much interest during the day, especially if we're doing research." Mac waved his hand at the first name listed. "Turn off towards Sylvia Park and keep going. We need to get off the expressway."

Tilly edged to the left of the carriageway and winced as she earned a blast of someone's horn for pushing into a narrow gap. Mac studied the concentration on her face and warmth spread outward from his heart. She gnawed her lower lip, a vertical line scored between her eyebrows. Her long lashes flickered as she played chicken in the borrowed vehicle. His face relaxed, and the tension left him as he admired her courage and determination.

"Stop grinning at me like a maniac." Tilly indicated and pulled onto the slip road. She joined the traffic crowding off the motorway like children escaping a forfeit.

"What?" Mac narrowed his eyes and dipped forward, his lips uplifted at the corners.

Tilly paused at the roundabout and glared sideways at him. "You know what I said."

Mac smiled and released a sigh. His chest deflated and a tick of happiness banished his fear. "I've always loved that about you," he mused. "You get me." He didn't watch her as he made the statement, not wanting to observe her reaction. But the car performed an unfortunate kangaroo action as she let out the clutch. It lurched onto the roundabout and hopped off at the correct exit. Mac stared through his side window and suppressed the bubble of laughter brewing in his throat.

The depleted data on Tilly's phone made finding the library difficult. Their generation knew no life without access to the information super highway, and it left them floundering. Mac resisted using her Google account to get directions, concerned it might leave them with nothing when they really needed it.

They found the library by accident as Tilly followed the signs to a medical centre and discovered the library nearby. She parked in the bays at the front of the stucco building and turned off the engine. She turned to face Mac, a wan smile on her lips. "All hail life without Aunty Google," she breathed.

Mac frowned and nodded. He glanced at his watch. "It opens at nine," he said. He dipped forward, his expression serious. "Am I shouting? I don't always realise."

Tilly shook her head. She lifted her left hand and cupped his cheek. "No." She smoothed her thumb over his lips. "Why are we here, Macky?" she asked.

Mac released his belt and screwed himself around in his seat. He dragged his rucksack high enough to pull a notebook and pen from its folds. He left his laptop inside it, unable to face the looming issues which opening it promised. "Let's make a plan," he said. "One that doesn't involve me logging on to Facebook."

61

CENTRE CIRCLE

The library opened a few minutes early, and the teenagers joined a queue of people eager to enter. A group of elderly ladies clutched hardback novels and avoided catching the eye of a homeless man. Mac carried the notebook and pen in his right hand, not objecting when Tilly slipped her arm around his waist.

Automatic doors slid open, and the queue snaked into the carpeted space. The ladies walked straight to the counter and dumped their books in front of a librarian. The homeless man shuffled towards the self-help section, yanked a book from beneath the shelf and hurled himself into an armchair.

Tilly placed her fingers over her lips in warning, and Mac nodded. They waited in line, but he jumped as a man appeared next to his elbow. His eyes flared in fear, but Tilly squeezed his wrist and smiled. Her lips moved at speed, sticking to the story they'd agreed. The librarian nodded and led them to the back of the library. He indicated a row of cubicles with his outstretched arm. Mac watched Tilly's lips curve up in thanks before she hauled out two chairs and slumped into the right one.

Mac sat next to her on an institutional orange plastic seat. He didn't need to ask what she'd said to the librarian. Tilly dug in his rucksack and retrieved the case containing his processors and charger. She handed it to him and he plugged it into a double wall socket. The unit's light turned blue and relief flickered through Mac's muscles.

The librarian returned with a battered laptop and waited while Tilly plugged it into the second socket. She nodded up at him, and Mac isolated himself from the conversation. Lipreading took energy, and he wished to conserve his and not waste it translating small talk and platitudes. Tilly waggled her eyebrows at Mac as the librarian left them.

She lifted the flap and pressed the power button. The screen flared to life. "We have it for an hour," she mouthed to Mac, and he nodded. His own device called to him from the depths of the rucksack. Faster and more powerful. In his panic, he'd left the screen open on his Facebook profile. He contemplated logging his own laptop onto the internet using the library's WiFi, but wasn't sure which of his accounts Bodie could trace. They'd had his phone for long enough to check all of them. It wouldn't cause them too much difficulty to dip back in and locate him. His mind flicked to the soccer girls, and he rolled his shoulders. He'd neglected them for long enough to guarantee their ire. It galled him he'd broken a promise, but circumstance helped him to rationalise it to himself.

The library's device booted up and presented a Google search box. Tilly pushed the laptop towards Mac, turning the keyboard so he could type. He extended the fingers of his right hand in a stretch and then prepared to type in a frustrating one-handed peck.

His first search turned up a recent article about a woman knocked off her bicycle in a hit and run six weeks earlier. Police officers caught the driver within hours and she pleaded guilty to reckless driving in an Auckland court. "That makes it easy," Mac mused. Tilly tapped his forearm, and he silenced. Too loud.

A guilty plea served to fast track the process and, after a quick trip before the magistrates, led to a sentence. Searching the court section at the rear of the newspapers revealed the name and penalty meted out to the driver. She'd lost her licence for six months and received a stiff fine. But it also gave the victim's name as per the court transcripts. Bodie had suggested Marie Andrews' ex-partner couldn't have killed her because she hadn't left the hospital. He hoped they might still find her there. He scribbled the woman's name onto a torn corner of the notepad and laid the pen beneath it. *Paulette Dunning.* Then he turned his attention to the online telephone directory.

Time marched on and a woman occupied the cubicle beside them. She spread a pile of CVs across the vacant seat next to her and used the library laptop to filter job vacancies. Tilly gave Mac an encouraging smile as he searched for an address and found nothing.

"Hospitals?" she mouthed, and he shrugged. He blinked as Tilly snatched up the note and stood. She created a waft of warm air as she whirled around. He turned to watch her stride towards the automatic doors, already lifting her mobile phone to her ear. Mac released a groan of dismay. Staff at the group home would have noticed her absence and notified the authorities. He didn't want them to triangulate her phone signal within the first few hours. Sighing, he turned back to the laptop. The woman in the next-door cubicle stared at him and he bit his lower lip, figuring his groan emerged louder than he intended. He ignored her and after a pause, she returned to her scrolling.

Tilly returned with a broad smile on her face. She slammed into her seat and used the pen to scrawl a message on the pad. 'Spinal Rehab Unit,' she wrote in her slanted handwriting. She underlined it and then added the address.

Mac opened a new tab on the laptop and searched Google maps for directions. Nineteen minutes by car took them through Ōtāhuhu to Middlemore Hospital. He leaned back in his chair with a deep sigh and nodded his head. The woman next to him stared again, and he winced. "Sorry," he said.

Tilly leaned across him and spoke to her. Her left breast brushed against his ribs and sent his mind in the wrong direction. He couldn't see her lips, but whatever she said caused the woman to look away and turn her chair so her rigid spine faced Mac.

But they'd found Marie Andrews' ex-partner. He hoped.

For the remainder of their hour, they completed online searches, which they'd never considered making before that moment. Arthur Darian's stupidity stretched to an address listing in the online telephone directory, plus a directorship for an IT company based in Mount Wellington. A Google search revealed a Facebook profile for Paulette, but they couldn't access it without logging into their own accounts. Mac resisted, but it irked him because the woman didn't appear anywhere else.

While Tilly used the bathroom, Mac closed the notepad and wound up the charger for his processors. He closed his eyes as he fitted them to his skull and braced himself for the usual cacophony to feed through his auditory nerve to his brain. He'd heard the effect compared to walking into a busy bar from the darkness of a silent street. The faint tapping of his neighbour's fingers over the keyboard trickled into his understanding, but the quiet library gave him time to adjust.

Tilly's smile stretched across her face as she returned and noticed the leads from the processors poking from beneath Mac's red curls. It added another dimension to their budding relationship but caused a flicker of resentment in his breast. Why should he need to accommodate the hearing world? Why couldn't they learn to sign or speak clearer for him? It seemed unfair that his disability marked him as the odd one in the herd and forced him always to make up the distance between them. Mac ran his hand over his face and scrubbed his eyes. The eternal issue caused him extreme tiredness.

Tilly returned the laptop to the front desk and thanked the librarian. The heavy rucksack rested over her shoulder and tugged her sleeve into a series of wrinkles. Mac carried his notebook beneath his right arm. His processor case bulged in his pocket and the cable dangled like a mouse's tail.

"I'm starving," Tilly announced as they settled back into the vehicle. She wrinkled her nose at him. "I just checked, and I got my allowance through this morning. We can use a drive through to avoid someone noticing us. What do you think? Then I'll buy some more data for my phone."

Mac nodded and clamped Alfie's hat back over his head. It tipped forward over his eyes, not designed to factor in the bulky processors behind his ears. He sighed and removed it. It offered him another excuse not to wear them. "The cops can trace your card," he murmured. "But you already used your phone, so I'm not sure there's much point in hiding." He spun the hat in his fingers, finding the action impossible one-handed. It pitched into the foot well and settled next to his right foot. Perhaps he should give the heirloom to Michael, after all.

Tilly didn't press him for reasons for his gloom. She offered a flat lipped smile of understanding and drove to a fast-food restaurant on route to the hospital. They chose breakfast from boards placed along the narrow lane which circled the building, and she paid using her card.

"Thank you." The server at the window paid them no attention. He didn't need to because a security camera captured both their faces through a wide-angled lens. The adolescent wagged his hand to his right. "Drive to the next window and wait for your order," he droned. The tiredness in his voice suggested he'd already said the same sentence over a hundred times that morning.

"Where to after breakfast?" Tilly turned to face Mac, studying his expression for clues. "The hospital website said visiting hours aren't until two o'clock." She rolled her eyes. "That's if they'll even let us in to see her."

Mac blinked as a paper bag appeared next to Tilly's open window. She took it before passing it across the vehicle to him. He placed it over his thighs, the warmth from the cheeseburgers and fries passing through the thin wrapper to heat his legs.

Mac's mood improved as the first bites of the soft bun and processed meat dropped into his stomach. The sun dappled the windscreens in the car park of the fast-food restaurant and created a cheerful aura. He spoke with his mouth full, reluctant to cease chewing. "Let's check out Darian's place," he suggested. "It's on the way south to the hospital. The business address is nearby, so we'll look there, too."

"Why?" A line of the plastic orange cheese snaked onto her chin and she wiped it off with her finger. Mac paused as she licked it clean and his mind plunged into the gutter again. His brain misfired and he no longer knew the answer to her question. Oblivious, she provided her own solution. "You're wondering why a sports teacher became linked to an IT company?" Her tumbling black fringe caused her eyelashes to stutter as she turned to face him. Mac nodded and turned his attention back to his food, willing his mind to play nice at least while they were in public view. He squirmed in his seat and Tilly frowned. "Don't you like it?" she asked. She held out her vegetarian imitation of his cheeseburger. "You can finish the cardboard version if you'd rather?"

He smiled and shook his head, forcing his brain to use its analytical skills instead of its sensory ones. "We have three hours and forty-five minutes before the hospital potentially lets us see Paulette Dunning. I need to go to the marae tonight or my absence will cast shade over my poppa. So we should use the hours we have to answer the most pressing questions." He crumpled the shiny paper from his burger in his right hand and used his index finger to point as he counted off their tasks. "One, let's see what Darian's up to when he's not harassing kids at school. The IT connection could add weight to my theory. He's behind the cameras." The thought caused a shudder to shake his torso. "Two, find out why Paulette Dunning scared Miss Andrews enough to block her." He shrugged. "Can we speak to your brother? I have questions about the BAC system and the cameras which he could answer."

Tilly nodded. "I can text him. We might need to meet him at school though, or nearby. His probation officer makes sure he attends every day. He can't risk bunking off lessons to meet us."

"Okay." Mac collected Tilly's wrapper from her lap and shoved it into the paper bag. He glanced around at the seats and carpet, keen not to create a food mess and draw suspicion when the social worker returned for his car. He left to put the rubbish into a nearby dustbin and returned to find Tilly plugging her phone back in the charger.

"I messaged him. He's pretty quick, so we should hear soon." She started the engine and waited for Mac to fasten his seat belt. He paused with his fingers caressing the webbed fabric. "What's wrong?" she asked. She mouthed the words with enough clarity to make his processors redundant. Her fingers tapped a nervous beat on the gear stick.

Mac leaned across the divide, reaching up with his right hand to cup her soft cheek. His lips brushed over hers, and he tasted the grease from her burger, overlaid by a fresh application of red gloss. "Come to my poppa's tangi with me?" he asked, his tone sincere. "I want you there. With me."

She nodded, and he knew she'd make it happen. Despite her imprisonment in the social care system and despite the difficulty. She'd be there. Her eyes crinkled as she tilted her head and deepened the kiss. Mac's stomach plunged into his boots and left him breathless. He realised in that moment that she represented everything he wanted and needed. Her severe but faultless makeup projected anarchy, but her kisses betrayed an innate sensitivity reserved only for him. *'Never underestimate the value of a good woman, Macky.'* Poppa Alfie's ghost whispered the words and Mac realised she'd been right under his nose the whole time.

62

HEADER

"Do you know where Sammy lives?" Mac frowned as he stared through the windscreen. An estuary snaked beneath them, meandering across low ground under the bridge as though it had all the time in the world. "Or can you call her?" He glanced at his watch. "She must know who controls the cameras because of her involvement."

"What involvement?" Tilly eased the vehicle behind a westbound gravel lorry and dropped her speed to match its steady plod.

Mac turned to her with a frown etched onto his forehead. It created a severe expression. "You said she got involved last year."

"Sammy?" Tilly's mouth hung open. "No, that's not right. She wouldn't do something like that."

"But you said she lured the older boys to the cupboard where they got filmed."

"I did not!" Tilly's body became spiky, her elbows and knees seeming to jut from her body like prickles. "You heard that from someone else and they're wrong!"

Mac narrowed his eyes and stared at the fabric ceiling. He forced his mind back through numerous conversations over the last few days. "Edin, then," he conceded. "She told me. That's why she threatened her to stay away from me. She didn't want Sammy luring me to the cupboard and ending up with grief and a porno movie."

Tilly shook her head and her black curls bounced against her shoulders. She raised an eyebrow and shot Mac a covetous glance. "If you dropped your trousers, I promise you Sammy would run."

"Oh." Hurt turned down his lips. "Nice."

Tilly clamped her teeth over her bottom lip and smothered a laugh. "Idiot! In a good way. I understand now why the Du Rose boys have such a reputation." She waggled her eyebrows before growing serious. Her mood darkened again, her chin jutting down in challenge. "No, Macky. I promise you're wrong about Sammy. She's a good kid. A total fruit loop, but not bad. Just because we've grown up in the care of social services doesn't mean we're all criminals. That's an unfair stereotype and I resent it. My mum chose drugs over me and my brother. She overdosed. He only started stealing to feed us both when she used all the money on heroin. And he's the exception to the rule. Many of us turn out okay, believe it or not."

Mac formed words with his lips, which he didn't release. "I don't understand this," he sighed. "If it wasn't Sammy, then who?"

"You're right about one thing," Tilly conceded. "We need to speak to Gray. I've texted him. Let's see if he calls me."

They continued their journey in silence. Tilly stopped once at a roadside dairy to buy a top-up card for her phone. She entered the code and waited for the text, confirming she'd added data to her account. Mac spotted a telecommunications tower mounted on a tall, flat roofed building and sighed. He figured he should just call Bodie and save him the bother of searching for him.

Tilly entered Arthur Darian's home address into Google maps and pushed her phone into Mac's right hand. "Hold this," she commanded. "I'll need help as we get nearer to his house."

Mac took it without argument. A sense of resignation settled over him as he balanced his forearm across his knee and tilted the screen so she could see it. The narrator's voice offered instruction in a robotic tone as Tilly drove to Mount Wellington. Mac plugged the phone back into the charger with a jerky movement as he noticed the drastic reduction in the battery level.

"Slow down. We're almost there," Mac cautioned. He stared through the windscreen at the passing houses. Hamlin Road overlooked a construction site with towering cranes moving in slow motion across the sky. The street rose at a steady gradient and Tilly steered the car towards a cycle lane, stopping before dotted yellow lines protected a sharp left-hand bend. She pointed ahead through the windscreen. "There's a school up there." She tutted at the robotic voice, which sounded louder as Tilly switched off the engine.

'You have reached your destination on the right.'

"It's there." Tilly turned towards a white house situated sideways to the street.

Mac leaned forward to see past her. "That one?" he asked with a frown. "It's smarter than I expected. Darian always looks like he's been dragged through a hedge." He sat back in his seat and twisted his lips. "There's something I didn't consider. What if he lives with someone else?"

Tilly shrugged. "That's better, isn't it? We can ask questions. We'll learn more than peering through windows." She winced and spun to face him. "What if he has security cameras? If he's set them up at school, it stands to reason he'd have them at home. Doesn't it?"

Mac blew out a breath. "I think you're giving him more credit than he deserves. The man's an idiot." He disconnected her phone from the charger and held it out to her. "Why don't we just knock on the door? What story can we tell?"

Tilly exhaled and sat back in her seat. "It's risky, Mac. It's bound to get back to him." She lowered her voice in a poor impression of an unknown bass male. "Oh, yeah. A punky girl and a guy with a hearing impairment popped in asking for you." She exhaled. "You don't think he'd work it out?"

Mac chuckled. "It's interesting how you settled on a male voice. Do you think Darian is gay? I kinda expected him to live with his mum."

"What? Like you do?" Tilly's eyes curved into almond shapes and she grinned.

"No." Mac scowled across at her. "I think little girls are safe around me, thanks."

Tilly tutted and slapped his knee. "Don't sulk," she said with a sigh. She dug her nails into his leg, their sharpness pinching the skin. "You know, I didn't mean to infer anything like that. And I'm not dwelling on Darian's preferences." She gave a visible shudder. "He's dodgy and I can't believe the headmaster didn't fire him after the last round of rumours." Then she gasped and turned to face him. "I've got it! Let's knock on the door and pretend we need to see him. We can't disguise ourselves enough to put him off the scent, so let's capitalise on your connection. You can say you want to speak to him about coaching the First Eleven."

Mac squirmed in his seat. "But I don't want to. And why wouldn't I approach him at school about it? Why go to his house?"

Tilly drew a blood red gloss from the top pocket of her jacket. She levered down the sun visor and drew around her lips in a single movement while staring at her reflection in the tiny mirror. Mac watched in fascination at her precision. She snapped the lid back into position and flicked up the visor. "Let's just wing it, Mr Du Rose." She lowered her chin and stared at him through the tops of her eyes. "If in doubt, blag it out."

Mac groaned. "That falls a mile outside my skill set." He shook his head. "I like a plan. It's too risky. What if he's at home instead of working?"

Tilly shrugged and waggled her head from side to side. Her black pigtails touched each shoulder like a subconscious tagging. "Then leave all the talking to me," she said with a smile.

Mac floundered as she exited the vehicle and her door clicked behind her. Despite her bravado, she'd parked facing south and avoided the easier option of Darian's driveway. She sauntered across the road and left him no choice but to follow her.

63

BLIND SIDE

"Who?" A woman with white hair peered at them from her doorway. Mac balanced on the second step behind Tilly as she knocked.

"Mr Darian." Tilly pursed her lips and pressed herself against Mac, an unspoken anxiety tell. He lifted his right hand and set it over her hip beneath the cover of her jacket. He pushed the sense of solidarity through his fingers into her psyche. Tilly cleared her throat. "Sorry to bother you," she said again. "This is the address for him."

The woman stepped onto her narrow porch in fluffy slippers. A checked housecoat covered a neat skirt and blouse. "The name sounds similar, but it wasn't Darian. Anyway, that man hasn't lived in this street for over six months." Exasperation speckled her tone. "I keep telling everyone. The bailiffs came for him last week." She jabbed a crooked finger towards the driveway leading past her house. "He lived at 26b. This is number 26."

"Ohhh." Tilly's exclamation contained understanding. "I get it now. He lived behind you?"

The woman nodded and stilled at the ping of a timer from the house. "That's my cookies. I need to take them out of the oven."

"Sorry to have bothered you." Tilly turned to leave.

"Where are you from?" The woman stopped with one slipper already over the threshold. "Does he owe you money?"

"No, nothing like that." Tilly paused mid-turn and Mac's fingers brushed her stomach. "He's our teacher. Mac wanted to speak to him about coaching the soccer team. It's fine. We'll catch him at school tomorrow." She spun on the step and clattered against Mac's chest. He hadn't moved backwards, still shocked by her use of his real name. He gaped at her in horror and missed the woman's question. Tilly whirled back to face her. Mac watched as she climbed to the level of the porch and held out her hand. "I'm Tilly Rae," she said, no discomfort in her tone. She turned to face Mac. "This is my boyfriend, MacGillivray. Would you like to see some identification? I have my driving licence here." She dug in a pocket hidden behind the waistband of her tartan skirt and pulled out the small card. The woman dipped forward to peer at it. Speechless, Mac watched the disaster unfold in front of his eyes.

"And you know where this man is now?" Crinkles showed at the corners of the woman's eyes and mischief twinkled in rheumy blue irises. "I'd appreciate somewhere to send the next lot who come searching for him. If it's the same man, though. Short, podgy, stringy hair pulled over his bald patch." She frowned. "He always wore a track suit of some sort. Matching top and bottoms."

"Yes. That's him." Tilly nodded at the accurate description of Arthur Darian. "Would you like me to write the address and phone number for the school?" She glanced around at Mac. "Please, can you grab the notebook from the car?"

"No need." The woman's demeanour changed. "I have paper and pens." She waggled neat grey eyebrows and grinned at Tilly. "And I also have chocolate chip cookies fresh from the oven. I'm a bitch," she said. Mac gulped. Her lips creased upwards at his startled expression. "A bitch who bakes. It's a charity. Someone will arrive soon to take the cookies to the women's shelter. But I can spare a couple for hungry visitors. Come in."

Before Mac could object, Tilly stepped over the threshold and into the house. She wiped her heavy boots on the mat with care as the woman disappeared along a narrow hallway. By the time Mac had jogged up the three concrete steps to the level of the house, Tilly had already removed her boots.

Mac followed with more caution. He leaned against the wall and struggled with his cowboy boots one-handed. Tilly's voice echoed from deeper in the house, her gentle tones carried to his auditory nerve through the processors. He paused a moment and listened, marrying the sound of her voice to the steady vibration it caused when she laughed. Mac locked the front door before retracing Tilly's steps to a kitchen at the back of the house.

"There you go." The woman smiled at him and placed a platter on the bleached pine table. Chocolate cookies speckled with melting chips spilled over the edges. She'd spared more than the promised few. Comfortable in her own skin, Tilly behaved as though she lived there. She leaned across the sink to pump soap into her palms and washed her hands. She looked over her shoulder at Mac and jerked her head towards the running water. Wrong footed and lacking courage caused a delay, and a frown bisected Tilly's forehead.

Mac obeyed, more from a desire for harmony than from agreement with their visit. He waited for Tilly to pump soap into his right hand before smoothing the foam across his palm with the fingers of his left. The bandage keeping the splint in place embarrassed him. The grey hue had spread throughout the fabric to create an ingrained dirtiness which pained him. Mac accepted the fluffy towel from Tilly before patting dry the fingers of his left hand and then hiding the splint behind his back.

"Tea or coffee?" The woman addressed Mac, and he faltered, not wanting either. He pursed his lips and considered his reply.

"Please, may I have water?" he asked.

She nodded, her curls bouncing at her nape. Tilly tapped Mac's elbow and tugged a chair from beneath the table. She jerked her head to encourage him to sit. "Judith had problems with Mr Darian," she said, sinking into the seat next to him. She widened her eyes and nodded, catching him up with what he'd missed. "Noise, accumulation of rubbish." She flattened her lips and stared at the cookies. "Gosh, these look gorgeous."

Tilly half rose to fetch a plate from the pile Judith had set next to the cookie platter. She placed one in front of Mac and laid a cookie on it. He observed her through the corner of his right eye, not sure he liked her mothering him. It added a new facet to their relationship and vied with his independence. But he ate the cookie anyway and closed his eyes with enjoyment as warm chocolate burst onto his tongue. As she rested her fingers over his thigh, he started.

"Mr Darian isn't a nice man," she continued with seamless timing, as though the conversation hadn't suffered a hiatus. "He wants to force Mac to coach the First Eleven, even though he doesn't want to do it."

Judith made a sound like a harrumph and shook her head. She concentrated on laying warm cookies into a cardboard box with care. "He's an asshole," she mused and Mac halted with a cookie half raised to his lips. A glance at Tilly confirmed he'd heard her right. "Back in a moment," she said, lifting the box and carrying it through the hallway to the front door.

Mac leaned sideways to whisper to Tilly. "I feel bad about this," he confessed. "I'm not comfortable."

Tilly nodded in response and schooled her face for Judith's return. To Mac's surprise, she fixed their drinks and slumped down at the table opposite them. He laid his cookie on the plate and lifted his glass. Condensation trickled over his fingers.

"How did you hurt your arm?" Judith sipped a mug of coffee and waited for Mac's reply.

"Fell off a horse," he managed between slurps of cold water. "I hurt it again yesterday and the doctor sawed off the cast." He frowned and cocked his head. "Actually, an ex-fire officer sawed it off. The doctor watched." Mac glanced down at the dirty bandage and frowned. "I'm waiting for an appointment with a surgeon to check for extra damage." The words poured from him like verbal diarrhoea and he couldn't seem to stop himself. Judith reminded him of Leslie with her solid frame and generous baking. His next revelation caused Tilly to give a sharp intake of breath. "I've lost the use of my little finger." He lifted his left hand and frowned at it. "My parents don't know yet." The glass trembled as he set it back on a waiting coaster.

He glanced up to find Judith studying him. The sharp edges softened in her expression. "I'm sorry that happened," she replied. She lifted her right arm above the lip of the table and gave him time to note the curled fingers. "Stroke," she added as an explanation. "I got rid of the limp, but the hand never came right." She shrugged and lowered her wrist to the table. "We just make the best of things, don't we?" Her eyebrows waggled. "Or we die miserable and make everyone else glad we're gone."

Mac swallowed, lost for a suitable retort. He considered pointing out his processors in case she hadn't already noticed, but it seemed too much like a one-up-man-ship. A pity party with no winners. He cleared his throat and concentrated on reading the room better. Tilly sat next to him, her gaze fixed on the cookie oozing chocolate chips onto her plate.

"You didn't like Mr Darian living next door?" Mac asked. He forced his shoulders to relax their tension. "And you said he moved out six months ago?"

"Yes. If it's the same man." Judith sipped her coffee and her grey curls tapped her forehead. "The owner inherited the place from his parents. He didn't want to sell, so rented it to a lovely couple for about two years. They moved to Australia, and this guy moved in. The problems started soon afterwards. He kept a dog which barked all day and night. Poor thing. The council took it away in the end. We have a refuse collection on Tuesday mornings, but he never quite got his out in time. Dustbin bags piled up in his yard and stunk out the neighbourhood." Judith's nose crinkled at the bridge and the action drew her eyebrows into a thin line. "He had people visiting every evening. My neighbours on the left suspected he dealt drugs." She frowned and shook her head. "I doubted that, although drug addicts come in every shape and form, don't they?" She searched Tilly's expression for solidarity and faltered at what she saw there.

Mac stretched his right arm behind Tilly's chair and rested his hand on her shoulder. He wondered at the mental images filtering through her mind. Pictures of a woman gripped in the thrall of heroine, cocaine, and anything else she could shove up her nose or into her blood stream. Emotional and physical neglect filled Tilly's childhood. Mac squeezed her shoulder, gratified when Judith changed the subject.

"I don't know what kind of business occupied him," she concluded. "Some of his visitors had nice cars with well-dressed owners. His rental agreement forbade running a business, but it didn't stop him." She exhaled. "The landlord got sick of the complaints and evicted him. It took almost a year to force him to leave. He hired a van and moved around thirty computers." She rolled her eyes. "But he must have used a dodgy credit card because the van company followed up a few days later wanting a forwarding address."

Mac squinted and studied the view through the kitchen window. An old-fashioned English garden stretched beyond the outline of a wooden shed. Hollyhocks bobbed their bulbous pink and purple heads as though agreeing with their owner. Geraniums snaked along the boundary fence, their petals crinkled and past their prime. "The computers must relate to his IT company," he mused. "We found a listing for him on the national website for registered companies. The address is for Mount Wellington, but a different street."

Judith nodded and set her mug on the table. "He came from somewhere local. I don't believe he owns much." She winked at Mac. "My neighbour keeps a pair of binoculars for his birdwatching." The amusement in her smile suggested no actual study of feathery creatures took place through their lenses. "That's how I know he shifted the computers when he moved. And I've seen him driving around in his vehicle when I take my evening walk. I don't think he moved far." She hitched her left shoulder in dismissal. "I can't imagine he got good references from his previous landlord, so the place he rents now must be very low budget with an ask-no-questions policy." She wrinkled her nose. "If he'd behaved nicer towards me, I might have sympathy. But I found him slippery and obnoxious."

Mac shot a glance at Tilly. She'd just described Arthur Darian with more accuracy than either of them hoped when they'd knocked on the door. Tilly dipped her body forward as she retrieved her glass from in front of her. Condensation welded it to the coaster, and she jerked to grab it as it lifted with the glass before plunging towards the table. She wiped it on her skirt before replacing it. "You think he used a similar name to Darian?"

Judith nodded. "Yes. I wish I could remember what he called himself. But not that for sure."

A knock sounded on the front door, echoing off the narrow walls of the hallway to reach the kitchen. Judith rose. "Won't take a second," she said. "I just need to give the cookies to the driving bitch."

Tilly pursed her lips together to avoid laughing. As Judith's footsteps receded along the corridor, she leaned closer to Mac to whisper. "Do you think we've learned all we can?" she asked him, mouthing her words to avoid raising her voice. He nodded in reply. By the time Judith had returned from waving off her visitor, they'd decided to leave.

"Oh." Judith wrinkled her nose and her shoulders dipped. "You could stay for lunch if you like?"

"Thank you. We have someone to visit at Middlemore Hospital." Tilly smiled at her. "Do you have that piece of paper? I'll write the address and phone number for the school."

Judith reached into the drawer of an old dresser and retrieved a pad and pen. She set it on the table in front of Tilly. Mac rose to leave, after glancing at his watch. Tilly used her phone data to find the number for the school's front office and wrote Darian's name at the bottom. Mac frowned as she added her own name and phone number. "This is me." She rested a black painted fingernail over her name. "Call me if you hear something else?" She shrugged, a strange motion of her shoulders, which betrayed an inner craving. "Or if you'd just like to chat."

Judith nodded, satisfied with the trade. "I'd like that," she concluded. "Perhaps you could come for tea?"

"Yes please." Tilly grinned. To Mac's surprise, she stepped towards Judith and wrapped her arms around the woman's shoulders. "Thank you for the cookies. I've tasted nothing that good for ages."

Judith beamed all the way to the front door. She strode ahead of them and Mac noticed the downward slope of her right shoulder and the banished limp which appeared on each second step. They parted as friends on the doorstep and Judith watched them cross the road to the car. She waved again as Tilly started the engine and pulled away from the curb.

"Why did you give our real names?" Mac demanded. "And your phone number?"

Tilly gave a wooden shrug. "She's lonely. And so am I. My mother fell out with her family and I never knew my dad's people. There's a vacancy for a kind old lady who bakes awesome cookies." She tapped her heart with her index finger, and Mac shrank back into his seat. Shame bloomed across his cheeks as he stared through the side window. The passing houses became a blur in his peripheral vision. He'd had it all. Alfred and Leslie

Du Rose provided a constant source of encouragement and love throughout his childhood. He shared no blood and only a distant DNA with one of them, yet never doubted their love for him. The new normal of a life without Poppa Alfie's curses echoing from the apartment's bedroom hit him afresh. He spent the next ten minutes pinching his thigh to stop the tears leaking onto his cheeks. At least he'd known the love of grandparents. Tilly hadn't.

She used her phone data again to find the route to Middlemore Hospital. "It's at the edge of the main campus," she commented, lifting her phone from the cup holder to peer at it. "Please, can you hold the map for me again?" She shoved it towards him without looking.

Mac took it and glanced at the digital display on the dashboard. They'd spent longer than he realised with Judith. He yawned and covered his mouth with his hand, the phone pulling taut against the charger cable. "We have an hour to wait before visiting time," he said, his voice distorted by a second yawn which followed it. "I'm stuffed on fast-food and cookies. And we didn't sleep much last night."

"Same." Tilly squinted sideways at the map but her lips quirked upwards. "Why don't we snag a parking space at the rehab unit? I bet it's limited, so if we're there early, we won't need to fight for a spot. Then you can nap for a while. I'll look at the information we've gathered so far."

Mac agreed, though he didn't imagine for a minute he'd sleep in a stolen vehicle in a busy car park in the centre of a metropolis.

64

Chip Pass

The ringing of Tilly's phone woke him. He'd removed his processors to sleep, but the vibration alerted him to the change of energy in the vehicle. The suddenness left Mac shocked and flailing. He couldn't work out his location, or why his spine ached at the angle of the seat.

"Sorry," Tilly mouthed as she answered the call.

Mac scrambled to reattach his processors, appalled at her acceptance of the incoming intrusion. Thoughts flew through his mind, assessing and dismissing the danger. Sound flooded his auditory nerve, and he lost valuable seconds as he separated the various strands. Tilly blinked at his alarm and tilted the screen towards him. "It's Gray," she mouthed, and he saw her brother's name written in a digital font.

Mac reached across himself and scrabbled beside the seat for the switch to raise it. The awkward twist so he could use his right arm hurt the base of his spine more. He utilised the seconds with his head shoved between the door and the armrest to school his expression into something less terrified. When Tilly disconnected the call, he turned to her with irritation in his frown. "What if that was my mother?" he demanded. "Or Bodie, or the school. What about the cops or someone from your group home?"

Tilly blinked at him, her eyes narrowing to slits. "Then I wouldn't take the call," she growled. She jabbed her finger at the digital clock on the dashboard, the motion spiky. "It's the end of lunchtime at school. Gray just saw my message and phoned me."

Mac swallowed and forced his anxiety into submission. He'd led such a peaceful existence beneath the mask of oblivion. He ached to drive home and hide in his safe bedroom on his father's gentle mountain. The real world beyond their gates held too much conflict and decision making to soothe his battered nerves. "Fine!" he snapped. "Will he meet us?"

"Yes!" Tilly's reply held an attitude and her pigtails gave a jerky bounce. "Five o'clock at the equipment shed. He has a tutorial with Mr Simms tonight. The social worker will fetch him on Alexandra Street afterwards. He walks across the field."

Mac groaned. "Of all the places I'd rather not go again." He slapped his right palm over his thigh. "Can't we meet him on the field instead?"

Tilly hardened her jaw and glared at him. "No." She blew out a ragged breath. "And while you slept, I checked out some of the online marketplaces for reconditioned computers. Darian has a legitimate business." She called up an image on her phone screen and turned it towards Mac. "But he's also stupid. Look, do you recognise this sticker?"

Mac leaned sideways and cupped her fingers with his, pulling the screen closer. "Yeah. Didn't we have an IT class during our second year where the teacher made us stick them onto the new laptops?"

Tilly nodded and her lips tightened. "Yes, in Year 10. That's what I thought, too. So, why hasn't anyone noticed him stealing school equipment?"

Mac dragged his knuckles across his scratchy eyes and sighed. "I'm not sure. Tech can't just go missing, can it? The teachers would realise they didn't have enough for each class."

Tilly tapped the steering wheel with her index finger. "You'd think so. But you've met the head of department. What I really don't understand is why Darian is so broke." Her tone held a note of incredulity. "It makes no sense. The man works two jobs and yet he gets kicked out of every rental he occupies."

Mac stared through the windscreen at the brick wall they'd parked against. "Judith said the complaints centred around his slovenly behaviour. Dogs, noise and rubbish. She said nothing about rent arrears."

Tilly nodded and reached a tentative hand across to lay her palm on his thigh. She tested his spikiness with the expertise of a horse whisperer. Mac bit back a smile. "The bailiffs," she reminded him. "Judith keeps sending them away, but they're looking for Darian."

Mac exhaled and ran a hand over his face. His sprouting beard scratched against his fingers like sandpaper. "Should we care why he's broke? We know he is, and it's perhaps dictating his behaviour. Desperation makes people do hideous things." His mind strayed to Edin's mother, and he shivered.

An ambulance arrived in front of the single storey building. The teenagers watched as the driver emerged without urgency. She opened the rear doors and her male partner appeared. Together, they extracted a gurney and wheeled it into the lobby. A fluffy grey head rose above the raised pillow and the driver reached into the vehicle for an overnight bag. Tilly blew out a sad sigh. "It's life-changing, isn't it?" she mused. "One minute you have everything, and the next it's cataclysmically ruined." She clicked her fingers to punctuate her observation, and Mac nodded.

"We take risks every day on the mountain," he replied. "We ride horses and manage heavy equipment. It only takes a second to get a kick to the head or not move aside fast enough when herding cattle into the crush for weighing." His frown created deep lines on his freckled forehead. "Pa gets mad when the stock hands don't take proper care. They think it's because he's afraid of prosecution, but it's because he cares about them." He swallowed and wrinkled his nose on one side. "I guess he doesn't want to end up in court, but it's not the only reason."

Tilly lifted her left eyebrow in a quizzical expression, which made him smile. "Yeah, I mean, you could fall and bugger your arm. Or lose the use of a finger. What would you do then?"

"Haha, funny guy." Mac stuck his tongue out at her, gratified when she leaned across and kissed him.

"Seriously, though." She reached up and smoothed his red fringe away from his eyes. "Talk to your folks about your hand. They deserve to know."

Mac nodded and pictured himself faltering through the conversation. He realised his biggest obstacle lay in knowing Logan would blame himself. When he shook his head and stared down at the splint peeking from behind the bandage, Tilly leaned forward to stare up into his face. "What?" she demanded.

Mac lifted his forearm and glared at it. "It happened when Miss Andrews died. My fingers all worked fine after I fell from Sassy." He swallowed and his Adam's apple seemed to lodge in his throat. His words held a strangled quality. "I lifted Layla and the tendon snapped. But everything leads back to Miss Andrews' death. All the bad stuff happened after that."

Tilly cupped his cheek in her palm. Her blue irises glittered with gentleness. "Yeah, but we've also brought some of it on ourselves." She sat back with a shrug. "If I hadn't rented the cupboard, we wouldn't have made an accidental porno." She waved her hand in the air. "And so on, and so forth."

"I hear ya." Mac jerked his head towards the entrance to the hospital unit. "I'm sure it's the best porno Darian ever watched." He shivered and released a grunt. "Yuk. Don't dwell on that image." The automatic doors slid open at the feet of the ambulance shuttle driver and her companion. They exited into the balmy air and walked to their vehicle. Mac slapped his right thigh, infusing himself with confidence he didn't feel. "Let's deal with one thing at a time. We'll visit Paulette Dunning and then speak to Gray. If we do nothing else today, let's vindicate Miss Andrews and nail Arthur Darian's nasty ass to the wall."

65

Attacker

"We're here to visit Aunty Paulette." Tilly fixed a smile on her lips and oozed confidence. Mac straightened his shoulders and watched her familiar acting routine. Faking it until she made it. He guessed it epitomised the sonata of her life, conjuring assurance where the relevant adults failed to create it.

"Let me see." The receptionist peered at a computer screen to her right. She squinted as though prolonging the moment where she admitted to her failing eyesight and bought glasses. The avoidance had gouged a furrow between her brows and caused crinkles at the corners of her eyes. Mac raised his right hand to touch the processor magnetised to his skull. He sighed, remembering when vanity became an issue, and he started removing them to negate the spiteful comments of classmates. The Disabled Du Rose. The name calling began in primary school.

"Paulette Dunning." Tilly continued in her even, unworried tone. "She moved here from the main hospital yesterday. A bicycle accident."

"Ah yes." The receptionist pushed a clipboard across the counter towards Tilly. "Fill in your details and I'll check she's available." She lifted a phone to her left and used pre-programmed buttons on the mini switchboard at her elbow.

Mac's brain ran riot over the various issues which might affect her availability. He suppressed the groan rising in his chest as Tilly's slanted handwriting spread lies across the page. A cursory step forward gave him the visibility of her expert form filling, and he inhaled in shock. Again, she'd betrayed their true identities. She laid the pen on the clipboard and edged it back towards the receptionist. Mac hooked his fingers around her forearm and gave a warning squeeze.

"Stop!" she hissed to him, mouthing the word without sound. Then she faced him and spun her wrist, so she caught his fingers in hers. "If you tell lies, you're responsible for maintaining them," she growled, her lips moving with clarity. "I'm leaving breadcrumbs in case someone gets upset with us."

The receptionist replaced the handset and rose. She left her seat behind the counter and walked through a doorway to her right, disappearing for a few seconds before arriving in front of them.

"This way," she said, her tone bright. "She's had her physio this morning and a nice shower. Her nurse says you can come straight through."

Mac's slower steps caused him to fall behind as he considered Tilly's statement. His mind whirred with the possibilities. As they tracked Marie Andrews' murderer, it hadn't occurred to him they might end up as the ones hunted. He watched Tilly's bouncing pigtails tap the tips of her shoulders and his heart quailed. His fists bunched and his left wrist protested. The scar hidden beneath the bandage tightened to remind Mac of his inadequacies. It seemed hopeless as he plodded the clinical corridor. In order to keep Tilly safe, he needed to understand more about Arthur Darian. How could such a ridiculous individual present such a cataclysmic threat? Mac faltered at the wide doorway to a bay housing four beds. Fear threatened him with the impropriety of surprising a woman who couldn't defend herself. "Wait!" he hissed to Tilly. "You should go in first."

"Why?" Her eyes narrowed in suspicion. "This is your idea!"

Oblivious, the receptionist kept walking into the room. She vanished behind a hospital curtain pulled around the bed furthest away from the door. Sunlight streamed through the vast windows lining one wall. It cast buttery shafts over the fluttering orange fabric, setting the curtain on fire. Mac shook his head and squeezed Tilly's fingers. "It's not fair," he whispered. "At least make sure she's dressed. Whatever she did to Miss Andrews, she still deserves some dignity. It's not like she can run away from a strange guy walking in on her, is it?" His own disability scored a cleft across his heart and created the abrupt turnaround. He wouldn't stamp across another person's choices as so many others had done to him. His jaw tightened, and he locked his knees to prevent Tilly from pulling him into the room.

The pressure released on his fingers and she rose onto her tiptoes and kissed him, her lips warm over his. "I thought for a second you got scared." She cocked her head, and a smile rose on her lips. "But you're a good guy, aren't you, Mac Du Rose?" she breathed. "Too good for me." She spun away from him and approached the furthest bed, beckoned by the curved finger of the receptionist. The woman cocked her finger and frowned at Mac. Tilly leaned sideways to whisper something and her face softened.

"It's fine," she called, waving him over. "Everyone is decent." The woman's outstretched arm encompassed the other residents in their various states of injury. One bed remained empty, its starched sheets waiting for a new victim of tragedy and accident. The other inhabitants watched his steady gait as he strode across the room. He saw them in his peripheral vision, but kept his gaze on Tilly and tried not to look at them. A lifetime of stares and comments made him leery of forcing others to endure the agony.

Mac thanked the receptionist as he stepped to the end of the last bed on the left. The curtain fluttered in his wake. He blinked in surprise as a man rose from the only visitor's chair and smiled at him. "Right then," he said to the woman in the bed. "I'll leave this exercise log on here." He placed a sheet of paper onto the night stand and tapped it with an index finger. By squinting, Mac noticed lined tables produced by a spreadsheet, with empty spaces for tallying. The man lifted two fingers to his temple and gave the visitors a casual salute. Muscular biceps bulged beneath his medical uniform of blue scrubs. Sensible shoes gave muted squeaks on the tiled floor. He drew bushy black brows into a line and pursed his lips, moving his gaze from Tilly to Mac. "Anyway, you know the drill. No running around and no ball games," he said with perfect seriousness. His face relaxed into a grin and he included the patient in his humour. "Not today, anyway. Maybe soon." He leaned forward and touched her fingers. "You'll progress faster over here." He left, dragging the curtain with him and shoving it back against the wall. Mac glanced at Tilly and blew out an anxious breath.

"Hi." Tilly jumped straight onto the offensive, stepping forward to introduce herself. She held out her hand, but it faltered in mid-air as though it occurred to her too late that Paulette Dunning couldn't take it.

"Hey." A pale hand lifted from the mattress, stopping a few inches from the sheet. The stunning brunette closed her eyes, and a frown crossed her porcelain forehead. "Sorry. I keep forgetting I can't do things."

In a smooth motion, betraying no awkwardness, Tilly turned the handshake into a downward movement and gripped the woman's limp hand. Instead of releasing it, she maintained the contact and slumped into the visitor's chair. The woman's shoulders relaxed.

"How can I help you?" she asked, her tone dull. "You aren't cops and I'm not your aunt." She turned her head and her long, mahogany curls covered the pillow like autumn leaves. "So, what do you want?"

Mac remained silent as Tilly explained in hushed tones. He focussed on the gentle lull of her voice as she told their tale in as few words as possible. Their teacher had died, and they wished to bring her justice. Mac's processors often failed to relay pitch or timbre and he shot worried glances at the other two occupants of the room. One read a book, turning pages with a swish at regular intervals. A sling supported her right leg from a hoist overhead, only the toes peeking from the end of a fibreglass cast. The other slept, her mouth open and her chest rising at a steady rate. Sheets drawn up to her chin gave her the appearance of a ghost with her deathly white skin. Mac leaned against the wall, one foot crossed over the other, and the splint balanced against his left hip. He'd brought no extra painkillers from home during his haphazard exit and a mind-numbing ache spread out from the centre of his palm. He knew his rucksack no longer contained relief. Forcing his mind away from the ugliness of yet another scar on his battered body, he tuned back into Tilly's monologue.

Tears streaked from Paulette Dunning's blue eyes, running across her nose and dripping onto the starched pillow with the angle of her turned head. Tilly still held her hand, a thumb caressing the backs of the woman's fingers in a comforting motion as she spoke about Miss Andrews' death. Mac blinked in confusion. Nothing about the woman rang true. His anxiety over the meeting seemed unwarranted. The fragile elf in the bed wasn't the frightening harridan conjured by his brain. So why did Marie demand he block her from her life? Why had he expunged her from the teacher's world as a potential threat? He glanced down at his dirty bandage and wiggled the injured fingers. The pinkie remained static, as though frozen in a photograph. He imagined telling his parents and caught the inside of his cheek as his teeth clamped shut.

Glancing up, he discovered Tilly and Paulette watching him. "Sorry," he said with a sigh. His chest deflated. In response to Tilly's narrowed eyes, he lifted his right hand and pointed to his processor. "I'm still here."

"How did you break your arm?" Paulette's right eyebrow quirked upward and interest drew her brows into a line. Mac swallowed, surprised by her willingness to swap injury stories with a stranger. He continued leaning against the windowsill but raised his left hand, an uncomfortable prickle blossoming from the raw graze trapped behind the frayed bandage. "I fell off a horse," he replied, sick of the sameness of his answer. It sounded so bland compared to her experience of eating tarmac after a shunt from a careless driver too busy on their mobile phone. Heat infused his cheeks, and he missed whatever Tilly said as she leaned forward to speak to Paulette. He couldn't read her lips. But the other woman nodded.

"Sorry," she said. Sympathy softened her mouth, and it shocked him she had any to spare. "I hope your finger improves. It can sometimes happen." Her chin dipped as she stared along the length of her prone body. The statement contained a universal wish for her own recovery.

"The driver pleaded guilty." Mac's tone held an uncharacteristic flatness. He realised part of the knot in his chest might ease if Caroline apologised for her outburst, which frightened Sassy. He also recognised hell would freeze over first.

"Yeah." Paulette's lip lifted on one side. "She's visited every week since it happened. I figured she'd stop after the court case." Her nose twitched. "Thought she just wanted to impress the magistrates." Her left shoulder gave an awkward shrug, her half-controlled movement thwarted by gravity. "Seems she's genuinely sorry. The doctors gave no notice before they moved me here. Maybe she'll stop now."

Tilly shook her head and squeezed Paulette's limp fingers. "We found you. If she's determined, it's easy."

Paulette frowned then, with a narrowed, pensive expression. "How easy?"

Tilly stiffened and Mac pushed himself upright. His muscular body cast Paulette into shadow. "Why?" he growled. "Is there someone you'd rather avoid?"

When Paulette swallowed, the sound reaching Mac as a strangled gulp, he sensed they'd hit gold.

66

DANGEROUS PLAY

They started at the beginning, Paulette's voice wavering as she grew tired.

She'd met Marie at Auckland University when they both studied for summer papers through the School of Education. Paulette painted a picture of friendship and then attraction. The Christmas period had ended with a loose commitment, and her world shone brighter than ever. She shifted in the bed and Tilly helped to adjust her pillows. "Everything seemed fine," she said with a sigh. "Term started, and we both got busy. We're teachers. We understood how intense termtime got, but things between us still seemed great. Then she phoned me late one night. She sounded scared. Marie said something happened. I assumed the problem occurred at work because she wanted to leave her job. She kept saying she couldn't stay there any longer and she needed to go back. But she wouldn't tell me why. I got a taxi to her place because she sounded so hysterical. But when I got there, she denied having a problem. She refused to talk about what happened, or why she got so upset. She told me it was a joke. So, we argued because I felt she'd wasted my time.

The taxi cost a fortune and she threw cash in my face to get another one home. She phoned me the next day to apologise for her behaviour and ask me to ignore it. Explained it away as a joke gone wrong. Anyway, I'd already bought tickets for a concert at Eden Park stadium the following weekend. Too short notice to get my money back. So, we met there, and I noticed she'd lost weight. She seemed on edge the whole time. I know she didn't enjoy the concert even though she'd seemed desperate to see the band. She struggled to concentrate and kept looking over her shoulder. Anyway, we arranged to meet the following Wednesday at a new restaurant on Quay Street. She promised she'd make it up to me, but then she stood me up." Paulette's jaw tightened. "She vanished. I never saw her again."

Tilly leaned forward, her fingers still stroking the back of Paulette's hand. "She disappeared?"

Paulette nodded. "Well, not physically. But she ghosted me online. She sent all my calls to voicemail." She licked her lips and Tilly rose to fetch a beaker of water. Without speaking, she held it to Paulette's dry lips.

Mac's mind ran down new pathways as it sought to crunch the data. He'd noticed no loss of weight, but then he'd seen her every day. His brain produced a kaleidoscope of images of their shared time with the soccer team. Had she seemed edgy or unsafe? Snapshots of conversations zinged through his mind as he sifted them for new evidence. Nothing. He tuned back into Paulette's weakening voice and shifted his position against the windowsill. The hook from a curtain tieback dug into his ribs and he moved again, the motion almost imperceptible. Guilt sent a flare of heat through his chest. He'd tried to kiss Marie without knowing the first thing about her. Foggy's words returned to condemn him.

Paulette cleared her throat. "I thought at first I could link the hit and run to whatever Marie got mixed up in," she said, her tone sad. "I figured the person she'd upset came after me. It's the reason I tried to contact her. To warn her." Her left shoulder rose in a shrug. "But then the driver handed herself in to the police and they dismissed everything else I said. It's just occurred to me that I should make it harder for someone else to find me here. Marie's dead. I can't help thinking she expected it. And you broke through the hospital system with a single lie."

Tilly nodded and hung her head. "Sorry. We didn't mean to make you feel unsafe. Perhaps the cops could speak to someone in authority at the hospital and prevent it from happening again."

Paulette snuffed out a laugh. "Like they care," she concluded. Her gaze switched to Mac. "Marie talked about you." She raised an eyebrow as Mac faltered. "Mac Du Rose." He held his breath and worry added to the swirling mix of nausea-inducing emotions in his gut. Tilly shot him a smile of encouragement and he clung to it. He stepped across the narrow distance and rested a hand over her shoulder, grounding himself in her confidence.

"About the soccer team?" Tilly offered encouragement, leading the conversation away from Mac's sore spot.

"Yes." Paulette smiled. "She liked you."

The guilt from Mac's error almost choked him. He licked his lips, though his tongue felt too dry to offer moisture. His brain bashed him with the knowledge he'd made a fumbling pass at a woman on the edge without considering how it might affect her. Or if she even wanted his clumsy adoration. "Yeah," he managed, his voice wavering. "I liked her a lot, too." He gulped and sadness sent a knot to block his throat. He wanted to tell Paulette about Marie's skill at herding the disorganised girls, how she'd cared for the rag-taggle group, and how she'd convinced them all they'd lift the challenge trophy at the end of the season. She'd carried them all forward on a wave of optimism. Her death had cast him adrift with the team. He didn't know how to lead them. His lips moved, but no sound emerged.

"The summer course we did together was an advanced coaching certificate. We both wanted to help girls' teams." Paulette dipped her chin to stare down at the outline of her legs beneath the thin sheet. "It doesn't seem either of us will fulfil that goal now." Her tears ran with an awful silence, soaking her hair and the pillow beneath her pale features. "I can't believe Marie's gone," she whispered, her voice hoarse. "Who would do this to her? Who made her so afraid?"

"We don't know." Tilly paused a beat to show sympathy. "But Mac found her." She covered his omission with consummate expertise. Mac cringed at the abruptness of the revelation to the already distraught woman. But Tilly curled her left hand around his thigh, sending an electrical charge through his body. He nodded, feeling outclassed and out of his depth.

She glanced up at Mac with a question in her raised eyebrows. He gave the slightest of nods and she continued. "Did Miss Andrews ever mention another teacher called Arthur Darian? Is it possible he made her scared?" She dipped forward and inhaled as she waited for the reply. Mac watched her spine arch as she held the breath.

"Yeah. She mentioned him." Paulette contorted her face and tilted her head to wipe her tears from her left cheek. Tilly leaned sideways and snatched tissues from a box on the nightstand. With extreme care, she wiped Paulette's face and brushed her hair back from her damp forehead. Paulette sniffed. "A handsy guy in the sports department? He gave her the creeps."

Tilly picked her words with care. "Did she act as though afraid of him?"

Paulette closed her eyes as she thought through her last conversations with Marie Andrews. Another tear escaped and plopped onto the starched pillow. "I don't remember," she replied with effort. "She only got upset over the phone. Marie brushed it off in person. Even after I went all the way to her place." She swallowed and didn't open her eyes. "But during the call, she said she felt unsafe. Whatever she discovered rocked her world to the core and made her want to leave a job she loved." Her eyes popped open, the irises swimming with salty tears. "After she stood me up at the restaurant, I borrowed a car from a colleague and drove to her school at lunchtime the next day. I only had twenty minutes to spare because I wasted time getting lost. I asked for her at the reception and the woman called the staffroom and gave my name." Her voice rose into a strangled wail. "She refused to see me. A dean came down and told me to leave." Her breath hitched and fresh tears coursed down her cheeks. A nurse passed the doorway and backtracked, curiosity in her brown eyes. She altered her trajectory and strode towards them with determination as concern turned to irritation at the visitors distressing her patient.

"It's okay, it's okay." Tilly patted her fingers as though attempting to smooth away Paulette's grief.

"What's happening here?" The nurse raised her eyebrows, and they disappeared into her fringe. Getting no answer, she snatched up the clipboard hanging from the end of Paulette's bed and squinted at a doctor's illegible notes.

Mac tensed, regretting the misery they'd caused but not yet having gleaned enough information to stop. He squatted next to Tilly and rested his right elbow across the chair's arm. "You said you'd called her in the last few weeks." He lowered his voice. "I'm sorry. She asked me to block your number."

Paulette shook her head, her hair swishing across the pillow. "My phone got destroyed in the crash. The nice physio you met worked with me over at the main hospital. I begged him to call her and let her know about my accident. He tried on the office phone but figured she ignored it because it showed up as a private number. So, he used his personal mobile."

"And?"

"I just need to check Miss Dunning's stats." The nurse moved closer to the bed, crossing to the opposite side of Mac and Tilly. She lifted Paulette's right hand and measured her pulse with a practiced finger over the vein.

"The physio said she'd blocked me." Paulette studied Mac with an intense stare. "But you did it for her?"

Mac inhaled. He rose and ran his good hand across his mouth. "She asked me to. I'm sorry." He glanced up at the nurse, who laid Paulette's hand back on the mattress with care. She reached into her top pocket for a thermometer device and capped it with a disposable plastic cover. Paulette became distracted as the nurse inserted the nozzle into her right ear. She winced as though in pain, but it may have been irritation. Mac held up his right hand. "Is it possible she wanted to keep you safe from whatever she'd gotten involved in? Perhaps she cared for you more than you think."

Paulette's eyes widened, and a light flickered, burning brightly from within her soul. "I never considered that!" she breathed. She released a disgusting sniff and stared at the ceiling for a moment. "One weird thing. During the phone call, she said she needed to go back somewhere. I thought she intended to return to her old job, but maybe that's not what she meant." She closed her eyes and her body rocked with a massive yawn. "Sorry, I can't remember more."

The nurse raised her eyebrows and shooed them away with a practiced glare. Tilly bent to place a gentle kiss on Paulette's cheek. "I'll ask Mac's mum to pray for you," she said, sincerity in her tone. "She's great at that sort of thing."

Mac gaped in surprise. His mind contained no memory of Hana imbuing her faith into a tiny, visiting Tilly. But somehow, she had, and it infused him with shame that he hadn't thought of it.

They allowed the nurse to herd them to the door of the ward, but Mac turned with a frown. He jogged back to Paulette's bed and leaned down to speak to her. "Can you remember the date Marie phoned you upset?" he whispered. "It might be important."

Paulette sighed and her thin chest deflated. "Not the exact date. But around my birthday. Two weeks after the start of term." She blinked up at him. "But then she denied it. I don't know what to think anymore."

Mac glanced at the door and saw Tilly trying to buy him time. She engaged the nurse in a one-sided conversation, but the woman had narrowed her eyes and turned her body to face Mac. "Did you tell the cops any of this?" he whispered.

He jerked backwards at her harrumph of disgust. "Why would I?" She raised her voice in agitation. "That loser wanted an easy arrest, and he had me in his sights. If I'd told him we argued or that something happened, he'd draw his own conclusions. He'd already decided I killed her. Only my watertight alibi stopped him in his tracks. I have enough problems right now without spending hours giving statements to morons. He dragged the poor physio down to the station and demanded to look at his phone. I'm surprised the poor guy still wants to help me with my rehab!" She coughed, and the motion rocked her body. "Besides, most of what I just told you only came back since I learned Marie died. It's all fragments and snippets mixed in with my accident."

"Okay. Thanks." Mac withdrew and pattered across the tiles to the door.

The nurse led them to the reception and stood over them while Tilly signed the visitor's form and added their departure time. She tugged her phone from her pocket to check the digital display, ignoring the massive clock above the receptionist's head. Mac gnawed on his upper lip before leaning across the counter and addressing the woman typing on her keyboard. Her fingers danced across the alphabet, not stopping even as she looked up at him. "Aunty Paulette is nervous about her security," he said, adding a booming seriousness to his tone. "How easy is it for someone to find out where she is and visit her?"

Tilly's head turned by slow degrees and her mouth opened in surprise. She dumped the pen onto the signing sheet and turned her body to face him. "Yeah Mac," she said, her tone a low growl. "How easy is it?"

Mac ignored her and kept his gaze on the receptionist. "Data protection makes it almost impossible," she concluded with a smile. "We can't give out personal details to people who aren't family."

Tilly's blue irises flashed a dangerous shade of aquamarine. She raised an eyebrow at Mac. They'd done exactly that just a few hours earlier and Mac saw her mind whirring. He pursed his lips as she delivered. As always. "Yeah," she said with a toss of her head. Silver earrings dangling from her lobes swung across to beat against her neck. "We've had calls from a journalist. He wants to run a story on Aunty Paulette. He told us he got her name from court records and phoned the hospital, pretending to be a relative. They said she transferred here yesterday." Tilly lied with such a straight face, Mac worried about their future. He studied the gentle curve of her neck and the rise of her breasts through her blouse. Discomfort flared across his groin and stomach as his mind wandered. He knew in that moment he'd accept every misdirection and untruth she threw his way. So long as she kept kissing him and only him.

The receptionist's head bobbled on her neck. Her fingers ceased their jig across the keyboard. "I'll make a note of it," she said, her tone serious. "That's not meant to happen." She sat up straighter. "We'll screen all visitors from now on."

The nurse rested a hand on the counter. "We check with the patient before we allow anyone in to speak to them." Doubt crossed her furrowed brow, and she glanced at the receptionist. "Don't we?"

"Yes!" The woman's eyes widened, and she bristled with affront at the veiled accusation. "A nurse checked with Miss Andrews before I took them to the ward." Her glare shone on Mac. "Didn't she?"

"That's true." Mac forced a smile onto his lips. "But the system should prevent people from finding out Aunty Paulette's whereabouts before they rock up here."

"Yeah, it's not fair." Tilly used her exceptional skill to spin the conversation. "You shouldn't need to protect patients as the last line of defence. It's shoddy."

"It is." The receptionist reached for her phone. Her redundant fingers tapped on the desk as though unable to cease their activity. "I'll escalate it to someone at the main hospital. It's not good enough."

Mac grabbed the visitor's sheet from Tilly and scribbled a name along the top. He turned it to face the receptionist. "This lady is okay though," he added, tapping the pen against the name. "She can visit as long as Aunty Paulette says she can." Tilly leaned over to peer at the slanted words naming the car driver who'd knocked the teacher off her bicycle. Paulette had said she'd visited every week, even after her guilty plea. Mac didn't want to place obstacles in the path of a woman seeking restoration. Tilly smiled and turned her gaze aside from him.

With their work done, Mac and Tilly exited into the bright sunshine. Tilly wore her smirk all the way to the car. But Mac's steps ground to a halt and she stopped with a frown to stare back at him. "What?" she demanded.

He cocked his head to one side. "Paulette said her phone got destroyed in the accident. But she asked the physio to call Marie."

"So?" Tilly stuck out her lower lip.

"Well," Mac began, running his right hand through his tangled fringe. "I lost my phone and can't remember a single number. Apart from the numbers you added to the contact list."

Tilly shrugged and used the key fob to unlock the car. "That's because you never bothered with a backup plan," she concluded with a smile. "Didn't you see the battered address book on her nightstand? I noticed it when I grabbed the tissues." She tutted and stuck her left foot inside the vehicle. Her body twisted as she stared back at him, her haunches already bent to drop into the seat. "Are you telling me you have no backup plan, Macky?" she demanded. "Tut tut."

Mac inhaled as she disappeared into the car and the door slammed behind her. "No," he whispered to the brilliant sunshine. "I have no Plan B." Heavy steps took him around to the passenger side. "But I guess you do."

67

ANGLE

"So, that seemed worthwhile." Tilly drove along the expressway, taking care travelling past a parked police vehicle. She checked in her rear-view mirror and her shoulders tensed. They passed without incident and she blew out a breath of relief. "Don't you think?"

Mac groaned. He supported his painful wrist in the palm of his right hand. "Not as much as I'd hoped. She confirmed Marie became afraid of someone, but not who. I thought at first we'd get more from her."

"I think we did." Tilly checked her side mirror before pulling into the right lane for the turn off towards school. Traffic backed up as parents began their after-school dash to clubs and activities, grid locking the city. "She recognised Darian's name. Her account of the phone call with Miss Andrews proves she discovered something amiss around the third week of the term. That puts it around the mid-February mark. I don't think Paulette knows about Marie's attempt to get her issued with a trespass notice. That means she didn't send her a copy, which is part of the process."

"So, why bother?" Mac watched her pigtails dance as Tilly turned her head to check her side mirror again.

"Because it put her on the radar." She wrinkled her nose. "Well, she wanted that to happen, but your brother said the notice got buried. So, it didn't work, did it? Any emergency call with Paulette involved should flag a faster response time, but it didn't work. I think Miss Andrews cut contact with her for her own safety and tried to place her name in the police system. Not because she wanted to get her into trouble, but so she got help quicker if the worst happened."

Mac blew out a breath. He ran his hand over his eyes. Pain radiated from his wrist as an incessant throbbing. "I should go to Bodie with everything we know." He stared at the road in front of them, a line of bumpers stretching into the distance. "But I can't remember his number."

"Dial emergency," Tilly joked. She grinned. "Maybe don't do that. But I can't believe how great you are with tech, and yet you never downloaded your phone contents onto your laptop." She flapped her left hand at him. "Onto a hard-drive even." Her lips drew back in a smirk. "I enjoy finding chinks in your armour," she declared with a flourish of her hand. "I feel less intimidated by your perfection."

Mac snorted. He turned his body to face her, the seat belt digging into his neck. "Have you met me?" he demanded. "No part of my entire existence gives the impression of perfection." He lifted his chin in a jerky motion. "I'm a deaf, freckled ginger, in a family of butch Māori." He shrugged. "Anyway, cloud storage is subject to hacking, as we proved by downloading that photograph. And I have a hard drive hidden from Edin, but no, I didn't think to include my phone contacts or data on it."

Tilly threw back her head and laughed, the light sound filling the vehicle. She glanced in her side mirror again and frowned. "Do you recognise that white car behind us?" she asked, her tone becoming serious.

"Which one?" Mac screwed his body around after the passenger mirror proved useless. He stared through the rear windscreen. "They're all white cars. It seems white is the new black."

"Does your father own a white car by any chance?" Tilly swallowed and raised an eyebrow.

"Na." Mac sat back in his seat and confidence infused his tone. "He drives a red truck with a massive scratch down the passenger side." He blew out a breath and contemplated what waited for him at home. Poppa's tangihanga and burial, followed by his father's displeasure and disappointment. "Pa won't lease white trucks. Our fleet vehicles spend too much time in the hills. The mud would send him crazy." The gravity of her question perplexed him. "Why? Do you think someone's following us?"

"Yeah," Tilly replied. "I think they are."

She licked her lips as she followed a line of traffic, making the turn off the expressway. Mac studied her serious expression with a frown. "Is it still there?" he demanded.

Tilly checked the rear-view mirror and nodded. Her gaze flicked to the sudden flash of brake lights in front of her and she stamped on the pedals. Their vehicle slewed to a stop and her fingers trembled on the steering wheel. Mac half-turned in his seat and stared through the back window. A transit van obscured his view, a wooden frame containing glass panels jutting from one side of its chassis. "Did it follow us off the expressway?" His voice sounded ragged even through the processors' unreliable relay.

Tilly closed her eyes and blew out a breath. She pursed her lips and didn't answer, pressing her foot to the gas pedal and pulling forward in rhythm with the leading vehicle. "I can't watch the white car and drive," she said after a moment's pause. "I'll crash." She stared ahead of her as though no longer wanting to know if a hidden foe trailed them.

Mac leaned his chin on the head rest, the action tugging his spine into an unnatural twist. "I'll monitor it. Do you remember the make and model?"

Tilly snorted. "Please hold, caller. Let me just check the manufacturer's guide book." Her voice altered to become a wail. "It's a white car, Mac! White! The plate number starts with the letter H. Just work with that, will you?"

Mac exhaled but kept his biting reply inside his head. Stress rolled from Tilly in waves, raising his heart rate to abnormal levels. His pulse pounded through his veins, creating a beat through the compression of his chin against the head rest. He spoke through gritted teeth, listing the vehicles behind them as far as he could see. "Glazier's white transit van. Blue people mover. Oh." He sank onto his right hip and faced Tilly. "The white car just turned off back there." He gnawed on his lower lip, not wanting to alert her to his doubt. "We're all good now."

Tilly's eyes narrowed, but she didn't reply. Her shoulders relaxed, and she concentrated on the road ahead.

"We're early," Mac commented as she braked and indicated left. Another vehicle pulled away from the curb in front of them, and Tilly edged the car into its vacated spot. It took three attempts for her to get it in line with the pavement, and Mac remained silent. He wanted to allude to the white vehicle but couldn't think of the right words. It scared him to imagine someone followed them from the spinal unit. But Tilly believed it and he didn't want to minimise her concern. His father once told him the road to disaster was paved with women who'd found themselves gaslighted by men. Mac watched him work hard not to negate his wife's anxieties. He'd once stripped down Hana's ute to the bare bones in search of a noise only she ever heard. If she said it happened, it counted as good enough for Logan.

Mac licked his lips. "Well done spotting the white car," he said, taking care of his tone. "Pa says I don't look in my mirror enough."

Tilly's facial features relaxed, and she released the steering wheel and stared down at her hands. "False alarm," she admitted.

"All good." Mac reached across and lifted her right hand to his lips. He placed a kiss over her knuckles. "What should we do now? We have just under an hour to wait until we meet Gray."

She lifted her phone from her jacket pocket. "Hey, why don't we see if we can find yours? Did you leave your location switched on? If I can trace it, we could walk up later and grab it."

Mac nodded. "Yeah, you can probably ping it." He shrugged and wrinkled his nose. "But leave it where it is. It has bad juju for me now."

Tilly's lips flattened into a sympathetic line. "Because you thought it belonged to Miss Andrews?"

"Maybe." Mac tilted his head and squinted through the windscreen at the rear of the vehicle in front of them. A sticker clung to the back wing. It depicted a father, a mother, and four stick children. He imagined the sticker which fitted his family group would occupy the entire width of the vehicle. Hana and her strays were legendary. The black iPhone flitted through his memory and he cringed. "It will always remind me of death. Miss Andrews'. Poppa's. I don't want it anymore. I imagine the battery died during the night. It didn't keep its charge for very long."

"Okay." Tilly slid her phone back into her pocket. She ran her finger along the flaking silver paint between the side window and the door panel. "I should get the car back soon," she observed, her tone dull. "Do you want a ride home or to the marae?"

"Not sure yet." Mac stared at the raggedy bandage which only just kept the splint fixed to his left arm. Frayed and filthy, it represented his fragile hold on sanity. He couldn't have picked a worse time to absent himself from the family's turmoil. Not if he'd tried.

68

Scoring Area

Tilly stood in front of Mac as they observed the First Fifteen rugby squad put to shame by a visiting school. The renowned Hamilton team left the Auckland contenders bloodied and dirty during a painful friendly game which exposed every weakness in the inferior side.

Tilly leaned back against Mac's body and he rested his forearms on her shoulders. During try after successful try by the visitors, he examined his damaged arm and used the pain to sharpen his mind. He'd sorted out all the moving parts of the mystery by the time the final whistle ended the slaughter. Arthur Darian needed cash for some spurious reason. He'd somehow hijacked the BAC system for his own ends. It didn't surprise Mac to find him playing an opposition role. They'd been at odds since Darian arrived at the school years earlier. Paulette had referred to him as 'handsy'. Anger budded in Mac's chest that Darian earned the label from a decent woman he'd obviously tested his charms on. Coupled with the fury came regret. Would she have labelled him the same after his fumbled pass?

He sighed and Tilly turned her head and tipped her chin to observe him. Her lips pulled back in a half-smile and he stroked her cheek with the side of his thumb. She knew the truth about him. He'd kept nothing back, splurging in a cathartic desperation. Yet she hadn't rejected him. Mac pursed his lips, feeling undeserving of her faith.

Tilly checked her watch as the battered rugby boys crawled off the field. The victors gave a hearty three cheers as reward for eighty minutes of forcing their opponents to eat dirt. "Almost five o'clock," she commented. She jerked as her phone vibrated in her top pocket. Her fingers slipped it free of the denim flap and she peered at the screen. "Unknown number," she remarked. Mac tensed as she answered, not waiting for his warning or approval. A smile broke across her lips and her tone oozed genuineness. "Hi Judith," she said. She stuck her left finger in her ear against the background din of the home side coach's harsh rebuke. A few steps took her behind Mac, and he spun to listen. Her brow furrowed. "No. That's not right." She shook her head and licked her lips. Her blue irises lost their lustre, and she glanced once at Mac. "Okay. I'd love to, yes, please." She blinked with the rapidity of a nervous tic. "The thing is, I'm in state care for now. Is it okay if I give your number to my social worker?" She pulled the phone from her ear and looked at the screen before putting it back again. "This number? Okay. I can do that. And thanks." After ending the call, she stared at the darkened screen with confusion drawing a deep furrow along her brow.

"What's wrong?" Mac stepped towards her. His body stiffened, and he touched her elbow in a gentle movement to indicate solidarity. "What did she say?"

Tilly slipped her phone back into her pocket and touched her fringe before facing him. "Don't go mad," she began, her tone tight. Mac studied her, his eyes narrowing and his gaze pensive.

"What?" he growled, wondering what Judith could have said to enrage him to the point it made Tilly afraid.

She licked her lips twice and straightened her shoulders. "Du Rose," she said, her voice carried away on a breeze blowing up from the south.

Mac dipped his head to study her features. "So?" His mind whirled with the possibilities. Why did she recount his surname back to him as though it meant something else?

Tilly swallowed. "It's the name Mr Darian gave to the landlord." She tapped her top pocket with nervous fingers. "Judith just checked with her neighbour. He's friends with the homeowner, so he phoned him. Darian signed himself as Arthur Du Rose on the tenancy agreement and provided a driving licence as evidence of his identity."

Mac shook his head hard enough to unseat his right processor. As he heard the revelation, he slapped it back into place. "He's not family!" he spat. "No way!" His lips curled back in denial, the notion too disgusting to acknowledge. His family name had entertained fighters, murderers, adulterers, philanderers, and cheats. But in their long history, he'd never encountered one so contemptuous as Arthur Darian. Mac shook his head again, refusing to accept the conclusion. "No," he hissed. "No."

Tilly exhaled and shrugged. "I'm sorry. It's what Judith said." Her expression brightened. "She invited me to tea."

Mac swirled away from her. He threw his shoulders back and rose to his towering height. His left wrist protested as he folded three of his fingers into a tight fist to match his right hand. His ring finger curved without tension and his pinkie stuck out like a passive observer. Mac's purposeful stride broke into a run as he covered the entire rugby pitch without seeing the spectators who dived out of his way. "Bastard!" he hissed from between his clamped teeth. His long legs carried him across two soccer pitches and a hockey turf as he headed towards the main building.

"You alright, mate?" A man hailed him from his right and Mac slewed to a dusty stop. He turned his head, recognising the adult voice and still programmed to obey authority while on the school premises. Keira's grandfather stood next to the equipment shed, balls and racquets surrounding his feet in a wide arc. Mac took a step towards the old man, wanting a reason to bow out of his hasty mission. He needed time to think, to digest this new revelation. His personal code abhorred violence but it bubbled in his chest like lava. His fists uncurled but his jaw remained clenched.

"I'm fine," he growled.

Foggy frowned as the heavy wooden door creaked closed behind him. He released a sigh of irritation, and the darkness swallowed his head and torso for a moment. Metallic clanks issued from the bag he dragged into the daylight. He shoved the door back on its hinges and dropped the heavy rucksack in the scrubby grass, edging it into place with a dusty boot. "That's good," he replied, sounding disinterested. Then he turned back to his job as though he hadn't just diverted an Exocet missile from its dangerous trajectory.

Without distraction, the Du Rose flame flared again. It burned in Mac's soul, handed down from the chief's formidable daughter to Jacob D'Arcy, to Rueben, and then to Logan. Mac had spent years damping its influence, but in that moment, it blazed like a wildfire. Vindication oozed from every stamp of his boot heels on the baked earth as Mac set off again. His fingers closed into fists and his gaze raked the landscape. Arthur Darian bore none of the classic Du Rose traits, he reasoned. The pause had given him a second of rational thought. The man's weedy, sagging existence provided an antithesis to Mac's treasured family name. It left another conclusion, one steeped in dishonesty. He'd used Logan's name for his nefarious activities.

A late start left Tilly far behind Mac's long stride. Worry etched her face and sharpened her features as she ran. She couldn't catch him despite his momentary stop to speak to the grounds man. She lost sight of him before the carpeted foyer beyond the open front doors. Anxious and panting, she whirled on the spot, her boots squeaking against the worn pile. The glass of the closed reception door faced her. "Why didn't I keep my big mouth shut?" she wailed.

69

FREE KICK

Grant Simms emerged from the headmaster's open doorway and frowned at Mac's frantic expression. "What's happened, Du Rose?" he demanded. "Why are you running around indoors?"

Mac ignored him. He took the main stairs three at a time, his long legs breaching the distance in seconds. His footsteps hammered on the floorboards as he ran along the second storey towards the staff room.

Mac flung open the door to the hallowed space without knocking. A cleaner blinked up in surprise, a vacuum bowing his spine under its weight as he carried it over his shoulders. He pushed the suction brushes beneath a cluster of battered armchairs. It cackled as it devoured crumbs and something metallic. Mac whirled on the spot, the door slamming shut behind him. Where would he find Darian at this time of day? His shoulders slumped as his rage built as a paradox in his chest. Perhaps he'd missed him.

Mac gripped the steel banister rail in his right hand, his fingers closing around its cool circumference. Choices paraded before him of rooms and locations where he might find the foolish teacher. He peered over the edge of the balcony to the lobby below and saw Tilly arrive. A flush of affection raced along his spine, paired with an innate need to keep her away from his inevitable confrontation with Darian. He didn't want his misdemeanours to taint her future.

Grant Simms' heavy tread breached the first landing and his body turned like a stiff rod to face the dogleg. The angle presented only his bowed head and thinning hair, but six years of familiarity with the tutor teacher communicated concern in his steady gait.

"Tutor teacher," Mac murmured. "Tutor teacher." Darian also taught a registration class and, therefore, possessed a designated classroom. Mac hadn't seen the First Eleven training and guessed the teacher wouldn't bother to step into the breach to offer coaching. A classroom presented the perfect hiding place. He'd remain on school premises for the sake of appearances, but do nothing taxing with his time. Classic Darian.

Mac's long stride took him through double doors and across a bridge, which joined two buildings. He shot down the stairs of the science block and rounded two corners before facing Darian's classroom door. A moment's pause gave him a chance to formulate a half-decent sentence before he tried the handle. It dipped beneath his pressure and the door opened.

"Ah, Du Rose." Arthur Darian's face split in a goofy grin. He jiggled his shoulders like a victory dance. An action video ran on his laptop screen and he jabbed his index finger over the mouse pad to halt it. Sylvester Stallone paused mid-shot, his mouth open and a white streak zinging from his automatic weapon. Mac frowned, his hastily crafted sentence wiped from his tongue. He'd expected a cupboard porn movie, not Rambo. It threw him off kilter for a second.

Darian leaned back in his chair. "You've seen sense at last," he concluded. He clicked his fingers as though in control of the situation. "I called your mother again this morning. Complained about your behaviour." Another finger snap, which Mac's processors relayed as an irritating wet click. Like a tongue smack. "You either do what I want, or I'll shower you with detention slips, kid. It's your choice."

A vision of Tilly flew through Mac's mind. She'd love that. He imagined her repurposing the green chits for her own ends. An evil smile lit his lips, and he noticed how the victorious expression slipped from Darian's face. Whatever he'd read in Mac's eyes put him on his guard. The mention of pestering a grieving Hana had pushed Mac beyond the point of no return. And Darian realised it too late.

Mac covered the distance in three strides. He lifted him from his seat one-handed, a tearing sound issuing from the sweat stained collar of the man's tracksuit. Darian coughed as the pressure increased against his throat. Mac felt his Adam's apple bobbing against his knuckles and squeezed harder. Bending forward, he issued his first grievance. "You used our name," he snarled. "Why?"

Darian's eyes bulged from their sockets like boiled eggs squeezed from their shells. An unhealthy blush rose into his cheeks and took up residence in his forehead. Gargling sounds came from his throat and Mac reasoned his need for answers trumped his desire to throttle the idiot. He dropped him into his seat and the chair rocked back on two legs.

Darian blustered. His cheeks flamed, his sickly complexion adding an oily shine. He didn't deny it, perhaps realising he couldn't con the angry teenager with lies. But his floundering caused Mac more frustration and unleashed the litany of complaints building in his throat. He leaned over Darian and slammed the laptop lid closed without care. Spotting a book of detention slips, he snatched them up before cuffing the teacher around the face with them. Spite and anger spewed freely, conveyed in a tidal wave of resentment and suffering. The Disabled Du Rose.

"You're a pervert!" He spoke through gritted teeth. "Why are you filming kids making out in cupboards? I'll make you sorry you ever abused the Du Rose name." He slapped him around the forehead, an unsatisfactory, papery waft. Without thinking, he stuffed the pad into his back pocket and grabbed Darian's greasy cheeks. The span of his right hand fitted around the man's face with ease. "You killed Miss Andrews," he snarled.

Darian's head jerked back on his neck as Mac shoved it hard enough to cause an injury. The man groaned and his ratty fingernails drew long scratches like railway tracks on the back of Mac's hand. He stank of sweat and fatty food, a nauseating combination. A pivotal moment arrived, like a crossroads in Mac's vision. He could either kill the man, or he needed to step away from him and regain control. The decision seemed harder than he expected. A wave of admiration struck him for Logan's coolheaded violence. He wanted to rip off Darian's head and display his body parts in gruesome dismemberment around the classroom, leaving no wall untouched by his vengeance. That's what Jacob D'Arcy would have done. Jacob, who'd held a gun on his vulnerable mother and her newborn. Mac didn't want to portray Jacob with his life choices. He wanted to emulate Rueben, Logan's father. A wily and calculating opponent, according to mountain legend.

Mac forced his fingers to widen like pincers, and Darian's cheeks sank from his grip. The teacher slumped into his chair like a sack of vegetables. Mac maintained his temporary superiority. He leaned over him, casting the man into shadow. Birdsong piped from the trees in the courtyard, like an anthem to Mac's rebirth. Sunshine speckled the windows and turned them into a sea of diamonds. "Talk!" he ordered. "Your threats don't scare me."

Words babbled free of Darian's lips like water cresting a waterfall. The delay between the processors and Mac's auditory nerve caused him a millisecond's anxiety before the pieces tumbled into place. "How did you find out?" he squealed. "It's just a name. Your dad taught here a few years ago. I liked it. I'll stop now, I promise."

A snort of disgust escaped Mac's lips. "Too late," he growled. "You owe money in our name. It's more than personal." He took a step away from the deflated man in the chair. The electrical current coursing through his body warned of a hidden lack of control. If he touched Darian again, he sensed he couldn't stop himself. Rueben and Jacob fought for the supremacy of his genetics. He needed Reuben to win.

"I didn't kill Marie!" Darian missed out any answers relating to the video footage and skipped ahead on the list of questions. "I liked her. We had a thing."

Another snort from Mac. This time, he watched the droplets cascade from his lips and shower the air between him and the teacher. "Pervert!" he snarled. "She liked women. If you were the last man standing, she'd still reject you."

Darian gulped. He possessed no reply to Mac's assertion. The teenager wondered if he'd even known of her preferences. Or if he cared. He gave himself a mental shake. Bodie could work it out later. If Darian survived to speak to him.

"You filmed me and Tilly." Humiliation flared alongside the rage and Mac's left wrist ached with the clenching of his fist. He longed to shove his knuckles through Darian's face until they met the wooden seat behind him. He imagined the satisfaction and his fingers closed hard enough to numb the weakened tendon and scar tissue. His injured left hand became like a boxing glove, an unfeeling extension of his body. One hit would do it.

But Darian sat higher in the chair and his neck twisted in a violent head shake. "Not me," he spluttered. "That's not me." His tone held such earnestness, it set a doubt ticking in Mac's brain.

"Keep talking!" he growled.

So, Darian did, his words tumbling free like a dribbling catharsis. He pressed his chubby palms together at his chest as though praying. "Okay, I run the BAC system. It provides little more than pocket money after I've paid the kids to man the cupboards." His wide-eyed gaze found Mac's icy stare, and he glanced away again. He'd painted himself as the lynchpin of the operation and realised too late it didn't impress the teenager. "I have debts," he offered instead, pitching for a sympathy vote. His chest rose and fell in a stuttering movement as though fear made breathing difficult. "I bought an IT business from a guy I met in a bar. He lied about a lucrative contract and falsified the company turnover. Then his creditors came after me because I didn't change the company name." His eyelashes fluttered. "He told me he bought cheap computers from hospitals and schools, reconditioned them, and sold for a profit. I believed him when he said he held an exclusive contract with them and he'd pass it to me." Self-pity oozed from Darian's expression. His hang-dog eyes appealed for sympathy. "He lied. After he sold the business to me, he set up in a different name and carried on as before. His guy works in procurement at the hospital and he puts all the old tech his way. It cut me out of the equation." His chest deflated, and he rubbed at the sore spot on his neck where Mac's grip left a red welt. "He owes money to some bad people. They took everything I owned and still want more. I can't convince them he's ripped me off as well."

"Boo-hoo," Mac sighed. "Go back to the film footage." A sharp pain zapped along his forearm and he forced his left hand to uncurl. A glance at his fingers showed his pinkie still drooped, as though sleeping. Raggedy strands protruded from the filthy bandage, a tendril floating in the air as he moved his arm.

Darian swallowed. "It's not me," he said again. "I promise." The self-pity returned to his tone. "Someone else sabotaged it. I only realised when Sal Richard sold me the old laptops from the IT department. It took most of the summer to format them and replace the worn parts. That's when I found the account linked to a cloud service. Someone had backed up the footage and forgotten to log out of the screen. It looked like they got interrupted half-way through editing but didn't change their password on all devices. I opened the laptop and found it already there." His blubbery lips shone as he passed a pink tongue over them. "It's not me," he said again. "I promise. Just the BAC system. I pay that new kid who started back this year. The one who spent time in juvie."

The ring of truth clanged in Mac's brain. But it left too many loose ends. He took a menacing step towards the teacher. "Miss Andrews found out about the BAC system. She threatened to tell someone, and you killed her." He swallowed, the scent of burning returning to his nostrils as a subconscious reminder. "You killed her somewhere else and took her body to the equipment shed. You tried to burn her." Another step put him beside Darian's chair and the man cringed. His body shrank into the seat like a deflated airbag. Mac's right hand darted out and grabbed the front of his tracksuit. The zipper scraped against his palm as he lifted Darian into the air again.

"Mr Du Rose." The steady, even tone brought a calm authority to cut through Mac's temper. Grant Simms closed the classroom door and turned to face him, feet spread and arms folded across his chest. Mac dropped Darian back into his chair, his thoughts scattering for cover. Reuben's spirit sighed into his brain.

'You wanted to leave school,' it soothed. *'You've done it now.'*

70

BACK HEADER

"He attacked me!" Darian sprang from his seat like a Jack-in-the-box. His recovery appeared instant.

The adrenaline receded from Mac's veins, leaving him shaking and wrong-footed. He fought the urge to shove Simms aside and bolt from the classroom. Perhaps Logan might save him if he begged for mercy. Darian used their name. It could prove enough motivation for his father to right his son's wrongs in one of his famed whitewashes. A flush of excitement startled Mac from his mental wrangling. He'd imagined Logan making Darian disappear. The random thought jarred with his pacifist values, spreading like tar over water.

Mac took a step away from Darian. The scent of sweat hung in the air between them. He couldn't discern whether it originated from him or the bedraggled sports teacher. A warning crackle told Mac his left processor required charging. Typical.

"What's going on here? Why are you yelling, Arthur? Sit down, Mac!" Simms brought instant calm. He jabbed his finger towards a desk in the front row. Mac resisted. He moved behind it but didn't sit. His nerves jangled at the weird energy surging in the room. It reeked of subterfuge and danger.

Then.

"He knows about the footage." Arthur Darian's fingers rolled together like sparring alligators over his protruding stomach, a constant, anxious motion. Rapid blinking completed the image of subservience.

To Mac's horror, Simms snorted. "The kid knows nothing. He's about as observant as a brick." Simms swirled his index finger next to his temple in a looping action. "I bet his hearing things aren't even working."

Mac gaped at him. Humiliation swathed him in a red mist of fury. The teacher he'd trusted most had just dismissed him as a non-entity. "I can hear you fine, thanks," he growled. He spun to face Grant Simms, an inner fire turning his irises into a curious emerald. "Say what you think of me. Don't hold back on my account."

The teacher shrugged his left shoulder and pointed to the vacant seat. Angled sideways to its desk, it appeared as though a student might have ejected from it just seconds earlier. "Sit!" Simms ordered. He blinked in surprise when Mac ignored him.

Simms appeared unconcerned. He dug both hands into his trouser pockets and squared his shoulders. "What does he know?" he demanded, focusing on Darian.

"Him and the Goth girl got filmed," he replied, his gaze darting from Simms to Mac.

"Oh. Really?" Simms dropped his lower jaw and two extra chins folded behind it. "You and Tilly Rae? Well, who knew you both had it in you?" He withdrew his left hand from his pocket and spread out his fingers, palm upward. "So, what do you want, Du Rose?"

Mac prayed with all his heart that Tilly's ten dollars had proved enough to expunge the embarrassing scene from the camera's memory card. But he doubted it, because he'd seen Darian follow them into the cupboard. Temper flared in his chest, and he turned his attention to the sports teacher. "You're harvesting the footage from the cameras," he declared. His eyes narrowed to angry slits. "I saw you."

Simms' body language altered in the millisecond it took Mac to swivel his gaze to face him. He straightened his shoulders and glared at Darian. "Did you now?" he drawled, his diction slow and menacing. "Tell me what you saw our friend do, Mac." He stepped away from the door, no longer blocking the teenager's exit, but still close enough to prevent him from leaving.

Mac took a deep breath and stood his ground, but he turned his boots so his toes pointed towards the door.

"After Tilly and I left the cupboard, I watched Mr Darian go into it. And he's always hanging around there after breaks and at lunchtime."

Simms released a long sigh. His jaw flexed and tightened beneath the skin, all his focus on the sports teacher. "I asked you outright if you planted the cameras," he growled. Darian seemed to wither in the chair. "So, you lied to my face."

Mac frowned with confusion. While Grant Simms knew about the existence of cameras filming pornographic footage of students, it appeared he didn't control them. He took a step towards the exit, making it look as though he just shifted his feet in a natural movement. But Simms had halted, his bulk still in the way. Mac's processor crackled again, and he swallowed. "He has a reputation with the younger students," he added, keen to drive Simms closer to the sports teacher. "And he killed Miss Andrews."

"What?" Mac realised his error as Simms turned to face him. The teacher's left eye blinked out of sync with his right. "You think he killed Marie?" Disbelief filled his tone.

Mac nodded. "Yes. She discovered the camera in the equipment shed. He killed her to stop her from exposing him."

"I didn't! I didn't!" Darian leapt from his seat, his arms stretched before him. He'd weathered the indictment of filming underage teenagers, and shown no distress at owning a reputation as handsy, but he objected when accused of murder. "She knew nothing about the cameras. That stupid girl told her about the BAC system. The blonde one with pigtails."

"Sammy?" Mac cocked his head. It made a strange kind of sense.

Darian left his chair and edged closer to Simms, as though tugged by an invisible fishing line. He pressed his palms together in front of him, his fingers still writhing. "The kid gave her the phone." His voice rose. "You know, the burner we use for the runners."

Simms' head jerked back on his neck. "You said you lost it," he growled. "Now, you say the kid gave it to Marie Andrews?"

A bulging pink tongue shot from between Darian's lips and swiped around his mouth. It resembled a coral creature investigating its doorstep. "You trusted me, Grant," he simpered. "I didn't want to let you down."

As the two men bickered over an illegal booking system for horny teenagers, Mac eyed the gap between Simms' back and the door. His left wrist sent a dart of pain to deaden his elbow and remind him of his own frailty. He focused on the pecuniary benefit of renting cupboards to kids. It added up to a small amount per day across the vacant spaces in the school. He shook his head and swiped his right hand across his eyes.

"Are we boring you, Mr Du Rose?" Simms growled.

Mac shook his head. "I just don't get it," he admitted. "What do you make each day? Fifty dollars? Split it between the two of you and then pay the kids who manage the bookings. That's less than ten dollars per day during term time. How is that worth your reputation and careers?" He stared at Simms, keeping his gaze steady. Logan advocated using logic wherever possible to throw light into confusion.

But Grant Simms snorted, a high, derisive sound. "Fifty bucks?" He turned his back on Darian to spew his bile at Mac. "Where did you get fifty from? There are nooks and crannies all over this site." He cocked his head and winked at Mac. "Kids come to school for six hours a day. That's a lot of time across a week."

Mac gaped. BAC wasn't just an interval and lunchtime scheme for wayward teens. It ran all day under the noses of unsuspecting staff. The dirty side-line was an industry in its own right. And someone had sabotaged it and created pornographic videos from the unsuspecting users of Simms' convenient service. Darian couldn't manage his own life and finances. Mac's naivety stung that he'd ever believed him capable of such masterminding. He worked for Grant Simms.

The stakes rose in Mac's mind as he gazed at the closed classroom door between him and freedom. He regretted getting involved and dragging Tilly into the catastrophe with him. His mind whirred through possibilities, standing them up like playing cards before dismissing each one and folding his hand. The subject of his focus became Tilly. He needed to keep her out of the mess he'd created.

In the end, it seemed as easy as just walking away. He crossed the classroom with his long stride and took the doorhandle in a decisive grip.

Simms and Darian stopped their bickering to watch him, as though with only a passing interest. The handle dipped, but the door didn't budge. Mac tried it four times before accepting his fate. He turned to see Grant Simms holding up a tarnished key.

71

Line of Retreat

"I'll ruin your life," Simms declared. He stretched out his arm, a bunch of other master keys swinging from the loop as he taunted Mac with the one to the door. "That's a promise. No university in the country will accept you when I'm finished with your reference. Hell, I'll make sure the halls of residence won't want you either. We play this my way, or I'll make you sorry."

Mac's future rushed before his eyes. He caught himself as his lips began their inevitable curve upward. His tutor teacher described the life he'd spent six years forcing Mac to consider. He'd rammed it down his throat until the words held the familiar staleness of an old cake. Simms had overplayed his hand and picked the wrong stake. Mac didn't care. He didn't want it. His father's mountain called to him, their ancestors whispering his name through the fronds of the canopy. Confidence oozed back into his shoulders at the lameness of the threat. "Is this how you treated Marie Andrews?" His jaw clenched so hard it caused his speech to slur.

Simms stared at him, as though waiting for the question to make sense in his mind. Then he replied, "Yeah. That's about the size of it. You can swap university rejection for that of a future employer if you like."

"So, which system do you manage? The cupboard booking one or the pornographic movies? Or both."

Simms shook his head. "Not the cameras. That's a step even too far for me and it's bad for business." He frowned. "But the last guy who tried it left in a hurry. I haven't worked out who picked up the baton yet, but I'll find out if it kills me."

Mac ran through a mental list of exiting staff from the previous year. His mind seized an obvious but missed clue. "Ian Fraser, the IT teacher," he mused. Sal Richard's throwaway comment during Mac's police interview indicated he'd left without notice. He took a deep breath, his brain still sifting and analysing the evidence.

Edin warned him Sammy got mixed up in the camera footage scheme, but Tilly denied it. Yet, Sammy recognised the phone he'd taken from the crime scene. The phone Darian said she gave to Miss Andrews. Mac released a hissed breath. The betrayal he'd seen in the girl's eyes when she found him using it made sense. She suspected he'd become part of the deception. And he remembered something else about that day, too. A tiny piece of the puzzle clicked into place. Another blonde girl with pigtails. "Layla," he said out loud. "Layla got messed up in the camera footage scheme. Not Sammy. And she took boys to the cupboards." He glared at Grant Simms. "Sammy told you about it to protect Layla because you're the Year 10 dean. And so, you got rid of the staff perpetrator, not because you cared about the kids, but because it interfered with your profits. You didn't realise Sammy kept the burner phone. Layla's smart. I think she worked both systems to her advantage and Sammy kept it as an insurance policy."

Layla had recognised the phone. She'd said, *'Lots of people have that phone.'* She didn't mean the model, she meant that actual phone with its chip on the top left corner of the screen. Frustration bubbled in Mac's chest at his own clueless blundering.

He jerked his head at Darian. "You already admitted runners used the phone for the BAC system. How did that work? Was it an early warning device for when the system became compromised mid-use? The phone contained no numbers, which means different lookouts must have dialled from memory and kept the call open while they needed it. A walky-talky would draw too much interest, but not a generic phone with a burner SIM card. The last user removed it from the device. I guess that's another safety feature. Sammy didn't understand that when she kept it as evidence."

The Year 10 dean dropped his bunch of keys onto a nearby desk with a clatter. He slapped his palms together in a slow, antagonising clap. "So, you listen sometimes," he crooned, as though speaking to a five-year-old.

"I'm not done." Mac's jaw created an angry line through his cheek. "Sammy heard the rumours again about cameras in the cupboards, even though you got rid of Ian Fraser. So, she figured you didn't fix the problem. She became scared Layla might get involved again. So, she gave the phone to someone else she trusted more. Marie Andrews." He groaned and threw back his head with exasperation. "I was there when Sammy asked her about it. I heard her with my own ears. She asked Miss Andrews if she'd spoken to you about the thing." He exhaled. "But the phone didn't relate to the cameras. It belonged to a different system." Mac shrugged. "Kids loved Miss Andrews. They'd give her answers to anything she asked. And anyone involved with the system would recognise that phone. Between what she learned from Sammy and from poking around, she'd uncovered your little scheme and your involvement by the third week of the term. It's why she paused before answering Sammy. Because the girl sent her to you and you threatened her. She'd failed. She couldn't stop it and knew Sammy trusted her. It drove her crazy. Paulette thought she wanted to go back to her old job, but that's not what she said. She meant BAC. Not back."

"Still didn't kill her." Grant Simms folded his arms. A nonchalant expression settled over his features. "My alibi is solid."

"So is mine." Darian stuck his chin in the air. He edged beside Simms, fancying himself as a brother in arms instead of a pawn in the other man's game. "Police cleared all of us."

"But your threats terrified her, didn't they?" Disgust filled Mac's tone. His gaze settled on Darian. "What did you do? Follow her home, make her feel unsafe? You threatened her partner too, didn't you?"

The smile slipped from Darian's lips. "I wouldn't actually do anything," he scoffed. "It's just words. We happened to go to the same concert at Eden Park stadium. Coincidence."

Mac jabbed his index finger at Simms. "But you answered the phone in the staffroom when Paulette visited. That's why Marie couldn't risk meeting her at the reception. But you went down and sent Paulette away. And so afterwards, she tried to protect her by getting a trespass order. To keep her away from you." He shook his head. "That's also why the receptionist couldn't find any record of the incident Miss Andrews told me about. Because it didn't happen like she made me believe. Geez!" he exclaimed. "You ruined her life! You made her hide from someone she cared about. Because of a stupid bloody cupboard system!"

72

BREAK

"It's not a stupid system for me." Simms pressed his lips into a stern line. "It's been a long time since I did this job for the love of it." He jabbed a hand at Mac. "A lifetime of kids like Syd Ross, for pity's sake! The boy doesn't have two brain cells to rub together. No, this stupid system is how I subsidise my income. It makes it worthwhile."

"So, it's just you and him." Mac's processor crackled its final warning. Any second now it would cease communication with his brain. He tilted his head and Darian's lower lip shot out, misreading the action as disrespectful.

Simms snorted. "He came to me about the footage he found. I figured I could use his computer skills." Darian pursed his lips and his head sank lower, as though the sentence held a veiled rebuke. Then Simms shrugged. "Let's just say I have assistance from others with alternate expertise."

Mac held his breath. BAC got bigger by the second. Darian's cowed body language told him someone scarier than Simms also belonged to their horrible club. How widespread did this thing get? The possibilities seemed endless. The older classrooms in the main building each had a store cupboard attached. Adding in the science and art rooms created a web of opportunity, but also demanded complaisance from the staff who ran those classes. Nausea roiled in Mac's stomach. Perhaps Darian told the truth. His part earned him pocket money. "You pay the kids?" He addressed his question to the sports teacher, and he gave a shallow nod. "So, why do you hang around the janitor's cupboard? The one on the second floor near the English department. It looks to me like you're harvesting footage."

"No." Darian's head shake almost detached his skull from his fleshy neck. "I'm searching for the cameras. We think they move them around from cupboard to cupboard to avoid detection. But I've found nothing yet." He clicked his thumb and middle finger in a show of bravado. "But I'm onto them."

Mac paused. The silence from his left ear created a lopsided effect. He hated it. To add insult to injury, the right one gave its familiar warning crackle. "Tilly paid someone to remove the footage of us in that cupboard." A deep furrow lined his forehead. "There's a camera in there. You walked in straight after us."

"Nope." Certainty caused Darian's shoulders to lift. "I check it at least six times a day. Me and Grant here pulled the entire space apart last weekend."

"But I saw the flashing light!" Urgency filtered through Mac's tone. He needed to conclude this meeting and leave before he lost all hearing.

Darian's nose wrinkled into a series of lines like an elephant's trunk. "Nope," he asserted. "That's a chargeable vacuum cleaner." He lifted his left hand and wagged his index finger in the air. "That caught me out, too. I thought I'd finally found it." His shoulders slumped. "We're losing that cupboard now, anyway. Everyone needs to move stuff around. The equipment shed is no longer available. The council is pulling it down. The grounds staff are distributing the cleaning gear around the site. We've lost a few cupboards in the main building to them."

Simms appeared bored. "Right," he said with a glance at his watch. "How do we fix this?" His gaze fell on Mac. "You'll say nothing to anybody, kid. Or else."

Mac swallowed the knot in his throat. He figured Simms' net spread a little further every time another unscrupulous staff member learned of his scheme. Ignoring his overwhelming desire to escape, he played the game to ensure his temporary safety. "What's in it for me?" he demanded.

Simms' lips curved into a goofy grin. "Aw, poor Mac. Is Daddy keeping you on short rations?" He shrugged. "Two percent of the profits."

Darian gasped. "Why does he get two percent?" Horror filled his voice and his mouth hung open. "I only get one percent!"

The tiny fractions offered stunned Mac. For Darian to make even pocket money from a one percent share suggested an operation mightier than he'd ever imagined. He gritted his teeth at another warning crackle from his remaining processor. "Three," he growled. "Or I take this to my brother." He raised a speculative eyebrow. "Detective Inspector Beaudain Singh Johal."

Darian hissed a curse, and Simms' complexion paled. He gave a decisive nod. "Okay, three percent," he agreed.

"What?" Darian pleaded. "That's not fair. You make me walk around the whole site and check every cupboard for my one percent. And I pay the runners and the kids who take the bookings and the cash." His lower lip folded over itself to create a shelf. "It's not fair," he repeated.

Mac hid his shaking hands behind his back, grimacing at the complaint from his left wrist. The unravelling bandage had left the scar exposed, and the splint barely clung to his forearm. He ached for Simms to unlock the door and allow him to flee. His first mission was to find Tilly and use her phone to call Bodie.

Mac held his breath as Simms stepped to the door with a surprisingly light tread. He lowered his chin and glared at Mac through the tops of his eyes. His sudden weight loss created sagging folds of skin, which turned his features into blobs of dough. "Don't cross me, kid," he whispered, and tapped the side of his nose. The key ground in the lock to create a satisfying click as his hairy fingers completed their rotation. He hauled the door open at speed and gasped.

Tilly Rae fell head first through the gap and sprawled onto the floorboards at his feet. Anger and misery reflected in her eyes as she glared up at Mac with pure hatred. Lips the colour of a satiated vampire drew into a furious pout.

73

Shadow Play

"How could you?" she yelled. She scrambled to her feet in a flurry of tartan fabric and stamping soles and whirled to face Mac.

His eyes communicated terror at her entrance. She couldn't have picked a worse time to throw herself into the perilous mix. Nothing the men said had convinced him of their innocence regarding Marie's death. Everything linked back to their reign of vice. And Tilly had tumbled into danger like an out-of-control soccer ball. Eavesdropping, but hearing only half the story.

Mac's right processor sent a sad cheep to his brain via his auditory nerve and died. An eerie silence filled his skull. He'd craved its familiar peace for so long, it seemed ridiculous that it now hindered his existence. He wanted to hear. Needed it.

Simms and Darian gaped for a second as Tilly launched herself at Mac. Darian recovered first. His clammy hands clawed at Tilly's shoulder, clamping over the bone with disregard for the gasp of pain she released. Mac saw her lips part in protest, her blue eyes wide and appealing.

As the scene he'd dreaded played out before him like a silent black and white movie, Mac sensed strength rise from his core and flood his torso. With it came courage and certainty. Mana. The ethereal, sought-after power and authority which generations of Du Roses had wielded for centuries. The blue threads, passed from Logan at his son's conception, twisted and merged with the gold ones bequeathed by Alfie at his death. They fused in MacGillivray for the first time since Kuia Phoenix Du Rose. Power filled his soul.

Silence aided him as the world slowed. Darian's filthy fingers clawed at Tilly shoulder, hauling her blouse higher until it exposed her belly. The collar tightened around her neck as she tipped backwards. Mac's right hand shot out with the skill and precision of a boxer. He felt the impact against his protruding middle knuckle, but Darian's nose caved first. The sports teacher's lips parted, a line of spittle remaining airborne in the seconds after he fell like a stone to the floorboards. Desks and loose chairs skittered around him like hens seeking seed.

Already overbalanced, Tilly fell with Darian. She disappeared from Mac's eyeline, leaving him to face Grant Simms. "You're sick!" he yelled, satisfaction blooming in his chest as the teacher reacted to the unexpected volume. Simms blinked and took a step backwards. He raised his hands to protect his head, seeing first-hand the damage Mac's right fist could produce. But Mac had passed the point of fighting fair. He swung his right foot backwards and planted his weight on his left knee. Then he kicked, driving his fury through his thigh and calf, and into the hard toe of his cowboy boot. His foot travelled upward between Simms' pinstriped legs and connected.

Grant Simms collapsed like an apartment block stuffed with dynamite. He sank to his knees and onto his face. His body arced around the testes which Mac drove into his pelvic cavity. He'd learned of the legendary Kane Du Rose kick from Toby, but never imagined he'd sink low enough to use it.

Tilly popped up beside him like a rubber ball. She grabbed at his forearm, her nails digging into his skin. Her mouth opened and closed too fast for Mac to read her lips as he readied himself to deliver another punch to whichever man rose first. Her head shook in a frantic motion and she shoved him towards the open door. She put her whole body into the movement until Mac found himself in the darkened corridor. He looked down to see her hands shaking as she produced Simms' bunch of master keys and turned the uppermost one in the lock.

"No cameras," he managed. An imaginary elephant sat on his chest and compressed his lungs. His right hand snaked upward to touch his useless right processor. Blood stains on his palm caught his eye, and he turned his hand over in surprise. Broken skin covered his knuckles from the force of his punch. The slap he'd given Logan paled in significance against the shattered cartilage inside Darian's nose.

Tilly placed both hands against his spine and drove Mac along the corridor as though she pushed a laden shopping cart. He turned twice, desperate to offer relief about their moment of fame as unwitting porn stars. It seemed ridiculous that the red light from a charging vacuum cleaner had spooked an entire community of thrill seekers. Laughter bubbled from his lips in the empty corridor, painting him as a momentary lunatic. And still Tilly pushed him.

She shied away from the main foyer, plotting a course through a less well-used route. They emerged into the sunshine through the rear door of the assembly hall, and Mac drank in the fresh air like a drowning swimmer. His silent world no longer held peace. It offered only restriction and missed opportunities.

"I'm sorry." He turned to Tilly and ducked out of her grasp, almost causing her to pitch sideways. He held his hands out in front of him. "I just needed to get away from them."

She shook her head and her lips curled back in an expression of disgust. Mac fell silent. When she gripped his wrist instead of his fingers, he knew he'd blown it. Their short but passionate relationship would end with the same speed with which it began. Numbness spread outward from his spine. It pushed the adrenaline and the mana back into their box and left him with a bone numbing emptiness.

They crossed the street and hustled to the social worker's silver hatchback. It stood alone, its passenger wheels occupying a cycle lane they hadn't noticed in the earlier bumper to bumper chaos. A parking infringement notice fluttered like a pinned butterfly from beneath the left wiper blade. Tilly released Mac's wrist and dug in her jacket pocket for the car key.

A figure stepped from the shadows of an overgrown wisteria bush. Snaking tendrils had climbed a dead conifer to create a purple fringe beneath which the man had avoided the sun's glare. Pollen and lilac petals dappled the shoulders of his black tee shirt as an indictment of how long he'd waited there. Mac swore, not needing the auditory capabilities of his processors to know he'd shouted the worst cuss word in his vocabulary into the quiet suburban street. When Tilly winced, he guessed it had echoed.

74

DEFENDER

Still, the silence filled his head. His lips moved with garbled excuses and he snatched at Tilly's left hand. His fingers closed around hers, not willing to let her drive out of his life without trying to explain. She blinked up at him, the key fob trapped within the cocoon of their joined palms as calamity descended.

He saw her turn towards the waiting man and her lips moved. Then his father reached Mac in three giant strides, grabbed his shoulders and spun him around. "Stop!" he mouthed.

Dark hair blackened Logan's jaw and chin. Exhaustion dulled his eyes, and a bone-deep sadness shrouded him. Cheap deodorant filled Mac's nostrils, and he recognised the emergency spray Logan kept in his truck. His dented truck. Emotion swirled in Mac's chest at the memory of Alfie's departure. The tightness prevented his lungs from filling and his throat constricted even as he gulped for air. He'd lost Poppa and now Tilly. Even the consequences of joy riding around Auckland in a stolen car paled into insignificance beside the overwhelming sense of robbery and violation.

And he couldn't hear. And he hated it.

Logan released his grip on Mac and his hands went into freefall. In a dizzying stream of movement, he signed to his stricken son. Over and over again, he asked him, "Are you okay?" His right index finger pointed to Mac's chest, before switching places with his thumb and circling anticlockwise through the air. "Are you okay?"

Mac got it. The clamour ceased in his brain and allowed him to read the concern in Logan's grey eyes. His father cared about nothing else but his son's wellbeing. The emptiness in Mac's tight chest swirled with a painful sense of love and acceptance. It hurt more than the grief. He didn't release Tilly's hand. The sharp edge of the key fob branded its imprint into their joined palms. But his reason returned. And he inhaled.

"I'm good," he managed, though he'd never felt less good in his life.

Logan's lips quirked into a reluctant smile. He turned his head to study Tilly, and they engaged in a conversation which eluded Mac. Tilly handed Logan the keys to the classroom, and he frowned, his head nodding as she added more detail to their exploits. When Logan reached into his pocket and pulled out his phone, Mac knew he would call Bodie. Their deeds stretched before him then. A list of infringements and potential consequences. He tried to read Logan's lips, but his father turned away and stepped back onto the curb.

Tilly dragged her hand free and stared at the dent in her palm. She stuffed the car key into her pocket and rubbed her hands together. Mac glanced at the identical imprint on his hand. He regretted how fast his body pressed blood back into the dent until it ceased to exist. Gone. Like his Poppa. There one moment and not the next.

Mac jerked in shock as Tilly dragged at his sleeve, awaking him from his stupor. She stepped into his personal space and forced him to face her, staring up into his eyes and waiting until he concentrated. "I'm not angry with you," she mouthed. When he didn't react, she repeated herself twice more.

It took a moment for her words to filter through his brain. With his hearing gone, his other senses crowded into the vacancy, clamouring to provide information which might help. The cloying wisteria fragrance clogged his nostrils and his eyes divided the surroundings into a series of vibrant lights and shadows. "I didn't mean it," he protested, eager to capitalise on any potential forgiveness. Her wince relayed important information. He'd shouted the words by accident. "I don't want two percent," he persisted. "I needed to get away."

Tilly's hand snaked across his mouth. A flicker of anger halted Mac's diatribe as it robbed him of speech in addition to his deafness. When she removed her hand, she rose on tiptoes and replaced it with her lips. She didn't reproduce Logan's signing, but her eyes relayed the same vein of information. "It's okay."

The cops came. Bodie sent a traffic patrol ahead of him and they moved through the school site at speed. Tilly led them to the classroom, where they discovered two injured teachers. Darian screeched to high heaven as paramedics loaded him into an ambulance, but Simms remained eerily silent.

Mac sank into the passenger seat of Logan's borrowed white vehicle, on the opposite side of the road to the silver car. He closed his eyes. The traffic cops had instructed him to wait for Bodie. His head tilted back against the head rest and he sifted through the alarming data he and Tilly had accrued. Images trooped across his inner vision as Logan used the vehicle's first aid kit to clean and dress Mac's knuckles. He removed the tattered bandage from his other wrist, ignoring his son's hiss of pain when it stuck to the oozing yellow grazes on his fingers and the heel of his left hand. Logan used a bottle of saline to wash away the strands of fabric and employed gauze and a fresh bandage to reseat the metal splint. He said nothing about the useless fingers. Mac wondered if Toby or David had relayed the news of his permanent injury. It didn't seem like the right time to mention it.

Mac's processors charged on the dashboard. Logan had used the car's USB port, and the unit emitted a flashing red light as it sucked power from the vehicle's battery to feed the devices. The diesel engine idled beneath Mac's seat, replenishing the little they stole. It took longer to charge them this way, but Mac nursed a futile hope as the battery indicator light slid to the top of the fifth bar and then back to the bottom of the scale.

He didn't recognise the car from any Logan owned. His father's subterfuge meant he'd trailed them for most of the day. A rosary clung to the rear-view mirror and a nodding doll rode the dashboard above the stereo. Wrapped in a slip of fabric bearing the pattern and colours of the Māori flag, the tiny mascot clutched a poi in each hand. They swung in the breeze, her plastic fingers curled around their strings and her bare feet glued to the dashboard. Mac turned his head and glanced into the rear seat. A flax basket lay on the cushion as though fainting. A folded headscarf nestled beneath the woven harakeke. Mac recognised it as belonging to an elder from the marae. He heard the echo of her karanga in his mind as she called visitors into their sacred space. His heart rose into his throat. Would she call his poppa home? Had she already done it?

The traffic cops secured the classroom and others arrived, converging on the school as though bored with the usual choice crimes Auckland city offered them. A sleek SUV with police markings slid behind the social worker's silver car and two new officers emerged. Mac saw a tall male draw handcuffs from his belt with a practiced sleight of hand. His body tensed with anticipation as the officer crossed the street. A female cop flanked him, checking the road before she proceeded. Mac couldn't hear the heated argument which ensued as his father refused them access to him, but the evening air carried the vibration of their raised voices.

Tension hiked as Logan slammed the passenger door and locked Mac inside the car. He jammed the key fob into his back pocket. The diesel engine continued to run, Logan's proximity with the key offering it no cause for alarm. Mac watched his father's head shake from side to side through the passenger window. "No," Logan repeated over and over. "No." Mac knew the signs and recognised Logan's determination as he readied himself for a physical fight if necessary. Power exuded from his angry profile, the beard shadow outlining his defined jaw. Mac watched as Logan raised his hands, his palms facing outwards towards the two cops. But his head continued to shake. Mac tilted his body to watch the cops through the side mirror. The officer kept the handcuffs in his left hand and drew a cylinder containing pepper spray from his belt. Mac read his lips backwards. "Suspicion of assault," the man growled through gritted teeth.

Mac sighed. "Enough," he said.

To Logan's horror, he unlocked his door and stepped from the car. He missed his footing on the gritty suburban street, and Logan caught his right elbow and righted him. Mac blew out a breath and shook his head at Logan. He planted his boots on the rutted asphalt. "I don't want them to hurt you because of me," he said. He put no effort into controlling his volume, no longer caring if he bellowed the sentence or whispered it. His body ached with the buzz of receding adrenaline. He craved exercise to burn off the excess and understood then why people ran from the police. They weren't just escaping the uniform and the consequences. They sought to flee their own bodies.

"I hit them," Mac admitted. He held out his left arm, bracing the splint against his right palm. The cop bearing the handcuffs stared at the bandage and Mac sensed his brain whirring. He wondered if they could cuff someone with his injuries or if it contravened his human rights. Wiri would know. Or Phoenix. If in doubt, ask a lawyer. "Let me explain," he tried. The cops glanced at each other and back at him. They couldn't understand his stilted speech.

Logan stepped in front of Mac, shielding him with his body. Mac blinked in surprise, watching the cops' resigned expressions over his father's shoulder. He wondered again when he'd exceeded Logan's vast height. The standoff continued. The cop with the handcuffs spoke into his radio. With his head down and his baseball cap covering his face, Mac couldn't read his lips. But he guessed the content of the conversation. "10-10. Officer requires immediate assistance. This one's trouble."

Hana's eldest son arrived at speed. He didn't bother parking his unmarked car in line with the curb. He abandoned it in the centre of the road and left the red and blue lights still strobing into the balmy evening street. They reflected off the windows of nearby houses. Mac turned his head and saw a family watching from their lounge. They didn't bother peeking from behind net curtains. They'd lifted them over their heads to enjoy the show, resembling a line of brides awaiting their nuptial kiss.

Bodie's body language oozed competency and business. He flashed a warrant card at the two cops and they retreated with backward glances at Logan. Smaller than either Logan or Mac, Bodie still exuded the authority of rank. The tall cop paused at his passenger door to replace his handcuffs. He offered no apology before sliding back into his vehicle. Bodie raised an eyebrow at Logan and his stepfather stood down. He turned, seeming surprised to find Mac so close behind him. Then he spoke, not resorting to sign language but mouthing the words to leave no mistake. "Brace yourself," he said, his lips thinning to parallel tracks in his brown face. "Your mother's on her way."

75

FAR POST

Logan estimated they had an hour's grace before Hana descended on the scene. He'd instructed Toby to drive her, adding both a decent delay and an element of safety. Bodie regretted his error, which amounted to admitting to knowing Mac's location.

"I'm sorry." He wrinkled his brown nose in discomfort. "She's called me at least once an hour since she noticed Mac's absence." He waggled his eyebrow at his half-brother. The expression contained sympathy back lit by the tiniest flicker of jealousy. Bodie Singh Johal struggled with his mother's second chance at love and family. Mac pursed his lips and imagined how he'd feel in Bodie's shoes. His gaze slid to his capable father and saw him through his brother's eyes. An interloper. Usurper of the sainted Vikram Singh Johal. He hung his head and disconnected from the conversation.

Detective Elliott kept Tilly for long enough to cause Mac concern. She sat in the front seat of his squad car, head bowed and giving the occasional nod. Both teenagers affirmed their belief that Simms and Darian had together somehow killed

Marie Andrews. Their motive was to protect the BAC system. Master keys to the sacred nooks and hallows of the school site provided ample opportunity. As a member of the management team, Simms would know the intricacies of the electrical refit, which left out the equipment shed. Even as he made the case against them, something nagged at the back of Mac's brain. He glossed over his misgivings based on his status as a schoolboy and not a cop.

The injured men rode to Auckland City Hospital in separate ambulances, a burly police officer accompanying each.

"How'd you follow us?" Mac pressed his left processor into place over the magnet affixed to his skull. He'd given up waiting for them to reach a full charge, impatient not to miss out on more of the excitement. His deafness had robbed him of the buzz of activity, watching it as though viewing an action movie with the volume muted. Tilly exited Elliott's vehicle and jogged across the street. She gave Mac a dramatic eye roll while unwrapping a nugget of pink bubble gum.

Logan dug into his jacket pocket and produced the iPhone with the chipped corner. His eyebrow quirked up at the sudden paling of the teenagers' complexions. He held it with his thumb pressed over the screen and the length of his index finger forming a brace across its dusty rear. Adventures in the bush had added a crack along the length of the screen. It wagged twice in his hand as Logan observed their discomfort.

Tilly's jaw worked at speed. She couldn't blow her trademark pink stress bubble yet. The gum hadn't softened enough. It seemed to leave her floundering. Mac shifted on his feet and focussed all his attention on seating his right processor. He cringed as his auditory nerve fired to life under pressure from the devices. They relayed Logan's bass back to him with a comforting familiarity. "Bo. Come here a minute, mate." He held the iPhone out to Mac's half-brother and Bodie wandered across without complaint. Two uniformed officers divided behind him. One carried a reel of crime scene tape and the other hunched as he spoke into a radio.

"Think you'd better take this," Logan stated. He shook his head as Bodie raised a hand. "Evidence bag," he commanded. "Their reaction tells me it's hot."

Bodie's eyes widened and his sweeping gaze took in Mac's guilty flush. It radiated from him in waves. "Stolen?"

Mac glanced at Tilly and then shook his head. "Not exactly."

Tilly exhaled. A giant pink bubble of rebellion obscured her expression. Attack trumped defence every time. The familiar mechanism infused Mac with the desire to protect her. Raspberry and something he couldn't name wafted around them like a sugary hug. He slid his right arm around Tilly's shoulders, noting the flare of curiosity in Logan's eyes. His father's lips flattened into a line of realisation which betrayed his interest. Mac turned his head to avoid connecting with Logan's intense and heightened study. He felt like a bug under a microscope. It embarrassed him and the flush intensified, crawling along his jaw and into his unshaven cheeks.

Bodie produced an evidence bag and dropped the phone into it. He sealed the lip and kept it in his left hand as he glared at Mac. "Start talking," he demanded. A glance over his shoulder at Detective Elliott conveyed the warning. They could talk to Bodie or to the officious career acolyte.

Mac tightened his grip around Tilly's shoulders. He realised too late it resembled a clumsy head lock and relaxed his muscles. After clearing his throat twice, he opened his mouth to speak. She beat him to it. "I don't get it," she announced. A red painted index finger jabbed at Logan without fear. "How did you find us?"

A smile of victory crept into Logan's stern expression, and he pushed his weight into his right hip. "I found Mac's phone in the bush," he said. "I took it down the mountain, figuring he dropped it during the chaos. When I still couldn't find him at home or the marae, I unlocked it." He shrugged. "A quick trip to Google maps showed he shared his location with one other person." He pursed his lips and met her confident gaze with something like disappointment. "A little sloppy, don't you think?"

Tilly wrinkled her nose at the rebuke, though Logan aimed it at his son. Mac's temper flared, burning his guts like a flash fire. He remembered their mutual location sharing days ago, when he wanted to clear Edin's name. It seemed ridiculous he'd ever suspected her. He wondered when Logan had made the discovery. Did he know he and Tilly spent the night together? Would he tell Hana?

Bodie released a groan of pain and Logan cocked his head. "You had this at the hospital, didn't you?" His tone held an element of begging. Then Bodie's eyes widened in accusation. "Please, tell me this isn't the teacher's phone?" His voice rose. Mac's processors relayed his antagonism. He rated their accuracy as Tilly shifted beneath his arm.

"Not exactly," he replied again.

Bodie's eyes bulged as though his brain might pop through the sockets. A vein pulsed beneath his right ear as his heart rate hiked to coronary inducing proportions. Logan turned his body to ally himself with his son. His loyalty only increased Mac's discomfort. He didn't deserve it. A glance to his right revealed the family still observing through their lounge window. The children ate snacks and drank from cans of fizzy. He'd become a spectacle. As usual. The Disabled Du Rose. His shoulders slumped, and he released a sigh which deflated his chest.

Logan pulled his own phone from his jeans pocket and squinted at the screen. "Toby," he announced. "They're almost here. You have five minutes, and then we're leaving."

Bodie folded his arms across his powerful chest. Antagonism and an old rivalry crackled like loose wires between him and Logan. Bodie shrugged, the movement wooden. "I'll just arrest him," he threatened, his voice a low growl.

Logan didn't miss a beat. "Try it," he suggested. His tone held a deceptive affability. Mac held his breath. He clutched Tilly closer. Her hair tickled his forearm.

"It's okay," he offered. "I'll tell you whatever you need to know." He lifted his left arm and stared at his hand. The pinkie finger curled around the edge of Logan's hastily fitted bandage. "But then, can I get help with this?" As though his words had flicked a switch, pain rocketed from the fused tendon and the partially healed bones. It arced through his forearm and into his elbow, like he'd given permission for its unleashing. He swallowed, fearing he might vomit on the pavement between his boots.

"Fine!" Bodie agreed. He jerked his head towards the expensive unmarked police car. "I'll run you to the emergency department now. I need to see the other two clowns after they're triaged. We'll talk on the way."

76

BLIND-SIDE

And so Mac evaded Hana's arrival and thwarted her maternal concern. He sat in Bodie's passenger seat as they cruised up the outside lane of the expressway at more than the legal speed. Mac half suspected Bodie intended to avoid their mother and diffuse the standoff with Logan. Either way, he'd separated him from Tilly and left her to more effusive questions of Detective Elliott. Mac regretted that with all his heart.

"What about Tilly?" he demanded, turning in his seat to observe his brother's stern expression. "She needs some kind of immunity."

Bodie snorted, a spiteful, aggressive release of air. "What do you think this is? You're not political dissidents, Mac! You're two stupid kids mixed up in something you should have left alone." Mac had poked the bear. "You lied to me, you little shit! I asked you about that phone." He ignored the road in front to turn his glare on Mac's face, his expression thunderous. "This isn't like you. It's that girl, isn't it?"

Mac bridled. "Don't blame Tilly for any of this! I dragged her into it. Miss Andrews found out about the BAC system and they killed her. Darian admitted he enjoyed following her. Simms saw off Paulette Dunning, and they effectively isolated Marie from anyone who might have helped."

Bodie's jaw dropped. "Why didn't she come to us? It's our job to help." His pupils widened to create black pits in his eyeballs. A car braked in front and found him scrambling. He left a week's salary in expensive tyre rubber on the expressway in his effort to avoid a rear shunt. Coarse swearwords burst from his lips as he slipped the heavy vehicle into the other lane and proceeded with more caution. Adrenaline surged through Mac's brain like a sugar rush. "How do you know anything about Paulette Dunning?" Bodie growled. His thumbs tapped an irritating beat on the steering wheel. It interfered with Mac's processors, adding a background noise he couldn't isolate from Bodie's question.

"Stop doing that!" he snapped. "I can't hear you."

Bodie repeated his question. His thumbs continued their frantic activity but in mid-air, not connecting with the smooth surface of the steering wheel. It gave the appearance of an essential tremor, just as annoying but at least soundless.

"We met her at the spinal unit," Mac admitted. "I blocked her from Miss Andrews' phone and social media accounts. But it wasn't because they broke up, but because Marie wanted to protect her." Mac shook his head. "I got it wrong."

Bodie sighed and tutted. He switched lanes twice more without replying. Then he said, "You'll need to include all of this in a statement. But I suspect you've buggered any chance we had as far as prosecution. You've tampered with evidence, Mac." His tone softened. "Don't you understand?"

Mac's chest tightened, and he nodded. He slumped in the seat and braced his painful left arm by cradling it in his right hand. Bodie reached across and squeezed his shoulder, a conciliatory show of brotherly solidarity which lasted longer than Mac felt he deserved. Tiredness, regret, turmoil and confusion pushed good sense aside as Mac cleared his throat. "That's not all," he whispered, his voice small and crackly. "It gets worse."

77

Injury Time

Bodie remained speechless as he marched Mac into the emergency department of Auckland City Hospital. Middlemore's proximity vied with his need to interview Simms and Darian, who'd gone further north.

Hana's porcelain genetics had muted the sepia tones Bodie inherited from his father, but Mac's confession turned his brother's complexion into a sickly taupe.

"Sorry," Mac pleaded. "I should have told you I'd made a stupid pass at her. I know the groundsman told Elliott about it. It's me he's looking for. And I can give you the SIM card from the burner phone. It's hidden in my soccer boot but it's empty."

"I've got nothing." Bodie held his hands in front of him as though Mac had pulled a gun and threatened him. The automatic doors closed behind them. "Don't speak to me." Mac's lips parted in protest and Bodie made a zipping motion with his brown fingers. "Not another word!" he growled.

Mac sank into a rigid plastic chair when ordered to, ignoring the man vomiting neat alcohol into a bucket opposite him. He tucked his boots beneath the chair to avoid the splashes covering the tiles between them. Bodie's shoulders held a warning stiffness as he spoke to the receptionist. He leaned on the counter with his elbows locked and talked through the plexiglass. A jerk of his head in Mac's direction resulted in a clipboard being pushed through a gap at the bottom.

Shame superheated Mac's cheeks. He wondered why Bodie didn't want to talk about his mistake. Perhaps Elliott hadn't told him about the student who'd made the victim cry and dragged suspicion onto himself. It seemed improbable the subordinate hadn't relayed the shadowy spectre of a mysterious suitor to his superior. Mac's shoulders slumped. He'd compromised his brother with his need to unburden himself. Bodie could no longer remain on the case. Hence his desire to silence Mac's confession. For fear of more hidden information which would exclude him from a murder case unfettered by the usual factors of domestic violence or sexual assault.

A woman waited behind Bodie, her right foot tapping with impatience. She held the hand of a small child who wore a camping kettle as a helmet. Mac released a low chuckle and leaned forward to get a better view across the waiting area. The child turned to face the reception desk, the spout protruding like a unicorn's horn. They'd wedged the handle under their chin like a helmet and tilted their head back to peer from the kettle's interior. Mac studied the child's clothing, unable to decide on its sex. He imagined a much younger Wiremu wedging his head into a kettle and nodded to himself. A boy, he concluded. With Phoenix, Edin and Tilly as a reference point, he figured a girl wouldn't do something so stupid.

Bodie slumped into the vacant chair next to Mac. He wrinkled his nose at the drunk and turned sideways in the seat. "You need to fill this in," he stated. He pushed the clipboard onto Mac's knee, bumping his damaged arm.

Mac released a hiss of pain. "I can't write!" he lied. When several people and the child's spout turned towards him, he knew he'd added too much heat.

Bodie huffed and pulled the clipboard back onto his knees. He filled in MacGillivray Du Rose but missed writing Logan as his first name. The pen wavered in his fingers as he paused over the date of birth. "How old are you?" he hissed.

"Really?" Pain reduced Mac's available patience. Bodie worked it out on his fingers and then filled in the right year but the wrong day and month. Mac leaned back in his seat and closed his eyes.

Having a police escort proved advantageous, earning assistance for Mac ahead of the drunk and the kettle-wearer. Despite his lack of a uniform, the nursing staff recognised Bodie from myriad visits to their department with various victims and prisoners over the years. He abandoned Mac to the care of a male nurse who, after stripping off the bandage, walked him towards a room containing an X-ray machine. "You in trouble?" the nurse asked, holding open the door for him.

Mac shook his head, changing the action half-way through to a reluctant nod. "Kinda," he admitted. "He's my brother."

The nurse gave a jovial upward jerk of his chin. "A different sort of imprisonment then, hey?" He waggled his brows, but lost interest when Mac didn't see the funny side.

A technician seated Mac beside the machine and forced him to twist his forearm into a series of uncomfortable positions. She stepped behind a screen while snapping each image, a lead covering protecting her bulging pregnancy. "All done," she announced, as the pain in Mac's wrist reached a dizzying crescendo. He collapsed forward and stared at the tiled floor beneath his boots. His right arm curved around the left and cradled it to his chest. "Sorry." Her tone held enough sympathy to sound believable. "The break is healing, but there's a tear on the tendon they fixed. I'll need to email the pictures to your surgeon."

Mac nodded and released a sigh. "Thanks." His left processor emitted a warning crackle, and he groaned. "Not again."

The technician cleared her throat. "A nurse will fit a back-slab to get you through the next few days." She lifted the sheet containing Bodie's appalling, crabbed handwriting. She flapped it in Mac's peripheral vision. "We can't seem to find you in the system. Are you a New Zealand citizen?" The technician gave a tight smile, filled with regret at the implications of her question. Mac glanced sideways at the form and his heart sank. He'd watched Bodie write the wrong date of birth, but missed the more serious and deliberate error. He glanced up at the technician as she grinned at him. "I've never met someone who lived at a zoo," she said.

Mac sighed. And decided he liked his older brother even less.

A horrible wailing drifted from the corridor to fill Mac's brain. The technician strode to the door and hauled it open. Miniature kettle-wearer stopped within Mac's eyeline, mouth open and tears coursing down rosy cheeks. The kettle dangled from the mother's limp hand by the stubby remains of its handle. Her lips formed a thin, pained line. Mac followed the child's gaze and saw two hands clenched into fists at the chest. Each clutched a severed pigtail complete with a limp and now useless pink bow. "Wow," Mac admitted to himself, regretting his unintentional sexism. "So, girls are just as stupid."

78

Sliding Tackle

"I need to know everything that happened."

Edin shuffled her chunky sleeping mat beside Mac's. The accidental jab to his elbow caused a ribbon of pain to shoot through his wrist and engulf his fingers. He groaned and squeezed his eyes closed, which meant he could no longer see her moving lips demanding answers. "Ouch!" he managed, more of an exhale than a complaint.

Edin tapped his shoulder, and he turned to discover her face a mere ten centimetres from his. He blinked in surprise. "Tell me everything!" Her lips moved in the semi-darkness of the wharenui. She breathed minty toothpaste over his face. Adults and children slept on identical sleeping mats around them. Phoenix occupied the space to Mac's right, Wiremu beyond her. Tama's mat remained empty as he took a turn keeping Alfie company in the meeting house. Logan stayed with him, his fingers strumming his guitar strings in a gentle stroking motion. Mac hadn't heard the notes he produced, but he wondered at his father's choice of activity as he hugged him before heading to bed. The ancient instrument represented more of Alfred's careful betrayal of Reuben. Perhaps in death, it no longer mattered.

The icy blue glow of emergency lighting shone from a nearby power socket, casting an ethereal halo around the carvings soaring overhead. The giant phallus belonging to an open-mouthed ancestor cast indecent shadows on the ceiling as the female below him birthed the next generation from between her splayed legs. Hana poked her head through the doorway and searched the room for her son. Dark circles underlined her eyes like smudged kohl as she assured herself of his presence. She gave him a tired smile and withdrew, heading back to the kitchen to prepare more food for myriad night visitors who would come to pay their respects.

"I can't!" Mac mouthed. He squeezed his shoulders up to his ears beneath his sleeping bag and shook his head. His processors charged on a multi-block behind Edin, too far to reach and besides, he lacked the energy.

Edin's lips turned down in a familiar pout. She stuck out her tongue and turned her back on him. Mac exhaled, imagining the sound emerging as too loud in the silent space. Mātua Kauri slept nearest the door. He'd arrived late after a shift at the meat factory in Horotiu, joining the throng of distant relatives keeping vigil over Alfred's body in an easy, familiar rotation. Mac sensed the vibrations of the uncle's snoring rumbling through the wooden floorboards as he slept until someone woke him for his turn. Perhaps the wharenui wasn't so quiet after all. He squeezed his eyes closed, grateful at last for his lack of hearing. The vibrations soothed him and he slept.

His bladder woke him before dawn. A silver light filtered through the open doorway and bathed a path between the mattresses. Mac slipped from his sleeping bag and padded outside into the fresh air. He stretched the kinks from his back on the deck, the soaring apex of the building casting faint shadows in his wake. His right arm reached for heaven as the joints cracked, but he didn't risk it with his left. The plaster back-slab weighed a tonne compared to the fibreglass cast. It tugged on his elbow joint as though he carried a dumbbell. His bare torso, with its dusting of red hair, seemed invisible in the moon's kiss. Like a fox, Mac thought to himself.

He'd wanted Tilly to stay at the marae, but the duty manager at the group home refused. Logan drove her back in the borrowed silver car and even topped up the tank at a garage on the way. Mac wondered if the social worker would notice the difference in the petrol gauge when he arrived home from Wellington. Tilly parked it back in the garage in the exact spot, according to Hana. Through a skilled series of half-truths and misdirection, she'd smoothed over her twenty-four-hour absence. She claimed another member of staff knew of her plan to stay overnight with a friend, placating the duty manager with frightening ease. Logan told Mac she planned to replace the car keys in the safe at the first opportunity. They hadn't discussed the parking ticket. Hana didn't approve of Tilly's easy lying, conveying her angst through pursed lips as Mac's father relayed the subterfuge with gentle appreciation. Logan liked resourceful underdogs. He'd been one once.

Mac jumped at a light touch on his biceps. Edin smiled up at him and held out his processors. She'd collected them from his charger, eager to gossip about his previous day's adventures. With a loud sigh of resignation, he took them from her palm and fitted them to his head. She stretched her arm around his waist, her touch feathery and sensual as her fingers performed a gentle stroking movement. Her fringe tickled his skin and she pressed a kiss against his bulging muscle. Confusion swirled in his gut. His brow furrowed as he gazed down on her. She caught his eye and discomfort blossomed behind her grey irises. The careful veneer of her smokescreen peeled back for long enough for him to see the truth. It still lurked behind her whirring thoughts, the possibility of them together. She'd hidden it in a unilateral decision taken when she jumped into a relationship with his friend. Her swallowed and watched her struggle to put the thing back in its box.

Birdsong and the eternal hum of nature piped through to his brain along the series of preordained connections. "I need the bathroom," he told her, his voice croaking.

Edin shrugged. "I'll come with you."

Mac rolled his eyes as he stalked towards the toilet block designated for tāne. Undeterred, Edin kept pace, forcing him to divert from the urinal to a cubicle. She leaned against the bank of four sinks, asking questions without waiting to digest his one-word answers. "So, where did they kill Miss Andrews, then?" she gushed. "Simms has hidden depths but Darian's gutless. I overheard Pa speaking to Bo on the phone last night. Someone coshed her over the head with something blunt. The post mortem showed flecks of paint." Her voice wobbled as though she'd shivered at the mental image.

Mac flushed the toilet and opened his door. He sighed at finding Edin blocking his exit. Skirting her bubble of curiosity, he noted how she turned in a slow circle and kept her gaze locked on him. She wanted every detail, even those he felt reluctant to repeat. But she wanted other things from him also, those he might have given once but couldn't now. Deacon loved her. He'd seen that. And he'd involved Tilly. They'd left it too late. They would never know if it might have worked.

Mac's mind flicked to his fumbled kiss of the teacher, who'd rebuffed him with such kindness. He washed his right hand under the tap and smoothed soap over the fingers of his left hand. His pinkie curled like a claw against his palm, atrophied and useless. Without hope. He splashed water over his face and hair, careful not to dampen his processors. His red beard scratched his fingers with its two-day-old growth. Mac hardly recognised the man staring back at him from the mirror. He'd told Tilly the whole truth with none of the shame and discomfort he'd felt while relaying details of the foolish kiss to his brother. Yet he couldn't tell Edin. He shied away from comparing her to Tilly. It seemed base, even for him. But he sensed Tilly got him. She accepted his faults and shortcomings without judgement. The thought stunned him. Perhaps she loved him. He pictured Tilly with her rebellious clothes, which hid luscious curves and silky-smooth skin. Her dark humour, quick mind, and bright lipstick thrilled and challenged him. His heart swelled until it grew large enough to stretch his ribs into tight, curved rods. He liked her. He more than liked her. And Edin had Deacon now.

"It makes no sense," Edin repeated.

"What?" Mac spun to face her, blinking as he struggled to pick up her thread.

"Why didn't they kill you?" Edin spread her hands. She wore a huge tee shirt which reached almost to her knees. The frayed ends of denim shorts poked from beneath like a frill. Deacon's shirt. Mac recognised the band name scrawled across the raised arcs of her breasts. They'd attended the concert together. He remembered. The sound and vibration proved too much for Mac. He removed his processors in the first ten minutes and suffered in stoic silence, plastering an inane grin onto his face for the torturous three hours until he escaped. He never attended another.

"I don't understand." He edged towards the door, skirting her and fascinated by how she turned as though he represented her true north. Mac corrected his random thoughts. Magnetic north. Deacon was her true north now. Best for everyone. Edin curved her fingers around his right biceps and exerted enough pressure to prevent him from leaving. His bare feet halted on the cool terracotta tiles and he shivered. The Disabled Du Rose. A gentle red giant. But she had Deacon now.

"Why did they kill Miss Andrews but offer you a cut of the profits? It makes no sense." Her brow furrowed, her black eyebrows joining into a single line. "Didn't they offer her a cut?" She shrugged. "Perhaps she refused. Did neither of them mention it? Why jump straight to murder?"

Mac's lips parted, and he stared at her. Playing cards containing information shifted in his analytical brain. His imagination added clunks and scrapes as they switched places and fluttered flat to form a different picture. This picture tied up loose ends, which until that moment made no sense. He swore then, a long, low hiss of exhaled air.

"What?" Her grey irises flickered with excitement as she pressed closer. Her shoulder bumped his left biceps, and she pressed a palm against his bare chest as though to prevent him from solving the mystery without her. An electrical charge sent shards of blue pain from her hand to his heart. Too late, Mac reminded himself. They'd missed their moment.

His lips formed an 'O' of pain as he flexed his healing wrist. The deliberate action killed the spark and it bounced off his ribs and fizzled to nothing. "Can you drive me to school?" he asked. A distraction. A missed opportunity. Desperation filled his tone. He pressed his hand over the fingers resting against his heart. Her warm skin offered solidarity, a willing partner in crime. Nothing else. She had Deacon now.

"Hell yeah," she replied. She licked her lips and devilment sparkled in her irises. It killed the other emotion, the deep longing she'd hidden but not banished. "I just need to steal some car keys."

79

Near-Post

"Please, can I use your phone to text Tilly?" Mac eyed Edin's phone resting upside down in the cup holder.

"Yeah, sure." She drove with extreme care as they navigated the winding roads towards the expressway. "Just understand that I'll read it later and laugh at your sloppy declarations of love." Her sarcasm had returned, but it lacked its usual bite. She'd seen the possibility in his eyes and regret choked any further retort.

Mac seized the device and tapped keys, missing Edin's frown of annoyance that he knew the code for her lockscreen. "I'm asking her what happened to Gray last night," he stated. "We arranged to meet him at five by the equipment shed."

Edin tutted. "And that's your first message of the day? Disappointing. You're not much of a romantic, are you cuz? Ask Deacon for some lessons." But her tone held less bravado than usual. Mac ignored the jibe.

"I ran past the equipment shed on the way to the main building to see Darian. Why didn't I pass Gray waiting for us?" He blew out a breath. "And why did he take Tilly's money to get the footage wiped when Darian spent the last month searching for cameras and found none? Do you think maybe Gray turned up but panicked when the cops arrived?"

"I don't know." Edin turned to face him, taking her gaze from the road for long enough to scare him. "But I want you to know I haven't slept with Deacon." Her revelation caused his skin to prickle with guilt. Neither of them voiced the inference that she'd waited for him instead.

"Edin!" he exclaimed as the vehicle crossed the centre line. She jerked the wheel and his mother's truck careened onto the right side of the road. Fear ticked like a clock in his chest, and he wondered if she'd buried the genes of the unhinged Caroline Du Rose deep enough to prevent her from killing them both. And the original reasons returned for his perpetual rejection of the sexual tension which swirled around their relationship.

Mac raised his right hand to his head and touched the processor's smooth plastic shell. But he couldn't disconnect from life anymore, even though he ached to wrench sound from his world. He cleared his throat and let his hand fall to his thigh, spreading his fingers and staring at the deep gouges across his knuckles. Despite a vow of pacifism, he'd hit three men in the last week. For one, he wished he could go back in time and undo the pain he'd inflicted. The other two he wished he'd hit harder.

As Edin pushed Hana's truck along the slip lane and entered the expressway, an image of Sassy rose into his memory and he missed her. The feisty mare didn't care if he could hear or not. They communicated through a primeval bond which superseded his senses. She heard and saw and felt for him. Logan had given her and Sonny the rest of the lawn to destroy in the family's absence. Time and nature would repair the grass from their hoofprints and the tearing of tender shoots from the earth. Mac promised himself he'd reseed it, revelling in the idea of nurturing something back to life from the desert which the horses would leave.

The air hung between him and Edin. He hadn't replied to her comment about her virginity, not wanting to unleash more of the emotion swirling in waves from her stiff shoulders. Instead, he focussed his mind on Alfie's gift, wondering where he last saw his hat. It became symbolic in a way he hadn't expected. Despite Alfred and Reuben taking wives, they had reverted to type and allowed the desire to ruin their lives and relationships. Reuben had crossed back for Miriam. Mac saw how the hat stood as a warning from beyond the grave. Henri Du Rose, their father's hat. It hailed from a time before they ruined the mountain and each other.

Mac glanced sideways at Edin, watching her from beneath his lashes. He sensed he could reach out and touch her and the dam would burst in an instant. It would carry them both into something explosive, wonderful, and devastating in equal measures. Sex with Tilly had woken him to a state far more dangerous than he ever anticipated. He imagined himself stroking Edin's inner thigh, his soft touch inching high enough to turn her into a quivering mess. As a fast study, he'd already learned how to cause the detonation of chemistry and physiology. He knew what he was doing now. Mac squeezed his eyes closed until his sockets ached. Instead, he pictured the hat. Alfie's warning.

Edin's phone vibrated in his lap and he pulled up Tilly's text. Guilt blossomed in his chest at the thought of her purity against the debauched thoughts he'd nursed about Edin.

'The little shit conned me,' Tilly replied. *'You're right. There are no cameras. He saw a way to trick me and took it. Wanted money for smokes. I'm done with him. Forever.'*

Her text held a note of finality. She meant it. Gray had crossed a line. Mac tutted and shook his head. He sent a flurry of replies to comfort her.

"What?" Edin glanced across at him, her brows knitted with concern. "What did she say?"

Mac released a sigh. "He wanted easy cash. I suspect he thought he'd meet us last night and concoct some issue with his techie mate. Then ask for more money." His teeth ground in his jaw. "There's no techie mate. And he's confirmed there's no camera." He imagined selling out Phoenix for pocket change and living with the consequences of having cheated her. But Tilly wasn't Phoenix. Mac's gentle sister might forgive him after a while, but not his sparky girlfriend. She'd defended Gray, painted him as a victim of circumstance and not the crook he appeared. He'd witnessed Tilly cut people off before and shivered. He never wanted to find himself outside her inner circle, not sure he'd survive the expulsion in one piece.

"So, Messrs Darian and Simms told the truth?" Edin's chin flattened as she lifted her head and gave a slow nod. "Well, that's a surprise. But they still lied about killing Miss Andrews."

"No." Mac shook his head, the action containing more certainty now. "They didn't kill her, but I know who did."

"You do?" Edin's eyes became round orbs in her delicate face. She turned to look at him, glee in her expression.

"The road!" Mac yelled again as she swerved onto the hard shoulder. The tyres produced a horrible squeal as she tugged the wheel. Grit sprayed across the crash barrier like buck shot.

"Tell me then!" she demanded, her tone petulant. Her lips turned down in a pout as Mac struggled to swallow his stomach and stop his fingers from shaking on the door handle. "Don't make me pull over, cuz. We're either in this together, or you can get out and walk!"

80

Drop Ball

Traffic increased on the expressway as office workers got a jump on rush hour. A fuming snake snarled beyond the turn after the airport, and Edin escaped from its clutches in time. She took the slip road towards Manukau and stopped at traffic lights. Mac glanced through the rails of the over-bridge and saw brake lights flashing on the motorway below. He imagined the bliss of quitting his bed, saddling Sassy, and riding the dewy ridges of the mountain before the world woke. It beat the prospect of angry honking and stress induced road rage starting below. A police car slid along the hard shoulder, skirting the waiting traffic as it responded to an incident at the front of the growing queue. It only took one minor ding to gridlock Auckland's primary artery.

Mac sighed and counted the remaining months left at school. Eight, if he didn't quit sooner. His relationship with Tilly complicated matters. He figured he'd stay for now.

Despite the brightness of the dawn, fewer vehicles dotted the back roads. Mac noted more early morning dog walkers and joggers than cars. Edin steered Hana's truck to the side street where Logan intercepted Mac and Tilly the previous evening. Without realising, Edin parked outside the same house. Mac stared at the lounge window. Sunlight speckled the uneven glass. The familiar net curtains hung as they should, no faces peering at him from beneath their folds. No one eating snacks and enjoying the entertainment of a dead woman, two injured teachers, and a few destroyed lives.

"This is a cycle lane," Mac announced with a sigh.

Edin peered through the windscreen. "How do you know?"

"Tilly parked here last night and got a ticket."

"Oh." Edin screwed her head around to examine their surroundings. "There's nowhere else to park. Double yellow lines are worse. What time do the school gates open? We could park in the visitor's car park if this won't take long." She turned to face Mac with a raised eyebrow. "I don't understand what we're looking for exactly."

"Trust me," Mac replied, sounding like his father. "I'll know it when I see it."

"You're wrong." She leaned her head against the seat and her hair stuck to the fabric like a static haze. It crackled as she turned to face him. "I've listened to your explanation and you're wrong."

Her phone buzzed against Mac's thigh. It had slipped between his legs and he frowned, having forgotten about it. "Sorry," he murmured. He handed it to Edin and released his seat belt. "Saved by the bell," he joked, his tone flat. "It would have smashed on the pavement when I got out."

He placed his right hand over the door handle, forced to reach across himself because of his useless left arm. Taps issued from Edin's phone as she unlocked the screen and replied to a text. Another vibration buzzed through the vehicle. Mac turned his head and waited for her to look up at him. "If I'm not back in twenty minutes, call Bodie. Stay on the call with him and tell him my theory. Ask him to come." He raised an auburn eyebrow. "Don't leave the truck. Ma will be angry enough at our joy riding without adding an infringement notice and a fine. We're lucky Toby didn't tell her about last time."

Edin's features screwed up, a look of concern involving every muscle. "Why twenty minutes?" she demanded. "I should just come with you."

Mac spoke through gritted teeth. "In twenty minutes, I'll either find it or I won't. Any longer and I'm in trouble." He jerked his head towards the steering wheel. "Stay with the truck. Move it only if a cop or a warden challenges you."

"Okay." She glanced down at her phone. "But you're wrong. I know you are. And I should come with you." She'd dismissed his theory and her interest waned.

Mac stepped from the vehicle. He raised his right hand to shield his eyes and peered into the distance. "The main gate should open soon for the rugby boys. They have a practice at six thirty. I'm guessing the gardeners and ground staff start super early. Only park at school if you absolutely need to move. Otherwise, wait here. This is where I'll come back to find you." He bent at the waist to stare into the truck's interior at her. "I still don't have my phone, remember?"

Edin exhaled and wrinkled her nose. "No, I forgot about that. Does Bo still have it?"

"Yeah. Stay with the truck, Edie." He used his pet name for her and her gaze softened.

Her phone vibrated in her hand and she frowned at it, her attention already wavering. "Deacon wants to come to Poppa's tangi," she said, her tone wistful. "Do you mind?"

"No!" Irritation laced Mac's voice as she dismissed his concerns. She expected him to return empty handed from his mission. "I don't care if he's there or not." The statement surprised him as his processors relayed it back to him. He didn't care. Deacon had aided Edin's false flag. He just didn't know it yet.

Her expression paled, and she winced at her screen. "Ma just texted. She said Pa knows where we are because of the truck's

GPS. She's given us an hour to get back to the marae with an explanation, or she's calling the cops."

"Great!" Mac sighed.

"I hope that means she's calling Bodie and not the actual cops." Edin peered out at him, holding the phone in her palm with the delicacy of a grenade.

"He is an actual cop," Mac replied. "We are so done." He slammed the passenger door and set off towards the school. He didn't glance back at her, sure he'd see her raised eyebrow of scepticism. The wide green expanse of paddock stretched before him, rugby posts giving their familiar two-fingered salute to the azure sky. Mac stepped over the chain-link barrier, which stopped teenagers using the school grounds as hooning circuits for their muscle cars. A shout caused him to spin around and face the road.

Edin had left the truck and stood in the centre of the street. "It's Tilly," she shouted. Her words echoed off windows and stucco in the early morning silence. "Gray did a runner in the night. I knew you'd got it wrong." Her lips curved upwards in victory. She waved her phone at him, perhaps hoping he'd abandon his reckless theory and return to argue it out with her.

Mac shook his head and continued his mission. Dew soaked the toes of his cowboy boots as his even steps carried him across the first pitch. Then he began his search, aware of the ticking clock, the coming parental storm, and Edin's complete lack of faith in him.

81

HAT TRICK

Four rugby pitches ruled the lime green front elevation of the school. They commanded the lion's share of the ground staff's time, the best nutrition for their hallowed turf, and the most expensive equipment. Like many New Zealand high schools, its reputation sank or swam on the success of its First Fifteen. The rugby squads took the pick of the best sponsorship and left the other codes to squabble over what dribbled through the cracks in their sizeable coffers. It wasn't fair or right, but as a soccer player, Mac knew no other ecosystem.

He trudged across all four of the rugby pitches without finding what he sought. But instead of disappointment, he experienced an uptick of excitement. He'd learned to hunt at Logan's knee, analysing the data and sifting the facts into rows of neat playing cards in his mind. This solution made sense, and only this one. He continued searching, tracking through his theory and ticking off the items. It only worked if he saw nothing until he found the one thing nobody knew to seek.

Because there was only one murder weapon, after all. And without realising it, Edin had told him what to look for.

Mac grinned with satisfaction when the rugby pitches offered no hidden treasure. The new dugout constructed from reclaimed timber and aluminium struts preened on the sideline like a silent spectator. Dark varnish cast a treacle hue over the wood and the support poles gleamed. His father's words echoed in his mind, accompanied by the quick hand motions, which repeated them in sign language. *'Start wide and close in real slow. Use all the data. Assess, assess, assess.'*

And so he did. The data told him the killer had overplayed their hand. A thorough hiding of the murder weapon in plain sight should make it impossible to link it with the death. They should have hidden it on the rugby pitches, blending its existence into the scenery with cunning seamlessness. A glance behind him showed he'd left dewy footsteps in the grass. They followed him in a dark, weaving line from one place to the next. A tractor fired up in the distance, its throaty roar relayed to Mac through a crackling in his processors. He turned to watch it as it set off across the first rugby pitch, its blades lowering by degrees like outstretched arms readying for an embrace. The sound changed as the sharp blades connected with the grass and damp clods shot outwards like green spray.

Mac reached the soccer pitches, noting the familiar red roof of the Alexandra Motel in the distance. The communication tower rose behind it like a stray hair caught in static. Its suburban placement had upset community groups who organised a petition. They hadn't wanted to live near it. Now they couldn't live without it.

Mac hit pay-dirt on the last pitch. His height gave him a distinct advantage as he ran the fingers of his right hand over the aluminium posts from bottom to top and front to back. He examined each of the joins where the aluminium posts butted to a mate at a ninety-degree angle. Rust covered each of them, telling a story of age and use, of games won and lost and trophies lifted high or grieved.

Mac knelt in the wet grass, the dew leaving a darker patch on the knee of his jeans and soaking through to his skin. A support strut left the top near side corner of the goal mouth at a ninety-degree angle, before bending at forty-five degrees and heading downward. It curved again to take it back to ninety degrees before joining two other crossbars. One of those ran forward to the front of the goal and supported the front left post. The other slid level with the ground at right angles until its junction with another bar. The rear supports acted as buttresses to the all-important goal mouth, maintaining the net's tension against the barrage of soccer balls travelling at speeds of one hundred and twenty-nine kilometres per hour. Rust spots ruined the patina of the paint, causing flecks to lift and reveal the decay hiding within.

But the bottom forty-five-degree bend in the back left bar didn't match its twin on the right. It had snapped in the last game of the season, pushed to breaking point by the opposition's failed attack on goal. The ball flew wide and hit the aluminium at just the wrong angle. One time too many. And it snapped. The crossbar dipped by thirty centimetres like a lopsided yawn, and the referee halted the game.

Mac sighed as he remembered the First Eleven manager wrapping the gaffer tape around the post. He'd married the two jagged edges together and fixed them in place while Mac supported the crossbeam. The man's chunky fingers shook with temper as he wrapped and wrapped and wrapped, using an entire reel of tape. Spectators had milled around the sidelines, checking the time or drifting to watch other games continuing on pitches with better equipment. The manager ranted as he worked, spittle landing on the flecked metal as he cussed out the rugby teams, which guzzled every available dollar for their higher profile games. Then he'd left, returning to the UK, to the beautiful game and the respect he hadn't received in a country where rugby posts and sheep outnumbered the people.

Mac stared at the bulging weld where someone had grafted a metal sleeve over the break and painted it white. The ridges stood proud of the metal, the wider circumference required to fit over the original aluminium pole. He didn't touch it, keen not to add his DNA and fingerprints to the mix. He rose and brushed grass chips from his jeans before turning to leave.

The tractor lay silent on the First Fifteen's hallowed rugby pitch. Engrossed in his task, Mac hadn't noticed its engine cough and splutter before silencing. The search had taken less than fifteen minutes, his long stride and keen eyes doing most of the work. He imagined Edin watching the digital clock in Hana's truck, not yet worried as she texted Deacon sloppy, romantic shorthand filled with emojis.

"Now then," growled Foggy. "You checking my workmanship?" The old man stood with his hands on his hips, a baseball cap clamped onto his head. The brim threw his expression into shadow.

"Something like that." Mac kept his tone light. "I hoped the sports department replaced the broken bar, but that's a great fix."

"Na." Foggy removed his cap and scratched his head. A flick of his wrist replaced it with an easy sleight of hand. "Glad you approve." His voice held a tightness, and the surrounding energy seemed to crackle and fizz. "That all you wanted then?"

"Yep, thanks." Mac took a step sideways, hoping to avoid the inane conversation and return to Edin. But Foggy matched his stride with surprising speed, arriving in front of him and blocking his path. Mac swallowed but didn't panic. Thirty-two acres of grass, longer legs, and the benefit of youth offered a raft of escape routes.

"You live out of town, don't ya?" Foggy adjusted the tool belt at his waist, hoisting it up as though imagining it could traverse his rounded belly. It reached an impasse at the level of his navel, and he dropped it back over his hips. "Long way to come just to check on soccer equipment." His gaze roved over Mac's jeans and tee shirt, taking in his lack of uniform and his unkempt beard.

"Just passing," Mac lied. "My poppa died. We're in town organising some things."

Foggy lifted his left hand and glanced at a wristwatch strapped to his hairy forearm. "Seems a bit early for that kind of thing," he mused.

Then Mac saw the hammer clasped in his right hand, the action with the tool belt a smoke screen to haul the weapon free. He ducked as the groundsman swung it in a high, spiteful arc.

82

GOAL KICK

The hammer flew towards Mac's head as though in slow motion. It took him by surprise, not least because he'd missed the adroitness of its extraction from the loop of the tool belt. On reflection, he shouldn't have lifted his left arm in self-defence, catching sight of the rugged white cast moving out and up in his peripheral vision to protect his head.

He'd expected the old man to dispose of the broken pole and replace it. But the burning scent kept returning to his memory. Not just seared flesh and an electrical sharpness but laced by the tang of melted solder. And then he remembered how the soccer goalposts went up first. They appeared overnight, erected at speed as though beamed there by aliens. Before the rugby posts. And after Marie Andrews died. A blow to the head killed her, inflicted with the loose upright now forming the ninety-degree angle stretching towards the sky. Foggy had welded a cuff of aluminium over the murder weapon and hidden it in plain sight.

Mac turned his shoulder at the last minute and withdrew his injured arm, self-preservation judging it unfit for sacrifice.

The hammer smashed against his ribcage, cracking two of the protective spindles and driving pain screaming into Mac's brain. His left lung inflated and then stopped, unable to press against the muscles panicking above and below the broken bones. Mac's knees trembled, threatening to drop him to the damp, loamy earth. Foggy lifted the hammer again, his eyes sparkling and strange as though their owner no longer lived behind the empty stare. Mac gasped for air, half bowed at the waist and his left arm hanging as though detached at the shoulder. Any movement to that side of his body caused his vision to blur with the red sheen of agony.

As the hammer fell again, he ducked aside, crabwise and awkward. He'd saved his wrist, but at a terrible cost. Mac struggled to rise, moving backwards as Foggy's blow fell wide. He propelled it with such force; it pitched him forward over the hammer for a fraction of a second as though the momentum might push him into a graceful forward roll. Holding his breath, Mac forced his torso to unwind and commanded his legs to move him back into danger. Foggy righted himself, foam leaking from the corners of his mouth. He lifted the hammer again, his eyes widening in surprise when Mac's left thigh blocked its trajectory. He blinked as the teenager's right fist drove through the air and contacted his veined nose with enough force to knock him off his feet. The old groundsman became the fourth person Mac Du Rose hit in a week.

Foggy collapsed back onto the grass like a rug unrolled and shaken into place. He stayed down, the hammer twitching in his right hand. Blood trickled from both nostrils to form a red moustache which stretched across his face to touch the grey hairs sprouting from his ears.

Nausea rose into Mac's throat and spilled from between his lips to douse the stubby green shoots and the baked earth. Pain radiated from his left side like a sunburst. He dropped to one knee, his right hand locked beneath his left arm and the fingers pressing against the source of the overwhelming ache. Foggy's feet twitched and Mac groaned, not sure he'd survive a second round with the hammer.

Then a Stygian shape appeared, powering across the soccer pitches like an angry rain cloud. Her lips parted in a shout of horror. Black hair streamed behind her in waves, which bounced with the rhythm of her footfall. A faux leather coat flapped in her wake, sable feathery wings which struggled to bear her off into the azure sky. She flew towards Mac like an arrow loosed from a bow by fingers, which became powerless to call it back.

And as Foggy pushed himself to a sitting position with his arms locked behind him, Mac held his breath and winced in anticipation of yet more pain. But the avenging angel rose into the air on her powerful wings and kicked the old man in the head with a heavy Doc Marten thud.

83

Far Post

Inspector Beaudain Singh Johal's vocabulary had increased with age and experience. A colourful litany of swearwords spilled from his lips as though released from an artery of bilge in his chest cavity. Even Tilly blinked in shock and interest as Mac's brother stood over him and yelled.

"Stop!" She rose from her kneeling position next to Mac and faced Bodie, no match for him in height but just as furious. She raised a black painted fingernail and wagged it near the police officer's nose. "He needs an ambulance," she growled. "Don't make me ask you twice."

"Far post," Mac said again. He gripped his side until his knuckles whitened, desperate to douse the flaming torch beneath his left arm. "Far post."

"What's he saying?" Bodie's black fringe had lost its coiffed appearance. It flipped into his eyes like a collapsed paperback.

Tilly's arm tightened around Mac's shoulders. "He's saying, *far post*' and pointing to that." She jabbed her inky fingernail towards the goal mouth.

Bodie's phone rang, a long, lilting peal of music which broke the silence of the soccer field. He hauled it from his shirt pocket and lifted it to his ear. "Yes," he snapped. "He's here. I've got him." His gaze roved across the groundsman and the nearby hammer which he'd kicked aside on arrival. Foggy lay in the recovery position where Bodie put him. Blood dripped from the end of his bulbous nose and stained the lime grass shoots below him. "Mac's hurt. And so is the other guy." His voice rose in irritation and fright. "I don't know what's wrong with him. He won't let me see." Bodie turned aside and Logan's bass tones rumbled from the device. "I don't know where she is!" he snapped.

"Edie." Her name huffed from between Mac's lips. He leaned sideways and tried to stand. Pure agony washed over him, stealing his breath again.

"Where is she?" Strawberry bubble gum scents stole through Mac's nostrils as Tilly leaned over him. "I'll find her."

Mac gazed up at her pretty face and believed her. Despite the early hour, she still wore her war-paint, the eyebrows drawn into deep blocks of matt and her sockets highlighted by a bruising blue. He imagined her stealing the social worker's car again, reacting to his hurried text on Edin's phone, which told her where he planned to go. And that he loved her.

"Truck," he managed. Bubbles of air and spit coated his lips and masked his words. "Alex."

Tilly released her arm from around his shoulders, pausing as though afraid he might crumple like an empty silk pillowcase. "I'll find her," she hissed.

Mac offered a jerky nod as she rose, her heavy soled boots clomping away in his peripheral vision.

"Where are you going?" Bodie demanded. "Get back here!" But Tilly sped into an effortless jog, heading towards Alexandra Street, determination in her thin shoulders.

Bodie couldn't make her stay and he couldn't leave his injured brother to follow her across the pitches. Her long skirt swished as she ran, billowing up to reveal slender calves and the back of shapely knees. Mac squeezed his eyes closed and forced his memory back to their night of passion at the house in the township. He focussed on the satin feel of her thighs wrapped around his waist and the vulnerability in the depths of her gaze. And he trusted her. And it lessened the blossoming pain.

In the distance, paramedics used a master key to unlock the padlock holding the chain links taut across the entry. It jangled as it fell and the ambulance rolled over it. Mac lay on his side in the grass as his breathing grew harder. Bodie tried to move him and he cried out and shoved him away. Grass stained the knees of his brother's smart trousers as Bodie knelt beside him, offering encouragement and hope. "They're coming, bro," he whispered. "Your dad sent me to look for you. What the hell happened?"

"Far post," Mac said again, his voice sounding weak. "Far post." A whistle accompanied his words as fluid trickled into his left lung. The cast scratched against his fingers as he pushed at Bodie's knee. "Murder. Far post."

Bodie inhaled with a hiss and disappeared from Mac's eyeline. After a moment, his shiny shoes returned. "The weld?" he asked, squatting next to Mac's face. "Do you mean the welded part of the goal post?"

Mac made a sound like a muted grunt. "Head. Kill."

Bodie swore. He spun, his soles squelching in the damp grass. "I can't understand what you're saying." Fear filled his tone. He rose again and Mac heard him speaking into his phone, his tone low and urgent.

Shouts issued from the edge of the soccer ground, high and female. Bodie's feet spun in Mac's eyeline until his heels blocked the view. The teenager focused on his breathing, realising if he kept it low and shallow, the pounding receded from his head. The cloudiness in his vision cleared to reveal a narrow window between the crinkled hems of Bodie's trousers.

Tilly ran next to the ambulance, towing a sobbing Edin behind her. Their arms swung like the ropes of a swaying bridge. A cyclist followed them across the field, his feet pumping the pedals. His helmet sat askew on his head, the brim covering one eye. He drew level with Edin and took a swipe at her, catching hold of her flying cardigan and yanking her backwards.

A paramedic leaned from the passenger window and yelled at him as Edin strained against his grip. And the wagon train continued its journey across sidelines and centre circles, penalty areas and goal mouths.

Bodie met them all with a loud shout, which held a surprising amount of aggression for a police officer. Fear made him antsy, and he lost his sheen of professionalism. He directed the paramedics to Mac and to Foggy before turning to face the cyclist.

"I'm sick of it!" the man raged, drawing up his sleeve to reveal a bleeding gash. "She opened her door onto me and I fell off. Look at the state of me!" The whiny edge of righteousness drove his hysteria as he pointed out a rip to his work trousers, which a broken cycle clip held around his ankle. "A cyclist almost died last month after a car knocked her down on her way to work. Community service, that's all the punishment the driver got."

Bodie sat the irate man on the grass, forming an orderly queue for the paramedics. He wrapped his arms around Edin and soothed away her shock, letting her cry against his crisp striped shirt. Tilly folded her knees and sank into the grass beside Mac. She reached for his hand and held his fingers in a death grip as the paramedic lifted his tee shirt to survey the damage.

"Ouch!" the man commented. Cool fingers touched Mac's skin, and he squirmed away from their intrusion. "You have broken ribs," he said, no hesitation in his diagnosis. "How'd it happen?"

"A hammer," Tilly growled. "That man hit him." Her words gushed free, and she fought to stop them tying her into a noose she couldn't escape. "He meant to hit him again, but I, but I…" She halted, clamping her pink tongue between her teeth.

The paramedic called across to his female partner. "He needs to go to Middlemore. What about yours?"

"Out cold." She looked up at him, a frown bisecting her brow. "And he's having a cardiac arrest."

Bodie released the sniffing Edin and swore. But Mac closed his eyes and guilt blossomed from a knot in his throat and joined the roiling waves of pain.

84

LINE OF FLIGHT

Foggy didn't die. Not right there on the green grass he'd tended for decades. Or by the goal post, which masked his crime. The paramedics worked on him until his heart rallied and then bore him away to the emergency room in their screeching ambulance. Tubes and pipes protruded from his prone form inside its high-tech bowels. Poor Bodie didn't know whether to go with him or stay with Mac.

He chose Mac.

But then wished he hadn't as Logan blasted over the fallen chain in his truck. Great clods of hallowed turf spat from the huge tyre treads, scattering behind him like surf as he crossed all four pitches at speed. He slewed to a messy halt, gouging long, earthy stripes in the grass and showering Mac with dust and seed.

Hana's yellow skirt appeared beside Mac's cheek, fluttering like butterfly wings next to his eye. He sighed with relief at her proximity, but the action hurt.

"Macky!" Gentle fingers pushed back his red curls to reveal his processor. Then the hand dropped to the earth and Mac recognised his father's scarred fingers. "He can hear us."

"Far post," he implored them, his speech garbled. "Far post." He sensed the swathe of silence fall around them like a curtain of awkwardness.

A second ambulance arrived to transport Mac to the hospital. Edin dropped to her knees next to Hana, seeking comfort and offering nonsensical explanations. He watched the shiny fabric of Tilly's skirt slither backwards and away from him, eased out by the unintended force of the Du Roses. His wrist protested with a dull stab, eclipsed by the searing, white hot splash of pure agony which his ribs sent to his brain as he reached out and snatched her hem. The useless pinkie became entangled in the slithery fabric. Mac didn't feel it, but it halted her escape.

"He knows something," she urged, her tone ragged. "He came here to find the murder weapon."

"Because her brother did it," Edin snarled. She jabbed a finger at Tilly. "Her brother killed Miss Andrews."

"What?" Bodie whipped to attention, his body straightening as if to deflect the anxiety bowing his shoulders. He glared at Tilly. "Her brother?" The police officer emerged from beneath the concerned mask of a frightened brother.

"Yes!" Edin wailed. "He's done a runner because he's guilty. I told Mac, but he just kept walking." She reached out a tender hand towards his curled body and then drew it away. "Why won't you listen to me?" she begged. "You never listen to me."

"Because you're wrong!" Aggression filled Tilly's voice. Her fingers shook against Mac's fist as he fought the pain which encircled his torso like a roll of rusty barbed wire. "Gray's a cheat, not a killer. He had no reason to hurt Miss Andrews. She never taught him. He didn't know her!"

"It's because of BACs." Edin gestured with her hands, as though attempting to fly away from the awful scene. "She found out, and so he killed her."

"He did not!" Tilly released Mac's hand and rose. Her boots clumped close enough to his fingers to make him wince. "Tell them, Mac!" she pleaded. "Tell them it's not true."

"Far post," he murmured again. "Far post."

"Everyone shut up!" Logan commanded. He knelt on the grass and bent to look into Mac's face. A farmer and a haemophiliac, Logan's familiarity with injury gave him a different view of Mac's pain. He recognised the urgency in his son's screwed up features. "Breathe in slow," he advised him. "Gentle, shallow breaths. Release your words as you let the air go, but don't hold on to it. Slow and smooth, son."

Mac concentrated on his directions, inhaling slower and less like snatching at the air. The breaths lengthened, and the panic in his brain lessened. "Far post," he exhaled, the words tangled in the whoosh. "Hit her," breath, "with the brace." Another inhale which tested the limits of his left lung. "Welded," breath, "far post."

"Got it!" Logan hissed. He relayed Mac's message to Bodie, whose eyes widened to glittering white orbs in his slender features. "The old guy?" he demanded, squatting beside Logan. "Ask him if the old guy did it?"

"Yes!" Finally! A sense of satisfaction filled Mac as his left lung struggled to inflate against the throbbing inflammation spreading out from the cracked ribs. He let his cheek sink into the grass and hoped they worked the rest out for themselves. The pieces clattered into a sordid picture in his mind as he heard his brother flailing to follow the fragments towards the same miserable conclusion. Bodie didn't yet know what Mac had realised. But he would. Saliva dripped from his open mouth and grass stuck to his tongue as he struggled. Struggled. Struggled to breathe.

85

Centre Spot

"There's nothing we can do. I'm sorry." The gruff voice held a steady resonance. Mac read the doctor's lips through slitted eyes still bleary from a drug induced sleep. An oxygen mask covered his face, making it difficult for him to turn his head. He forced his eyes to search the room for his mother, finding her expression more irritated than the devastation he'd expected. His eyelashes fluttered as he watched her, resisting the urge to drift away from the heat consuming his left side and sleep.

Her face brightened, her soft pink lips curving upwards as she caught him studying her. 'It's okay,' she signed to him, repeating the movement twice until he gave a long blink of acknowledgement. He looked for the lie, his pupils like pinpricks in his emerald irises. The doctor couldn't help him. He'd said so. That meant death, and yet he felt strangely peaceful.

'You're coming home,' Hana signed. 'Tomorrow.'

Mac pushed his right hand free of the bedsheet and held it palm upwards between them. When he flipped his hand over like a dead fish, the bed shook and the movement elicited a groan of pain from between his lips.

"Who's dead?" Her face moved close enough to kiss if he'd wanted to, her brow furrowing in concern. Then she shook her head, misunderstanding. "Oh, the groundsman?" Her red curls bounced as she turned her head from side to side. "No, he didn't die."

Mac groaned again and closed his eyes. He'd meant himself, but saw she wouldn't acknowledge the lack of hope. Something warm rested on his left shoulder, the pressure of gentle, steady fingers. Mac forced his eyelids to part and looked up at his father. No sadness eclipsed Logan's stormy irises, just worry and exhaustion. "You're okay," he mouthed, pausing until he saw his words hit home. He held up both hands and tapped the fingernail on his left index finger with the pad of his right. 'Can't.' The wrapping motion which followed it offered Mac reassurance. Logan made a hammer action with his fists, the right one uppermost and bumping the lower. 'It'll mend,' he told his son.

Realisation rushed through Mac's brain like cold water. The medics couldn't fix his broken ribs. He would return home to allow them to mend naturally. He released a sigh which stretched the bruising on his left side, but a broad smile broke across his freckled face. Somewhere in the annals of his mind, he had known this about broken ribs.

Mac lifted his right hand and tapped the space above his ear where the processors magnetised to his skull. Hana blinked in surprise and bobbed out of sight. She popped up again, her handbag settled on her knee. She dug into an inner pocket and produced his processor. It took two attempts for her to fit it on his head. Mac closed his eyes to give himself a moment to adjust to the sounds of the noisy hospital flooding his auditory nerve as crackles and hissing. He tilted the oxygen mask just below his chin and, amid the whoosh of the pure air, he demanded to see Bodie.

His brother arrived, his black hair sticking up at the front where he'd run his hands through it. A colleague relieved him, waiting outside the room where Foggy roused from his surgery and found himself under police guard. "Right," Bodie said, all business, as he drew a notebook from his jacket pocket. He licked the end of a tiny biro and poised it over a new page.

Mac held the oxygen mask in his right hand, ready to breathe in the fortifying air when the ache in his left lung demanded assistance. But he told his story regardless, keen not to repeat himself. "Foggy killed Miss Andrews," he began, his voice hoarse. "She intended to drop his granddaughter from the team. He didn't think Keira could take any more pain after losing her mum last year. She had friends in the team, Layla and Sammy." Mac broke to gulp at the air whooshing from the mask. "Foggy and Miss Andrews argued in the equipment shed and he hit her with an aluminium brace. I remembered the goal post snapping last season. It needed replacing, but there's no money for soccer. Just before I found Miss Andrews' body, I noticed someone had installed the soccer posts overnight. I thought it unusual because the rugby posts always go up first." Mac coughed, and it took time for the pain to subside.

"Foggy spent the night welding the murder weapon onto the post. He assembled them all, eight goals in total. The management team knew about the decommissioned equipment shed and the old power line, but Foggy told me about the nail which negated the need for a fuse. He's worked at the school for decades. I'm guessing he hammered in the nail years ago. He ripped down the overhead cable, attached it to the body and left, putting distance between himself and the crime scene." Mac exhaled, blinking as Hana used a tissue to dab at the corners of his mouth. "Foggy told me about a student making a pass at Miss Andrews. It was a threat, and I missed it. Perhaps he saw me, or more likely, made a lucky guess about my feelings for her. He spent a lot of hours on the field watching people. But he intended to warn me off. He also mentioned the presence of a rogue trolley in the equipment shed, intimating someone used it to move the body. I thought he told the cops both things, but Bodie's reaction made me doubt. Foggy told me Marie didn't die in the shed, not Bo."

Bodie paused his scribbling to give a decisive shake of his head. "He didn't mention either thing to us."

Mac took a moment to breathe from the mask. His head cleared more with every sentence and the weight, which bowed his shoulders into the mattress, was lessened by degrees. "Miss Andrews had two phones in her possession, the one Sammy gave to her, which she believed contained evidence of the BAC system, and her own. But perhaps before they argued, Miss Andrews placed the iPhone on the corner of a ball crate. Foggy didn't see it, and after she died I pocketed it, believing it was hers." Mac raised his right hand at Hana's hiss of horror. "I had my reasons, Ma. And it's blown back in my face a hundredfold."

"All good," Bodie growled. "We've covered it." He used the end of his pen to scratch his brow. "Your girlfriend retrieved the other SIM card from your locker last night, thanks."

"Your girlfriend!" Hana's green eyes widened, and she shot a glance at Logan. By the way her lips turned down in sadness, Mac knew she regretted his independence and growing distance from her.

"No," Mac wheezed. He returned his gaze to Bodie. "You haven't covered all of it. I thought someone took the photo on the day I kissed Miss Andrews because I still believed in a blackmail scam attached to the BAC system."

Hana gasped again and Mac hid his face behind the cloudy plastic mask. "You kissed your teacher!"

Bodie waved his hand to indicate the need to move on with his evidence gathering. Grateful, Mac obeyed, avoiding his mother's horrified glare. "I figured I saw my rucksack holding open the door of the equipment shed in the photo. That entire line of thinking took me down a rabbit hole and I went way off track. Because there's a bag containing weights, which Foggy uses as a door stop. Sammy will confirm she took the photo of Miss Andrews during a sports class at the start of the year. Marie's hair is longer in the picture and it's a mixed team of boys and girls. I believe it's the day she handed the phone to Miss Andrews. Without meaning to, she sent the picture to the cloud storage attached to that phone. The SIM cards get switched around and wiped to avoid detection, but all data goes to the cloud. I believe Darian strips everything daily, but for some reason, he missed that photo. It's just a random picture of a sports class, and he's interested in spreadsheets of cash collected and room usage. It's a booking system. They don't take photos. But if you can get Sammy to admit she took it on that phone, you can perhaps link its ownership to Darian and BACs."

Bodie nodded and jabbed his pen in the air. "Yeah, he may have accidentally downloaded it to his own device. That'll give us continuity of evidence."

Mac inhaled through the mask again. "It's stored somewhere strange, like in a file folder buried under the Documents tab. I only discovered it because I searched every single one. I hacked into it through a back door using software from the grey web."

"Please tell me you copied it and didn't open the original?" Bodie's expression sharpened, his features becoming hawklike.

Mac's nod reassured him. The teenager continued. "Your forensics guys might get a date stamp from the cloud. I couldn't see one." He sighed and the hand holding the mask shook. Hana supported his wrist with her cool fingers and offered him an encouraging smile. A hiccough built in Mac's chest from the oxygen and he tensed, dreading the pain which releasing it promised. "Get your tech guys to search Darian's laptop and his classroom. I found him watching a movie, which meant he'd already downloaded and deleted the information from yesterday's activities in the cloud storage. He knows what he's doing, so I doubt even your forensics guys can retrieve the originals, but he'll keep copies on a hard drive somewhere. Try his classroom."

Bodie tutted. "If you left an online trail, then Darian could say you planted the photo. He could claim you're a party to whatever scheme he's running." He lifted his lips on one side in thought. "We'll include everything in your statement and hope for the best." He made a clicking sound with his tongue. "Our forensics guys are good. If there is even a ghost of these files, they'll find it."

Mac continued without acknowledging Bodie's sifting of legal loopholes. He'd already confirmed he didn't touch the photo in the cloud storage. Resentment burgeoned in his chest at Bodie's reliance on his evidence to prove the case to a jury's satisfaction. His tone developed a bite. "Layla has Miss Andrews' phone. Foggy removed it from the teacher's body and took it home. He must have destroyed the SIM card. But I think Keira found the device at his house. She lent it to Layla when the cops confiscated hers after we found the body. I recognised the crack in the screen and the distinctive pink case because I handled it when I blocked Paulette's number and social media profile. Layla told me Tilly got the phone for her, but she didn't. Keira is desperate for friendship, especially with Sammy and Layla. I bet she told Layla she stole it to hype up the drama and asked her to lie if anyone noticed it. Layla has no idea who it belongs to. Tilly procures certain items, and it makes her vulnerable. I imagine she gets blamed for a lot of things she hasn't done."

Mac turned his gaze on his father. "I thought at first that Edin killed Miss Andrews," he admitted. His voice croaked and exhaustion nipped at the frayed edges of his consciousness. He dipped his chin and observed Logan's discomfort. "You told Toby you suspected her. I only started this to prove her innocence."

"Me?" Logan's face screwed into a series of lines underscored by shadow. "I didn't think she killed your teacher." He blinked down at Mac until a flicker of some distant conversation crawled across his inner vision. "Oh, I know what you're talking about," he breathed. "Your painkillers went missing. She'd started acting up again, and it caused me to wonder if she'd stolen them." He shrugged as his lips flattened into thin, parallel lines. "We pulled the pantry apart and found them. They'd slipped down the back of the shelf." Logan rolled his eyes and blinked at Hana before settling his gaze back on his son. "Mate," he sighed, sounding tired. "You can't base your life decisions on half a bloody story. You could end up on the wrong side of the damn world!"

Mac let his head sink into the soft folds of the pillow and closed his eyes. The statement held a note of irony in view of the speaker. Irony and double standards. He drifted to sleep, spent after recounting his tale for the benefit of Bodie's fast, illegible shorthand. His dreams contained Poppa Alfie telling his favourite story of how Logan travelled to the other side of the planet in search of his soulmate, only to find her right here in New Zealand on his return. "Half a bloody story," he murmured, as the oxygen mask slipped from his limp fingers.

86

Counter Attack

Mac endured a painful ride home the next day, missing the comfort of the oxygen mask and the modern conveniences of the hospital. Most of all, he missed the mattress with its electronic settings and remote control. Sitting and laying caused him more agony than his broken wrist and the surgery which had followed.

Logan drove him to the marae to visit Poppa Alfie. The wāhine of the community had spent two full days weaving a harakeke casket, which encased the old man's twisted body like a flax sleeping bag. Mac gazed at the waxen features visible through the neck of the casket. He'd thought until that moment that he might like to kiss Alfie's forehead, but changed his mind. Logan sighed next to him, and his lips quirked up in a sad smile. He turned to face Mac and raised his hands.

"I can hear you." Mac touched the red curl hiding his right processor. He saw his father's blink of surprise.

Logan lowered his voice. "Guess which bit your ma wove," he whispered.

Mac frowned. A gasp left his lips as he shrugged. "Dunno."

"Sorry." Logan's nose wrinkled on one side. "I shouldn't make you laugh."

Mac's gaze raked the casket, assessing the gentle ara of the flax as the strands flowed in a graceful arc around Alfie's rail thin body. Despite himself, he smiled. Hana's weaving efforts caused much hilarity, but never in her hearing. He stiffened as her yellow skirt appeared in his peripheral vision. Floral scents filled his nostrils and soothed his aching heart. "That's my bit," Hana whispered. She didn't ask if he could hear her, using her fingers in quick movements to sign to him. She leaned forward and pointed to a wonky line covering Alfie's right hip. More experienced fingers than hers had attempted to cover the error. "I missed a stitch." Hana's fingers wiggled as she mimicked the motion of weaving. She frowned. "Kuia promised she'd put a decoration over it. We wove it as one complete basket. I almost buggered the whole thing."

Mac groaned and pressed his right hand over his ribs, willing himself not to laugh. He stepped back and almost trod on a distant cousin who kept vigil in a sleeping bag beside Alfie's casket. The man slept with his mouth open, one hand gripping the leg of the gurney to maintain contact. Sadness crashed over the bubbling laughter like a breaking wave. Mac wrestled with emotions which were scrambled and confusing. "I need some air," he muttered. He stepped over the cousin's legs, nodded to the man's wife, and navigated the camping chair she occupied. It seemed a mission to make it to the doorway before releasing the tears aching behind his eyelids.

Fresh air engulfed him as he poked his bare feet into flip-flops outside the meeting house. He closed his eyes and fought for control, struggling beneath the heavy weight of his ancestors, who swirled around his head like a spiritual fog. Edin glanced up at him from the steps. "Uh oh," she commented. "I know that look."

"I need to go to the township." Mac pressed his fingers over the horrific bruising covered by his tee shirt. "Can you take me?"

Edin snorted. "What do you reckon? Pa grounded me for the rest of my life. He already banned my great-grandchildren from driving." She lifted her chin and stared at the scudding clouds. They raced across the blue expanse like cotton balls. A plane above them marked the azure purity with an ozone wake. "Toby still hasn't told them I nicked his truck, too." She sighed. "I paid him off. David Allen set him up on an online dating site, but Toby can't read the girls' bios or messages. He's making me do it for a month." She waggled her eyebrows and mischief turned her irises into a diamond grey. "He never learns, does he?"

Mac nodded. "The guy has faith. Gotta admire his bravery."

Edin sniggered. "He didn't realise swiping right meant he liked them. An eighty-year-old from Christchurch sent him sexy messages."

Mac groaned. "That's older than Nonie," he breathed.

Edin snorted. "Did I say they were female?"

He smiled. "Poor Toby." The silence between them held a familiar strain. His right hand fluttered towards his processor and he stopped himself. He cleared his throat. "When does Deacon arrive?"

As though he'd pressed a detonator, Edin's expression changed. It became a hard, grey mask. "He's not coming." Her tone held the tightness of a guitar string wound too taut.

"Oh?" Mac's brows furrowed. He wanted to ask her why, but she dropped her chin and her neck held a warning stiffness, so he didn't.

Mac took care on the steps. His soles grated against the gravel. He spied a group moving towards the heavy gates and an idea formed in his mind. "See ya later," he called to Edin, before attaching himself to the knot of distant family members. He stood out like a red rooster against their sombre clothing and black hair and skin, but they didn't notice him until they arrived at their vehicle.

"Hey cuz." The driver blinked up at him as his passengers clambered into the transit van.

"Do you have room for one more?" Mac's tone contained hope as the man's gaze took in the plaster cast on his left forearm. He kept the fingers of his right hand pressed over his ribs. The muscles ached as though threatening to explode from beneath his armpit.

The man winced and leaned across the vehicle to speak to his front passenger. "Get in the back, Jez," he told him. "We're taking Logan's tamatāne home."

"No, not home." Mac took a step forward. "Just to town is fine, please."

"All good." The man smiled at him and Mac waited while the passengers switched places in the back of the van. He clambered into the front seat, but struggled to close the passenger door. It required him to lean sideways and use the sill of the open window to edge it shut by degrees. When it didn't catch properly, someone popped out from the sliding side door to do it for him. Embarrassment hung over Mac's head, the familiar flush snaking up his neck and into his cheeks. He managed the seat belt by himself, although every miniscule movement jolted and jarred his aches.

The van careened around the tight bends towards the township and Mac held his breath for most of the journey. He expected to die at any second. Voices babbled behind him and he resisted the desire to disconnect himself by turning off his processors. The driver chatted without reserve, but Mac remembered nothing of the conversation by the time the van arrived in the township. "You want some kai paraurehe?" the cousin offered, pointing to a fast-food restaurant on the main street.

"No, thanks, I'm good," Mac reassured him. "I'm not hungry." The thought of junk food caused his stomach to growl as though to prove him a liar. He waved at the other cheerful faces and turned away, his steps heavy with exhaustion and pain.

The arched doors stood open, anchored to their posts by giant black hinges. Mac took the steps at a slow pace, his mind whirling with facts and figures, images of straight roads and cul-de-sacs. His past had led to this moment and this set of decisions. Only one man could help him sift them.

87

Wall-Pass

"An eventful week then." Pastor Sam nudged the glass of water closer to Mac's fretting fingers. "I'll pray for healing." His lips pursed before issuing their next promise. "And clarity."

Condensation wriggled down the glass like tadpoles. It slid to the table and created a ring on the dark wood. Mac pressed painkillers from their blister pack one handed. They skittered onto the table and one landed in the growing pool. It stuck and began dissolving. He snatched it up and pushed it into his mouth, dousing it with a slug of the icy drink. "Even swallowing hurts," he breathed, waiting for the pain to subside.

"Take small mouthfuls then, you idiot." Sam sounded like his father. He crossed his long legs and Mac spied a pair of expensive shoes peeking from beneath the black shroud covering him from neck to ankles. Grey and covered in pink flowers, the shoes' presence came as a surprise. It made Mac want to grin, as though he'd found a hidden stash of happiness in an unlikely place. Under a priest's cassock.

"I've arrived at a crossroads," he admitted. He downed the second tablet and prayed it worked fast. The bruising super-heated beneath his armpit as though tiny people there stoked a furnace in his blood. His skin prickled as they stamped around in jackboots made from porcupine spines. "I'm fed up with school, but I've met a girl there. I'd like to give us time to develop our relationship, but I'm not convinced it's the best place to do it."

Sam nodded, as always, without judgement or condemnation. He didn't pry, and Mac experienced a flood of gratitude. The pastor's stuffy vestry occupied the more rundown side of the church. It intimidated Mac less than the vaulted ceiling of the nave and the pretentious incense which clung to every surface. He'd needed peace, and he found it with the faded theological tomes and the battered armchairs. His childhood included happy memories of hanging out in Sam's office. The pastor understood him when few other people bothered. "So, question the premise." Sam sipped at a mug of black coffee, his only known vice. "Why did you go back to school for Year 13 if it's not what you wanted?"

Mac blew out a breath and then regretted it. He clamped his elbow to his side, realising it made more sense than twisting his torso to use his right hand. "Pa wanted me to finish school," he hissed, praying Sam would hurry on his promise of prayer for healing. "And I wanted to please him."

"And now you need to please this girl by staying at school?" Sam shrugged. "What does MacGillivray Du Rose want?"

Mac sat up straighter and blinked at the cleric. He considered the question. Nine more months of school would culminate in a series of gruelling exams. He told himself he liked exams, even pointless ones. "I started wearing my processors more," he said, taking the conversation in a different direction. It appeared as a tangent to the priest, but Mac saw the flare of a connection in his mind's eye. "I did it at first because I noticed other people's disappointment. But I've missed key things, events and conversations I needed to hear." His mind drifted to his futile attempts at reviving Alfie. The old man had dreaded an earthly resurrection enough to force Logan to inform the family not to bother.

Mac's shoulders slumped. The action caused more pain. "It's confusing," he concluded. "I want to please them and make them proud of me, but they say they already are." He stared at a picture of the crucified Christ clinging to an apex wall. It hung at an angle, evidence of the hundreds of harmless earthquakes which rippled across New Zealand daily. Mac gave a definitive nod. "That's an okay goal, isn't it? I want to please the people I love. Is that daft?"

Sam smiled. "Only if it doesn't conflict with what you know in your heart. It's still okay to tread your own path, Macky. You're almost a man. You have autonomy. Logan wouldn't deny you that." He pushed his spectacles further up his nose. "I think it would destroy your father to discover you did something you hated just to satisfy him."

Mac nodded and realised he'd always known that. He narrowed his eyes and faltered before the next of Sam's pointed questions. "Why do you think he asked you to stay in school until the bitter end?"

Mac stared at the tortured Jesus for inspiration. It came easier than he expected. "To give me options," he reasoned. "Pa made a mistake with Tama and Wiremu. He wanted them both to help him with the farm and the bloodstock business. Tama bombed out of agricultural college and Wiri lied to him." His sigh caused him pain. "I've always said I want to stay on the mountain. Perhaps he doesn't believe me."

Sam shook his head. He leaned across and rested a gentle arm on Mac's shoulder. "He doesn't dare to believe you, Macky," he whispered. "For him, it's too good to be true. The disappointment might prove overwhelming if he lets you throw yourself into it and then you decide it's not for you. Where does that leave him, then?" He spread his hands before him, palms facing the ceiling. But he'd opened his fingers and Mac silently wondered if Sam knew he'd signed that he needed something.

He snuffed through his nose, discovering it allowed him more control over his breathing. "It's all I've ever wanted," he replied. "Pa should know that." And then he thought of all the lies he'd told in the previous week and wondered why his father should ever trust his word again. He'd shown a teacher unwelcome affection, lost his virginity in a cupboard, hurt two men and put two more in hospital, and ridden shotgun in two stolen vehicles. "What a mess," he whispered.

Sam smiled at him through eyes narrowed in a sage expression. "Let me pray for you," he offered. He rested his hand on Mac's shoulder again and closed his eyes. The teenager squinted sideways at him, desperate for the peace which settled over the pastor's handsome features. He stared down at his right hand, flexing the fingers and turning his palm to face the fly spotted ceiling of the tired vestry. As Sam's gentle prayers washed over him, Mac relaxed his hand and spread his fingers, signing to heaven that he also needed something.

88

RED CARD

"You'll never believe this." Bodie sounded excited, but the processor distorted his words into lost tones and crackles. Mac glanced around him in the quiet street, the phone pressed against his right ear. He sank onto the church steps with a grunt and touched the screen to activate the phone's speaker. He appreciated having his own device back in his possession, but wished he'd thought to carry the amplifier with him. Another glance around him took in the closed front doors to the nave. Sam had gone home for lunch after ensuring Mac had a ride back to the mountain. He'd lied again, keen to enjoy the peace and to visit his ancestors in the graveyard before he called his father. The marae would fill with more family from the north until it resembled an ant fortress. It challenged Mac's need for silence and personal space.

"Say again," he said to Bodie. "I didn't catch that."

"We got a warrant and raided the groundsman's house," he began. "We found nothing."

"Oh." Mac closed his eyes against the glare of the sunshine. It licked the delicate skin across his nose and cheeks where it planned to dot more freckles. He'd hoped for a conclusion to Marie Andrews' murder. The groundsman's fingerprints covered the equipment shed, but then he worked there. Mac's theory centred around Marie dying in the dusty shack, but apart from the blood which had dried in her hair, the police examiners found nothing to support that premise.

Bodie's tone grew serious. "Mac, he's saying you attacked him. He lashed out with the hammer in self-defence and then suffered a heart attack from the stress. If we find no evidence to support your theory, you'll face prosecution."

Mac closed his eyes and arched his neck until his chin touched his chest. "What about Layla, Sammy and Keira?" he asked. "I saw Layla with Miss Andrews' phone."

"They're denying it, mate." Bodie cleared his throat. "I tried to call you a couple of times to warn you."

"Sorry." Mac sighed. "I only picked up my phone from the watch house an hour ago. Then I went to church."

"Right." If Bodie felt surprised, he hid it well. "Look, you're my brother and I'll do my best to protect you, Mac. In the meantime, we'll keep searching for evidence."

The call ended, and Mac stared at the blank screen resting on his knee. He lacked the effort required to clamber to his feet and walk the few hundred metres to the urupā beside the catholic church. But the sun continued to beat down on his auburn head and Mac wondered again what happened to Alfie's hat. He lifted his phone and texted Tilly. *'Got my phone again. Do you think Poppa's hat is in the social worker's car? Can't find it.'*

She replied within seconds. *'Yey! Welcome back, dude! And no, I checked we hadn't left anything before I parked it in the garage. He collected his car this morning. Gutted for you.'*

Mac rubbed his right hand across his eyes. "Sorry, Poppa," he murmured. Failure struck at his heart and added to his pain. Eliza and Michael Du Rose had arrived already. The judge and the doctor wouldn't deign to sleep at the marae. Logan's half siblings had demanded rooms at the hotel, forcing the manager to move conference guests around to suit them. Mac suspected they were the vultures Alfie referred to. He touched his chest and remembered Sam's prayers. Perhaps the hat should remain lost until after Michael departed again.

He dragged himself through the gates of the graveyard, wandering the gravel paths towards the familiar graves. Reuben's headstone offered something to lean against, and Mac eased himself down until his bottom touched the warm earth. Sadness shrouded him, held at bay only by the fragile prayers of the faithful Sam. Mac closed his eyes and leaned his crown back against the stone reminder of his grandfather's existence.

A sound woke him much later, relayed as a clatter through his processors. Mac jumped and gripped his side, pursing his lips to control the ragged breaths which rattled against his ribs. A yellow digger glinted in the sunshine, the serrated edge of its bucket scoring the grass and curving it into rolls. Mac watched it from between Reuben and Miriam's headstones as two men worked to dig a fresh grave. Alfie's. He turned away from the sight, a fresh wave of grief crashing over his head. An ache in the pit of his stomach urged him to find and hug his mother while he still had time. Mac pulled his phone free and dialled her number, his fingers shaking as he made the call.

She answered on the first ring. "Hey, baby." Her bright voice filled his processors and comfort soothed the gnawing in his guts. "Uncle Hone said he gave you a ride to town. Are you okay?"

"Yeah," he managed, though he lost the last syllable in his sadness. "Please, can you fetch me?"

"Sure." Cutlery clanked in the background like kettle drums. "Are you anywhere near the fish and chip shop on Main Street? Kelly promised to dice ten kilogrammes of carrots for me in her potato chipper." She gave a cheerful giggle. "I hope nobody finds out I cheated. They think I'm doing them at home."

Mac smiled at his mother's exploitation of loopholes. She'd only survived on the stronghold of Du Rose mountain through wit and shortcuts. He realised he admired her. Very much. "Sam prayed for me," he said, knowing it would please her.

"Oh, good lad," she breathed. "I'll see you soon."

Mac used Reuben's headstone to steady himself as he clambered to his feet. Every movement caused the breathing muscles around his damaged ribs to panic and tighten. Both gravediggers jumped in fright as he appeared from behind the stone. The driver jerked on his domed handle and sent the soil cascading back into Alfie's last resting place. The other man recognised Mac and gave him a curt nod. They watched him walk across the grass towards the path, tiny, measured steps lessening the impact on his chest. "Carrots, carrots, carrots," he murmured to himself, as though losing his mind. Because Hana's errand had reminded him of something important.

Mac dug his phone from his jeans pocket and dialled Bodie's number. "Carrots!" he shouted into the phone as the policeman answered.

89

Injury Time

Though the police officers had raided Foggy's city apartment, they'd found no trace of Marie Andrews' blood or her missing belongings. But a search of the council's records revealed an allotment in the name of Daniel Kohu-Parker. Bodie's warrant permitted him to search it. Beside a locked tin shed, the forensics team disturbed an incinerator made from an old oil drum. The fragments of a melted rubber mat smouldered at the bottom. Laboratory tests revealed traces of Marie Andrews' blood on the tiny, tell-tale strips.

And just like that, the pending charges against Mac disappeared like the morning mist which hung over Alfie's tangihanga. A sobbing Keira admitted to Bodie how she'd visited the allotment to dig up more carrots for the soccer girls. She found the phone in her grandfather's shed and borrowed it to impress Layla with her friendship and devotion. She'd intended to replace it once the police finished with the girls' phones. Accompanying Bodie to the newest crime scene and after digging around behind forks, spades and a rusty toolbox, she revealed the missing keys, the SIM card, and Marie Andrews' handbag and wallet.

"I'm glad it's over," Hana commented after hearing Bodie's recount. She shook her head. "That poor woman." A glass of orange juice tilted in her hand as Mac bent to kiss the top of her head. "Don't take long," she advised, glancing up at him. Her gaze slid to Logan and then to his scruffy jeans. "You both need to change before we go to the marae. Leslie wants everyone suited and booted to see off Alfie."

A vein twitched in Logan's cheek, and he didn't acknowledge her warning. Mac waved to Jas and Hope as they ate bacon and eggs at the kitchen table. Phoenix and Wiremu had slept at the marae again, but the concept of communal living unnerved Bodie and Amy. Mac's processors fizzed with the busyness of the house and the ring of laughter. He followed his father to the front door, waiting as Logan pushed his feet into his cowboy boots. Mac copied him, but the ache in his ribs prevented him from bending to fasten the zippers.

"Do you mind?" he asked as Logan fired up the truck. He hauled his seat belt around him and clipped it into the socket one-handed.

"Mind what?" Gravel spat from behind the heavy tyres as the truck moved forward.

"Mind that I invited Bodie, Amy and the kids?"

Logan snuffed. "You can't call them kids, mate. Jas is older than you."

Mac wrinkled his nose. "Jas is a jerk. He behaves like a child."

Logan's eyebrows waggled and his lips pursed. Mac sensed him biting back a comment about the boy's jerk-laden origins. He opted not to poke the bear. "Sorry, anyway," he murmured.

"No worries." Logan's lips twisted, his body language conveying the opposite message.

"Have you seen Aunty Liza and Uncle Michael?" The urge to chat surprised Mac. The silence of his deafness seemed different from the burdened air of the vehicle.

"No." Logan sniffed, a warning tell. Mac ignored it, a need bubbling from his chest cavity.

"Pa," he began. "I've lost Poppa's hat." He choked on the confession and a bank of tears tightened his chest. Darts stabbed through his ribs to constrict his breathing.

Logan stamped on the brakes, and the truck slewed to a halt. He shoved the gear lever in Park and jammed on the handbrake. The truck pointed downwards at a dangerous angle on the steep slope, the belt tightening around Mac's body as though fearful he might disappear through the windscreen.

He glanced sideways as the driver's door slammed shut. His right hand shook as he covered his eyes and cussed at himself, bad words which turned the air blue. Sam had urged him towards speaking his truth, and this happened when he tried it for size. He'd broken his father's heart. A click as the lid to the flat bed released and then another as it closed. His father's unpredictable temper meant he'd fetched anything from a tissue to a shotgun. Mac clamped his eyelids shut and breathed against the grip of the seat belt.

Logan grunted as he climbed into the cab and closed the door behind him. Then nothing. Mac's fingers fluttered over the fabric belt, desperate to deactivate his processors and escape into his own thoughts. "I'm sorry, I'm sorry, I'm sorry," he breathed into the silent vehicle.

Logan cleared his throat, forcing Mac to look at him. He held out both hands, palms upwards, and in them sat Alfie's hat. But it looked so different. The leather shone, no longer a faded tan but a gleaming brown. A shining knot of twisted threads wound around the brim in a leathery embrace. Logan's words emerged in the stuttering pattern of shotgun pellets, betraying embarrassment and a heavy, hidden emotion Mac couldn't name. "Hemi in the township made it nice for you." He turned it over, his scarred hands trembling. "I asked him to make it so you could wear your processors. So he took it apart and added these pockets in both sides." Logan flipped it over again, holding the brim between thumb and finger with reverence. "I gave him some tanned leather from our herd. He's hidden the alterations under this braided part." Logan held the hat out towards his son, an offering and a gesture of peace and acceptance. "Your ma isn't pleased with me. She thinks I should have asked you first because I've destroyed its provenance."

Mac's voice held a strained gruffness as he thanked his father for his generosity. The bespoke leather work turned the hat from a faded heirloom into a practical, treasured thing. Henri Du Rose's scrawled name still nestled beneath the crown. Mac no longer had to choose between wearing the hat or hearing the world's noise. Logan had removed his last excuse.

Mac placed the hat on his head. It fitted with more snugness than before. A new thong dangled beneath his chin to stop the hat from ever flying off his head during a madcap downhill gallop. And Hemi's beautiful stitching meant his processors tucked into their pockets with ease. Better still, he doubted Michael or Liza would recognise it as belonging to their father's estate.

"It's marvellous," Mac breathed. His face lit up, his green eyes like sparklers in his pale face. "I love it."

"Righto," his father replied, returning to his usual blank state. But Mac saw his lips curve upwards in an uncharacteristic smile and recognised the moment he considered Hemi's exorbitant invoice for work few men in the twenty-first century could still perform.

Down in the paddock adjoining the stable yard, Sassy greeted Mac like a long-lost friend. She tossed her scrubby mane and flicked her tail, waving it upright like a flag on its wiry spindle. Toby leaned on the fence, his amusement hidden in the shadows of his hat brim. "Got a tail like a dog," he commented. Three-day-old stubble turned his angular chin to a craggy ridge. "She's missed you then."

Logan rested the sole of his cowboy boot on the bottom rung and said nothing. Sassy performed another lap of the paddock, her head tossing from side to side and a high whinny rising from her powerful chest muscles. Dust and precious clods of new grass peppered the air behind her. Pleasure infused Mac's throat at a compliment he would have missed with his processors in his pocket or flung onto his bedroom floor. Sassy snorted as she slewed to a messy halt in the grass before him. She splayed her front legs like a dog waiting for a thrown ball. Then she turned tail and gave a hefty buck as though giving Mac a two-fingered salute. The men laughed and even Logan smiled. He turned to his son, disregarding the broken ribs and the bulky plaster cast protecting his wrist. "Go on then," he said, and jerked his chin towards the paddock.

Mac shrugged. Knowing his mother would pitch a fit when she found out, he clambered over the fence with a grunt of pain. He stepped towards the crazy white mare with the mismatched eyes and the feisty personality. And he sensed his father's pride reaching out to him across the baked earth, thinking of another time and another crazy white mare with mismatched eyes and a feisty personality.

90

Foot Trap

"You're so lucky." Tilly gazed around the marae in wonder, her eyes raking every detail. The family had descended from far and wide, occupying every centimetre of the grassy space to pay their respects to Alfred Du Rose. A social worker sauntered from group to group, seeking a responsible adult so he could hand over temporary care for Tilly. He'd stayed for the pōwhiri, the funeral procession, the haka, and the long speeches in fluent Te Reo Māori. Mac had recognised the car they arrived in, pursing his lips with guilt at the mysterious parking ticket winging its way through the postal service. But the man had eaten his body weight in free kai, and grease still shone on his moustache from the delicious meat cooked in the hāngī. Mac called it fair, though knew it wouldn't seem like it.

"I'm lucky?" Mac frowned, confused by Tilly's assumption he liked the hustle and bustle of loud conversation and frenetic activity.

"Yeah," she breathed. She gnawed her lower lip, her blue irises sparkling in the sunlight. She grinned with delight as a group of children surged past her like a tidal wave. A toddler brought up the rear on tottering feet and an older boy stooped to collect the flailing human into his arms. "Don't you love it?" She turned to face him and her expression dropped as though swiped from her face by an invisible hand. "Sorry." She licked her lips. "You don't like crowds and fuss."

"But you do." His tone held sadness. He balanced his cast over his left hip and faced her, steeling himself to ask the pivotal question and really listen to and absorb the answer. "What do you want, Tilly? From life, I mean." He swallowed, the sound returning to him as a series of awkward crackles as he awaited the catharsis of a painful rejection. His mind told him she couldn't want anything from him long term.

She inhaled, her black blouse rising and falling with her long breath. Her heavy mask of vibrant makeup failed to conceal the latent craving in her eyes. "I want acceptance," she declared. "Family and chaos. I want to rule a tiny group who thinks I'm amazing. But above all, I need safety and a place of my own." Her brow furrowed in an angry line. "Gray conned the ten dollars from me. He knew the camera didn't exist." Her jaw tightened as she disconnected all emotional loyalty from her brother. He'd intended to meet her at the shed and extort yet more cash from her. Until he'd seen the rage on Mac's face as he sped past the groundsman. He'd misinterpreted it as intended for him and slunk away to his waiting social worker's car.

Mac forced himself not to dredge up Tilly's aloneness by glancing away and allowing her a moment's grace. He gave a slow nod and paused until a wry smile crossed her lips. "You're a matriarch in waiting," he concluded, the statement surprising even him as it left his tongue. "You want what my mother has?"

Tilly cocked her head and frowned at him. A light flickered on behind her irises and a smile spread her lips wide. "Yeah," she whispered. "I guess I do." She smashed the moment with a shrug, perhaps afraid of its depth. "So, I just need a family with a vacancy."

Everything in Mac recoiled. He wrapped his arm around her and squeezed, closing his eyes to avoid the knowing smiles of passing aunties. He rested his cheek against the top of her head and waited for the crash of emotion to incapacitate him. A cousin wearing a long black dress chased after the surging children as they navigated the meeting house where Alfred Du Rose had laid in his harakeke casket. But he wasn't there any longer. The gravediggers worked a few kilometres away to seal him into the hole they'd dug just a day earlier.

Mac sensed the air change as the woman passed. The children circled the building, the decibels increasing as they became infected by the thrill of the chase. Tilly wanted everything Mac hated most in the world. Noise, chaos, and disorder.

A hand clamped around his elbow and caused him to jerk. Tilly got crushed against his chest as he reacted with surprise and then aggression. She extracted herself and smoothed her curls into order before smiling at Edin. "Hi," she said. "Your family is amazing, isn't it?"

Mac glared at his cousin, for both shocking and embarrassing him. His anger bounced off Edin like a rubber ball. "Ma needs you to help her shift chairs in the whare kai," she announced. Her wide grin told him she enjoyed his discomfort. She jerked her head towards the dining hall where everyone had eaten their fill and restored noa or normalcy after the stress of Alfie's departure to the graveyard.

"I'll help," Tilly offered. "I'd rather be useful."

Edin slipped her arm through Tilly's and tugged her close. She shot a covetous glance over her shoulder at Mac. "No. We're needed in the kitchen," she said. "It's just washing the plates, but the aunties tell stories and sing songs. You'll love it." She steered Tilly away without giving her a chance to farewell Mac. They left him standing on the grass alone like a maypole as the community whirled around him in a well-worn dance.

A light touch on his shoulder caused him to turn. It brought him face to face with Nonie Leslie. Her puffy eyes and downturned lips caused his chest to tighten. She wore her grief like a veil over her face, ethereal and delicate with her fragility glimpsed with every flutter of her eyelashes. "You okay boy?" she asked him. Her voice wobbled.

Mac wrapped his arms around her, his cast bumping her shoulder. He squeezed as though to excise the unhealable pain. "Poppa loved you, Nonie," he whispered, tilting his face to rest his cheek on her fluffy head.

"Yes," she replied.

A crowd of nannies and aunties had accompanied her like a rear-guard, holding her hands and walking her through the trauma of Alfie's tangihanga. They took a propitious step back to offer privacy, but remained close enough to catch Nonie in their loving embrace if she needed it. Leslie rested her cheek against Mac's broad chest and linked her fingers in the small of his back. His ribs protested but he suffered the stabbing darts of pain, afraid of the offence which releasing her might cause.

Leslie Du Rose tilted her chin to peer up at Mac. Condensation from her tears created a mist on the inside of lenses, which sat in heavy black frames. "You're a good boy, Mac Du Rose," she said, her voice sounding feeble but determined. "Alfie loved you best."

Mac nodded. Edin had said as much. He wished he'd known that fact while Poppa still lived and breathed. He wished he'd hugged him more while he had the chance. His grip tightened around the old woman, his cast bulky and restrictive as he tried to fill her with his love. She swallowed as words bubbled up from her throat and spewed from reluctant lips. She didn't want to say them, choking them out as a warning as though divinely possessed. "Be careful," she whispered. "There's a storm coming."

The nannies and the aunties bore her away on a sea of black fabric and gentle hands while Mac stared after her, his mouth open. A kaumatua waited for them near the edge of the marae, his body gnarled and bent like an ancient tree. They moved towards the car park, bound for the loft apartment over the hotel. They would stamp and sing through the rooms, cleaning, and throwing open the windows to chase out the spirits of sickness, sadness and death. Ready for Leslie's new life of solitude and emptiness.

Mac's shocked mind returned to Tilly's answer, and it lodged in his chest. She wanted the very things he possessed, but didn't need. Family, noise and chaos. He ached for the loneliness of the mountain. Of riding out by himself to count steers or move fences. She wanted laughter and busyness. They were opposites. He'd known before she said it.

Yet the expected pain dulled as fast as it began. Because he realised with a jolt of excitement how their paths converged in the centre of a mental Venn diagram to create an intersection of possibility. He'd seen only two separate circles until now. But it didn't represent the complete picture.

As he watched Edin lead Tilly away from him towards the kitchen, he sensed his heart lurch. They'd stopped to herd more baby cousins into the care of a responsible adult. Tilly threw her head back and laughed at the tidal wave of tiny, marauding humans. Instead of scraping her black curls into severe pigtails, she had left them to roam across her shoulders. A silver clip held most of her fringe away from her eyes and exposed her high cheekbones and pretty features to scrutiny. Mac recognised the courage it took for her to attend the gathering and to reveal so much of herself. Vulnerability gave her a softer appearance, despite the muted harshness of her black blouse, skirt, and the heavy boots which formed her silent armour.

So, Mac redrew the Venn diagram in his mind's eye and allowed their unique attributes and desires to converge and fill the leaf shaped segment in the middle. She'd told him she wished to be at the centre of someone's world and for them to find her useful. They both wanted acceptance and peace in their respective dream lives. Perhaps they weren't so different after all.

Toby's truck pulled into the car park and Mac turned his feet towards it. By the time the stock man had killed the engine and opened his driver's door, he found Mac standing before him. "I need a ride," the teenager gushed.

Toby's brow drew into a line and he cocked his head, a denial already on his lips. "I just took one group to the bus station at Papakura!" he grumbled. "I want some kai!"

But urgency filled Mac's chest with courage. "Please," he added, infusing his tone with authority. "Now."

91

FORWARD PASS

"Would you do me the honour of becoming my wife?" He stammered over the sentence, despite rehearsing it on the roof while Toby fidgeted in his truck. Glancing at the ring held out at arm's length, Mac noticed compost beneath his fingernails where he'd scrabbled in the blue pot. The ring had survived the fire which killed Miriam, a jeweller later restoring the gleam to its platinum surface. One of two family heirlooms, one for each daughter. Antoinette's had become lost in time, but Miriam's survived. Mac had imagined Alfie sliding a jeweller's box beneath the surface of the soil and patting it flat with his arthritic hands. But the old man hadn't made it easy for his heir. No box protected his most prized possession. A pile of muck now graced the centre of the roof garden, where Mac upended the pot onto the paving slabs one-handed. It cracked into two halves like an egg, and he'd sifted through the dirt in a panic. Guitar music and singing drifted up to cover him in his ancestors' approval and the plan had felt right. He'd sneaked back down the stairs and through the secret door while the mourners stamped and sang through the bedrooms of the apartment.

Loamy streaks covered his best shirt and trousers. He gulped and ignored the hundreds of pairs of eyes turned towards him as he knelt on the floor of the dining room.

"Sorry?" Tilly's cheeks flushed scarlet through her heavy foundation and she stared at Mac as though he'd lost his mind. She glanced at his outstretched hand and her brows met in a single black line.

"Marry me," Mac said. He forced authority into his voice, ignoring the hushed narrative inside his head which urged him to whisper it. "I love you," he concluded, his words echoing off the apex ceiling and repeating themselves. "I've always loved you." He couldn't look at Edin, though he felt her horrified gaze boring into the side of his face. Logan took a step forward in his peripheral vision, but Hana's hand on his forearm halted his protest. They'd wasted twenty-six of their own years. She wanted her son to make his own adult choices.

Tilly's lips parted, but a chime from Mac's right processor obliterated her reply. Panic caused sweat to bead on his brow and he growled low in his throat. "My battery's going," he whispered. Agony burned in his chest. He'd spent a lifetime disregarding his processors. Their spectacular revenge added the ultimate irony. Of course, they'd fail him right then. He'd never needed them more as he knelt on the floorboards of the dining hall in full view of his entire family. His right knee punished him as he pushed his weight into the joint. A tingle began in his calf as it headed for numbness. Mac pictured himself tipping over sideways with the ring still held aloft. The laughter would follow him to his grave and his stupidity become the stuff of legends.

Soles ground against the floor and Michael Du Rose appeared next to them, his face turning a sick shade of violet. Mac held his breath. If Tilly didn't accept the ring, he'd lose it, anyway. Alfred's eldest son would take it, along with the Jackaroo hat.

Just as his poppa predicted. The vultures. Or one whatura in particular.

"I love you too." Tilly's fingers clasped his, and the ring poked above their joined hands as though floating. She leaned down and pressed her lips over Mac's. "I'd love to marry you," she said. He waited for the but, surprised when it didn't come. Tilly held out her left hand and waited for him to push the ring onto her fourth finger.

"No!" Michael shouldered Tilly aside, his voice already raised in contention. "No way! I want what's mine! All of it. I'm owed thousands." He grabbed for her wrist, his bony fingers closing around her delicate joint. Despite the precariousness of his kneeling position, Mac tensed. He pushed his full weight and energy into the foot still flat on the ground and launched himself skyward. He arrived between them, a wall of muscle and fury cutting out Tilly's view of Michael. His right shoulder caught the man in the chest like a rugby tackle, catapulting him backwards until he clattered with a dining table and bench.

"No!" Mac snarled. Michael returned for more, popping up like a boxer and wading in against a teenager with a broken wrist, two smashed ribs, and a useless pinkie finger. So Mac drew back his dangerous right arm and aimed it at the fifth man in a week.

Wow!" chuckled an old kaumatua, leaning crablike over his walking stick. Michael cleared the table backwards without touching it, landing with a heavy thud at a surprised Wiremu's feet. "I knew Reuben wouldn't stay dead for long," the old man cackled. "Well, who guessed he'd pick the red boy?"

92

REFEREE'S FLAG

Liza Du Rose's sense of humour didn't stand out as her primary virtue. In fact, it's something she kept well hidden. But as Michael hit the floorboards, she lifted her chin and roared with laughter. Mac's processors relayed the sound as a cackle, filled with the famed wickedness of legend. "You are joking?" she snorted. She pressed her fingers against her thumb to create a beak and waved it as she lectured her brother. "You seriously believe our father owned anything more than the clothes on his back? He gave the ring and the hat to the boy. Just leave it."

Michael's head wobbled on his neck as he pushed himself to his feet. The scene had attracted the attention of everyone in their immediate circle. People flooded from outside to watch a legend unfold. They'd speak about it for generations.

Mac experienced a flicker of gratitude as Tilly's arm slipped around his waist. The sun lit him through the wide window. It bounced off his smart shirt and super-heated his armpits and spine. The dispute offended the sense of propriety his mother brought to the family. She hated what she called *'doing their dirty washing in public.'*

"I want what's owed," Michael growled. The blonde, elfin girlfriend accompanying him moved away on stiletto heels, as though seeing his true nature for the first time in their brief relationship. He jabbed a finger at the Jackaroo in Mac's hand. "I want my pa's hat and my mother's ring. And I deserve a half share of his hotel. It belongs to me." He clenched his jaw and then, remembering his sister's legal status, included her in his claim. "And Liza. We're his rightful heirs. It's only fair. He owned the farm and everything. We want it."

Mac risked a glance at his father's expression, dreading what he might find. Only amusement lifted the corners of Logan's lips into a sardonic smile. Michael Du Rose wouldn't know fairness if it bit him on the ass. His demand had bypassed Leslie's claim as though she didn't exist. Perhaps to him, she didn't. Mac cringed in his skin, wishing he didn't need to hear Michael put straight about what Alfred did or didn't own. It amounted to a big fat zero, and he prayed his father didn't say it in public. He clamped the hat over his ears, the processors snug inside the cushion created by the saddler's skilled fingers. The brim threw his expression into shadow and the new string dangled beneath his chin like a hammock.

But it wasn't Logan who put Michael straight. Liza did it for him with her usual brand of spiked realism. "Our father didn't even own his own shit, Mike!" she snapped. "And you know it. He lived on Logan's charity for over three decades, you idiot!" She took a step towards her brother, no sympathy in her expression. Mac felt glad he'd never face her across a courtroom, not just because he'd work to avoid legal woes, but because she'd recuse herself from family cases. "Crawl back into your hole, brother," she hissed. "Stop embarrassing yourself."

"The hat." Michael set his gaze on Mac. "It's mine. The ring belongs to my sister."

Mac opened his mouth to speak, but then something else happened. Hana appeared in front of him, her spine ramrod straight and her auburn curls tapping the waistband of her black dress. Tilly released her grip on Mac's waist and joined her, their fingers touching as they stood guard. The diamond from Miriam's ring glittered in the sunlight. Logan's cowboy boots grated on the floorboards as he stepped forward, obscuring Mac's vision of Michael Du Rose. Hana spoke first. "Go away," she growled.

Logan lifted his right hand and pointed towards the car park beyond the window. "Bye Mike," he said, his tone flat. "We need never meet again now Alfie's gone. I'd like to say it's been nice knowing you, but I'm not a convincing enough liar."

Liza shook her head and turned away from the scene as though it bored her to witness it. She stepped aside to engage in conversation with an auntie from the north, her smile bright and her manner unconcerned. Michael glared at the back of her head for support and his shoulders slumped as he received no expected solidarity. Defeated, he turned on the spot, the movement slow and calculated. "You don't rule here, Logan!" he called over his shoulder. But he'd missed his opportunity to retreat with dignity. "I'm coming back for my pa's stuff!"

"Na, bro. Not happening." Tama's voice issued as a low growl. Michael walked straight into the broad expanse of chest encased in a fire officer's uniform. Tama reached out to grab his shoulders and right him as he listed sideways. The action held the dispassionate courtesy of a stranger. He waited until Michael collected himself before adding, "Bye Daddy. Drive carefully now." Sarcasm laced his tone.

With a dramatic huff, Michael steered around the son he'd denied, and beckoned to the blonde woman standing near the periphery of the gathered mourners. She clip-clopped towards him on unsuitable stilettos.

Edin arrived at Mac's left shoulder. She didn't look at him, her proximity communicating solidarity enough. He'd thrust Tilly between them now like a buffer zone. She would keep them all safe.

Mac's teeth ground in his jaw. Michael's retreat marked the first victory. The platinum ring sparkled on Tilly's left hand, a MacGuffin or a Holy Grail radiating peace. For the time being, anyway.

Edin sighed, her lower lip turning down as she raked Mac from head to toe. "Well played, Mac," she whispered, her tone calm. "You surprised us all." She gave a slow blink. And then, as the air crackled between them, she fixed a mock familial smile onto her lips. Her face changed, the features sharpening. She became a carbon copy of the woman in the high heels who'd spooked Sassy a lifetime ago. Caroline Du Rose, with her insatiable desires and her spirit of destruction. She'd caused his broken wrist and walked away without a flicker of guilt. "I hope you know what you're doing," Caroline's daughter said. "You know we're not done."

Mac watched as she strode away, a glass of orange juice clasped in her delicate fingers. The temper fizzled in his chest as though doused with icy water. He needed to redraw his image of himself, and he knew it. But he feared letting go of the old Mac while embracing the new. He'd used his deafness as a shield of oblivion. A lifelong struggle stretched ahead of him, just as it had for Jacob D'Arcy Du Rose. And for Reuben. He forced his shoulders to straighten, and the held breath to expel from his lungs as a painful whoosh. They'd both failed. Mac refused to accept anything less than a black knight's courage to become his legacy. This battle he wouldn't lose.

He watched his mother's red hair reflect the sunlight through the open ranch slider and cast his mind back to her stories of her brave mother. Judith MacGillivray, his namesake. She hadn't enjoyed the crackled sound brought to her by implants or the momentary relief of comprehension. Like Jacob, her life comprised silence and lipreading. But where he'd become a recluse, Judith was known and revered. She'd worked as a librarian and served as a vicar's wife. Everyone loved her.

Mac closed his eyes and channelled his image of Judith, finally rejecting his likeness to Jacob. He held his own future in his hands and, for now, he seized it and held on tight.

93

FINAL WHISTLE

Some of the visiting family stayed overnight at the campground. They filtered away from the marae as the emerging mosquitos attacked exposed skin. People from the township drove home or to the local tavern, to continue remembering an old man who'd fallen from grace long before most of them were born. Only the northern whānau remained, eager to catch up on family news. Mac searched for his father amid the departing crowds, a new humility settling on his broad shoulders. He discovered him in the car park.

Logan touched a gentle finger to the line of gouged paint on the wing of his truck. A dent in the passenger door showed where Alfie had bounced off once and then gone back for an accidental second go as he steered the quad bike on its haphazard trajectory.

Mac touched a finger to his right processor, where it nestled beneath the hat, and then dropped his hand. "Poppa didn't mean to do it." He gnawed on the inside of his cheek.

"Liar." Logan squatted in the gravel to inspect the damage, his mouth twisting on one side. Mac held his breath at the sight of the bruising which had bled into the skin between his lower lip and chin. He watched his father's fingernail scrape against the flaked paint and then rise with a sigh. "Bet the old bugger enjoyed it," he mused. His brow lined in a frown. He exhaled and turned to Mac with an unexpected smile. "Think I'll leave it. I guess it's the last message he'll ever give me."

Mac swallowed. His fingers twitched against his cast. "It isn't Pa." He sniffed and waited for Logan's full attention. His father turned towards him as though squaring off for a fight.

"I don't wanna hear it," he growled. "He had forty years to tell me the truth and almost twenty to make up for it. He did neither."

"I know." Mac raised his right hand, palm outwards as a sign of peace between them. Then he pressed it over his heart. "I wish he'd never involved me, Pa. It wasn't my business." He inhaled and blew out a ragged breath. "But he wanted to make sure I told you he loved you like his own boy. And he said to tell you he was sorry. For everything."

Logan swore and covered his eyes with his right hand. His clenched fingers massaged the tension from his temples. He made a clicking sound with his tongue as he fought for control. Mac held his breath, no longer afraid of his father's disappointment but of the swirling grief energy circling Logan's head. Anger lit a flame in his breast. Alfie should have passed on his own message while he lived and breathed, not second-hand through a kid who had his hat, but not his DNA.

Mac took a decisive step towards his struggling father and wrapped his right arm around Logan's neck. He pulled him tight against his body. "I love you, Pa," he whispered into his ear. He tilted his head and pressed a kiss to his father's weathered cheek, surprised he needed to lower his chin to do it. "I'll learn from it," he whispered, before releasing him. "We won't make their mistakes, will we?"

Mac turned away and began walking back to the meeting house, where Tilly waited for him. She stood with one leg crossed over the other, awkward in the unfamiliar surroundings. Her left foot pointed towards him as though summoning like a ballerina. He smiled as his mother appeared, linking her arm through Tilly's elbow and collecting her up into her swirl of activity. She led her towards a knot of family members from the north and he watched as she introduced them. Tilly nodded and smiled, her teeth white against plum lipstick. Nobody eyed her with disdain or condemned the rebellious streak betrayed by her outfit. An elderly matriarch of that family pulled her close, pressing noses in a hongi of acceptance. The rest followed in a willing cascade of foreheads and noses. Acceptance by decree.

A wave of gratitude caused Mac to falter, his heart filling in his chest. His lungs inflated, making his aching ribs tighten to the point of pain. He glanced back at Logan to see if he'd noticed, expecting to meet his wise grey eyes flashing in the fading light.

But the ready smile slipped from Mac's lips as he watched his stricken father pull up the hem of his shirt and dry his eyes. Love caused heat to prickle Mac's skin as he witnessed the only show of weakness he'd ever observed in the King of the Maunga. And he recognised in that moment that he needed to stop trying to please anyone else.

The mountain needed MacGillivray. Just as himself.

As he walked back towards Tilly, a breeze slipped through the leaves of the upper canopy. It formed an unseen portend as the mountain settled and readied itself for the future. Cool air blew up from Antarctica, promising an early blast of winter to scuttle the mild autumn. The ghosts of two brothers drifted on the updraught, united and free, but not without enmity even in death. They tousled the dark curls of Edin Du Rose and witnessed the better path chosen by the new King of the Mountain and his Du Rose matriarch in-waiting. Old battle lines rose to meet them as the jealous, grey-eyed girl glowered at the ring on Tilly's finger. Black poison seeped into the intersection of their Venn Diagram.

As clear as words printed on the grass between Edin and Mac, he saw how she had followed a well-worn pattern of behaviour in her relationship with Deacon. Her mother had tried it first, decades earlier, when she'd bounced between Logan and anyone who might cause him jealousy and force a commitment. Including Michael. Mac realised Deacon's place in their relationship now. A tease, a cattle prod, an inducement. She watched him from the fringes of a knot of extended family members. She stood with them but her feet pointed towards Mac as though poised for him to beckon her. Like a dam about to burst she pivoted with her weight in her toes. Just the tiniest provocation would wash them all away on a dangerous a loop of passion and regret. Deacon should have come. But for whose protection?

Mac removed his gaze from Edin's tortured expression and concentrated on Tilly, his fiancé, as he strolled towards his future.

"Nāna anō tōna mate i kimi," Reuben Du Rose whispered into the trees.

"Āe. Too bad," translated Alfie. "He just dug his own grave."

Dear Reader,

I would love it if you could leave a review at your usual retailer.

I find the opinions of readers helpful and constructive. Reviews are the Holy Grail to an author as they cause our work to sink or swim. It is the bench mark for other readers and can determine whether our work will be successful and reach many or none. It doesn't have to be an essay or a literary criticism. A few words about what you liked would be most appreciated. The shortest review I ever received for my work was, 'Great,' accompanied by five stars and the longest was a whole video from a gorgeous woman in the USA. My favourite to date has to be the lady who said, '*I read until my eyes fell out.*' I keep looking at that one because it makes me laugh.
You can review on my website, ktbowes.com.
Go to the book's buy page where you can follow through to your own retailer and leave a review for me.

And hey, let me know when you've done it. I'd love to hear from you.

Join our In Crowd

I have a reading group which you're very welcome to join.
You can do that by signing up on my website ktbowes.com
In return, you'll receive four free eBooks sent to your inbox and
an email from me once a month.
I'd love for you to join us.

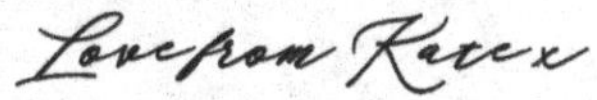

Love from Kate x

About the Author

K T Bowes is a bestselling teen and women's author. Her novel, *A Trail of Lies*, was the winner of the genre award for Author's Cave in 2014.

Phoenix Du Rose was considered for the prestigious Ngaio Marsh awards for 2021 and *Her Quiet Legacy* in 2022.

K T Bowes is an Englishwoman in exile in New Zealand, swapping rugged cosmopolitan for mountain ranges and terrifying rivers. She loves Māori culture and has learned to weave flax using traditional methods. Her other passion is Rongoa Māori, which involves creating medicines from native plants. She is a student of Te Reo Māori.

You can find her hanging out on social media in the following places.

Check in and say hello. Maybe suggest she gets back to writing and stops watching cat videos.

FACEBOOK

https://www.facebook.com/NZauthorKTBowes/

INSTAGRAM

https://www.instagram.com/k_t_bowes

Also by this Author

The Hana Du Rose Mysteries Series:
Logan Du Rose
About Hana
Hana Du Rose
Du Rose Legacy
The New Du Rose Matriarch
One Heartbeat
The Du Rose Prophecy
Du Rose Sons
Du Rose Family Ties
Du Rose Vendetta
Du Rose Blaze
The Hana Du Rose Mysteries; Generation Z
Phoenix Du Rose
Wiremu Du Rose
The Calculated Risk Series:
The Actuary
The Actuary's Wife
The Actuary in Trouble
The Heart of The Actuary

Troubled series for teens:
Free from the Tracks
Sophia's Dilemma
A Trail of Lies
Gone Phishing
Escaping the Back Country NZ Series:
Pirongia's Secret
Deleilah
Standalone novels:
Artifact
Demons on Her Shoulder
All Saints
Her Quiet Legacy
Humorous Cozy Mystery Series from New Zealand
Dead Straight
Bad Hair Day
Side Parting

www.ingramcontent.com/pod-product-compliance
Lightning Source LLC
Chambersburg PA
CBHW011025190726
48290CB00011B/2704